THE
ASCETIC
OF
DESIRE

THE
ASCETIC
OF
DESIRE

A NOVEL OF THE
KAMASUTRA

SUDHIR KAKAR

THE OVERLOOK PRESS
WOODSTOCK · NEW YORK

First published in paperback in the United States in 2002 by
The Overlook Press, Peter Mayer Publishers, Inc.
Woodstock & New York

WOODSTOCK:
One Overlook Drive
Woodstock, NY 12498
www.overlookpress.com
[for individual orders, bulk and special sales, contact our Woodstock office]

NEW YORK:
141 Wooster Street
New York, NY 10012

Library of Congress Cataloging-in-Publication Data

Kakar, Sudhir.
The ascetic of desire / Sudhir Kakar.
p. m.
1. Våtsyåyana—Fiction. 2. India—History—324 B.C.–1000 A.D.—Fiction.
3. Sex customs—India—Fiction. 4. Young men—India—Fiction. I. Title.
PR9499.3.K273A3 2000 823—dc21 99-059585

Manufactured in the United States of America
ISBN 1-58567-007-3 (hc)
ISBN 1-58567-280-7 (pb)
1 3 5 7 9 8 6 4 2

To my wife Katha,
the beginning of another story

Author's Note

All we know of Vatsyayana, the author of the *Kamasutra*, is that he lived somewhere in north India between the first and sixth centuries of the present era, although most scholars tend to narrow this date further to the fourth century. His life and times are thus a part of the Gupta period, widely regarded as the 'Golden Age' of Indian history for its achievements in art, literature and science, and for the general flowering of an urbane sensual and cultural life.

THE
ASCETIC
OF
DESIRE

Chapter One

Of what use is the practice of virtue, when its results are so uncertain?

Kamasutra 1.2.21

Whenever I pass a group of prostitutes strolling in the streets or on the bank of the river, I am overwhelmed by a rush of confused feeling dominated by a mounting sense of panic. I fear I will not be able to stop staring at their glossy skins, their high coiffures studded with jasmines, and the wave-like movement of their bodies, nor check the impulse to cup a proud breast or stroke the curve of a hip. I flush with embarrassment as I move away from them. The back of my ears burn, the nape of my neck tingles and I cringe, certain that I will be followed by a peal of knowing laughter which has divined my shameful yearning. I hate the women's invasion of me. I hate what they do to my body without my consent. I resent the unbidden erections they cause. I feel I must hide my arousal from them by surreptitiously tucking the top of my erect penis in the fold of the tunic tied at my waist. I ache with unfulfilled desire. At the same time I am angry that this part of my body, the fount of such exquisite sensations, seems to belong more to them than to me. And I wonder—do most young men of my age feel this way?

My friend Chatursen had tried to help by persuading me to accompany him to a brothel. He assured me that an attractive young prostitute, skilled in the sixty-four arts and in making virginal young men lose their inhibitions, would take away my dread of women. The result of this visit was disappointing. First, I was intimidated by the opulence of the establishment. Chatursen had selected one of the town's best brothels for our evening's entertainment. It was to cost him a full gold dinar even at the lower, summer rate. The artful lotus ponds and fountains in the garden, the silver birdcages in the verandas, the silk hangings and soft carpets in the rooms, were forbidding enough for a poor brahmin scholar, but what left me inwardly quaking were the women themselves. Dazzlingly beautiful through a combination of nature and artifice, their bodies translucent through diaphanous summer cottons, the women overpowered my senses with their soft presence and the riot of their scents—flowery perfumes mixed with the intoxicating smell of female perspiration. I hardly paid attention to Chatursen's negotiations, and whispered instructions to one of the women who detached herself from the group and approached me with downcast eyes. With a shy smile she offered me a garland of jasmines. 'Come,' she said, addressing me in the third person, her tone conveying nothing more than studied respect.

On the way to her room she asked me polite questions about my well being and did not seem at all put out by my monosyllabic answers. Before entering her room, she stepped aside to give me precedence. 'I will follow you,' she said, and then added with the first hint of sexual banter, 'I will always follow your lead.' Even later, after she had brought me a basin of perfumed water to wash my feet, and we had changed into the love-making garments provided by the brothel and were reclining on the bed, the ritual erotic offering of betel nut was done with a timidity that made me feel more and more relaxed. I realize now, and even knew at that time although I kept it a secret from myself, that her modesty was feigned, her languorous gazes and tender words were selected from a collection of erotic stances designed to suit different types of lovers—in my case, the diffident one.

She succeeded. I was feeling at ease, sufficiently relaxed for whatever awaited me this night, when she finally asked me to blow out the lamp. 'I can only undress in the dark,' she said, as she took my hands in hers, gently guiding them in the unknotting of the string of her skirt and the unclasping of her necklace and bracelets. By the time she lay back on the bed, completely naked except for a thin ankle chain hung with a row of tiny silver bells, her body awash in the moonlight streaming through the latticed window, my senses were screaming with desire. Abandoning myself to a feast of touch made even more exciting by the accompanying medley of sighs, groans and the tinkling of anklet bells, I stroked her hair, kissed her eyes, caressed the top of her shoulders and kissed her eyes again, my hands and lips moving up and down her face but not venturing further in their explorations than the base of her neck. Yet my surrender remained incomplete. In all my excitement I still remembered to keep the lower part of my body firmly flattened against the mattress. Even as I pretended to ignore the press of her breasts against my chest, a part of me was vigilantly guarding against the possibility of my erect penis inadvertently striking her waist or thigh, thus betraying an embarrassing maleness.

At this point the woman decided she had had enough of my diffidence. She took my hand and placed it on a plump yet firm breast. To the task of keeping my erection a secret was now added the dilemma of what to do with her luscious breast. Suck when in doubt—a solution she greeted with genuine pleasure. She now became urgent in her demands, no longer content to wait till I gathered courage to take the next step. One hand firmly wrapped around my penis, her other hand took one of mine and placed it between her legs. To my credit, although completely surprised at what I found, I did not flinch at the shock of all that warm wetness. Could she have urinated in her excitement? It did not feel like it, the viscosity of the liquid smeared so generously on the inside of her thighs seemed more like oil than water. Had she massaged oil into her thighs when she had gone to the bathroom? Surreptitiously, I even sniffed at my fingers to help solve the puzzle. For a moment I thought it was blood, that I had somehow injured her in my vile male lustfulness.

Impatient with my hesitations, the woman finally took over. She roughly pulled me on top and guided my penis inside her where, to my utter horror, it instantly shrivelled, popping out of her as if forcibly evicted. It drooled weakly on her pubic hair. The woman was silent, though she was breathing hard. The image of a tigress coiled to spring flashed behind my closed eyes. Gradually, her breathing slowed to normal, and my own stomach muscles unknotted. Her training in the sixty-four arts took over.

'You are so strong. There are bruises all over my body,' she said coquettishly.

'I am sorry,' I mumbled, still dazed.

'Don't worry. It is all that goes on before which gives a woman pleasure. Making love is more than shoving a fleshy cucumber into her.'

The woman—I hate to call her a prostitute and I wish I could call her by her name which, alas, I did not register in my initial nervousness—was infinitely more sensitive to the nuances of a man's mood than to niceties of language.

After we had bathed and dressed, she invited me up to the terrace to sit and watch the moon, a recommended sequel to intercourse, especially on full moon nights during the summer. Sitting on a thin cotton mattress and reclining against plump round pillows in one corner of the terrace, we ate the traditional fortifiers—cold meat broth, grilled meats, sugarcane juice with pieces of tamarind fruit, peeled and seeded lemons with lumps of sugar—brought up by a maidservant. A low murmur of conversation came from other parts of the terrace where two prostitutes were similarly entertaining their clients. After we finished eating and were chewing betel, she moved closer, leaning her back against my chest. The smell of her hair was sweet in my nostrils as she pointed out the various constellations in the sky.

'That one is Arundhati who is hard to see; however anyone who is unable to see her will die within six months. And there is Dhruva, the unmoving polestar. If you can see it during the day all your sins will be washed away. And look, there are the Seven Sages!'

I listened with less than full attention. I knew I had failed her. I wondered what she had felt when we lay intertwined in bed. What is the nature of a woman's pleasure which I should have helped provide?

I was young at the time, no more than twenty-one years of age, although in the year that had passed since I returned home after finishing my theological studies I often felt either younger, almost a child, or immeasurably older, beyond any possibility of rejuvenation. In my last year at the hermitage, I had found myself becoming increasingly impatient with my Veda studies. In fact, I despised them heartily. Nevertheless, I am aware that my theological studies have bored deep within to give me that smug feeling of superiority towards the useful arts, especially the erotic.

I dislike this smugness in other scholars; I dislike it in myself. In fact, my friendship with Chatursen was in part a result of this dissatisfaction. We were friends because our sensibilities intersected. He was a merchant's son who had little taste for making money but much interest in the arts and poetry. I was the son of a brahmin scholar travelling in the opposite direction, lightening the load of my intellectual inheritance and of a preordained ascetic lifestyle with as yet hesitant explorations of the sensual life. I did not have a natural gift for what I was trying to become. My inner irreverence could not breach a painfully correct exterior; the spontaneity I often felt, even intimations of a passionate nature inclined towards excess, did not undermine the stilted movements of my body and my terse, much too deliberate speech. I winced when Chatursen proudly introduced me to his other friends as a man of letters, a kavi. I knew I should be flattered at this imputation of literary prowess, although I had never produced a written text. I was aware that nothing brings greater honour to a man than the status of a kavi, so that even kings aspired to this title. But I no longer coveted the rewards of a literary career, having retired from it even before I had started. I told myself that I would rather be a consumer of texts than their producer.

My father, who was the chief assistant to the royal chaplain, naturally expected me to follow in his footsteps. I would learn the finer points of all the rituals and the correct way of performing them, thus putting into practice what I had only studied in theory. And since the royal chaplain had no children, it was speculated that one day I might take his place at court. My father was ambitious for me. In his mind's eye he saw me holding the first place among the kingdom's great men. As the chaplain, I would be the tutor of the princes, serve as the king's counsellor in both temporal and spiritual matters, administer the palace in his absence and have the privilege of being his opponent at games of chess and dice.

Although I tried hard to show interest, my father sensed my indifference to his plans. His obvious disappointment weighed heavily on me. It was not as if I did not try. For a few weeks I accompanied him daily to the palace and worked along with him in the rooms reserved for ritual specialists. I helped in the preparations for the rituals—of which there were a large number—which kept the royal chaplain, my father and six other assistants busy from early morning till late into the evening. There were the various rites of passage for the king, the three queens and their eleven children. There were the court rituals on festive occasions and public ones such as offerings to the seasonal deities in which the king took the lead. Of course, in my short stint at my father's profession, I did not have a chance to participate in the preparations for the most solemn occasions: rituals on the eve of the king going to war, the anointment of the crown prince, the royal consecration, the horse sacrifice. I learnt to judge the quality of darbha grass and to select the right kinds of lotuses, rice, cakes, ghee and roasted grain used for different offerings. These ingredients—the colour of the lotuses, the quality of rice and the kind of grains, the composition of cakes and the unctuousness of ghee—depend upon the nature of the ritual and its presiding deities. What is acceptable to the god of fire and the goddess of speech at the first feeding of the infant is different from the child's initiation into learning when offerings are made to Ganesha, the remover of obstacles, Brihaspati, the teacher of the gods, and Saraswati, the goddess of knowledge, music and poetry. In the daily, seasonal and annual rituals, Ganga water is mixed with water of other sacred rivers, ocean, wells and pools. The particular source and correct proportion of the waters is laid down in minute detail, and has to be memorized.

Yet I did not derive any sense of accomplishment from these activities. My brief apprenticeship with my father's younger brother, one of the better-known astrologers of Varanasi, was equally unsatisfactory. As I learnt to colour the diagrams he drew for the casting of horoscopes, I sensed within myself a vast inner distance from the surrounding world. I did not feel I was living my life but that life was happening to me. On some days I was gripped by a sense of urgency, of unknown matters that somehow demanded my attention, unformulated plans I needed to realize, strangers I must meet, while on other days time simply disappeared as a dimension of my existence. For a few weeks I read day and night, almost read myself blind, although I was unable to concentrate and could not remember what I had read. I found it hard to go to bed and to surrender to sleep but equally hard to get up in the morning and confront the prospect of being awake.

This painfully heightened state of isolation finally provoked me to break loose of familial and ancestral expectations, and to spend more and more time with Chatursen and his friends. Full of fun and youthful high spirits, they were nevertheless generous men who accepted me without question and even deferred to what they regarded as my superior learning. Given to an uncomplicated pursuit of pleasure, their lives lived for the most part unfettered by any obsessive self-scrutiny. If they did not relieve me of my agonizing, at least they succeeded in numbing it for a while, although lately I had again found myself getting restless.

Thus when my friend Chatursen gave me the news that Vatsyayana had come to live in the Seven Leaf hermitage on the other side of the river, and suggested an excursion to meet the sage, I readily agreed. Besides the hope of getting answers that would untangle some of my own confusions in relation to women, I was intrigued as to why such a man would choose to give up a life of luxury and influence to come and live with bark-clad and often rank-smelling hermits.

If there was one person in the central countries, indeed in the whole Gupta empire, who knew about the nature of woman's pleasure and the subtleties of her desire, it was Vatsyayana. I was surprised to hear he had chosen to come to Varanasi and live in one of our more undistinguished hermitages. I was aware of his honoured position at the court in Kausambi, his great influence with the queens and the king, Udayana. We had heard rumours that Vatsyayana was an ascetic who had never known a woman. His knowledge of sex, it was widely believed, came from austerities and prolonged periods of meditation over many years. In Kausambi, the credulous believed that he wrote his famous text at the dictation of the goddess Rati herself, who was so smitten by the man that she revealed to him the secret knowledge entrusted to her by her consort Kama, the god of love. This, of course, is nonsense. The authority of any treatise comes not from any divine grace, the fame of the author or the amount of information it contains, but has a subtler source: the author's intimacy with his subject, which is reflected in his writing in a myriad ways. Whatever the merits or faults of the *Kamasutra*, fiercely debated by all sorts of scholars, Vatsyayana's intimacy with erotic life was unquestionable.

In spite of its great popularity, Vatsyayana's *Kamasutra* was not yet a text used in the education of all castes. Babhru's ancient work on erotics was still the standard text although a casual student like myself found its hundred and fifty chapters heavy going. But among the younger, more advanced students of erotics Vatsyayana was already a cult figure, perhaps also because our venerable teachers thought so little of him. My own guru Brahmdatta was an exception. In the late afternoon, after the morning instruction was over, when the guru rested and the students began lighting the fires and preparing the evening meal, there were sometimes visitors from other hermitages who came to talk to Brahmdatta. For a few weeks, some years ago, I had sat in on the conversations, fanning my guru and his guests, where the merits of the *Kamasutra* were vehemently analyzed. I could not participate in these discussions, not only because of the impropriety of offering an opinion in an assemblage of venerable teachers but also because of my ignorance of the subject.

I remember that my guru's friends were scandalized by the book. Some of Vatsyayana's opinions went against all established principles of erotics. Vatsyayana was respectful of older authors on the subject, it was grudgingly conceded, and his scholarship was impeccable. What made the sages so disapproving was the tone of the treatise. Vatsyayana's subversive intent was transparent. For instance, contrary to Dattaka's standard work on prostitutes, Vatsyayana claimed that in their liaisons courtesans were also moved by considerations other than money.

'It is a vulgar popularization, fit for dull-witted princes and the sons of merchants,' the excitable Palaka had said in his urgent voice, spraying a mist of saliva over his listeners as well as his bobbing white beard. Palaka's wrath was especially directed at Vatsyayana's notions about the sexuality of women.

'Since ancient times every sage has confirmed that a woman's desire mirrors that of the man. It is the intensity of man's excitement which arouses a corresponding passion in the woman. She is only kindling, the man provides the fire. This fellow says there is no difference between male and female desires. That each follows an

independent course. Is this not a recipe for anarchy, I ask
you? Will it not undermine dharma which holds the world
together and which even this man agrees must always
remain superior to kama?'

Most of the others seemed to agree.

'It is destined to be forgotten soon,' someone else said.
'It will end up in libraries. The only human hands that will
handle the *Kamasutra* will be those of the keepers of books
who must occasionally moisten the cloth in which the palm
leaves are wrapped.'

My guru Brahmdatta had disagreed.

'I do not say it is a great treatise which will replace that
of the Babhravyas. But it will be read because it is
pleasingly written and summarizes a great deal of
information. It is only a few scholars who want anything
more in a book.'

I remember my venerable teachers' talk of Vatsyayana's
subversion making me want to read the book. I promised
myself I would soon do so, but the promise remained
stored with others as the stack of unread books continued
to grow higher in my mind.

For more than a month, our plan to visit the Seven Leaf
hermitage remained just that. Chatursen kept reminding
me of our intention but my wish, and my curiosity, had
begun to contend with a mounting hesitation. Theological
studies tend to dampen spontaneity and strip one's
language bare of feeling. I have to make a conscious effort
to say that the idea of meeting the author of the *Kamasutra*
both attracted and scared me. My sense of purpose
alternated with trepidation. I visualized Vatsyayana as an
irascible old sage, not unlike Palaka, with a long white
beard and tufts of white hair sprouting from his ears. I
imagined vertical frown lines in the middle of his forehead,
bushy eyebrows and piercing eyes that could delve deep
into my mind to ferret out its last shameful longing. I

wanted to wait till the prospect of being in his presence did not threaten my composure so immensely. Given Vatsyayana's stature in the field of erotics, I told Chatursen, I needed to thoroughly study the *Kamasutra* to prepare myself for the encounter.

Chapter Two

Not only in erotics but in all fields, few know the theoretical aspects. Theory is fundamental, even if divorced from practice.

Kamasutra 1.3.5-6

*I*t was not difficult to locate a copy of the *Kamasutra* in Varanasi. Because of my access to the royal palace through my father, I could even take the book home from the palace library. In one extended period of single-minded concentration of which I am occasionally though erratically capable, I memorized the text from the first verse: 'Praise the three aims of life: virtue, prosperity and erotic love. They are the subject of this work' to the last: 'A wise man, versed in all things, must not be a sensualist craving sex but consider both his ethics and material interests and establish a stable marriage', with which Vatsyayana concludes the *Kamasutra*. It was only later, with a more careful reading that I began to comprehend that although Vatsyayana does not challenge the basic framework of dharma he also follows a purpose of his own: the celebration of pleasure.

My father, who saw me trying to memorize the text by chanting its verses in the prescribed manner, looked at me reproachfully every time he passed my room but did not make any comment. Like most educated brahmins in our kingdom, he looked upon erotics as a regrettable discipline which had to be both studied and practiced in one's youth, but which was definitely inferior to the other branches of knowledge, especially dharma, the science of virtue and ethics, the Law. Vatsyayana's suggestion that a man's action should not only be determined by the prospect of increasing virtue but also by the promise of pleasure would have horrified him.

The sutra form is mnemonic, hence I memorized the text within three days. This is not as difficult a feat as it might appear since special attention is paid to the mnemonic techniques in the Varanasi gurukulas. At the beginning of my Veda studies I had learnt the basic method of repeating each word independently, then together with the word preceding it, then in the reverse order, with each verse repeated once again before the following was tackled. My guru Brahmdatta, who placed great store by memory, kept a special slot in the day's timetable for his own favourite system of training. After the exposition and discussion of a paragraph from a single text on any subject, he would ask me the next day to repeat verbatim what had transpired between us in our previous conversation. He would point out my memory lapses, correct my errors, and the next day I had to reproduce the first conversation together with the additions and corrections made by the guru in the second. This would go on for some time in a unique and skilfully designed frame of infinite regress. Like the effort involved in the perfection of a conjuring trick, a good memory is merely a matter of practice.

The *Kamasutra* consists of seven parts, thirty-six chapters, sixty-four paragraphs and twelve hundred and fifty verses. The first part, 'General Observations', consists of five chapters: contents, three aims of life, acquisition of knowledge, conduct of an elegant townsman, and intermediaries who assist the lover. The second part, 'Amorous Approaches', comprises ten chapters: stimulation of sexual desire, embraces, caresses, scratches, bites, copulation and special tastes, blows and sighs, mannish behaviour, fellatio, before and after intercourse, sexual variations, and lovers' quarrels. Part three, 'Getting a Girl', consists of five chapters: forms of marriage, relaxing a girl, obtaining the girl, managing by oneself, and marriage. The fourth part, 'Rights and Duties of a Wife', consists of two chapters: conduct of the only wife, and conduct of chief wife and other wives. The fifth part, 'Other Men's Wives', has six chapters: character of men and women, getting acquainted, scrutinizing feelings, the go-between, king's pleasures, and harem behaviour. Part six, 'On courtesans', comprises six chapters: choosing lovers, looking for a steady lover, ways of making money, taking up with a former lover, occasional profits, and profits and losses. The seventh part, 'Secret Practices', consists of two chapters: success in love and increasing sexual prowess.

Vatsyayana does not present his book as an original work but as a compendium of opinions of ancient authorities on the subject, beginning with Shvetaketu Auddalaki who composed the first text on erotic love in five hundred chapters (I am excluding the contribution of Lord Shiva, whose bull-companion Nandi originally dictated a thousand verses on the subject). Although Shvetaketu's text is lost, I had heard of the sage during my studies. According to our guru Brahmdatta, this book was responsible for putting an end to unbridled sexual coupling and a certain profligacy in relation to intercourse with married women which is so prominent in the *Mahabharata*. Prior to Shvetaketu's treatise, both married and unmarried women were viewed as items for indiscriminate consumption, like cooked food. Shvetaketu was the first to make the novel suggestion that men should not generally sleep with the wives of others.

Shvetaketu's treatise was condensed into a hundred and fifty chapters by Babhru of Panchala and his sons. This text by the Babhravyas remained the standard work for generations of students. Monographs were written on different sections by various authors: Suvarnanabha on erotic advances, Ghotakamukha on the seduction of girls, Gonardiya on the duties and rights of a wife, Gonikaputra on sexual relations with other men's wives, Dattaka on courtesans, and Kuchumara on occult sexual lore. Vatsyayana used these monographs together with the Babhravyas' work to further condense the extant knowledge of erotic love in thirty-six chapters, which he arranged in the same seven parts as the older text. The *Kamasutra's* merit, according to those who are favourably disposed toward Vatsyayana's work, is that it combines completeness with conciseness, clarity with knowledge.

Of course no one should take Vatsyayana's claim about his own lack of originality seriously. Apparent modesty is part of a hallowed literary tradition wherein even the most boastful of savants is compelled to present his work not as a product of his own mind but only as a derivation, a mere commentary on what has been thought and written before him by illustrious predecessors. Vatsyayana is like other scholars who deliberately avoid all claim to originality, preferring instead to attribute their innovations to sages of yore and passing them off under the guise of received wisdom. My fascination with the man, with the person behind the name, ensured that his own opinions, heralded by *iti vatsyayanah* (so says Vatsyayana) in the text, received my searching attention. I discovered that his voice is not tentative at all but full of self-confidence, even self-assertion. This reassured me greatly. Perceiving a lack of these qualities in myself, I needed this evidence of self-confidence in a man who, unbeknown to me, I was choosing as my new guru.

The *Kamasutra* is also a commentator's delight. It often contains hidden meanings not immediately apparent to the casual reader, as well as allusions which need further explication before the richness of the sutras and the subtlety of the author's mind can be fully appreciated. For instance, a general reader would be puzzled by the number sixty-four which occurs with some regularity throughout the treatise. There are the sixty-four arts which every man or woman who aspires to be a sexual adept must first learn. One can understand the relevance of the knowledge of singing, dancing, gymnastics and poetic composition if one wants to be a good lover, but why are the arts of cock, quail and ram fighting on the list of erotic arts? Why chemistry and mineralogy? Then the chapter on foreplay is called sixty-four, although the elements that constitute foreplay are nowhere near this number. Now, as Vatsyayana well knows but does not elaborate, sixty-four is a natural number. Ayurvedic medical texts list sixty-four main diseases of the body. This number also occurs in the ancient law books. *The Laws of Manu,* pronouncing on the transgressions by the different castes, say that the guilt of a thieving shudra is eight times, of the vaishya sixteen times, of the kshatriya thirty-two times and a brahmin sixty-four times. In the initiation rites, the circle symbolizing the universal spirit of Brahman is divided into four quarters, every quarter again into four parts to indicate that the initiate is to receive sixteen branches of knowledge. If each of these sixteen branches is again divided into four, we get the sixty-four arts which cover the whole circle and are an expression of totality. Sixty-four is not only a natural and revered number but so large in relation to the limited possibilities of sex that it becomes an ideal. It tells us not only what is but what can be. It is a number that tests the limits of our sexual imagination. Vatsyayana's lists of the sixty-four arts, of the sixty-four positions of intercourse and the elements of foreplay, are efforts to include all that is even remotely possible in the realm of sexual love, even when some of the items on a list appear improbable. His is a search for infinity in love, an attempt to reach completion through the inclusion of everything that could be relevant.

Although he was respectful, Chatursen made it clear from the way he listened to my findings that he did not share my scholarly excitement with the *Kamasutra*. He seemed especially bored with my discoveries about the secrets of numbers in the text. Like other members of his caste, Chatursen's natural deference to scholars coexists with an equally ingrained impatience with the subtleties of their craft.

'Tell me,' he said, 'are there any hidden meanings in the names Vatsyayana gives to the different sexual types of men and women?'

Like most lay people whose interest in the *Kamasutra* is limited to the section on intercourse, Chatursen was aware that regarding the length of the penis and its corresponding thickness, Vatsyayana talks of the hare man, the bull man and the stallion man with penises which are respectively six, nine and twelve finger-breadths long. Similarly, according to the width and depth of the vulva, he speaks of the gazelle woman, the mare woman and the elephant woman.

'Yes, indeed!' I replied, delighted to have my friend's attention. 'The animal names he gives different types of men and women are not random. That the names convey the dimensions of the sexual organs is a primary intention but not his sole consideration. I have noticed that the only animal species in his classification which represents both a man and a woman is the horse. This is because among all the animals we know, the sexual behaviour of the horse is nearest that of a man. The stallion's large penis, of immense interest to every little boy who has watched it gently swinging under the beast's belly, becomes erect slowly like that of a man, stiffened not by muscles but by the rush of blood. Like a man and unlike other animals of comparable size, the stallion dismounts rather soon from a mare. The mare's vulva, like that of a woman, has a large clitoris nestled in the soft fold at the entrance which is massaged by the stallion's thrusts. A mare, of course, opens and closes her vulva in spasms, holding and letting the penis go, an ability a woman can develop with much practice, and to the great delight of her partner.

'Vatsyayana chooses to call the large-penised man the stallion rather than elephant man because an elephant's penis, though large, has a peculiar, snake-like, curved shape when erect. It confines itself to shallow vaginal penetration, sometimes missing it altogether to happily thrust in and out of the female's anus. The bull, on the other hand, conveys not only size but also potency since he can ejaculate almost twenty times during a single coupling.' The look of pure admiration in Chatursen's eyes was highly gratifying.

What intrigued me most in the *Kamasutra* at the time was not its scholarly challenge but its content, especially its views on women. The interest was very personal, and not just because I felt an overriding literary need to compare Vatsyayana's opinion on women with those in the many treatises on dharma. This was easy enough to do since my scholarly training was impeccable. It was not in the textual but the real world of women where I tended to flounder. In the world of textual comparisons, I move easily. The dharma texts believe it futile to instruct women in *any* of the sciences, including erotics, implying that women are not entitled to study a shastra since they are intellectually incapable of understanding it. Vatsyayana expressly recommends the study of the *Kamasutra* to women even before they reach puberty. He would have them study it even after marriage but, realistically, admits that this will depend on the attitude of the husband. Two of the seven parts of the book are addressed exclusively to women—the fourth to wives and the sixth to courtesans—while the third part tries to make men understand a young girl's sexuality and the need for gentleness in removing her inhibitions and fears before intercourse.

Where Vatsyayana differs most from the dharma texts on the question of women, is in his attitude towards the courtesan. The treatises on dharma look down upon a prostitute of any kind. The texts maintain that no lotus will grow on a mountain top, no rice where barley is sown, no woman pure that is brothel born. The prostitute is one of those individuals from whom no one, especially a brahmin, should accept food. Mentioned in one breath with thieves, the courtesan's house is one of the places to be watched and patrolled by the police because a variety of scoundrels are likely to congregate there. In contrast, it is the courtesan whose welfare is close to Vatsyayana's heart. Even at that first reading, I wondered why.

My critical engagement with the *Kamasutra* had the effect of reducing my tension about meeting its author. Without my being aware of it, the balance of archaic hopes and ancient fears with which a prospective disciple approaches a guru, any guru, had decidedly shifted towards the former. All I could guardedly tell Chatursen when he commented on my new-found eagerness to meet Vatsyayana was that I hoped the sage would help calm some of my inner turbulence—not by providing answers but by clarifying the questions that lie at the heart of all restlessness.

Chapter Three

He who wishes to obtain virtue, prosperity and
sexual love in this world and the next must know
this text thoroughly and, at the same time, become
a master of his senses.

Kamasutra 7.2.58

On the day we finally selected for our expedition, the
white bullocks with their grey horns gleaming with sesame
oil were still being yoked to the carriage when I reached
Chatursen's house. Cushions were stacked on the floor of
the carriage, the soft carpet still rolled up, as were the
purple silk flaps on the sides. It was a spring afternoon
when we set out for Vatsyayana's hermitage. For me, this
is the best time of the day in the best time of the year,
although some may dispute my preference. Chatursen, for
instance, always waxes lyrical about late winter mornings
when the early fog has been dissipated by the sunshine,
pale yet warm, 'like the golden skin of a Kashmiri woman
flushed by rising excitement'. I try hard not to wince at the
metaphorical excesses to which sensualists are especially
prone. Some of Chatursen's other friends, with perhaps
greater poetic sensibility but equally small talent, prefer
the first days of the monsoon and insist on describing them

with tired old clichés of stormclouds as dark as a herd of buffalo, beating drums of thunder and the shooting shafts of rain suddenly cooling the land that has baked throughout the summer months. I am not impervious to the charms of the first showers of the rainy season when the moist earth smells of promises, hinting at the coming lushness and the bright green grass shoots and new leaves that will soon be all around us. But I prefer the cool male dryness of spring. I like the dewless balmy breeze of early spring mornings. I like the busy hum of honey— and bumblebees around flowering trees and sprays of mango blossoms. I like what spring does to rocky hilltops, inlaying them with a lace of tiny white and yellow wildflowers.

Coming out of the western city gate, we crossed the Ganga at the ghat next to the village of the weavers. The boatman was a loquacious old man, obviously struggling with his conflicting desire to know all about us and to tell us everything about himself before the short crossing was over. I left the business of making a polite show of interest to Chatursen as I closed my eyes, shut my ears to the persistent stream of words and dozed off in the warm sunshine to the craft's gliding motion. I confess to an impatience with men of lower castes. I do not like the way they talk with that mixture of obsequiousness and carefully disguised impertinence. I am repelled by their beards which is always a stubble, the cheeks neither clean shaven nor luxuriant with hair like those of venerable hermits and sages but looking perpetually like the undergrowth after a forest fire. Chatursen gets along much better with the lower castes. It is due to his merchant blood. Merchants, I have discovered to my surprise ever since I began to consort with Chatursen and his friends, are more sensitive to other people's needs and moods than are poets, musicians or scholars. To be successful, they must learn to get along well with everyone; Chatursen's very tolerance betrays his lack of refinement.

Another carriage, much less ornate and with wheels that creaked loudly, was waiting for us on the other side of the river. The road leading to the hermitage was not a main highway and was thus neither raised above the surface of the adjacent land nor bordered by a ditch backed with sand. It did have trees along its edges, though, shading travellers from the sun. Its flat, hard mud surface was scarred by a few potholes and ruts over which our carriage rumbled along like an old pig. In the countryside around us, spring ploughing was in full swing. Little mud embankments bordering narrow water channels and hedges marking the boundaries of small fields gave the land the appearance of a monk's patched cloak. Scarecrows fashioned from buffalo skeletons set up on poles dotted the fields. Dark, wiry farmers, naked to the waist, bodies burnt by the sun to the colour of rosewood, urged their oxen-pairs forward with whip in one hand while they gripped the plough handle with the other. The ploughshare pushed its sharpened lower end in deep furrows through the earth. Soon the fields gave way to large vegetable gardens, the source of cartloads of gourds and cucumbers which had passed us on their way to Varanasi.

Beyond the vegetable gardens, before the forest began, we passed the village of fowlers, home to the long-haired, bearded men with silver hoops dangling from their earlobes—who come daily to the city with their cages of parrots, mynahs, cuckoos and other birds so dearly loved by our women, hanging from both ends of a long pole balanced at the shoulder. The hermitage was a couple of leagues further from this village, not quite in the forest but at its very edge. As hermitages go, this one was neither particularly big nor otherwise impressive. The right word for it would be 'charming', especially now when dusk was settling in, the sinking sun the space of an arrow—shot above the crimson embers of the horizon. Above us, rows of cranes, bright as a snake's belly just slipped from its slough, were advancing steadily along the clear sky. Now stretching in an even line, now wide apart, now soaring high, now sinking low, crooked in its twists and turn, the line cut the sky in two.

There were perhaps a dozen circular timber huts in this hermitage, separated by carefully cultivated patches of darbha grass needed for the various rituals and by groves of seven leaf and wild lemon trees. Each grove also had a couple of ingudi trees, which people in our part of the country call hermit trees since their nuts provide these recluses with oil for their lamps and medicinal salve for wounds. At the bottom of such a tree there is invariably a large moist stone half sunk in the earth, glossy from the oil of the ingudi nuts split and pounded on it. On the left, sloping down towards an unseen stream, was a large grassy field where during the day tawny cows from the hermitage and black antelopes from the forest grazed quietly in perfect amity. In the early part of the evening, when dusk begins to settle, there tends to be a good deal of activity around such a place. The trees are alive with birds returning to their nests but not yet settled down for the night. The cows are being milked, the cooking fires lighted and sacrificial fires replenished with wood and incense. The scented smoke from the altars, mixed with the tangy fragrance of lemon leaves and flowers, wafts pleasantly through the hermitage. We asked for directions to Vatsyayana's hut from a greasy old hermit, his long grey hair plastered down with oil, who had just come from his bath in the stream and was hauling down a bark-garment hung out to dry on a tree branch.

'It is the last hut to your left,' he told us with a marked show of interest. 'Its walls are marked with fresh handprints of sandalwood paste. He is a famous author, I hear.'

We thanked him, he blessed us perfunctorily, and we were on our way.

Vatsyayana was a tall man, stately without being stout, with shoulder-length wavy grey hair complementing the iron-grey curls on his bare chest. Not yet having taken to the coarse bark garments of the forest dwellers, he wore wrapped around his waist a thin white cotton cloth with pleats that reached down to the ankles in a fashion preferred by men of Kausambi, Avanti and other western countries. An undecided grey stubble covered his chin and cheeks, either the beginning of a full beard favoured by the hermits or the maximum growth permitted to the cultivated citizen. Since we had arrived unannounced, his greeting of welcome had an understandable reserve which he sought to mask with a grave courtesy. Would we like a glass of madhupalaka? I declined the ritual welcoming drink but Chatursen nodded eagerly. I find this mixture of sugar, ghee, curds, herbs and honey barely palatable even if it is quickly gulped down at one go. The enjoined sipping in six mouthfuls makes its cloying sweetness quite unbearable. Would I like some cold lemon and barley water instead? He called out the names of our drinks in a loud though polite and not unpleasant voice. He was answered by the distinctive sound of tinkling anklets as an unseen woman busied herself in the kitchen.

As we sat on low wooden stools in the small clearing outside the hut, the sacrificial fire crackling to our right, the glow of other hermitage fires glimpsed through the groves like immense, still fireflies, we exchanged obligatory courtesies. I was mostly silent, awed by his presence, while Chatursen told him about our great admiration for the *Kamasutra* and our desire to meet its author. Vatsyayana listened quietly, his impassive face betraying not the slightest sign of self-satisfaction at Chatursen's paeans. His noticeable and characteristic reserve was not grounded in distance but in a deep shyness. I sensed this at our very first meeting but I fully experienced the dimensions of this restraint only much later. Although his relative silence made us feel uncomfortable initially, we soon relaxed for he did not have the forbidding exterior with which many famous scholars equip themselves to go along with their learning, and which can so intimidate the casual visitor.

Sitting there that evening, slightly anxious but nonetheless fascinated by my host and our surroundings, I could never imagine that in the next few minutes I was going to experience two emotional upheavals as powerful as earthquakes, which would permanently alter the topography of my life. I felt the first one clearly, its shudder of excitement and the sudden rocking of the senses, as one of the most beautiful women I have ever seen came out of the hut bearing our refreshments on a simple wooden tray. When I say 'beautiful' I do not mean a conventional, physical beauty—although Vatsyayana's wife Malavika was beautiful in any sense of the term. I could, as Chatursen later did, truthfully describe her in metaphors favoured by his untalented poet-friends: large fawn-like eyes under eyebrows arched like Kama's bow, a wide mouth and soft full lips as if swollen by the sting of a bee, slim waist with a hint of three folds, shapely hips and achingly long and tapering thighs like the stems of banana trees. These metaphors are conventions of poetry, desinged more to summon a youthful erotic fantasy than to describe a real person. Malavika was no longer a sixteen-year old girl on the brink of sensual life but a woman in her late twenties, glowing with the secrets of her sexuality rather than the promise of its fruition. The images engraved on my mind are not of Malavika's face and body but exquisite details that will be forever unique to her. I remember the sparkling web of beads of sweat at the corners of her mouth, the bracelet of white jasmines around her left wrist, the pale delicate silk draped around her full breasts and unable to dim their golden glow, her bold glance pouring into me like delicious wine as she offered me my glass. My impression of her was not defined by the fact of her physical beauty but by an incomparable femininity animating her face and her limbs.

The tremors of my second reaction shook my mind long after the event. I cannot even place it within a precise moment, although I suspect it occurred sometime after Malavika had gone back inside the hut and Vatsyayana turned his attention towards me.

'You look more like a student than a merchant,' he said.

'I have just completed my studies, Acharya.'

'And now?'

'Oh, I don't know yet. I was thinking of various things,' I said.

'Perhaps you will come again another day and tell me,' he said in a gentle voice.

The conversation seemed superficial, even banal, but at that moment his clear brown eyes were the kindest I have ever seen. They looked at me as if they understood everything—my past, my future, the fears I did not know, the dreams that lay hidden within me. His eyes recognized me. It was a recognition full of compassion, like the wounded Jatayu being seen by Lord Rama. On the battlefield of Kurukshetra, when Arjuna was full of doubt on the dharma of killing his kinsmen, Lord Krishna convinced him to fight not by wise counsel, as is commonly believed, but by looking at him in just this way. I felt a sharp tug in the region of my heart, the melting of something which had lain there encrusted for a long time, and unbidden tears welled up. Tears, of course, are the manifestation of feelings, but I could not then, nor can I even today, give a name to my emotion. To say that I felt happy or sad is to artificially isolate one feeling from the others woven into it. Looking back, I can only say that my emotional confusion was further aggravated by the sexual excitement which still coursed through me, and my mortification at my shameful desire for the sage's wife.

My agitation persisted throughout the return journey. Thoughts whirled together with feelings, changing from one to the other, as if an old barrier between the two had collapsed, or at least become permeable. As the carriage rattled along the road under the radiant silver canopy of the spring night, the bullocks involuntarily increasing their speed as they neared home, I was grateful for Chatursen's unrelenting eloquence. I even endured his lustful description of Malavika without losing my composure at its salaciousness. Why does the desire of others appear coarse, while one's own is always sublime? As I dozed off, I thought I would ask Vatsyayana this question in one of our next meetings. With a shock I realized that I had unconsciously decided that there were going to be further meetings. Of course, I had not the faintest inkling that I would devote a large part of my life to the composition of Vatsyayana's biography and the very first commentary on the *Kamasutra*. At that particular moment, I was only aware of the urgent need to understand the manifestation of kama in women so that I could free myself from the distress and guilt they repeatedly caused me.

Chapter Four

Vatsyayana's opinion is that a woman, like a man, experiences the same sexual pleasure from beginning to end.

Kamasutra 2.1.23

'Long have I pored over ancient texts and commentaries on how a woman experiences sexual pleasure and whether it is different from that of a man,' Vatsyayana said. 'I have also asked this question of many women. A few years ago, when I visited my aunt Chandrika at her retreat, we had a long discussion on the subject, the most frank I have ever had with a woman, perhaps also because now, as a Buddhist nun, Chandrika could look back at pleasure dispassionately. My considered opinion is that though we know a great deal about how a woman experiences sexual intercourse, the essence of her pleasure, her female rasa, will always escape a man and vice versa. Ultimately the very source of this pleasure, our bodies, get in the way of our knowing. What drives us towards union is the wish to experience the partner's pleasure, and the tragedy is that we have to be satisfied with our own.'

This was my tenth visit to the Seven Leaf hermitage in the past one month. A nascent pattern was already shaping these visits. I would leave Varanasi at dawn in the carriage Chatursen had placed at my disposal, spend the morning with Vatsyayana, share his frugal mid day meal, write out the notes on our morning conversation while he rested and after some more talk in the afternoon, this time of a more general nature, I would return to Varanasi.

At the time, I also did not see it fit to wonder why Vatsyayana generously gave me so much of his time and patiently answered my questions on his work. I took for granted his assent to my adoption of him as my guru, even though the transaction was one-sided and took place in an unknown part of my mind. Today, I can only shake my head at the arrogance of my presumption and marvel at the generosity of his spirit. After all, I was a callow youth, barely emerging from the student stage of life, with neither achievement to my credit nor a demonstrable proof of my potential. Vatsyayana, on the other hand, was already a recognized though controversial figure in the science of erotics. Later, when I came to know him better, I believe I understood some of his reasons better. He was lonely, not just because he had cut himself off from his friends and his life at Udayana's court in Kausambi but also because he was cursed with that special kind of loneliness in which fame cloaks those it blesses. He was also struggling with the question of whether the time for him to become a forest dweller had come, a step involving a radical renunciation of the interests and concerns of an earlier, householder stage and a deliberate turn towards the spiritual ends of life, with which he had little affinity. He had the example of many. poets before him who continually vacillated between the forest and the city, between renunciation and sensual indulgence, finding them equally attractive and equally deficient. In their forties, at the beginning of old age, the poets often agonized over what they should attend upon, 'the sloping sides of wilderness mountains, or the buttocks of women abounding in passion'.

In me, he recognized a version of his younger self-perplexed, irreverent, wanting to commit himself to something outside the predestined flow of his life, if he could only find it. I resemble that part of his former self he needed to get reacquainted with; I was a place in his life he needed to revisit before bidding it a final good-bye. I would also like to believe he discerned a spark of creativity in me, or at least a deep curiosity—they are perhaps the same thing—which he wanted to nurture as a gift from one generation to the other; I would repay the debt by making his person as immortal as his work is destined to be. For a long while, my idealization of his person, the eyes of love with which I continued to regard him for many years even after the terrible way it all ended, did not permit me to guess that he could also have another, hidden purpose in welcoming me so warmly to his hermitage home and his temporarily suspended life.

'How does a woman's need for intercourse compare with that of a man, Acharya?' I had asked further.

'There is little doubt that woman's need for intercourse is greater,' Vatsyayana answered. 'It is said:"Neither the god of wind, nor he of fire, nor the other thirty-three gods are so dear to a woman as the god of love". And in another text:"Lack of sexual enjoyment is decay and old age for women", and at yet another place in the same text," Mankind is made old by worry, the warrior by fetters, women by a lack of coitus and clothes by the glow of fire".'

Vatsyayana paused. At the beginning of our conversations, it was his habit to look questioningly at me whenever he quoted from a text and to wait for a while before proceeding further. He expected me to give some indication of my familiarity with the source of the quote, wanted that I not only demonstrate I was educated enough to understand but ready to receive knowledge with proper deference. Sometimes he would deliberately misquote, and smilingly acknowledge my tactful correction. Whenever he cited a passage from a text, his voice became grave, the tone sonorous.

'Quotes link us to our ancestors as much as the rites we perform for them every month at new moon,' he said once. 'We can only think what has been thought before. If you ever start believing that you have a new idea, remember that you have merely forgotten its source.'

Later, as he became more convinced of the seriousness of my purpose and the adequacy of my preparation as a student, this kind of testing—and teasing—became less frequent.

'How well the sage Vyasa puts it and, of course, like all great scholars, Chanakya was not only well-versed in the science of politics but also of love and of ethics,' I replied, correctly identifying both the sources.

Vatsyayana gave a nod of acknowledgment and proceeded further.

'A woman's sexual hunger is also much greater than that of a man, although I do not agree when it is said, "Fire is not satisfied by all the wood in the forest, the ocean by all the rivers, the god of death by all the living beings and a woman by all the men". Whether a woman also enjoys greater pleasure in the act of love than a man is a more difficult question which can only be answered by someone who has had the experience of being both the sexes. From history, we know of only two persons, both men, who were changed into women and had a woman's experience of intercourse. I am not including Lord Shiva here who, on insulting a procession of barren women, was cursed by the women with a change of sex. Later, transformed back into his original state but now familiar with the sexual sensations of both men and women, he is said to have dictated Dattaka's text to that great teacher of erotics.

Among men, Ila, the king of Bahlika, was the first to experience life as a woman. He was out hunting in the forest when he came to a glade where Shiva was sporting with his wife. To satisfy a whim of the goddess, Shiva had changed himself into a woman but to hide his embarrassment cast a spell which changed the sex of all the male animals and even the male trees. On entering the glade Ila, to his horror, found that he had become a woman. Deeply troubled, he appealed to Shiva but the god only laughed. The goddess had more compassion and decreed that Ila would be a woman for a month and a man for a month. The moon's son fell in love with Ila as a woman and they enjoyed each other till he changed back into a man after the month was over.'

'And how did Ila compare the sexual sensations of a woman with that of a man?' I asked.

Vatsyayana smiled, pleased to have caught me out in a lapse of memory.

'Unfortunately, we do not know because he could not tell. When the goddess decreed that Ila would alternate between a woman and a man, she also added that in neither state would he remember the other.'

I had noted that Vatsyayana had begun to occasionally smile as our conversations and familiarity progressed, although the smile had yet to take the next step into open laughter. His was an infectious and deeply reassuring smile, contradicting my first impressions of the sage as a terribly serious, even sombre man. The smile had the effect of both lighting up and calming any turbulence in the space around him. It was like the sudden appearance of the moon from behind heavy clouds in the rainy season, sending the demons of the night scurrying back to their hiding places of the day.

'But not everyone who has crossed the borders between the sexes has remained silent about the sexual experience,'

I said, continuing our discussion.

'You are right to draw my attention to the only personal testimony on the comparative experience of sexual pleasure, that of King Bhangasvana,' Vatsyayana said with a courteous nod of acknowledgment.

I knew the story well. The king had earned Indra's enmity because he did not invite the god to the sacrifice which was intended to give him a hundred sons. Indra avenged the slight by putting a spell on a lake in which Bhangasvana was bathing so that when he came out he found he had become a woman. Greatly troubled by this change, Bhangasvana left for the forest where, in course of time, he married a hermit and had a hundred sons from him. Bhangasvana then took these sons to the city so that all the sons, two hundred of them, could live together and rule the kingdom in amity. When Indra saw this, he was furious that the king was not suffering. He caused enmity between the sons so that they fought each other and all of them were killed. Indra then disguised himself and went to the hermitage where Bhangasvana was mourning and lamenting. The god finally took pity, revealed himself and told Bhangasvana that she could have one hundred of his sons restored to life, either those he had fathered or those he had as a mother. Bhangasvana, saying that a mother's love is more tender than that of a father, chose the hundred sons he had given birth to as a woman. Indra was pleased and offered to change the king back into a man. Bhangasvana refused, preferring to remain female because, he said, as a woman he had experienced much greater sexual pleasure than as a man.

'King Udayana told me,' Vatsyayana continued, 'that he once dreamt he was a woman having sexual intercourse. As the unknown man in the dream parted the king's thighs dripping with the liquid of the love god and entered her, Udayana said that he experienced pleasure so intense, it has never been matched in his waking experience of intercourse as a man. This has been confirmed by other men who have dreamt of being women, while no woman has reported the opposite experience.

'The texts also say that a woman's boldness in matters of love is six times as great as a man, and her delight in its pleasures eight times as great. Therefore, given the authority of the texts, Bhangasvana's personal testimony, men's dreams of being women and the common observation that in her loud groans, sighs, sharp intakes of breath and facial expressions a woman shows much greater evidence of pleasure in the sexual union, it is fair to say that a woman enjoys sex more than a man. Because of the pain she has to go through during childbirth, the gods have compensated her with greater pleasure in the act that initiates it.'

'But is her pleasure of the same kind and does it follow the same course as that of a man?' I asked.

'This we know with less certainty because Indra forgot to ask Bhangasvana,' Vatsyayana said. 'In my own sutras on the subject, I convey a greater certainty than I now feel.' I was ready with the relevant quote:

> Vatsyayana does not believe there is any difference in the pleasure itself. Difference of sex is a matter of birth. It is generally held that man is active and woman passive. The man's actions in intercourse are therefore different from the woman's. The man thinks he is enjoying the woman, while the woman thinks she is being enjoyed by him. The difference is thus of attitude and experience, not in enjoyment.

Vatsyayana liked to hear his own sutras quoted back to him as long it was done in a reverential rather than critical spirit. Apart from his thick gray hair which he wore fashionably long, this was the only sign of vanity in the man. But then, wisdom and vanity are more closely associated than we are willing to recognize or accept when we are young.

'When you try to understand my sutras,' Vatsyayana said, 'you must always remember their context. My opinions also take their meaning from where I stand at the time. One cannot have a view from nowhere and from everywhere. At this particular place in the text, I was engaging with the opinions of my illustrious predecessors on the course taken by woman's pleasure. Often they contradict each other and themselves, attesting to even the wisest of men's confusion on the subject. The venerable Shvetaketu Auddalaki believes that a woman finds her true pleasure in signs of affection, kissing and caressing, whereas the pleasure given to her by the man's organ comes from a partial calming of her vulva's itch which continues after the man's ejaculation. According to the Babhravyas, there is a marked difference in the way sexual intercourse is experienced by men and women. A woman experiences violent pleasure when the male organ slides into her while the man experiences the highest bliss at the moment of ejaculation. They compare the woman's reactions to the action of a potter's wheel, slow to start with, then fast in the middle, and slow at the end, but with a continuous movement. However, all agree that a woman finds greater pleasure in kisses and caresses and, when fully excited, in bites and scratches than do men. Kisses and caresses are necessary to arouse her desire.'

'Acharya, why are a man's kisses and caresses so vital for the woman's desire?' I wanted to know, genuinely curious.

'This is a question which neither Shvetaketu, nor the Babhravyas, nor Suvarnabha nor even Dattaka have addressed,' Vatsyayana answered with what I thought was more than a tinge of self-satisfaction. I had noticed that his voice became vibrant whenever he discussed the opinions of other scholars. There was a distinct light of combat in his eyes at such times, confirming my opinion, already formed during studies with my guru Brahmadatta, that scholars are not at all as detached as popular perception would have it. There is a barely concealed blood lust in their disputations, exultation in the wounds they inflict with their words, while finishing off an opponent by annihilating his best argument is one of their chief pleasures.

'There is no part of the encounter between man and woman where a woman feels more cherished, more enveloped in the man's desire than in the preliminary kisses and caresses that lead to intercourse,' Vatsyayana began to explain. 'From the lightest of a man's kisses that alights on a closed eyelid or flutters along the surface of her lips, to the firmest of caresses that kneads buttock cheeks in urgent entreaty, the woman feels herself at the centre of intense male desire, an ardour that ignites her own. Once the intercourse actually begins, much of the man's desire retreats into his body's own sensations. There is a reluctance in the woman to give up the state of being so passionately wanted and shift into the realm of a wanting of her own. Most men fail to understand these moments of reluctance just before intercourse, and are baffled by what remains beyond their understanding.

'Apart from their different experience of caresses and kisses, I have opined that there is no difference between men and women. Yet, if you ask me to enlarge upon this view today, I will only say that women's bodies are more open than those of men. They are accustomed to receiving, being invaded by, even used, by their babies as much as by their men, and this circumstance gives their pleasure a different cast. A woman's receiving body is reflected in, indeed shapes, her receptive awareness. During the act of love it lets in a greater number and variety of images of union. Imagination is crucial for the experience of pleasure, and women are naturally endowed with a superior bodily imagination than are men. Even at climax, when all past births and future rebirths collapse into an instant, a woman's openness to the flood of pleasure is greater and its waters recede more slowly than in a man.

'Most scholars believe that imagination plays an important role in a woman's pleasure only in the beginning. As intercourse progresses, they say, the body takes over and by the end of the encounter, her consciousness is subsumed in her physical reactions. There is a verse by Dattaka on the subject:

> First she trembles in anticipation. Later, there is neither trembling nor anticipation, not even thought.

In the full flow of intercourse with a loved man, imagination may not always be dominant, but this does not mean that the woman's experience is merely corporeal. From its dwelling place in the deepest recesses of the body, the soul rises to the surface of her skin as the man and woman strain toward and against each other. In the best kind of intercourse, instead of the body being the sheath of the soul, it is the soul, in becoming skin, which sheathes the body.'

As self-absorbed as any other youth, for a long time it did not occur to me to ask Vatsyayana about his life at the hermitage. From his stray remarks, I had gathered that the hermits and their wives were curious about the new couple in their midst but apprehensive of his notoriety. They generally left Vatsyayana and Malavika alone, but exchanged polite courtesies whenever they chanced to meet on the grounds. It was as if Vatsyayana's work clung to his body like highly polluting animal fat which could permeate the sanctity of the hermitage, defiling the inmates and endangering their spiritual pursuits. Former priests and ritual specialists for the most part, with an odd merchant and retired state official thrown in, the hermits were seeking to renounce the pleasures and objects of the senses. Vatsyayana was an unwelcome reminder of Kama's presence in their own nature, a presence they needed to deny if they were to serve the purposes of other gods.

'I do not mind it for myself,' Vatsyayana said, when I finally asked him about his isolation, 'but my wife feels lonely and unhappy. Some of the other wives, even though much older, would like to be friendly with her but fear the disapproval of their husbands.'

I did not think to ask why the couple had chosen to live in a hermitage at all, in discomfort and isolation.

Except for a brief appearance to serve food during my third visit, I had not seen Malavika at all. Vatsyayana had mentioned that in this balmy weather which had just begun to heat up, his wife went out for long walks in the forest to gather wild flowers. She also spent hours just sitting on the bank of a pond inside the forest, watching the kingfishers, the herons, and the ripples that the light spring breeze caused on the surface of the water.

Frankly, I was relieved that I never caught even a glimpse of her. My turmoil in relation to Malavika had subsided in the week that had elapsed before I came back to the hermitage. My feelings of shame certainly contributed to this, as did my increasing preoccupation with the *Kamasutra* and my slowly intensifying resolve to write the first commentary on the treatise. Sutras, after all,

are only mnemonic devices to assist in recapitulation of the
main arguments of a much larger, unwritten text. The
value of a sutra lies in its brevity. That is why it is said that
the author of a sutra text would sell his grandson to save
a single syllable. Sutras cannot be understood without a
commentary; the verses and their exposition form a unity.

In my mind, Vatsyayana's wife was now just another
beautiful woman, not the promise of a magical
transformation. I would be lying if I said I was not acutely
aware of her when she briefly appeared to serve us the meal
during my third visit. But this time I was not struck dumb
and blind by her physical beauty. I saw the intelligence in
her eyes and the confidence in her movements, observed
that she and her husband exchanged very few words and
rarely looked at each other, an avoidance of contact rather
than indifference, and that Malavika seemed eager to serve
the meal quickly and get away from the hut.

'I hear you like to spend your days in the forest,' I said
as she was pouring water while I washed my hands after
eating. She looked up at me and once again I felt the full
impact of her beauty which sharpened my senses even as
it dulled my discrimination.

'Yes. Do you like the forest?' she asked in the friendly
but distant voice that wives of famous men use toward
their husbands' young admirers.

'Well, I am more of a city man. Like the Buddhists.'

'I have never been to Varanasi,' she said, suddenly
wistful. 'But I should now leave you to your work. Please
treat our humble abode as your own,' she added formally.

As I watched her walk away, I noticed with relief that
the quickening of my senses and the racing of my heart
were much less pronounced than on that first occasion. It
was like the falling of a few pebbles after an earthquake
was over.

Chapter Five

She must always be beautifully dressed so as to attract attention from passers-by on the royal road. But she should not exhibit herself shamelessly which would reduce her market value by half.

Kamasutra 6.1.7

The very next morning after his discourse on a woman's pleasure, Vatsyayana began to talk of his life. I was late in reaching the Seven Leaf hermitage that day. My father, who had so far determinedly ignored my preoccupation with the *Kamasutra* and its author, finally decided to convey his disapproval that particular morning. To do so he took upon himself the sin of interrupting his morning prayers. He came out of the puja room just as I was about to step out of the house, looking stricken and disapproving at the same time. Rather than using words, he allowed the act of the incomplete ritual and the expression on his face speak of his disappointment in me. I greeted him respectfully, pretended an ignorance of his feelings and climbed into the waiting carriage. As the carriage drove off, I had to tell the driver to slow down while I regained a measure of equanimity.

To judge from the warmth of his greeting, Vatsyayana

must have been eagerly awaiting my arrival. It was an agreeable sensation to have the sage so keenly anticipating our encounter.

Vatsyayana's discussions of the *Kamasutra* had been interspersed with personal snippets but on this morning he seemed to have decided to venture deeper into his memory. The process of concentrated introspection and narration was punctuated with long silences wherein he seemed to commune with voices from the past. His face, too, became more mobile, as his forehead furrowed in anger, creased in remembered guilt or smoothed over in the recollection of love or flattery.

Mallanaga Vatsyayana, to give him his full name, was born in Kausambi, the capital of the small kingdom of the Vatsas which was sandwiched between the powerful neighbours of Avanti and Magadha, although all three of them were now a part of Samudragupta's empire. At the time of his birth, this kingdom was ruled by Rudradeva, a feudatory of the Gupta emperor. Vatsyayana was born the same year as Udayana, Rudradeva's only son and successor, named after his illustrious predecessor, the hero of the famed Vasavdatta romance, who ruled Kausambi at the time of the Buddha.

'You have not visited Kausambi? It is smaller than Varanasi, of course. But the smallness of Kausambi was of a perfect pearl as compared to the large diamond brilliance of your city. The impression of a pearl's symmetry was reinforced by the king's decree that the sun-dried brick facades of all the private dwellings and public buildings must be whitewashed every two years. Visually, the city was harsh and blinding in the afternoon when the sun is high but became insubstantial at night, no more than the whispering play of silvery shadows. The pearl is now flawed, though, because Kausambi is becoming overcrowded even as it becomes more prosperous. The changes are especially noticeable on the four main streets that lead from the city gates to the central square on which the royal palace abuts. On the king's highway connecting the eastern and western gates, the files of porters and the caravans of bullock-wagons loaded with goods on their way from the ports of Saurashtra to Pataliputra and other great cities of the eastern kingdoms, jostling for space with the pedestrians, troops of cavalry, palanquins of nobles and courtesans with their trains of servants—all this would make you think you were in one of the great cities of the empire, Mathura or Varanasi, for instance. Of course, we do not have even a quarter of your one hundred Shiva temples, and only two Buddhist monasteries as compared to your thirty. Nor are there so many ships, boats and rafts on the river; but, then, as compared to our Jamuna, your Ganga is not a river but a veritable ocean.

'When I was growing up, Kausambi was a more leisurely, even a sleepy place. Besides the royal park, there were only the slaughterhouses, the village of salt-makers and the village of butchers outside the city walls. Nowadays, because of Udayana's passion for building and beautifying the city, the overflow of carpenters, smiths, bricklayers and labourers has settled in a ring of slums outside the town's walls. Around these walls the moat, a hundred feet wide, which also serves as a diversion channel whenever the Jamuna floods, is becoming filthier and smellier by the day. But if you approach Kausambi through the eastern gateway, as do the trading caravans on their way to seaports on the west coast or to the lands beyond the mountain ranges to the northwest, then you will still pass through miles and miles of our magnificent royal park which is both a forest and a park, wilderness as well as civilization. The forest, with its herds of spotted deer and wild boar, the hunting lodge of the king, pavilions of nobles and isolated hermitages, covers much of the larger area and was out of bounds to Kausambi's citizens except with special permission or invitation of the king. But even the public park covers an area greater than that of many large towns.

'As a child I spent whole days in the park, watching cock and ram fights on special feast days in the sporting arena. At other times, I wandered on the undulating grassy slopes by the river or explored the wilder parts of the park near the forest. We often took picnic meals with us during these outings which we ate in a clearing at the edge of one of the many ponds that dot the park. Watching the saras cranes with their red heads and neck under white feathers standing motionless on one long thin leg, surrounded by the kusha grass which bears long silky plumes of pale silver drifting fluff, one had to be careful that these did not fall into the food like an unwanted garnishing.'

From Vatsyayana's description, even if gilded with nostalgia, the house he grew up in must have been truly magnificent. He was almost seven, though, before he realized that his home was also a famous brothel, the establishment of Kausambi's celebrated courtesan sisters, Avantika and Chandrika. Located in the southern quarter of the city, traditionally the quarter of the courtesans, it occupied over an acre of grounds and overlooked the highway leading from the king's palace to the royal park.

'For a child it was a miniature, enchanted world with none of the dangerous unpredictability of the real one. Here I could even trust the shadows, which came alive each evening when the lamps were lit, to stay as shadows and not suddenly become full of the menace which can paralyze a child with fear. Coming through the gate, one entered the outer courtyard with stalls for animals on both the wings. There was always a great deal of activity going on here. Twice a day, the bullocks had to be fed their meal of grass and chaff and their horns oiled. The buffaloes and the cows were milked, the horses' manes combed, the stalls cleaned, the animals washed—all of this accompanied by the incessant chatter of the keepers as they went about their tasks. For about a year, when I was around four, we also had an elephant tethered to a post in the middle of the courtyard. I remember the dignity with which it quietly shovelled stacks of hay into its mouth with the help of its trunk while occasionally swishing its tail to keep the flies away. On special occasions, days of whose significance only the elephant's mahout was aware, it would be treated to a meal of sugarcane stalks, while once a month it was given a dinner of boiled rice oozing oil, kneaded into white balls as big as melons.

'The private bedrooms reflected individual taste. My mother's bedroom was austere, with a plain bed, a chest containing her clothes and a stool with one small box of ornaments. Chandrika's bedroom, on the other hand, was cluttered with jewel boxes piled on top of each other in crooked rows. Other presents given by her many admirers were strewn all over the floor. I especially remember a fly-whisk made of soft yak-tail hair and set in a ornamental handle. It lay in one corner, unused, for many months. The couch in the room, in spite of her maid's best efforts, never seemed to be quite free of discarded clothes. Beside her drawing board, next to the mirror, there was a small round table, its marble top covered by pots of perfumes, salves and creams. A birdcage hung from an elephant tusk mounted on a wall. The birds—mynahs, parrots, koels—kept varying according to the course of Chandrika's fickle affections, the discarded bird banished downstairs to one of the cages lining the walls of the inner courtyard. These birds, a little boy's perpetual delight, were not the only ones we had. There was also a house peacock who generally preferred to strut around the terrace every morning and early in the evening, sweeping the terrace with its regal tail, waiting for an interested peahen to alight. The peacock was a nuisance during the rainy season when it shrieked its love incessantly, the cries especially raucous between thunderclaps.

'The third room was occupied by Kanchan-mata, the old nurse who had brought up both the sisters and held a special position in the household. Chandrika and my mother shamelessly used her to convey unpleasant messages to unwanted suitors, or to make excuses:"Kanchan-mata won't like it", "Kanchan-mata won't allow me to do this". They let the clients think she was their mother. Her room was cluttered with bottles, flagons and vials containing powders, pills, ointments, lotions and oils. Besides a fondness for gossip about the peccadilloes of Kausambi's leading citizens, the ruling passion of the old bawd's life was the preparation of various aids to enhance female beauty and sexual allure.

'Downstairs in the east wing we had three large rooms where the clients were entertained. One room had a gaming table while the other two were used for music and dance. Musical instruments—the vina, the flute and the drums—protected from dust in their cloth covers, were stacked against the walls. The musicians did not live with us but came to the house every evening from the Quarter of the Entertainers. The larger of these rooms was also used for the vocal concerts of visiting maestros, or of our own Jaivanti who had a great reputation as a singer in those days. Like many old men whose sexual performance and desire move in opposite directions with age, Jaivanti loved to come to our house, ostensibly to sing but in reality to approach Chandrika who he contrived to brush against or touch in what he hoped would be understood by others as a paternal caress. Whenever Chandrika complained after he had left, my mother explained the sexual needs of old men to her, adding that they became more and more like little babies as they aged, with a heightened need to touch and be touched.

'Chandrika, who had little patience with babies, old men, or for that matter with any one else who did not play an active role in her sexual theatre, would make some sarcastic comment about men—of all ages—and then flounce away in a concert of swishing skirts and jangling bracelets, tinkling anklets and tiny bells which hung in a loop from her girdle.

'Oh, how I loved her! A beautiful girl just stepping into womanhood but still wearing the slightly flustered expression of someone who is surprised by her own beauty, Chandrika was not yet at home in the realm of desire; she was still surprised by the effect she had on men. Her high spirits and glowing skin were not only revelations of youth but were also provoked by the lustful eyes that caressed her as she walked on the street, her head held high, looking straight ahead while her body soaked in a quiet excitement from the erotic field in which it moved so knowingly. I have seen more than one Jaina monk, renouncers of desire, clothed only in modesty, who walk with a hesitant gait with their eyes on the ground lest an imprudent movement hurt an insect, look up and falter in their step, their ceaseless waving of the fly whisk coming to an abrupt halt in mid-air when Chandrika brushed past them on the street. Her instinctive sensual wisdom never dimmed even when she was alone or with me, a little boy.

'Every day, just before her bath, Chandrika stood naked in front of a mirror of burnished copper, an import from Damascus. Her eyes would roam in pleasure over the reflection of her slender limbs, sheathed in a golden-brown skin without a blemish, her thick black hair with a hint of curl cascading well below her narrow waist. The only unwanted guest at her feast of self admiration, a frown, appeared when her green-gray eyes settled on her breasts.

Covering them with her hands, she would squeeze them a little, as if estimating their size and firmness.

'"You don't think they are too small, Malli, do you?" she would ask, not so much of me as of the empty room crowded with the eyes of invisible males.

'"They are perfect, Chandrika masi," the five-year old lover would reply.

'Indeed, looking back now with the knowledge of the adult man, and contaminated only by the virginal longings of little Malli, I can see how Chandrika's small high breasts were perfect for her slender frame. From the strict dictates of classic beauty, though, they were smaller than the heavy orbs eulogized by the poets. But then, in my long experience I have yet to know a woman, including the most gorgeous of her sex, who was convinced that she was beautiful, who did not grieve over some secret shortcoming magnified in her own eyes into a grave defect. For years Chandrika pestered Kanchan-mata for remedies to enlarge her breasts. She would bathe them in antimony and rice water for a month, tell herself every day before the mirror that there was a slight but unmistakable increase in their size, and then one day acknowledge that the proud breasts were also stubborn, refusing to change their shape. She would then switch over to another remedy, such as the paste of pomegranate seeds in white mustard oil, which she asked me to rub into her breasts. None of the remedies was ever effective, though Chandrika tried them over and over again. That is one reason why in my treatise on kama I have kept away from the subject of increasing the size of a woman's breasts in spite of the availability of much ancient lore on the subject.'

Remembering some of the conversations in my guru Brahmdatta's ashram, I interrupted him. 'Acharya, I have heard some learned men criticize you for the seventh part of the *Kamasutra*. They question whether you really believe in the remedies you give there for attracting and sexually enslaving a member of the opposite sex, for increasing sexual vigour and penis size.'

Vatsyayana looked pensive for a moment before answering.

'I can only repeat the answer I give in the book. Good looks, good qualities, youth and generosity are the chief and most natural means of making a person agreeable in the eyes of others. It is only in their absence that a man or a woman must resort to art and artifice. No means should be tried which are doubtful in their effects, which are likely to cause injury to the body, which include the death of animals and which come in contact with impure things. "Ah, Mallanaga," mocked a poet-friend once, "You do not really believe that if a man, after anointing his penis with a mixture of the powders of the white thorn apple, long pepper, black pepper and honey, engages in sexual union with a woman, he makes her subject to his will?"

'"Yes, I do," I answered in all honesty.

'I admit I have not tried any of the recipes myself. Poets often fail to realize that personal experience counts for little in textual scholarship, a tradition they are wont to mock without understanding its complexities. They are strangers to the pleasures of registering, systematizing and classifying, preferring to believe that all we scholars do is make books out of other books. Like poetics, scholarly writing has its own conventions. It is not that one simply quotes the opinions of other scholars on a problem and then gives an opinion of one's own. One must explain what others have said, the assumptions on which their opinions are based, the weaknesses in their arguments, look at other possible solutions to the problem and then choose the best one while giving reasons for this choice. Unlike the poet who reveals himself in every line, the person of the scholar is perhaps only revealed in his conclusions. If you want to know Vatsyayana, read carefully the last verses of each chapter.

'The remedies I give in the seventh part of my work have to be cited in at least two standard works on erotics. None of them should be a direct quotation and there must be inconvertible evidence that the author has consulted the medical and other authorities of his times.

'I told my friend that the recipe he mentioned is originally found in Babhravya Panchala's great work, and then again in the text of Kuchumara. Increasing sexual vigour by drinking the mixture of rice and sparrow eggs boiled in milk and sweetened with ghee and honey is a remedy found in Shvetaketu and is repeated by Dattaka and Kuchumara in their texts. The recipe for sexual enslavement of a woman by dressing pieces of arris root with oil of mango, placing them for six months in a hole made in the trunk of a sisu tree and then grinding them into an ointment which is applied to the penis before intercourse, is to be found in works of Svetaketu, the Babhravyas and Kuchumara. The only recipe where I had doubts and agonized over its inclusion in my text concerned the enslavement of women by anointing the penis with the remains of a kite who had died a natural death, ground into powder and mixed with cowach and honey. It was not only the authority of the Babhravyas which tipped the scale in the favour of its inclusion but my consultations with other experts, especially doctors, who gave scientific explanations for the efficacy of this particular ointment. I am proud to say that there is not a single sentence in the book which is not supported by authorities in other disciplines. If my book has merit, it lies in its endeavour to go deeper into erotic life by going beyond the science of erotics.'

In our next day's meeting it was as if Vatsyayana had not re-emerged from his immersion in the memories of his childhood. I was again late that morning—Chatursen's carriage driver, bleary eyed and reeking of stale mahuva liquor, had turned up two hours after the appointed time—and Vatsyayana's greeting was short as he impatiently motioned me to my seat. Without waiting for my questions which normally initiated our conversations, he began to talk, continuing his story from where he had left it the previous afternoon.

'When I think it over, I got to touch and hold Chandrika's ˙ breasts more than any of her regular customers and occasional lovers. In addition to the rubbing in of various breast-enlarging salves and creams, I was an ardent assistant in her toilet for the evening entertainment. The preparation started in late afternoon and easily took three hours. When I was small and could still wander into her bedroom without waiting for her permission or invitation, I remember Chandrika stepping out of her bath and standing naked in front of the mirror, staring at her reflection with frowning concentration. Her long black hair glistened with minute drops of water while her fingers skimmed lightly over the shaved skin around the vulva, spying out any tell-tale prickliness needing the immediate attention of the pumice stone. She would send me out to the veranda for this part of her toilet, but she was aware that I watched her through the window.

'Besides helping to hold and spread her hair as she leaned back to perfume it with black aloe smoke, I assisted her in the adornment of her breasts, the only part of her body Chandrika treated as if it did not quite belong to her. She watched me closely as I first scented them with liquid sandal and then lightly rubbed them with saffron dissolved in water to give them their golden glow. Although I was only a little boy, I noticed her eyes smouldering with that wine-intoxicated look I came to know and remember so well. Her small nipples would harden and her breathing quicken. Embarrassment was a word unknown to Chandrika. In any case, I was too absorbed in my own sensations of the soft flesh under my palms and the fine line of down above the navel rising up to meet my caressing fingers to notice her excitement or discomfiture.

'Only after I had completed this part of her toilet was the maid summoned to tint the soles of her feet and decorate the insteps with lines of red paint. The maid also dressed her hair, twining thin garlands of fresh flowers in the tresses artfully coiled high at the back of her head. After brushing her lips lightly with coral lac-dye, rimming her eyes with lampblack and rubbing a perfumed ointment under her armpits and the upper parts of her thighs—perfume matching the season although jasmine was her favourite—Chandrika would drape a long skirt, held fast by a gem-studded girdle, around her waist. The material of the skirt, again depending upon the season, varied from a light, almost gossamer-thin cotton muslin to delicate silks woven with gold threads. Except for winter, when her breasts were held tight by embroidered bodices of raw silk, she generally threw a thin stole over her shoulders which covered her breasts as often as it revealed them. As a finale to the worship of her body, she then put on her favourite ornaments: gold earrings the shape of yellow lotus flowers, a gold chain with a ruby at the centre around the neck (in summer, a long necklace of pearls falling in strings upon the rise and fall of her breasts), ruby-studded gold armlets and bracelets, and rings decorating her slim fingers, their designs varying according to her mood, although a serpent-shaped one on her left index finger remained a perennial favourite.

'A very different kind of memory of Chandrika's ceremonial preparations for the evening's entertainment is my recollection of the perfume of her body, a fragrance so intoxicating that it made me dizzy if I inhaled too deeply. In spite of its restricted repertoire and lack of elaboration, my sense of smell has always been the brighter lamp into the vaults of my memory than my vision. Chandrika's scent was not singular but a glorious composite of subtly shifting smells. The essence of her perfume was a heavy female odour, not unlike the smell of mossy earth after rain. This mysterious, dark scent was dispersed by the fragrance of sandalwood from the paste rubbed into her breasts, and then further overlaid with the flowery lightness of lotus blossoms and the somewhat sharper tang of night jasmines she often wore in her hair.

'I realize that the utter precision with which I can recollect Chandrika's body rituals is the consequence of a small boy's forlorn effort to reach into the depths of a woman's soul through mesmerizing physical details. Even as a child, whenever I watched Chandrika preen before the mirror, smiles of delight and frowns of concern drifting across her face like the shadows of monsoon clouds, I wanted to enter her mind and experience her emotions. In the hot afternoons of the summer I became seven years old, I often prowled the veranda of the upper floor. Unable to sleep, listening with my ear pressed close to the door to the sound of my mother's soft snores, or hearing Chandrika's sighs, purring and suppressed laughter through the window of her bedroom where she lay with her lover, I wanted to crawl into the heads of the women, curl myself into their hearts. From the age of four or five, I was in a state of constant longing, almost unbearable at times, as I watched the women in our house, these creatures whose bodies were not only different but whose each limb was animated by a mysterious female force. And there I was, a little boy, acutely aware that I was not one of them. I pushed myself into the exile of my maleness, wondering if they felt the same sensations and the same emotions I did as a boy, or even whether one could feel the same feeling differently if one was a woman?'

As I listened to Vatsyayana reminisce about the household of accomplished and vibrant women in which he had grown up, I could not help thinking of the women of *Kamasutra*. Whether servant girl or queen, go-between or courtesan, all of them were proud of the beauty of the female form, boldly 'loving with naked breast'. Yet there are occasional verses on women in the text, on their passivity, which convey a feeling contrary to its dominant tone. For instance:

> Vigour and boldness are male qualities. Weakness, sensuality, and dependence are characteristics of the female.

'Perhaps you did not notice that this verse was a quote?' Vatsyayana was reproachful for the first time. 'And although it is true that one generally quotes with approval, this particular quotation is an exception to the rule. A woman is not passive but receptive, a crucial difference indeed, since one can be both active and receptive at the same time. In the four kinds of preliminary loveplay that I have described, the woman takes the active part in two. In one, she encircles her lover like a vine does a tree, offering and withdrawing her lips for a kiss, driving the man wild with excitement. In the other, "Climbing the Tree", she rests a foot on one of the man's feet and the other against his thigh. Hooking one arm around his back and clinging to his shoulder and neck with the other, she makes the movement of climbing him as if he was a tree.

'Then I have a whole chapter on virile behaviour in women, on the inversion of roles, where I recommend that when a man has spent his strength after repeated intercourse and the woman is not satisfied, she lie on top of him and insert a dildo in his anus. Actually, Chandrika was an expert at perceiving a lover's hidden wish that she play the man. There are some men, she told me later, especially among the rich and powerful, who are capable of intercourse only after the woman has used the dildo on them. Chandrika was very much on my mind when I wrote those particular verses.'

On cue, like a docile student, I quoted.

She is determined to unite him with the instrument she is inserting into his anus, so that he gets a taste for different pleasures. This is one way of proceeding. Tearing the flowers from her hair and laughing until she is breathless, she presses her breast hard against the man's chest, forcing him to lower his head. She imitates all he did to her, dominating him in turn. Laughing, she mocks and insults him. If he shows modesty and wishes rest from his exertions, she climbs on top and sodomizes him.

'Yes,' said Vatsyayana. 'This is certainly not recommending weak, passive feminine behaviour in lovemaking. I further instruct the woman that although a man may want the dildo in his anus he is often embarrassed about this wish. To avoid the embarrassment, distract his attention with inconsequential chatter while stealthily untying his undergarments. If he clenches his thighs out of modesty, she must caress the inside of his thighs, slide her hand into the cleft of his buttocks to widen it and then insert her middle finger or the instrument.'

The morning silence was beginning to disperse. Voices came drifting in from other huts as women became busy in the preparation of the midday meal, focused on the tasks of cutting vegetables, cleaning lentils and lighting the cooking fires. The easy syllables of ordinary dialogue and the comforting clatter of ritual domesticity gradually infiltrated Vatsyayana's concentrated discourse. It was time to end the day's session and go into the kitchen for the lunch of tamarind rice and curds with black peppercorns that Malavika had laid out for us.

Chapter Six

It can happen that in pursuing profit, one ends with loss. A sexual relationship must be approached with prudence.

Kamasutra 6.6.1

It was almost the beginning of summer when I finally ventured into the forest next to the hermitage. In the countryside, the earth was heating up as if in a low fever. Bled dry by the rays of the sun, the cracks in the earth's baked surface had begun to widen ominously. The trees, robbed of their discoloured leaves, had begun to look as if struck by a wasting sickness, casting doubt on their capacity to survive the arid winds of high summer which would soon seek to grind them down with fiery sand.

That particular morning Vatsyayana had appeared listless. Dark smudges under his eyes accentuated the fine lines at their sides. As we sat in our accustomed places in front of the hut, he was unusually quiet. His eyes often glazed over and at times he seemed to be looking through me into the depths of the forest behind my back. Images of Malavika alone in the forest flashed through my head. I forced my mind back to the hut and the calmer vision of a guru instructing a reverent student. It was a struggle, though, and noticing my growing discomfort, he made an effort to pull himself together.

'I slept badly last night,' he said. 'After many years I again had a nightmare I used to have as a child.'

He lapsed into silence. After a few minutes, without my prompting, he began to narrate the dream, more to himself than to me.

'I am climbing up the gentle slope of a hill. It is just before sunset. The hilltop is bathed in a rosy light which drifts toward me in swirls. The lake at the bottom of the hill is a motionless sheet of water glinting with the colours of the setting sun. Suddenly it becomes dark. The hillside becomes pulsatingly alive. Tree branches extend toward me like twisted arms. The ground below me starts to heave like ocean waves. I cannot keep my footing. I am falling. I am falling into a lake of water blacker than any seen by a human eye, blacker than an ink spot in a pile of black beans.

'In childhood I used to wake up screaming from this nightmare. Whichever bed I was in—my mother's or Chandrika's—became a place of agony. The woman would try to comfort me but I shrank from her touch. The only person who could soothe me was our cook, Ganadasa. He had to be woken up, and would bring me a glass of hot milk with sugar, almond slivers and saffron. He would sit next to me while I drank the milk, quietly feeling his solid presence.

'And then?' I asked.

'Oh, nothing much happened after that,' he said. 'I would go back to sleep. On waking up in the morning I had to carefully wash my face to ward off the dream's baleful influence. I still do.'

Sensing his reluctance to go on, I put off asking questions about the text with which I had come prepared.

I was content to wait. When he suggested that we talk later in the afternoon and that I spend the morning in the forest, I readily agreed.

Today I wonder whether it was his intention that I meet his wife alone since Malavika spent much of her day there. In any case, it was at his encouragement that I walked into the forest. Perhaps it is more exact to say that as I walked away from the hermitage I gradually found myself in the forest. Hermitages straddle the space between cultivation and wilderness and it is not easy to say where one ends and the other begins. There were a few markers, though. The initially wide and almost straight path narrowed and broke up into small crooked trails which meandered away from each other even as each in its own way followed the lay of the land, skirting thick scrub, a thicket of tall grass or a dense grove of trees. Except for the closely clustered bamboo trees with their slim spear-shaped leaves, indifferent to summer as they are to other seasons, the forest showed distinct signs of fading. Most sal trees had already lost the fresh green leaves of spring to a darker foliage. Grass was turning into clumps of dried stalks. At randomly chosen spots, however, the forest, as if bored with its different shades of bilious green and brown, had impulsively decided to break into flames through trees covered all over with orange and red flowers.

As I walked further into the forest, it became more dense. The foliage overhead straining toward the sun and perpetually hungry for light, allowed less and less of it through. The dun-coloured anthills, imitating sheer cliffs and needle-thin mountain peaks seen only in dreams, became rarer. Spotted and swamp deer gave way to antelope that bounded away at any close approach. Then, suddenly, I found myself in a clearing, exactly where Vatsyayana had said his wife would be.

Malavika was sitting on a grassy knoll that sloped

down gently into a large pond. Half a dozen ospreys were lined up below her at the pond's edge, staring fixedly at the dragonflies skimming close to the surface of the water. Malavika took my intrusion more calmly than did the birds. As I sat down next to her, the indignant cries of the ospreys fading into the distance, she was at first very much the guru's wife, kind but reserved. I will not pretend that I was unaware of her physical presence. Much of the time I looked at her feet while we exchanged polite pleasantries. For more than a decade of their exile together, Lakshmana never once raised his eyes above Sita's ankles and hence could not recognize her necklace and earrings which had fallen off when Ravana carried her away. My own difficulty was that feet, especially those as shapely as Malavika's, can become the repository of all of a woman's beauty, a distillate of all her charms. The problem lies with the gaze, not its object. Given my strong attraction to her, conflicted and suppressed as it may have been, I would have even found Malavika's toenail irresistible. Only a few years older than me, yet she was absolutely unapproachable. As described by Manu, the punishment for intercourse with the wife of the guru, even if Vatsyayana, strictly speaking, was not my guru, is unambiguous . . . and chilling:

> The mark of the vulva will be branded into his forehead; he will be forced to embrace the red-hot iron image of a woman till he become pure by dying; or he may cut off his penis and testicles and taking them in his joined hands go on walking in the south-west direction till he falls down dead.

I discovered at our very first meeting that I could comfortably assimilate my different feelings for her. To my surprise, neither desire nor fear came in the way of my being at ease as we began to talk, impersonally at first and then with a mounting intensity and lack of reserve which is the singular blessing of youth. In the beginning, our conversation was mostly about trees. Malavika loved trees and flowers. She was never as animated as when she could tell me things about them which I did not know before. I knew that a sal forest of the kind we were in was sacred because the sal tree is associated with Vishnu in his incarnation as Rama. To convince a hesitant Sugriva to ally with him, Rama had demonstrated his strength by shooting an arrow which pierced seven sal trees standing in a row before it returned to his quiver. I did not know, till Malavika told me, that Lord Buddha was born under a sal tree. On her way to her paternal home for childbirth, Mayadevi, the Enlightened One's mother, rested in a grove of sal trees. As she stretched her hand upward to pluck flowers from a branch, the baby was born and the tree shed flowers on the newborn child.

Malavika described the erotic significance of the red dye made from the flowers of the flame-of-the-forest, and how at one place in the *Kamasutra* her husband compares the spring buds of the tree to nail marks made by a passionate woman on the body of her lover. There were yet other trees and flowers on whose significance we differed amicably. The five arrows of Lord Kama through which he excites the five senses and inspires passion, Malavika held, are made of flowers of the ashoka tree. I agreed that ashoka is indeed dedicated to the love god and is closely associated with women, especially forest nymphs. But I knew that the arrows of the love god are made of five completely different and much more fragrant flowers: blue lotus, jasmine, mango flowers, champaka and sirisa.

In all this talk of trees, flowers, gods and nymphs, time flew with the speed of Krishna's discus and it was well past noon by the time I returned to the hermitage, lightheaded with the fresh air of the forest. Observing my somewhat exhilarated mood, Vatsyayana gave me a quizzical look and only nodded when I told him about meeting his wife by the pond. I was happy to see that he had recovered a measure of his usual equanimity, although when he began to talk it became apparent that he was still engrossed in remembering his early life.

'I have often wondered whether my mother disliked me, not for what I was—for they tell me I was a sweet-tempered, plump and cuddly baby—but for what I did to her beautiful body. Barely thirty, in her youth she was renowned in lands far from our kingdom as the jewel of Kausambi, the incomparable Avantika.

'"Your mother had no rival in all the kingdoms," Ganadasa used to tell me. "She knows by heart all the poems sung during a dance and has mastered the language of gesture by which the various moods of love are expressed. She knows how to play the drum and how to adjust the tightness of its skin to regulate the sound. She knows the flute, as also the art of playing ball. She can prepare dishes almost as well as I can, according to the recipes of the best cuisine. She is skilled in the manner of bathing, in the body's sixty-four positions of making love, in seeming reluctant and in anticipating men's desires. She knows how to write elegantly with a cut reed, to draw and paint. She knows the language of flowers and how to arrange magnificent bouquets chosen for their form and colour. She has studied astrology, mathematics and poetics. Very few people are aware that it was your mother who invented the well-trick which is now taught in the best brothels of the central countries."

'"The well-trick, Ganadasa?" I asked.

'"Like any great innovator who gets a reputation by solving a long-standing problem in his field, what your mother did was to find a solution to the courtesan's dilemma.

'"Now, listen carefully. A good courtesan must make her lover believe that she is truly and passionately in love with him. Yet however much the man wants to go along with her pretence, he cannot quite forget it is a measure of the courtesan's skill to make him believe precisely that. Her loving glances, passionate cries and poetic declarations of love will never quite succeed in removing the last residue of doubt in his mind. That is, if the man is sensible, and generally men who amass riches are sensible.

'"Many years ago, a wealthy merchant became your mother's lover. He liked her well enough, even after the initial infatuation had worn off, but looked sceptical whenever she professed her great love for him. 'I would die if you ever left me, even for a month,' she would say, but the merchant would only touch her arm and smile, as if humouring a child.

'"One day, the merchant announced that he was going away on a business trip and would return to Kausambi after six months. Your mother wept, imploring him not to leave her. She tore at her hair and clothes, crying all the while that she could not bear the separation, but the man took it as a game and smiled his disbelieving smile.

'"She clung to him as he was leaving, weeping piteously, and when he reached the gate she ran into the garden, crying, 'I cannot bear it anymore! I want to die!' Suddenly, we heard a shout, 'The mistress has jumped into the well!' All of us rushed toward the well. There was much confusion, with people milling round, women crying—Kanchan-mata's wails were the loudest. A servant was lowered into the well by a rope tied around his waist.

After a few anxious minutes, we heard him call out, 'It is a miracle! The mistress is alive!'

'"Your mother was pulled up, soaking wet and only half-conscious. By this time the merchant was besides himself. He was rolling on the ground in his grief, crying, 'Oh, my love Avantika! How could I have ever doubted your love!'

'"After that, he was her slave, opening up his heart and his purse without reserve. Your mother left him after a year, much poorer and, I suspect, heartbroken. What your mother had done that day was to have a net secretly tied under the surface of the water to break her fall into the well.

'"Of course, by now the well-trick is so well-known that a courtesan can only use it with a lover who is a stranger to the Middle Kingdoms, and even then she needs to be sure that the man is unaware of your mother's innovation."

'Somehow I did not like the end of the story.

'"Why did she leave the merchant if he loved her?" I asked.

'"Because he had become poor," the cook was patient with me. "A good courtesan would rather touch a corpse than a pauper, and your mother was the best. It is a very rare courtesan who is honoured by the king, as she was with the title 'Lady of the Court'. You should be proud of her."'

Well past the first flush of youth when he was born, Vatsyayana's mother had not taken well to motherhood. For all her accomplishments, she found it hard to reconcile herself to the loss of freshness in the beauty of her face and to the gradual blurring of lines in her sculpted form. What

Vatsyayana remembered most clearly about his mother while he was growing up was her preoccupation with the rejuvenation of her fading looks. Two classes of objects increasingly claimed her full attention: those which held out the promise of enhancing her beauty—lotions, salves, oils, scents, powders—and those which reflected the results of these efforts, primarily mirrors, not only of the highly polished copper kind but also, and especially, the eyes of men.

'I can now imagine the strain the obsession imposed upon her, particularly when she was out among people on the street. Even at home my mother must have been uncomfortable when clients came for the evening entertainment where Chandrika was the star attraction. Letting her sister be at the centre of the stage while she kept herself in the background, my mother's desperate eyes must have scoured—without appearing to—the eyes of the assembled men, for a glimmer of that desire always sent a shiver of well-being coursing through her. Her search became more frantic with each passing year as the number of indifferent eyes, each capable of inducing a succession of small inner collapses, increased.

'Unlike Chandrika, my mother had no use for the eyes of a small boy, my eyes. The only men she granted access to her special world were those who could facilitate her obsession. Essentially, these were only two: the doctor who came in once a week with the herbal medicines of rejuvenation which Ayurveda prescribes for a person entering the thirties and thus the beginning of old age, and Ganadasa, whom my mother consulted for hours on the preparation of potions from fruits, vegetables and meats which served as her daily beauty draughts. The rascally doctor, with his dyed hair and beard, whose infallible science was ever at the service of profit, was well known for ogling his fairer patients, and though old in years and experienced in conspiratorial seduction, often played the young man for them. All my mother needed me for was to pluck out the gray hair that had begun to appear on her head, paying a cowry for every five I could find—a task I hated in spite of the cowries I began to accumulate. I feel sad about it now, but at that time I accepted her indifference to my existence as the natural way of a mother with her son. But my mother's indifference was more than mitigated by Chandrika, who welcomed me into her self-absorption. She was an altogether different goddess—who did not spurn my adoration.

'Just before I felt asleep last night, I remembered something else—the stretch mark on my mother's belly which she often told me was my "gift" to her. It was the faintest of marks, a short thin line a shade lighter than the golden brown of her skin. Barely noticeable, it nonetheless looms in my memory like welts left by the blows of a cane on a thief's naked back. I remember that when she finished examining herself in the mirror, my mother would lightly rub her right palm against the mark I was responsible for. I imagined I could see the mixture of repulsion and duty as she did that, as if caressing the cratered face of a pock-marked husband one no longer loves, and I cringed along with her—I, the wrecker of her beauty. And then, as she put on her favourite long red skirt and tied the girdle high on her hip to hide the mark, I wished I could give her back the perfection of her beauty, her unalloyed pleasure in her body, give them back to all women.'

'Acharya,' I wanted to protest, 'you have given so much to so many women! You gave them permission to be active in love, encouraged them to be fearless in seeking pleasure. You unshackled their erotic life from prohibitions imposed upon it by generations of sages since the time of the epics. Is freedom any less important than beauty?'

I remained silent, receiving Vatsyayana's pain even as

he masked it by carrying on his narration in a neutral, almost bemused voice.

'I know my mother would have preferred a daughter. What could she do with a son who was only a guest in her home for a few years? A son belongs to the father and she knew that when I turned ten he would take me away. She could not afford to love me with all her heart; it would have broken when I went away. With a daughter she need not have fought her feelings, not deliberately forced the fading of the glow in her eyes at the sight of the child. A daughter would have taken her place, inherited her profession. She could have remained a part of a daughter's life. She would have loved teaching the girl all she had learnt, prepare her for life with her own experience. What could she do with me?

'My mother's unhappiness touched with wintry frost what I otherwise remember as a lively house full of music, dance, laughter and the bustling flow of a stream of clients. There were no financial worries even though the expenses were considerable. The monthly wages of the musicians, maids, cooks, the mahout and the keepers of other animals, the gardener and the washerman, must alone have come to fifteen hundred panas. If I add to this the cost of animal fodder, food and clothes for the servants and all other household expenses, then the total amount we spent every month must have been over three thousand panas. That is sixty gold dinars in your Varanasi money. Yet money was never a concern, although Kanchan-mata constantly grumbled about our expenses and the need for thrift. Chandrika alone paid four hundred panas every month to the king's treasury, the amount which the tax inspector had fixed as being equivalent to two days of her income. For the wealthy and the powerful men of the city she was a prized trophy, universally accepted as the seal of great success. The fact of being her lover could be flaunted to arouse the envy of other men; after all, what good is success if it does not arouse envy?

'At the time of which I speak, between the fourth and sixth years of my life, she was living as wife to the jeweller Madansen, a man whose financial generosity was matched by his possessive jealousy. Not counting tradesmen, servants, musicians and dance teachers, the only male visitors Madansen tolerated were the chief of prisons and my father, who divided his occasional affections between the two sisters. The jeweller did not permit my father's visits out of sentiment but because my father was one of the most respected leaders of trading caravans throughout the central countries. "The great sarathvaha of Kausambi", as he was often called, carried Madansen's more valuable consignments in his personal care. It also helped that since he was on the road most of the year, my father's visits to Kausambi were infrequent. Since my birth, or rather from the time I can remember and till the age of six, my father visited us but four times.

'Why did my mother continue the connection with my father? It had nothing to do with me, their son. My father was wealthy, and brought expensive and exotic gifts for us from foreign lands. The copper mirror from Damascus was one of his presents. My father's continued liaison with us provoked Madansen to keep his own ardour and generosity at a high pitch, and prevented him from forming other liaisons.

'The chief of prisons, a small, plump and fussy man—his name was Nitigupta—came more often, perhaps once a month. I knew of his impending visit by the sight of Madansen's unsmiling face at the evening entertainment a few days before Nitigupta came to spend the night with Chandrika, and the solicitous attention my mother paid Madansen during these evenings. As a tradesman, however wealthy, Madansen was in no position to alienate the chief of prisons. His protest was confined to sulking, from which he had to be coaxed by the two women—both experts at the task of coaxing sullen men. On these evenings Madansen would refuse to stay over for the night, and a contest of wills took place between him and Chandrika to see how near the beginning or after the end of Nitigupta's visit she could seduce the jealous jeweller. Nitigupta too paid well, but of course not on the same scale as Madansen and even less than my father. The liaison with him was useful for reasons other than money: it protected us from unscrupulous tax collectors, avaricious policemen and the other human vultures who hover around the establishments of courtesans.

'Madansen made large presents of money as well as ornaments. The gold pieces came in beautifully embroidered silk bags tied with a red string and the jewellery in carved wooden boxes padded with dark red velvet. But, of course, as a courtesan it was a point of professional pride for Chandrika to see how much she could get out of him through her own artfulness. In my *Kamasutra*, this is one of the points where I hold a different opinion from previous scholars.'

'What I say about money, however,' Vatsyayana continued, 'is for the ordinary prostitute, not for the most accomplished practitioner of the courtesan's calling. In Chandrika's case it was not the money that was important but the exercise of her professional talent. It was a matter of pride to extract as much as was possible from her lover. What she did was to excite Madansen's competitiveness with the most expansive, generous part of himself, not with other possible lovers. I remember overhearing their conversation one summer afternoon when they were in her bedroom. They were lying in bed and Chandrika had opened the window toward the veranda where I had been prowling around for a while waiting for her to do so.

'"Chandrika, what can I give you?" Madansen had asked.

'"Yourself, as you did just now," she replied.

'"But I want to give you something else too," he said.

'"Whatever it is can never be more than you. I am sure that whatever you give will match my worth in your eyes. The preciousness of the ornament will reflect my value for you but will always be less than yours for me."

'The exchange I overheard through the bedroom window was perhaps not in such a serious tone, as I remember it now with the memory of an older man. The couple was young. They had just made love on a summer afternoon. Perhaps they giggled as they talked. Perhaps she tweaked his penis when she spoke of the "preciousness of the ornament". I do not know. The next day, just before we were sitting down for our noon meal, Madansen's servant arrived with a silk-covered box. In it was a most exquisite filigree necklace, its gold reflected in the emeralds and green aquamarines like the afternoon sun in small forest pools.'

'Then one day Madansen left Chandrika. To be precise, from one day to the next the jeweller stopped coming to our house. It happened on an evening when preparations for the entertainment were almost complete. The little lamps in the wall-niches had been lit and the odour of burning ghee-dipped wicks was mixing pleasantly with that of sandalwood incense sticks and the perfume from garlands of flowers hanging from the windows and doors. Fresh paans wrapped in moist muslin cloth were stacked in a silver plate next to the warm flickering light. Jaivanti, who was to sing that evening before Chandrika danced, had not yet arrived but the accompanying musicians had finished tuning their instruments. They were now amusing themselves, the vina player plucking brief anticipatory glides on the strings of his instrument while the drummer tapped out quick flurries of pleasure. Two of Madansen's friends were already there, reclining on the carpet against silk-covered cushions, chatting idly as they sipped at their glasses of sugarcane liquor, perfuming it occasionally with mango blossoms heaped in a tray in front of them. I had come into the room with a message from Ganadasa for my mother—I forget what it was—and was about to leave, impatient to get away to my marble seat in the bower.

'"Mother!" the maid called from the door.

'There was a whispered conversation between the two before the maid hurried away.

'"But first ask Chandrika to come down," my mother called after her.

'Chandrika must have been on her way, for she entered the room almost immediately after the maid left.

'"Madansen's accountant is here with a message," my mother said.

'Chandrika frowned. Always late herself, she hated to be kept waiting by others. Although not a slave, the accountant was still a servant and the short conversation between him, my mother and Chandrika took place in the veranda outside the doorway. Madansen was not coming and had sent a present for Chandrika.

'"I hope his enemies are not ill?" my mother inquired politely about Madansen's health.

'The room had become quiet. The musicians and Madansen's friends were listening intently.

'"My master is well," the accountant replied. "He asks me to convey his greetings and to say that he is leaving Kausambi. He has also instructed me to give this box to the young lady and asks her to accept his last offering at the temple of the love god."

'Chandrika was trembling with anger. She took the box and threw it into the room. A necklace of blue sapphires spilt onto the carpet. The stones were inlaid in thin wires of gold entwined like snakes, their blue light intensifying, exploding into stars and then contracting to pinpoints before their radiance erupted again. It was the most beautiful piece of jewellery any one of us had ever seen. Without turning back to even look at it, Chandrika rushed off upstairs.

'For a few days. Chandrika refused to believe that Madansen had left her.

'"There were no signs of the waning lover in him," she constantly repeated to my mother. "He always gave me what I asked for, neither less nor something else. He did not forget his promises nor did he postpone their fulfilment. I cannot believe he has gone back to his wives or to another woman."

'It turned out that Chandrika was right. Madansen had left her because he had to get out of Kausambi in a hurry. He fled the city for Avanti because his creditors were closing in and the jeweller naturally did not relish the prospect of spending time in the prison run by his rival for the favours of his mistress. Sharp in business affairs, Madansen was naïve in personal ones. Generous even when he knew he was being exploited, as he shamelessly was by the relatives of his two wives, Madansen was unable to say "no" to people he felt had a personal claim on him. In any case, once Chandrika knew that Madansen had left Kausambi, not her, the clouds of self-doubt—her small breasts? her skin's fading lustre? hidden deficiencies in the arts of love?—lifted and she became as radiant as the moon. Later, whenever she remembered Madansen, which was seldom, it was with a distant fondness.

'"Even with the dimensions of a hare, he was a bull among men," she'd say, and both the sisters would laugh.

'Chandrika was always wholeheartedly in love with the man she was with at any particular time,' Vatsyayana continued. 'This, and not her beauty or youth, was the true secret of her professional success. That she only fell in love with rich men, the love waning rapidly if he happened to become poor, does not speak against the sincerity of her feelings. Some women fall in love with poets, others with warriors. Why should not some fall in love only with rich men?

'In the *Kamasutra* I give a long list of what a courtesan should do to gain a man's favour. Chandrika did not need this instruction. It came to her naturally. In the same list, I recommend that the woman be in high or low spirits according to the state of the lover, that she express feelings of dejection and sorrow if he sighs or yawns. Chandrika did not have to act to reflect the mood of her lover, she entered it naturally. But was Chandrika only acting? I do not think so. If she was acting, she was acting a truth, not a lie. For you must know that Chandrika not only *behaved* as if she was attached to her lover, she really was. It was difficult to know with her whether the behaviour or the feelings came first. She did not know it herself. She was a woman of that rare genius who could not separate her acting from her sentiment, her nature from artifice, her genuineness from her hypocrisy, and thus had no conflict between her wishes and her wants, between what her practical intelligence told her was good for her and the impulsive direction in which she was thrust by her emotions.

'I know she was naturally flirtatious. She practiced her wiles of seduction as a musician practices on the vina, with purpose and concentration. But even the half-smiling sidelong glance, the sudden enlargement of the pupils of her gray-green eyes which signalled her surprise at being overtaken by desire, the hint of a stutter to her words and a broken rhythm to her sentences, meant to indicate her helplessness in the realm of kama, were never done for a man to whom she was indifferent. Her skills needed an actual environment, where the possibility of a lover existed in the man, where she could at least totter on the brink of infatuation.'

Chapter Seven

*According to ancient teachers, she should prefer a
lover who pays well rather than one who is
passionate.*

Kamasutra 6.5.9

I arrived at the hermitage earlier than usual the next
morning. During the entire trip from Varanasi I had felt a
pleasurable sense of anticipation, though I could not quite
think why. Perhaps it had to do with my eagerness to hear
Vatsyayana continue Chandrika's story and to feel the
excitement in his voice as he recollected those particular
memories of his childhood.

'Didn't you meet Malavika on the way?' he asked after
we had greeted each other and sat down to begin the day's
work. 'You must have just missed her.'

'She has already gone to the forest?' I asked.

'Yes. But she left this for you,' he said, looking at me
with a distinct fondness and pointing to a brass tumbler
on the ground next to my seat. 'She said you prefer lemon
barley water to madhupalaka.'

Beside the tumbler lay a large lotus leaf, glistening with
scattered droplets of water and with a sprig of red ashoka
tree flowers in the middle.

'The first non-wealthy man—although he was quite comfortably off—that Chandrika ever fell in love with was from a foreign land, a Greek merchant whose caravan had stopped in Kausambi for provisioning. Kausambi, as you know, lies on the main trade route that cuts through the central countries. Merchandise of all kinds from across the seas—red coral, yellow amber, silver vessels and lamps, bronze jars and containers from the lands of the Yavanas, emeralds from Egypt, glassware from Alexandria, Tyre and Sidon—is unloaded from ships at the western ports and carried by caravans which pass through Kausambi on their way to other central countries and farther to the eastern kingdoms. Caravans from across the mountain ranges to the north-west, carrying silks and saddles, lacquered and copper objects from China, and casks of wine from Bactria, Kapisha, Kashmir and as far away in the west as Laodica and Arabia, also pass through Kausambi on their way to the eastern countries. There is constant traffic in the opposite direction too as caravans carry our ivory, fine woods, precious stones, perfumes and spices to the western ports, or to Peshawar, Kabul or even farther north to join the great route that connects the Syrian coast to western China.

'Much of Kausambi's prosperity is based on its location on the main trade route. Its wealth not only derives from the toll levied on the value of goods in a caravan or on the herds of horses that dealers bring during the summer months from the north-west, from across the mountains, for the royal cavalry. A caravan must also make a stop to rest and collect fresh provisions. The merchants, drivers and servants must eat, drink, sleep. There are inns and taverns next to both the eastern and western city gates which cater almost exclusively to the caravan trade, as do a few cheap brothels at the outer edge of the Quarter of Entertainers. We are thus used to the sight of foreign goods in our shops and of foreign men in our streets. When I was a child, we even had female Greek slaves in the houses of the prime minister and the commander of the king's army, each of whom spent a good deal of money and effort to match the other's possessions. Although King Rudradeva made an exception in case of these high officials, he did not approve of the city's nobility possessing foreign female slaves and any caravan that carried such a consignment was forbidden to camp on the designated sites within the city walls.

'To the eternal anguish of the prime minister, one of the senapati's female slaves was not from the Greek and Bactrian kingdoms to the north-west or even from the homeland of the Greeks far, far away to the west. She came from a land even farther away, we were told, a cold land of dense forests, home to bears and wild men and women who lived in caves and clothed themselves in bearskins. It is well known that the farther the place of origin of a Greek slave, the higher her value. The prime minister, we heard, asked many foreign merchants to provide him with just such a slave, promising them both official favours and a high price, but he never got one—the girls were unable to survive the heat and rigours of a one-year journey from the land the Greeks called Germania.

'Many people laughed at this aspect of the rivalry between the commander and the prime minister. They attributed it solely to envy. I believe they underestimated the significance of sexual desire in the affair, the role played by the female slave on Kama's stage. For the attraction of the girl lay in her utter foreignness and thus in her inaccessibility. She was a body a man could enter, but a consciousness—formed in a very different crucible of experiences, of climate, food, gods—which would always remain impenetrable. I was thinking of her when in the *Kamasutra* I advise the courtesan not consent to a union immediately, because men are apt to despise things which are easily acquired. A courtesan should always have a shade of strangeness, a hint of aloofness, even if this goes against the woman's very nature which wishes to surrender and reveal herself completely to the lover.

'I do not know what the slave felt toward the commander, but I do know that the senapati went to great lengths to keep her foreignness intact. The supervisor of his female slaves, a middle-aged widow with lifeless gray hair, a sly look and a mouthful of crooked teeth stained brown with betel juice, was Kanchan-mata's friend and visited us often. She was a mine of gossip about all the aristocratic households of Kausambi. It was she who told us that this slave was forbidden to be outdoors when the sun was high so that her skin did not darken.

'"I don't know why he wants her to keep her revolting colour—if it can be called a colour," Kanchan-mata's friend had sniffed. "I could not bear to touch her skin if I was a man. Like caressing an albino! Then her hair must be left open at all times. It is thick and hangs down to the waist, mostly uncombed, but again what an unappetizing colour! Lighter than dried wheat stalks! Her eyebrows and eyelashes are also the same pale yellow, as is the hair on her legs and under the arms. Only her pubic hair is a little darker, more the hue of dried sunflowers."

'"You mean she does not even remove the hair around the vulva?" my mother exclaimed, scandalized.

'"No. It is the custom of her land that men and women keep all their body hair. The senapati wishes her to remain in that barbarous state."

'"Men can be so disgusting," Chandrika gave a delicate shudder. "To want to have sex with a hairy woman!"

'"Not only that," Kanchan-mata's friend continued. "The cook has been instructed to only feed her the revolting food of her land-pork boiled with salt or, as a special treat, wild boar roasted in its own juices on a spit. Nothing properly cooked."

'She now lowered her voice and gave the women a meaningful look. "Send the boy out."

'Without waiting for my mother to say so, I got up and left. At the door, my ears still straining to catch what was being said I only heard the word "aupratishka", which, I found out later meant "mouth congress"; I now know what Kanchan-mata's friend must have said: that the senapati was especially fond of mouth congress and found the odour of this slave's vulva particularly stimulating.

'The different odours of the vulva, and their importance for mouth congress is not a subject I have discussed in the *Kamasutra*. In the absence of previous writings on the subject, it was the difficulty of treating this topic as exhaustively as I would have liked which held me back. The odour of the vulva, like body smell in general, is closely connected to a woman's food regimen and is thus characteristic of different nations with different food habits. Women who only eat fruit, vegetables, rice and lentils, lightly spiced and without onions, garlic and especially meat, will tend to have fragrant vulvas. The love fluids of a brahmin woman of the Dravida country even have a faintly fruity perfume, much remarked upon by connoisseurs of mouth congress. The vulvas of the women of eastern countries have a musky, marshy smell, not unpleasant to many noses. The vulvas of the meat-eating women of Tibet, the lands around the Indus, and of Persian, Greek, Parthian and Bactrian women, have the strongest odour, redolent of the sea and some of its smallest creatures—shrimps, oysters and mussels. These are the natural odours but, of course, artifice can give the vulva any desired scent, at least for a short while. I have listed some recipes for perfuming the vulva when the smell is odious because of congenital factors or a disease. Together with pills made from crushed lotus stalks and milk which increase the elasticity of the vulva, every courtesan in Kausambi also kept a bottle of mustard oil in which jasmine buds, muscat nut and liquorice had been cooked over a slow fire. But this oil was applied vaginally only when the genitals smelt foul.

'I will let you in on a secret I did not reveal in the text. A lotus petal, anointed with the love nectar of each type of woman, has strong medicinal properties when eaten at full moon. The love liquid of the gazelle woman is astringent, cold, eliminates the conjunction of the three humours and is effective against consumption, dyspnoea, cough, hiccups and loss of appetite. The vulva nectar of the mare woman calms wind, excites phlegm and bile and stimulates the digestive fire. The sexual fluid of the elephant woman is hot, acid, corrupts bile, calms phlegm and wind, increases a man's virility and works as a diuretic.

'Which vulva odour, which particular redolence of the woman's secretions will excite a man is a question of individual preference. Like many other matters in sex, as I keep reminding my readers at the end of almost every chapter, when passion is high whatever stimulates the pair further into ecstasy is certain to have the blessings of the love god. In the case of the senapati, I would say that together with the feel of an unexpected silky fuzz on a woman's skin, it was the odour of the female slave's vulva, especially strong and entirely different from the woman—smells of our own countries, that aroused him, an arousal he tried to sustain by insisting that she preserve her foreignness.

'It was the foreignness of the Greek merchant that attracted Chandrika. He represented a new challenge.

Chandrika had the nature of a conqueror who is drawn further and further into unconquered lands. In normal course, Chandrika might never have met Mitras—that was his name. Not that we were unfamiliar with Greeks or other foreigners in Kausambi, although not many lived in the city. In contrast to Ujjayini or Pataliputra where a special feast day in the year is reserved for their foreign residents, the foreigners in Kausambi were either a few slaves or itinerant traders and merchants who came to our city with the caravans, stopped for a few days, and were then again on their way. In the evenings, unless invited to their homes by their business contacts, they normally kept to themselves, drinking in the taverns near the eastern gate and visiting the cheaper harlots in the same quarter. Ignorant of the arts of a courtesan and thus undiscriminating in matters of love, a foreigner would never have been received by any self-respecting courtesan.

'Mitras, however, had a letter of introduction from my father which a servant presented to my mother one spring morning, a few weeks after the departure of Madansen. The Greek and my father had met in Mathura where their caravans had crossed. I imagine the two men drank and whored together in the camaraderie that develops between men who are far from home but share the same profession. In any event, "the Greek" as my mother continued to call him even later, was duly invited for the noon meal the next day.

'"What is a Greek, Ganadasa?" I had gone running to the kitchen to ask.

'Ganadasa, our portly middle-aged cook, was sitting on a low stool, supervising the bottling of a lemon pickle by one of the apprentices. He smiled a welcome and motioned me to take a seat in his lap. Leaning against his solid stomach, I contentedly sniffed in the wonderful aromas of the kitchen. The acrid smell of the mustard oil in which the lime slices were dropped was gradually prevailing over the older smells of fried spices and meat cooked for lunch.

'Ganadasa conducted the proceedings in his domain with the help of three young apprentices and the seriousness of a Vedic sacrificial rite. Naked to the waist, the sacred thread sliding up and down his glistening, sweat-lathered paunch, his instructions and explanations to his helpers were given in the same sonorous tone that is used by a venerable teacher expounding the principles of Sanskrit grammar. Although Ganadasa openly showed his displeasure if anyone except the apprentice-cooks entered the kitchen, he made an exception in my case. I wonder now if this was not out of compassion for a child he thought was an emotional orphan. As he moved around the kitchen with ponderous dignity, supervising the correct storing of cereals and lentils in large earthenware jars, the bottling of relishes, pickles, jams and syrups, occasionally tasting the gently simmering sauces in the pots on the hearth with a long silver spoon that hung by a chain from his waist, he let me follow him around.

'Ganadasa had been apprenticed to a vaid for two years before he decided to give up his study of medicine and follow the equally arduous regimen of becoming a cook.

'"Both the preparation of medicine and cooking are processes of mixing and perfecting of substances," he often said. "As in pharmacy, the art of cooking lies in combining those materials whose properties are complementary, avoiding incompatibilities, and perfecting them through cooking to imbue them with properties other than those with which nature has endowed them."

'Ganadasa had an elevated view of his calling with which he tried to imbue his student-helpers.

'"Food", he maintained, "is the basis of all activities—of those leading to prosperity, to the pleasures of sexual love and even of those whose aim is a deliverance from the cycles of birth, since the ascetics engaged in them must only eat a vegetarian diet. Every meal is a sacrifice to the gods. Like the pure ingredients used by the priest for the sacrificial fire, a cook must also provide wholesome offerings to the digestive fire within man. That is why just as a priest must be a brahmin, only a brahmin can be a cook."

'As he proprietorily surveyed his kitchen, cradling his paunch in his lap, occasionally stroking it as if it were the downy head of a baby, Ganadasa would tell us that life is nothing but a chain of food.

'"Those that do not move are the food of those that move," he would quote Manu, "and those that have no fangs are food for those with fangs. Those that have no hands are food for all those with hands, and cowards are the food of the brave."

'Every time one eats one is celebrating a victory, Ganadasa was fond of saying. Sacrifice to the gods, celebration of survival, food that has been eaten with reverence always gives strength and vigour, but food eaten without respect destroys both.

'In Ganadasa's vision, the universe, too, was nothing but a kitchen. The fundamental savours—sweet, acid, salty, acrid, bitter and astringent—were being constantly diluted or heightened to feed one or other of nature's realms: the stars, waters, the earth, the plants, the fauna. These savours may be invisible as sugar and salt are in water but they pervade all of nature. To a person with a discriminating and educated tongue, an organ which has seven thousand nerves of taste, the savour of a spring breeze is quite different from the taste of summer or winter winds. Each rock has a special savour, as has the sap coursing through a plant or the juice of a particular meat.

'From Ganadasa I learnt that sex is like cooking. Not that he ever made the comparison himself. He was much too dignified a man to talk about sexual matters in the presence of a small boy. There is nothing an accomplished man or woman can, like a good cook, do to each other which will not heighten the savour of passion; but equally, just like a bad cook who destroys the taste of the best ingredients, a man ignorant of the erotic arts will turn all excitement into ashes. As in cooking, where the ideal is to hit on the right choice—quantities and mixtures of meats, cereals, fruit, vegetables and spices which are then transformed by curdling, boiling, frying, roasting and other methods so that the nature of what is eaten is rendered appropriate to the nature of the eater—in sex, too, the test is to hit on the right choice and combination of caresses, kisses, bites, scratches, sounds and bodily positions which, cooked by the heat of passion, are transformed to be exactly appropriate to the sexual nature of the partner.

'From Ganadasa I also learnt that people have different tastes in food, a momentous discovery for a small boy who had so far only been instinctively aware of differences in gender, age and social position. Whereas we, the people of central country, the land between the Ganga and the Jamuna, have a food regimen whose basis is barley, wheat and cow's milk, the regimen of people living in the wet marshy lands to the east is based on fish. Like the Tibetans, the easterners make an excessive use of alkaline substances. The habitual diet of the Dravidas is rice gruel while the people around the Indus put salt in their milk. The fierce inhabitants of the countries to the north-west, the Persians, Bactrians, Kushans and Huns, have a diet centred around meat, wheat and madhvika alcohol which makes them so devoted to the fire and the sword.'

'Acharya,' I interrupted him, 'You are silent on the connection between sexual and food regimens in the *Kamasutra*.'

'It would have been premature,' Vatsyayana said. 'Even today, I can only speculate on some of the links. For instance, the women of eastern countries are full of impetuous desire and their love fluid falls in such great quantities during coitus that there are always large wet patches on the sheet under their thighs. Is their greater wetness connected to the eating of fish? Also, like the women of the land around the Indus, the Persian, Greek and Bactrian women love mouth congress. I believe this taste comes from a food regimen in which meat is central. The eating of meat is the basis for the taste for sexual eating and for being eaten, although in mouth congress the biting, chewing and swallowing are only hinted at rather than actually carried out.'

'Not always, though,' I respectfully interjected, 'Susruta's treatise on medicine describes the wounding of the penis with teeth as one of the causes of a disease treated in that work.'

Vatsyayana acknowledged the correction and continued.

'But why should we be surprised at the close connection between food and sex? After all, the words for making love and eating derive from the same Sanskrit root-bhuj.'

'As I had expected, Ganadasa knew all about the Greeks. Over the years, he had met some in the tavern he frequented, near the eastern gate, and once even had a long conversation with a Greek cook who was attached to a passing caravan of Bactrian merchants.

'"They are not as civilized as we are, although not as barbarian as our forest-dwelling tribes who live on berries and roots," Ganadasa said in answer to my query.

'"What is a barbarian?" I immediately asked.

'"Barbarians are people without cooks. The Greeks are little better since they do have cooks, but they are not quite civilized since their cooks are uneducated and of a low status."

'I had wanted to know more.

'"The Greeks eat poorly. Their main food is stomach-filling gruels of barely and wheat or flat breads seasoned with a salad of bitter herbs and onions. They are also eaters of fish, but have no knowledge of spices or the subtle art of mixing them so as to being out the hidden, essential nature of food rather than its superficial taste. This cook told me that one of their biggest delicacies is the tail of a fish found in their seas, which is sliced, baked, sprinkled lightly with salt and brushed with oil. The slices are then eaten hot, dipped in sharp brine.

'"I do not mind the simplicity," the cook continued, "but I am appalled by some of the things they eat, like sow's wombs. But the worst thing about the Greeks is their eating of the cow. I was told that they sacrifice a cow outside their temple and divide the meat among themselves. It is then roasted, sprinkled with salt and taken from the spit when still undercooked, with bloody juices dripping from it. Can you imagine? Eating a cow! The mother of the Rudras, the daughter of Vasu, the sister of Aditya, the womb of immortality, the very goddess of earth!"

'We were silent for a moment, sharing our internal shudders of disgust. The vision of Greek faces smeared with brown juices burrowing into the vast belly of a cow shimmered before my eyes. The apprentice tried to lighten the gloom that seemed to have descended on the kitchen.

'"Sir, tell Malli about their gods and the cow," he said, having obviously heard the story before.

'"The separation between Greek men and their gods happened because of the cooking and eating of a cow,"

Ganadasa said. "In ancient times they lived together with their gods in heaven without the need to eat. Once, after sacrificing a cow, the men sought to deceive the gods by dividing the cow into two parts: the inedible bones and gristle covered by appetizing fat and the edible meat covered by unpalatable skin. Their Indra, the king of the gods, was aware of the intended deception but still chose the inedible part as the share of the gods. Then the men, wanting to cook the cow's meat, stole the fire from the gods. The second trick was too much for the king of the gods, who created a woman so that from then onwards the men had to procreate, work to feed their families and became mortal.

"'So you see," Ganadasa summed up the moral of the story, as much for me as for his student, "cooking is a meditation which, like all meditations, demands complete purity of mind and body. To cook dishonestly, with bad thoughts in the mind and deception in the heart, will have disastrous results for the cook.'"

'I remember it was a late spring day when Mitras came to our house for the midday meal. We had celebrated holi earlier in the week and were now preparing for the great festival of the love god, celebrated by courtesans and all others engaged in the business of love—the various classes of prostitutes and those who depend upon them, the pimps and other go-betweens, the pithamardas who manage a courtesan's affairs, the teachers of painting, singing and dancing—as the most sacred of all festivals. The preparations for the great festival of Lord Kama had begun. The swings, stored away at the onset of the monsoon, were brought out and set up in the garden and in the outer courtyard where the daughters of the servants competed with each other in swinging higher. Earthen lamps had been bought and the children of our household were busy rolling cotton wicks for the night of the festival when each house in the quarter would struggle to outdo its neighbours in brilliance. I was already looking forward to the day of the festival. After the morning visit to the temple where effigies of gods were placed in cradles and swung to and fro to imitate the course of the sun, we would put garlands of fresh flowers around each others' necks and go for a picnic to the royal park outside the city; my own love of flowers comes from their intimate connection with the festival of the love god.

'What I most enjoyed on this day was watching groups of persons of the third sex dance with abandon in the park. As you know, this is a traditional dance, first performed by Kama himself when he disguised himself as an invert to rescue his son from the demon Bana's prison. Wearing short garments which came down to the middle of their thighs, most of these beings had slim figures and small, high, pretty breasts. Their sexual organs were tied artfully between the legs to emphasize their protuberance. Depending upon the angle of one's vision, one could view the bulge as either the pubic mound of the love god or as a penis snared in a tight sheath with the testicles. I was fascinated, trying to see first the one and then the other in the same dancer. With their curly beards and long black hair, mouths painted coral red, large shining eyes outlined with kohl and eyebrows arched like crescent moons, I thought they were exquisitely beautiful—more than most men and women I had seen.

'I don't know about Varanasi, but in Kausambi all the normal rules of conduct are suspended, and a lover will not complain of the use the woman makes of her freedom on this night. In our house, my mother would send letters to the suitors who had sought Chandrika's favours over the year—which she could not otherwise grant because she was living as a wife with one lover—informing them that Chandrika would spend this particular night with whoever reached our house first with certain presents. The required gifts would be listed in detail; for instance, the quantity of gold and the quality of rubies in a necklace would be exactly specified and even the shops from which the presents could be bought were named. Although Chandrika never did so, this was also the night when a courtesan sometimes invited suitors in a group. She could then be possessed by two or more men simultaneously or taken in turn, each man giving her a lavish sum of money since money given to a prostitute on the day of the festival of Kama comes back ten-fold to the giver.

'Ganadasa was the only person in the household who did not share in the excitement caused by the impending visit of the Greek merchant. He was a conservative man who disapproved of an outsider, and that too a foreigner, joining us for the mid day meal at which only a long-term lover could be present as an exception. Guests, however, are treated as gods, and Ganadasa's disapproval did not stop him from preparing one of his magnificent festive meals. Heaped at the centre of the banana leaf and forming the base of the meal was boiled rice with curds and three ground spices—cinnamon, cardamom and mace. On the side, served in small silver bowls, were Ganadasa's other specialties for the festival: roasted quail wrapped in bitter leaves and in a thick sauce made of ghee, mango juice, salt and pepper; slices of gazelle meat fried in sesame oil, chili pepper, cardamom, cloves, cumin and salt. There were the obligatory fresh basil leaves and sliced ginger to stimulate the palate and encourage thirst, while on another side of the banana leaf were balls of wheat fried in butter coated with sugar, thin slices of coconut and various spices. This guest may have been a barbarian, almost certainly ignorant of the finer points of cooking and the subtleties of texture and taste, but Ganadasa's own pride in his skill would never allow him to exercise it with anything less than his full attention. He did insist, though, that the Greek be excluded from the ritual before the meal at which Ganadasa, as the man of the household, presided.

'There was an air of excitement as we gathered around the sacred fire at midday to chant prayers to our family deities, ancestral spirits, earth and fire, while Ganadasa threw samples of food he had cooked into the flames as an oblation. Looking forward to meeting my first barbarian, I was impatient to get through my own routine tasks of taking small packets of the food up to the terrace and outside the gate for insects and, finally, at the end of the ritual, washing my mother and Chandrika's feet as a mark of respect on behalf of the household.

'Mitras arrived punctually. He was also good-looking, although later Ganadasa would sniff at the ruddiness of his fair complexion, comparing it to the colour of a monkey's behind. I do not know what I expected, but I know I was disappointed that a barbarian looked almost like one of us. When offered water to wash his feet, and the special guest-seat woven from cane, his hesitation and clumsy movements indicated that his knowledge of civilized manners was rudimentary. While he ate, and talked to mother with much waving of hands and curling of fingers as he tried to mould the words of a foreign tongue to the rhythm of ours, I saw Chandrika staring at him raptly. I, too, watched him or rather his eating habits, first with disgust and then with fascination, the one quickly changing into the other. Mitras would pick up a quail by its legs and tear the bird apart with both hands. He would then stuff a whole leg into his mouth and noisily crunch away at it with all signs of obvious pleasure. In between mouthfuls he smiled often, his curly black beard parting like curtains to show his strong white teeth. Later, much later, when I visited Chandrika in the nunnery and we were talking about those years, she recalled her state of sexual excitement on that day. As she looked at Mitras smiling at her sister or eating slices of gazelle meat with the spicy juices smeared till his elbow, Chandrika saw his bearded face burrow between her thighs and the two wet mouths fasten upon each other—one all active tongue, probing, agitating the lush folds; the other soft and swollen flesh, moist and yielding.

'In the beginning, my mother indulged Chandrika's infatuation. Mitras was a distraction she allowed so that her sister could cope with Madansen's absence. Not that Chandrika had grieved unduly over the jeweller's departure. All that had happened was a slight drop, noticeable only to the most discerning eye, in Chandrika's faith in the omnipotence of her beauty. She was still as ravishing as ever. With Madansen's desertion, there was a host of suitors jostling to replace him. A large part of my mother's time was taken in composing courteous notes of refusal (careful, though, to contain the hint of a future promise) and in returning gifts sent by aspiring lovers through their servants. The evening entertainments were reserved weeks in advance by the rich and powerful citizens of Kausambi who came with small parties of friends to admire Chandrika's dancing and fabled charms. But she was hesitant to choose a steady new lover. To my mother, it seemed that Chandrika was content with brief, temporary liaisons and was shying away from the serious business of selecting Madansen's replacement. An affair with a foreigner, my mother thought, with its odd sensual delights and unexpected sexual twists and moments, would be just the right medicine for her sister's full recovery.

'The remedy almost turned into poison. Mitras's effect

on Chandrika was disastrous. From a great courtesan she sank to the level of a merely good one. Mitras disturbed her in a profound way. Both the days of their union and of separation—Mother would not let him spend the night at our house—had equally ruinous effects on her. The brilliance of the smile with which she greeted her clients began to falter on its way to her eyes. There were lapses in the total absorption with which she listened to men. There were brief and unexpected retreats into an abstracted inner state which her suitors found deeply insulting as they suddenly became aware she was not listening, whereas they had paid a considerable sum of money for Chandrika to conjure a convincing illusion of intimacy.

'My mother was alarmed. The Greek merchant had affected her sister in a way totally alien to her experience but one which was powerful enough to crack the shell of her professional discipline. My mother believed she understood everything about the effect of sexual passion on a young girl. She knew that the anticipation of intercourse can make a girl, as the poets put it, "reel, stammer, cry, shudder, gasp". She was aware that separation from the lover could make the body grow thin, choke the speech with tears, make the girl sigh, moan and weep. All these states and expressions were normal, serving to heighten erotic passion and, ultimately, its pleasure. What Chandrika was experiencing with Mitras was something quite different. For one, she was too quiet, too silent. What she felt seemed to take place somewhere deep within her, normally the dwelling place of religious fervour rather than of sexual passion. Mitras was not only the source of excitement and delight, arousing Chandrika's senses. This my mother could understand. What baffled her was that the Greek had become a subject of entrancement, even devotion.

'I, too, felt Chandrika's reaction to Mitras was

excessive. Now she often looked through me rather than at me when I helped her with her toilet in the afternoon. Her nipples still became erect when I rubbed sandalwood paste on her breasts, but this stiffening was no longer accompanied by a quickening of the breath or an answering glint in her eyes. My mother frantically consulted Kanchan-mata and some of Kanchan-mata's friends, including the supervisor of the army commander's female slaves. Their diagnosis was that Chandrika was possessed. When a woman becomes addicted to a man, when only one special lover dominates her thoughts and her imagination, when every sexual consummation, every slaking, only serves to increase the thirst, when most of the time the woman seems to be present only somewhere deep within herself, surfacing to the world and its reality with shocked reluctance, she clearly manifests the symptoms of possession. This particular possession is generally by one of the minor spirits in service of the love god, most often the spirit of a man or woman who died suddenly during the act of love. In these cases it is not the doctor, only the exorcist who can help. It was also the consensus that ordinary, average exorcists who stood at dawn in the street howling imprecations at the evil spirits living in the trees, were not equal to this task. They were perhaps strong enough to combat the ghosts that threaten pregnant women or new mothers and their babies, but would find Chandrika's case beyond their expertise. Kanchan-mata was deputed to engage Kausambi's best-known exorcist, a middle-aged man with a surprisingly mild demeanour very different from the frightening, wild-eyed look cultivated by his less qualified colleagues, who lived on the premises of the temple in the cremation grounds.

'To a child, the cremation grounds were a terrifying place which not only lay outside the city but also outside all dreams of safety. From where we lived, I was aware of them only as a distant haze which sometimes changed into a darker pillar of smoke, waving like a flag on windy days. In one part of these vast grounds, surrounded by high stone ramparts with entrances opening to the four cardinal points, there were brick mounds of smaller or larger sizes—tombs of famous scholars, members of the royal family and of women who had followed their husbands onto the funeral pyre. On certain days, while passing these grounds on the way to the royal park, one could hear from within a continuous deep murmur as Buddhist monks recited the merits of their deceased companions. From time to time, echoes of the crash of drums accompanying the funeral chant reminded the mourners and the passers-by of the end of their own mortal journey. To the lamentations of mourners were added the barking of long-muzzled jackals, the hooting of screech owls and the silence of the brown-necked vultures as they patiently waited to feed on uncharred pieces of flesh they could scavenge from the smouldering pyres. In one corner of the grounds was the temple of the city of dead, dedicated to the black goddess who lives in the desert. The temple was surrounded by trees whose branches, the servants said, bowed under the burden of the severed heads of fanatical devotees who sacrificed themselves to the goddess. Here, on the temple grounds, over a period of the fortnight of the dark moon, exorcism rituals were carried out to free Chandrika from her affliction.'

'And did the exorcist succeed, Acharya?' I asked.

'How could he fail?' Vatsyayana countered rhetorically. 'For one week Chandrika was ill with a violent fever that refused to subside. When she recovered, all signs of her infatuation had vanished. Mitras quickly became a memory. It also helped that the Greek too had disappeared while Chandrika was bedridden. Perhaps he rejoined his trading caravan. Later, I heard rumours that he had been murdered at my mother's behest. My mother was certainly ruthless enough to have commanded the deed if it ever took place.'

A dark shadow gradually eclipsed the radiance of Chandrika's memory, which had so vividly bathed Vatsyayana's face all morning. The day's session was clearly over. I stood up and bowed down to touch the sage's feet in a wordless farewell, leaving Vatsyayana to his brooding communion with the spirit of his mother.

Chapter Eight

To get money, sexual attraction may be real or feigned. In either event, she should pretend that she is besotted with her lover. She must make the man believe in her infatuation.

Kamasutra 6.2.2-4

*I*n the next few weeks I often went into the forest after Vatsyayana's morning talks, an undertaking he encouraged. He said that his wife, separated from her sister and her friends in Udayana's harem, was starved for company in the hermitage which, after all, was an asylum for older people in the last two stages of life and meditatively preparing for its end. Unaware of their life in Kausambi and of all that had transpired between them, I admired Malavika for the sacrifice she was making. For a young woman like her, I thought, there could be no greater demonstration of the love she bore her husband than to live uncomplainingly in the Seven Leaf hermitage.

There is a sensual quality to the forest, Vatsyayana once said, which is absent in both cultivated spaces and in the arid, deserted land of the jangla. For one, the ground is springier, convulsively releasing the soles of the feet after seeming to clutch them for the briefest moment. Forest leaves are darker, as if the sap coursing through them is thick and turgid. The hum of the bees, the chirping of crickets and the sounds of other insects combine to form a steady background drone to the calls of lapwings and blue jays, the cries of parrots and the screeches of small groups of monkeys as they swing from the branches of one tree to those of the next. In temple courtyards the monkeys are almost human. In the forest, they manifest a sinister quality, as well as a sense of abandon. I remember stories of women carried off by lustful monkeys and choosing to live with their simian lovers rather than return to their husbands. The unseen power of the forest, Vatsyayana said, made a woman sexually more attractive to men, transforming an ordinary pretty girl into a ravishing yakshi. Poor Ravana! Although aware of the potentially disastrous consequences of his ill-conceived passion, he still found Sita sexually irresistible in the forest, where all forms of life are pushed in the direction of impulse and freedom. I too felt it infiltrate my own hesitant and inhibited nature.

I doubt whether I could have talked to Malavika as easily as I did if we had not been vulnerable to the influence of the forest. When I am in human spaces, the presence of young women makes me painfully shy. In such natural spaces as the forest where the only time is the present, where both the woman and I were without histories or expectations deriving from our real lives, I was free of all fear. Indeed, I was in an exalted state where my mind, heart and speech effortlessly combined together to surprise me with my own eloquence.

To preserve the space of gods which has spontaneity as its distinctive marker, a space which the poets tell us is transiently experienced, if at all, in the sexual encounter, I tried to enter the forest without hope or desire to meet Malavika, straining each time to erase the memory of our previous meetings. Memory and expectation prevent us from living wholly in the present. They disrupt and destroy our experience of ecstatic communion, and mire us in the anarchic realm of emotional turbulence. Whenever I did encounter Malavika, which was often, we effortlessly fell in together to stroll along a forest trail. We talked or were silent in unexpected sequences. When we parted, we did not fix a time or place for our next meeting. Lately, though, the mood of our meetings had begun to register a subtle shift. We could both sense a disquieting inner struggle as we tried to keep our awareness of a growing mutual attraction from breaking through poorly locked vaults of the body and the heart, and begin to seep into our eyes. We would quickly turn our faces away whenever our seeking eyes met in what our minds wanted to believe was a chance encounter. Afterwards, in the carriage which took me back to Varanasi and the literal facts of human space, desire and shame came crowding in, easily overwhelming my inner protests that I met Malavika only so that I could learn more about Vatsyayana.

'A few weeks before my seventh birthday,' said Vatsyayana, 'there was much excitement in the household at the arrival of a mysterious letter. Written on birch bark and wrapped in the coarse saffron cloth preferred by forest and cave-dwelling ascetics, the letter was addressed to my mother.

My lady Avantika, you do not know the yogi. He is writing to you on the instructions of his guru. The guru desires the yogi to tell you that you did him a singular service in your previous birth and the time has now come for the guru to repay the debt. My lady, the next few years are full of danger for you and your family. These are the worst years of the Saturn period of your life since the moon is entering the sixth house and your ketu is in a debilitated condition.

The yogi knows that your old nurse is even now lying seriously ill. Her time has come and she will not survive beyond the second full moon. Do not grieve. This world is one of comings and goings and she who is going now will return later. Your son should not be sent to a gurukula for schooling till he is eleven years old. Otherwise, there is danger to his life. My lady, fate is an unbridled mare and there are dangers ahead, but with the help of the yogi and your own efforts they can be averted. The yogi will warn you in time of the dangers, as also disclose the means by which they can be avoided. My lady, know the yogi wants nothing from you but is only carrying out his guru's command to protect your welfare. You should not try to locate or write to the yogi. He will contact you whenever time so demands.

'The letter caused considerable astonishment in the household. No one doubted its authenticity. The writer's knowledge of my mother's horoscope and of Kanchan-mata's condition was too exact for the letter to be anything else than a genuine product of prescience. Only Ganadasa was less than enthusiastic.

'"Mark my words," he said to me glumly, "the first thing yogis do when they get involved in the welfare of a household is to change its eating habits. In the name of purity, the food will become blander and my cooking skills rust away."

'Even the yogi's prediction that Kanchan-mata would not survive for more than twenty-one days did little to dampen the high spirits of the household at the thought that it had powerful protectors watching over its welfare.

'Kanchan-mata had been ailing for many months with a low fever that refused to subside and left her weaker with each passing day. She knew she was dying. It was not consumption that was killing her, Kausambi's best known doctor told us. Her time had simply come. Where time is not the accomplice of disease, medicine has the power to conquer sickness and stave off death. But the pulse that throbs at the wrist signals death when one's predetermined time elapses. Medicine exists to fight disease, not death. When death approaches holding hands with disease, all a doctor can do is prepare the patient for its arrival. Kanchan-mata had accepted the diagnosis. She wanted the doctor to predict the exact time of her departure from this world, a prognostic skill more highly regarded than therapeutic expertise, and for which this particular doctor was famous throughout the kingdom. Like other experienced practitioners, he could not only see the condition of every important organ of the body reflected in the beat, movement and temperature of the pulse, but in an illness of long standing he could predict the time of a patient's death to within a specified number of hours. In the afternoon of the second full moon day of this month, he had told Kanchan-mata. She wanted to spend her last days on the bank of the Ganga at Varanasi. Thrifty to the very end, she wanted to know the exact number of days she would have left in the city. She could then take just the right amount of rice and oil with her, since prices at the pilgrimage site were known to be exorbitant.

'The yogi's letter and the doctor's prognosis were in total agreement on the time of her death, and Kanchan-mata was content. One morning, accompanied by a maid, she was carried out on a litter to the carriage that was to take her to Varanasi. All of us came to the gate to bid her farewell and to receive her last blessings. My mother and Chandrika, both dressed in the courtesan's ceremonial attire of red garments and wearing jewellery of red gold, recalling the god of death, sobbed loudly as the litter was lifted into the carriage. Holding hands, Ganadasa and I were weeping silently, my own tears occasioned more by the grief of others than an understanding of Kanchan-mata's approaching death. By the time the carriage moved, a fair number of onlookers had gathered. The rare sight of a courtesan dressed in her traditional finery in the morning was harbinger of assured good luck.

'For me, the yogi's letter was a reprieve from the gods. In the last months there had been much disturbing talk about my being sent to a gurukula fifteen leagues outside Kausambi to begin my studies. I was told how much I would love being with boys my own age, of the joys of learning and a healthy outdoor life. The more the household tried to reassure me, the more my dread mounted as my seventh birthday approached. I could not understand why I had to leave home except for the fact that most boys my age did so. I did not want to be separated from Chandrika although she had begun to restrict my participation in her daily toilet. I did not want to leave Ganadasa who tried to convince me that the food at the gurukula, although it could not compare with the tasty fare produced in our own kitchen, was nourishing and wholesome. I would miss our birds. I would miss the peacock's morning visits to the terrace, I would even miss the smell of the elephant's steaming mounds of olive-green dung. The yogi's letter meant that I could begin my studies, initiated by the recognition and writing of the letters of the alphabet with a piece of chalk on a wooden board, to be later followed at home by three hours of grammar and phonetics with a tutor in the mornings.

'My seventh birthday also meant the entry of my father into my young life. With his height and erect carriage, shoulder-length curly black hair that had begun to glint with gray bound in a white turban encircling his head, my father cut an imposing figure. Although there was a web of fine lines at the corners of his eyes, the sheen of his skin, highlighted by the tiny pearls studding his earlobes, was still youthful. Earlier I had registered his presence through the marked changes of mood that took place in our household whenever he came to visit us,the visits coinciding with the halts made by his caravan in Kausambi for rest and provisioning. Chandrika would brighten perceptibly even as my mother's visage darkened. These alterations in their moods had little to do with his shift from one woman to the other as a lover. Or perhaps they did. I do not claim to know all the secrets of the female heart. Over the years, Chandrika later told me, he had become less of a lover than an old friend with a remarkable gift for intimacy. In fact, she could barely wait for the lovemaking to be over so that they could peaceably lie together in bed and talk, their naked bodies touching each other in affection rather than desire. She shared with him the worries and transient sorrows of a young heart while he calmed her anxieties by placing them in a perspective fashioned from an older man's more encompassing sense of time. It helped that he loved women and had a palpable need of them. Nothing else in the three worlds so quickened and heightened his sense of life.

'"Your father was a wonderful listener. He actively fostered our intimacy by talking of his own defeats, but in a way which took the sting out of *all* defeats."

'In my mother's case, perhaps my father's visits reminded her of a loss of closeness which she never re-established with any of her subsequent lovers.

'For others in the household, my father's visits were a

source of excitement because of the generous gifts he brought them from different countries. There were Chinese parasols and lacquered knickknacks for the maidservants, small, tightly sealed onyx jars of Tibetan musk oil for Kanchan-mata, Malayan nutmeg and Persian grape wine for Ganadasa, to which the cook was quite partial. My father entered into long discussions with Ganadasa on the recipes he had collected during his travels, patiently listened to complaints of profligacy Kanchan-mata had stored up against the two sisters, and flirted with the maidservants, young or old.

'As a child, I received my share of attention but sensed that it was perfunctory. On entering the house, my father would pick me up in his arms with a flourish but then set me down equally promptly. He would ruffle my hair but his eyes were already searching for Chandrika in the group that had gathered around to welcome him. I was just a little too old to play with the wooden toys he brought me as present, or wear the embroidered woollen jackets from China which were always one size too small. All of this was to change with my seventh birthday. Afterwards, whenever he came to Kausambi, my father made it a point to spend time alone with me. The attention he gave me now almost rivalled Chandrika's share.

'At the age of seven, then, I fell in love for the second time. I fell in love with my father. Perhaps love is an odd word to use in relation to one's father, an infinitely superior being who the boy admires and holds in awe. Fathers, we believe, are there to be obeyed, men to whom sons willingly subordinate their own desire. Doubtless, all these beliefs and feelings nestled close together in young Malli's soul. But when my father took me along to the resting site of his caravan and we walked between the unhitched wagons and carts, the drivers breaking their conversations and getting up from their games of dice to bow low in respectful greeting, I felt some of my father's self-assurance and male swagger seep into my own body through my small fingers clasped firmly in his large hand. At the same time, I felt waves of adoration course through my body and flow toward him through my fingers, gently bathing this sacred being in my devotion.

'When he was away on his travels, my imagination seated me in the lead carriage of the caravan as it wended its stately path on the royal highway, or behind him in the saddle clasping his waist with both my arms as he reconnoitered a dangerous stretch of road with a posse of the caravan's mounted guards. He told me stories about encounters with fierce tribes of the jungles, their men and women naked except for a string of leaves around the hips, who shot poisoned arrows at the travellers with the aim of procuring a human sacrifice for their savage gods. He told me of bands of brigands who roamed the forests and uninhabited stretches of land between the towns, attacking passing caravans at dusk when they believed the guards had relaxed their vigilance after a hard day's journey. He talked of the demons of the desert, especially fond of devouring corpses, howling in the distance at night, waiting for a caravan to lose its way so that the travellers perished from hunger and thirst.

'I could barely wait for the arrival of my eleventh birthday, so far into the future as to be almost unimaginable if I did not keep its promise alive by constantly thinking about it. My father had promised to take me along with him on one of his journeys across the mountain passes to the northwest, veering east to cross the Pamir mountains, and finally reaching the great market city of Kashgar in the Tarim basin of Sinkiang. He would have done so earlier but another letter from the yogi had put a stop to my cherished desire.

My lady Avantika, for the next three years, Saturn has entered its most baleful phase. There are a host of dangers threatening your family: grievous injury to your sister from a client, a great sadness that may overwhelm you, danger to your son's life from any travel. My lady, pride and vanity are the mental states in a human being which provide the channels through which Saturn acts. You and your sister must guard against both. Begin to follow your dharma as courtesans by giving your body to all comers without distinguishing handsome from ugly, old from young. The yogi says all this only for your benefit.

My lady, all of you must also renounce the eating of meat and the drinking of liquor except when they become unavoidable as part of your professional duty in the entertainment of clients. Begin to be more disciplined by setting up small rules to govern your daily life. Eat only at fixed times even if hungry. At meal times, when food is served, wait five minutes before taking the first mouthful. Set apart a time in the evening for the recitation of the three mantras that calm Saturn's ire. My lady, the Vedas say knowledge comes from renunciation. If you and your family begin with these small rules you will store up the energy and will needed for the more difficult renunciations that will be required of you later.

After exactly one year, ask your priest to calculate two auspicious days in the brighter part of every lunar month. On these days, every month for the next four years, you must recite the Vedic verses which I will send later. They have to be recited one hundred and one times at sunset. Fast on both these days and offer oblations to Saturn. Follow this discipline for the welfare of your family.

You must also immediately burn the enclosed leaf on which the yogi has written down a mantra. Put the ashes in an amulet. This should be tied around the upper portion of your son's right arm. It will protect him from danger.

'The yogi's letter had immediate consequences, although these constituted less than full compliance with his instructions. Meat was banned from our meals. To everyone's surprise, Ganadasa's protests were perfunctory and without passion. Having foreseen the effects of the yogi's abrupt entry into his life, Ganadasa was almost relieved that the only proscribed food was meat and that, too, only partially.

'"Imagine!" he said to me. "The yogi could have forbidden the use of all spices or the eating of everything which grows underground or cooking with any kind of fat. You can never be sure with these people."

'Ganadasa now turned his energy and ingenuity to the invention of new and the refinement of traditional fortifiers served by brothels after lovemaking, which had the yogi's express sanction. The sounds of frying in the kitchen began to be replaced more and more by those of simmering as he searched for that elusive, perfect broth. Which particular unctuous, acid and acrid additives combined best with the hot, sweet and rather heavy meat of partridge to produce a broth which nourished a man's body as well as his virility? Were ghee, pomegranate seeds and black pepper the best ingredients to use with fragrant, light and astringent deer meat to bring out the delicate fusion of savours and virtues particular to each ingredient? I was allowed to taste, in secret, the results of Ganadasa's experiments whenever I wandered into the kitchen, thus circumventing the yogi's injunctions on both the eating of meat and of adhering to fixed mealtimes. I did get to wear my new amulet, though I assumed that like the one I had worn at the wrist since babyhood, this one too could change into a serpent and bite anyone who tried to attack me, even if the assailant was the god Saturn in disguise.

Setting apart a few minutes every evening for a collective recitation of Saturn's mantras was more a dull chore than an unacceptable imposition. But to ask Chandrika to give up her rituals of vanity was like asking the sun to give up its fire. To voluntarily become as humble as the lowest woman in her profession, who has no choice in the selection of her lovers and must accept all as long as they pay her price, was to invite certain rebellion from the girl. My mother did not even try, contenting herself with reading the yogi's letter aloud to her sister. It was much easier to postpone the plans of my travel with my father, a decision with which—to my regret—he, too, agreed. I had to wait till the worst years of Saturn's malefic influence on my mother's life were over.'

Vatsyayana's disappointment did not last long. Looking back, he could see that the next few years were some of the happiest of his life. He studied hard, discovering with astonished pleasure as one screen after another was lifted, the awesome play of human knowledge. He enjoyed most of the subjects the tutors gradually added to his curriculum in the traditional system of education.

'I cannot say I was excited by the study of grammar and phonetics, the preliminary requirements and aids to the Dharmashastra studies I would engage in after my eleventh birthday. But to compensate for the pedantic dullness of these subjects, the study of the Great Epics was a source of delight although, again, not all the sections. Like most boys my age, I was not exactly enamoured of the narratives concerning the evolution and dissolution of the universe and the sequence of its eons and millennia, leading to the genealogies of kings and sages, which had to be memorized. What I loved in the epics were the wonderful stories and legends and their fascinating excursions into the most varied areas of knowledge—from astronomy to sculpture and dancing.

'I played, too, although mostly within the grounds of our house, with the gardener's son who was a year younger and became my inseparable companion. Climbing trees to eat unripe mangoes that inevitably led to stomachaches, trying to hit pigeons with pebbles from a slingshot, agitating the pond for non-existent fish with a thread tied to a twig at one end and a piece of dough impaled on a thorn at the other, kept us happy enough.'

Vatsyayana also recollected these years being pervaded by a heightened, almost frantic gaiety. Except for a lull in the hottest summer months, Kausambi's citizens were like a tippler habituated to debauch, staggering from one festival to another, from one public entertainment to another celebration. Once his mother agreed that an outing to the royal park outside the city did not constitute 'travel' in the yogi's sense, he was free to attend the grand festivals which took place in this park. Accompanied by his friend, Vatsyayana was utterly happy to wander around the public section of the park, sampling the feats of the jugglers and the acrobats, the contests between itinerant wrestlers, the ram, peacock, and cock fights, the shows put on by folk dancers and singers, sword swallowers and snake charmers, mongoose and monkey handlers. After the rains were over and the last clouds of the season had drifted away, there was the annual regatta on the river in which the king and the court enthusiastically participated.

'I can still feel the excitement of that day, recall the sight of the magnificently decorated royal boats, the ships with white sails, galleys, barges and the smaller boats shaped to look like birds, fish or sea monsters bobbing on the water under the freshly washed blue of a clear sky.'

During these years, Vatsyayana also discovered his fondness for theatre. Together with a still sleepy Ganadasa who had to be cajoled each time to accompany him, he would reach the temple at sunrise, when a travelling troupe usually began its performance. Of course, during spring, the time of the year when theatre companies came to Kausambi to present their new works in public halls rather than in temples, the whole family made it a point to be present at the performances along with other members of the town's elite. To Vatsyayana's great regret, there was no permanent repertory company at the court in those days—that would come later when Udayana became the king—since Udayana's father, derisively called 'soldier-king' by some of Kausambi's fashionable citizens, much preferred to be on horseback among his soldiers, riding from one frontier to another in the outer reaches of his kingdom, rarely coming back to the capital for longer periods to sample the pleasures of court and palace life. Later, when he became a feudatory of Samudragupta after his defeat in battle, Rudradeva spent even longer periods away from the court, fighting with his troops in the imperial army as that illustrious emperor went about the business of carving out an empire.

There is little that delights the heart of a boy more than the spectacle of an army marching out of the capital to begin its annual campaign. Each autumn, when the rains were over, the roads had become dry and the rivers fordable, when the oxen pulling the carts loaded with supplies were full of spirit and the rutting war elephants full of fight, Vatsyayana looked forward to the day when Rudradeva's army would leave Kausambi. Days before the event, bells tolled in various temples where the king prayed to the gods for their blessings. On the auspicious day itself, Kausambi's citizens began to line up on the royal highway from the early morning onwards.

'We only needed to climb up to the terrace of our house which lay on the route of the army's march,' Vatsyayana remembered. 'I loved the music and the beat of drums, the men running on both sides of the road shouting "Victory to the King! Here he comes!" The women threw parched rice from the balconies as Rudradeva on his magnificently caparisoned elephant passed by. Behind him came the phalanx of war elephants, the cavalry and the columns of infantry, with the tail brought up by a line of oxen carts carrying supplies and covered wagons carrying the army's prostitutes. The last always raised a special cheer from the onlookers.

'My absorption in the discovery of the world outside the home almost made me miss the changes that were taking place in my mother during these years. In the beginning, the changes were subtle. There were no marked alterations in her behaviour. I felt them without being able to put my finger on what had exactly changed. One could even say that before the yogi's letter my mother ate, slept and went about the household tasks. After the letter, she still ate, slept and went about the household tasks . . . but differently. She had always been the quieter of the two sisters, taking herself and her responsibilities too seriously. Now, she became even more remote. The invisible wall which had always enclosed her went up by another layer. She began to spend more time in her room surrounded by her collection of mirrors: highly polished circular copper and gold plates ranging in size from five to twenty finger widths and decorated with lines at the rim and with images of goddesses at the back. She had stopped taking lovers a while ago, but now even refused to go on picnics or for festivals in the park with the rest of us. Instead, she preferred to attend Buddhist discourses at the Goshitarama monastery or listen to Jaina monks at the old temple which has existed in Kausambi since the sixth tirthankara. Today I can see her choice of Buddhist and Jaina spirituality rather than our own as revealing. Like some of our—now thankfully discarded—ascetic sects, Buddhists and Jainas have a sombre view of life and are vehement foes of Kama: the Buddhists even equate the god of love with their god of death. In her choice, Mother was giving up the quickening of sensual life, excitement and passion, although the mirrors stacked against the wall around her bed revealed that it is more difficult to give up vanity than sex.

'However, what she got instead of peace was sadness. Both lie close together in the mind and perhaps the yogi's prediction was fulfilled after all, although in a quiet vein rather than in a dramatic fashion.

'And Chandrika? The yogi seems to have been more successful in divining her particular misfortune. At the time the yogi's letter arrived, Chandrika was struggling with her choice of a new lover.'

Chapter Nine

Sexual intercourse can be viewed as a kind of combat, and eroticism both as a contest and a perversion.

Kamasutra 2.7.1

*I*t had not escaped my attention that the *Kamasutra's* discussion of the prostitute's dilemma in choosing a lover does not mechanically proceed to cover all possibilities, as in the older works of Uddalaka and the Babhravyas. Personal experience glimmers through the screen of Vatsyayana's scholarly dispassion. The older texts have considered a courtesan's multiple relationships almost solely from the viewpoint of profit and loss in terms of money. When there are many possibilities, they say, those involving money are always to be preferred by the prudent courtesan. For Vatsyayana, the issue is more complex. According to him, the actions of a prostitute, like those of the rest of us, are not solely motivated by the prospect of obtaining wealth. He maintains that the prostitute will have doubts where there is a conflict between money and sexual love, love and ethics, or ethics and money.

'Ethics was never really an issue with Chandrika,' Vatsyayana said. 'Her conflict at the time was between love and money. Although all her education, upbringing and my mother's exhortations should have pushed her towards the latter, Chandrika's stubborn streak, perhaps a consequence of the ascending Saturn in her life, asserted itself.

'Love was represented by Kirtisen, a perfume merchant who had recently lost most of his fortune through a series of mishaps. A large consignment of his wares on the way to Ujjayini was washed away in a freak accident when the trading caravan was fording a sandy stretch of the Narmada river. This loss was followed by a bitter dispute with his partner who withdrew his capital from the business, a signal to the creditors to foreclose their loans. A middle-aged man with undistinguished looks except for his large liquid eyes which now looked more sad than soulful, Kirtisen had been attending Chandrika's evening dance recitals for many weeks. He sat quietly in the same corner every evening, his gaze raptly following each of Chandrika's movements, adoring her every limb. The presents he sent through a servant—pieces of old family jewellery, talking mynahs and parrots—were far from lavish but Chandrika did not seem to mind. Kirtisen's gentleness, his respectful and silent adoration, so unlike Mitras's swagger, were having a powerful effect on her. On a couple of occasions, after the evening's music and dance were over, she tried to engage the merchant in flirtatious conversation, giving broad hints on her availability for the night, but Kirtisen, content to worship from afar, did not take up the offer. This further whetted Chandrika's interest.

'Wealth was represented by Suvira, a young and handsome poet who had recently come into a good deal of money upon the death of his father. Utterly charming and brimming with a self-confidence that comes from the conjunction of youth, talent, wealth and beauty, the contest between him and Kirtisen for Chandrika's favours would have appeared hopelessly one-sided to any outside observer.

'The observer, however, would have missed a vital factor in the equation—that quality my mother called Chandrika's "capriciousness". Chandrika would have laughed at sage Auddalaki's assertion that there are a hundred and ninety-two questions with regards to an erotic union which need to be reflected upon before a courtesan chooses a lover. She deliberately spurned the advice of the sages, who claim that between a serious, faithful man—such as Kirtisen—and a fickle one, like Suvira, the prostitute should favour the fickle lover. More inclined toward astrological explanations, Ganadasa attributed Chandrika's eventual choice of Kirtisen to the reigning planetary constellations in the horoscopes of the three protagonists of this sexual drama.

'At the onset of her affair with the merchant, Chandrika was deliriously happy. Much later, sitting in her narrow cell of the women's section of the Goshitarama monastery, she told me that she had begun to feel at the time that however sensitive a particular lover may be, he was ultimately intent on traversing the path that led to his own pleasure. It was a matter of professional pride for her to make this journey as exciting and pleasurable for him as she possibly could. Kirtisen was the first man she knew whose goal was not pleasure but adoration. When both of them lay naked in bed, he would spend a long time in worshipping her body with his hands, lips and tongue, oblivious of his own erection. All he asked from her was stillness rather than active participation, and an acceptance of his homage. He partook of her bodily secretions—sweat, saliva and the love fluid—as if it was prasada in the worship offered to a goddess, to be ingested with the solemnity of a devotee rather than licked with the urgent greed of the lover. After making love, he bathed and dressed her, braided her hair and adorned her with ornaments—just as a priest does to the idol of the goddess after the morning and evening puja in the temple.

'"There is no greater homage to a woman and often, although not always, no greater pleasure," Chandrika said.

'I must have looked nonplussed, for she laughed. In that aching moment, I again glimpsed in my old aunt the youthful Chandrika of my childhood memories, emerging from her bath, proud in her nakedness, giving me a searching look as I began to rub sandal paste on her glistening legs. "I know you have become a famous man," she continued. "But you never knew much about women, Malli. You were so enthralled by their bodies, by the way the female form occupies space, that you never wondered enough about what goes on inside a woman when she is with a man. You always confused the idol with the divinity."'

Vatsyayana fell silent, and I longed to reassure him. Scholars have attacked the *Kamasutra* chiefly because of its liberal advocation of women's sexuality, I wanted to say. But then I paused. Is it possible for advocacy to be divorced from understanding? I shook off the disquieting thought. Of course, Acharya had understood the nature of woman's pleasure like no one else before him! I remembered a morning, many weeks ago, when he had summarized the physiology of female enjoyment in a short masterful discourse not included in the *Kamasutra*.

'Perhaps men cannot enter woman's sexual imagination; but they can know her body, especially the abode of Kama,' he had said. 'I do not agree with Suvarnanabha when he talks of four kinds of vulvas: one as tender as the inside of the lotus, another with small knots under the flesh, another which is finely wrinkled and yet another that is like a cow's tongue. I have not included Suvarnanabha's classification in my exposition because the texts teach us that a classification is only as helpful as the usefulness and clarity of its criteria. It is not enough to maintain, as Ghotakamukha does in his commentary, that Suvarnanabha is classifying vulvas according to the texture of their insides. This criterion lacks a critical dimension, its usefulness to man . . . or woman. Or is Suvarnanabha classifying vulvas according to the degree they are pleasing to the penis? If so, then his classification is inaccurate with regard to facts.

'It is, therefore, best to start with a description of the vulva from the viewpoint of woman's pleasure, a description I left out in my own text not only because of the goal of brevity I set myself but also because I did not want to strengthen the widely held belief that sexual pleasure is a matter of body alone. Now, you should know that the vulva is the most enduring part of a woman's body. It keeps its elasticity and smoothness of texture well into old age when the rest of the skin has become loose and wrinkled.

'The first source of female pleasure is the "umbrella of the love god". Shaped like a nose in the upper part of the vulva, it is connected to many small veins through which the love nectar flows to make the vulva oily wet during union. Spread throughout the vulva and invisible to the eye, there are three kinds of worms made of blood, which are of high, average and weak power, and which create a corresponding itch in the abode of the love god. Some women produce more blood worms of high power, so their vulvas are naturally itchier than others. The combination of these vulva worms keeps on changing since the increase or decrease of each kind depends on many factors: phases of the moon, the time of the woman's menstrual cycle, seasons of the year, time of day, age of the woman, physical stimulation of the vulva by the woman herself or her lover—and of course by the woman's imaginings about a desired man.

'The second source of pleasure, embedded in the inside wall of the abode of the love god and rising towards the navel, is the nerve called saspand. The rhythmic pressure of the penis against this nerve causes Kama's nectar to flow in large quantities. When excited to a sufficient degree by the friction and pressure of the penis, it induces the final paroxysms of love during intercourse.'

'For a woman to reach this highest state of bliss, the sexual union has to be just right. Yes, I know that in the chapter on union, I have treated the subject too tersely. My intention was to make it easier for beginning students and householders to memorize the text. It is easy to remember the three-fold formula of success in a sexual union: size, time and temperament. An advanced student like you, aware that sexual intercourse is a more complex phenomenon, will doubtless need a more subtle discussion than the one I give in the book.'

I had winced at his description of me as an 'advanced student', my thoughts inexorably drawn to the memory of my first encounter with the prostitute. Could a man who possessed so much knowledge about female bodies not know women? As if reading my thoughts, Vatsyayana gave me a rueful smile and continued with the story of his aunt.

'Perhaps it was only now when she was older that Chandrika could explain her choice of Kirtisen as her lover, a choice which left everyone bewildered. Youth's very thirst and capacity for assimilating new experiences works against its effort at balanced judgement, whereas the danger of old age is that it tends to foreclose experience through too rapid a search for explanations.

'Sitting cross-legged on the floor of her narrow cell, my

old aunt had gone on to remember her months with Kirtisen.

'"The communication of our bodies and feelings was so complete that each time we made love I felt I had conceived," Chandrika said, "and I would have the most intense orgasm. My vagina felt vibrantly alive. The feeling would spread through my limbs and for the first time I felt I was experiencing my body as a whole, with life coursing through its each pore. It seemed I had vulvas just about everywhere and could experience pleasure anywhere."

'After a few weeks, though, Chandrika felt a subtle change in Kirtisen's touch. Sometimes, while he lightly stroked her arm, a shiver of gooseflesh ran through her. The potential violence she began to sense in his caresses was not unpleasant; on the contrary, it was rather exciting.

'"The violence was such an ephemeral whisper, the merest hint of a suggestion, that I noticed it with my skin rather than my mind. My shoulder reacted to his lips with a tensing of its muscles and an increase in blood flow to that part of the body, as if expecting to be bitten. When his fingers skimmed lightly over the inside of my thighs, the flesh would pucker in expectation of a painful twist."

'My mother, ever the realist, tried to persuade her younger sister to end the affair.

'"We have all the wealth we are likely to extract from him. I hear he has nothing left. It is time to send him away. Remember, the beauty of a courtesan is shortlived, like that of a sunset which lasts only till twilight," she said.

'"I will, soon," Chandrika promised.

'But she did not. Pursuing some subtle purpose of her own, she needed a lover like Kirtisen who she believed she could mould to the needs of her obscure undertaking.

'Chandrika first tried to remove Kirtisen's inhibitions by talking about her own preferences in the arena of love's playful violence. "I love to see the necklace of coral jewels at the top of my breasts when I wake up in the morning," she said to him. "It makes other women so envious."

'She then went on to explain to this man, who was ignorant of the sixty-four arts, that a coral jewel was the red mark made on the same spot of the flesh when it was squeezed several times between the upper teeth and the lower lip.

'The violence in Kirtisen's lovemaking became more pronounced. The first time he went over the edge was when he seized the skin at the base of her left nipple with the nails of his right hand and pulled it while pinching it savagely at the same time. She had cried out in pain and he was profuse in his apologies. Thinking this incident was caused more by clumsiness than malice, she remembered telling him that this particular caress—I have called it the "hare's jump" in the *Kamasutra*—should be done lightly so that it does not wound but only leaves a mark.

'"That is all I want," Kirtisen had said. "I want to mark your body for the time I am away from you. The marks will remind you of my love. Bodies are otherwise so fickle, so quick to forget, so shamelessly without memory."

'In the days to come, there was a marked increase in Kirtisen's overt violence. Chandrika noticed that he had begun to grow his nails long and shaped some of them into two, and others into three points. His bites became harder, the nipping of her lips and earlobes more painful. The rashes on her body from the friction of her breasts, belly and thighs became deeper. They were still welts, though, for Kirtisen had not yet cut her skin with either his nails or teeth. The pain no longer enhanced her feeling of pleasure as it had done at the beginning. She felt that Kirtisen's temptation to inflict even greater quantities of pain was becoming irresistible, and she was afraid.

'The first time he really hurt her was when he slashed the side of her neck hard enough with his nails to draw blood. Chandrika screamed with pain and jerked convulsively, bruising her knee against the wall. Kirtisen showed an immediate concern with the bruise even as his fingers went on raking her side with his razor-sharp nails for another couple of seconds. He was abject in his apologies, begging her forgiveness. The expression on his face was once again that of the devotee. With his eyes closed, he licked the blood he had drawn and the tears of pain he had caused to flow. Chandrika forgave him although she knew within her heart that the affair had to be speedily ended. She no longer felt like a goddess but more like a chunk of meat worried over by a tiger building up an appetite. Most of the time now, she felt, Kirtisen's violent use of her body seemed not a manifestation of overwhelming passion but of almost a peculiar flaring hatred.

'Disaster struck during Kirtisen's very next visit, before Chandrika could end the liaison. My mother, Ganadasa and two other servants rushed to her room on hearing her terrified screams. Kirtisen had lost all control and was biting her chest and shoulders like a wild dog while she struggled to free herself from his body, which had pinned her to the bed. Strips of flesh had been gouged out by deep slashes from his nails, and her blood was all over the sheet. The "tiger's claw" and the "nibbling of the wild boar" were no longer rituals of foreplay from manuals of the erotic arts. They had manifested themselves in their original bestial incarnations. After Kirtisen was pulled away my mother lay down on the bloodstained bed, trying to comfort her sister and bring some light back into her empty eyes. Chandrika's face, thankfully left unmarked, was devoid of all colour, a lotus plant struck by frost, while a low whimper arose from her gashed throat. It took many months before her wounds healed completely, although she carried their scars on her shoulders, the side of her neck and the top of her breasts for the rest of her life.

'Kirtisen did not last long in the prison he was taken to straight from our house. For one month he lived on a small plate of gruel and a bowl of water given to him every day in the dungeon. On informal instructions from the chief of prisons, he was then poisoned. For Nitigupta, it was a matter of honour; no one could treat his former mistress so barbarously and still stay alive.'

Later that afternoon, with the story of Kirtisen and Chandrika still fresh in our minds, it seemed natural that our discussion of the *Kamasutra* focus on 'Blows and Sighs', the seventh chapter of the section on amorous approaches.

'You begin this chapter by calling sexual intercourse a combat and a perversion, Acharya,' I said. 'Does the opening verse not contradict many of your earlier ones on the tenderness and playfulness of erotic love?'

Indeed, this chapter as well as the previous one on scratching and biting had made me uneasy with its seeming sanction of the cruelty rampant in Kama's domain. Nails boring the cheek, striking a woman's breasts and pubis with an open palm or bunched fist, bruising her flesh by twisting it in a pincer-like grip—these and other such aggressive acts, Vatsyayana seemed to say, led to greater sexual pleasure than gestures of tenderness.

Vatsyayana smiled. 'It is a folly of youth, regrettably shared by many elders who should know better, to believe that a person cannot entertain disparate and contradictory ideas at the same time.'

I settled down to listen, my ears and mind alert.

'The combative nature of sexual intercourse is clearly seen in many animal species. The male captures, mauls and bites the female who in turn uses her teeth and claws freely, as the mating pair often emerge bleeding and mangled from sexual encounters. Sexual contest is subtler in human beings. Its battlefield is less the bed than the imagination of lovers engaged in intercourse. Many of these fantasies are of a violent nature. Without brutality, however minimal, attenuated and distant from awareness, a man will not be gripped by powerful sexual excitement. It is his wish to dominate and subjugate a woman, as much as his wish for pleasure, which gives him an erection and makes penetration possible. Aggressiveness towards the woman is as much a factor in his potency as his loving feelings. One of man's major fantasies is of taking by force that which is not easily given. Some men imagine the woman not wishing to participate in the sexual experience but then being carried away by the man's forcefulness despite herself. Every good courtesan knows this—after arousing the man, she feigns reluctance at the beginning of intercourse and then, with a carefully constructed medley of sighs and groans, proceeds to play-act a surrender of her will. In an accomplished practitioner of the craft, such as Chandrika, the pretence will often become a reality and the woman *is* carried away. Whether play-acted or real, this surrender reassures the man that the woman is feeling what he wants her to feel, that she has not escaped to a place somewhere deep inside herself where she is watching his passion and judging his performance.'

'And women?' I asked. 'Do they, too, require violence to enhance passion?'

'Yes,' Vatsyayana answered. 'A woman's passion increases in proportion to the sexual frenzy she can induce in the man. That is her victory. Excited as much by her triumph as by desire, the woman inwardly gloats at the illusion of supremacy she perpetuates for the man. Whereas one of the man's violent fantasies is of penetrating the woman, in the woman's imagination the insertion of the penis into the vagina is not only a loving acceptance but a seizure—for some, even a wrenching off of the lover's organ, to be retained inside her as the victor's trophy. Aggressiveness in sex blurs the boundary between the male and female and allows each sex to experience the violence of the other.'

'Of course, this crossing of boundaries is only temporary. The man and woman must soon resume their sexual natures,' he added.

My need for his approbation reasserted itself, and I quoted:

> Sometimes, out of passion, custom, or temperament, the woman inverts the situation. This is only temporary; nature will always reassert itself in the end.

He rewarded me with a smile.

'I agree with Suvarnanabha that the violence of sexual intercourse, although indispensable to its excitement, poses danger of serious injury, especially to the woman. Chitrasena, the king of Cholas, struck the courtesan Chandrasena so hard on the chest with the blow called the "nail" that she died. Naradeva, the chief of army in Pandya country, aiming to strike the courtesan Chitralekha's cheek with the "borer" missed his aim and gouged out one of her eyes. That is why I have compared lovers making furious love to a speed-maddened horse, flying at a gallop and unmindful of obstacles in its path or the nature of the road.

'In classifying various scratches, bites and slaps, I have tried to bring some order to the disorder of violence in love, made an effort to ritualize the cruelty of sexual intercourse. When I identify the different cries a woman makes under the blows of her lover, it is also to make the man aware that he can control his violence by judging from his partner's cries whether the woman wants to be hit harder or whether his blows are already too hard and must stop. My aim was to civilize the violence of sex, and that is why I end this particular chapter with the verse:

In his sexual behaviour, a civilized man takes into account his own strength and the fragility of the partner. He knows how to check the violence of his impulses and is aware of the girl's endurance limits.'

'And sexual intercourse as vamashila, as perversion, Acharya?' I asked.

Vatsyayana became thoughtful. When he spoke again he was uncharacteristically tentative.

'I know I have been accused of subverting virtue by not taking a clear-cut position on the relation between two goals of life, kama and dharma. Indeed, many verses in my text are ambiguous in this respect. I will let you in on a secret. I now doubt whether eroticism can ever serve virtue. The violence released in sex, which goes against the core of the virtuous man's desired control of the senses, especially his aggressive impulses, is one reason for my doubt whether increased sexual pleasure is compatible with human virtue. Yes, I do say causing suffering is not an Aryan practice and is not suitable for respectable people. Yet at the same time I assert infliction of pain is a part of sexual pleasure.

'Besides aggressive behaviour and fantasies of violence, there are other perversions inherent in the very nature of sexuality. Perhaps the most perverse is the fact that our awareness of violating the precepts of virtue makes the edge of excitement even keener. Another perversion is the need for variety in intercourse, which inevitably dehumanizes the partner:

> When they adopt an unusual position, whoever they
> might be, the courtesan and her lover are
> depersonalized. Whatever be his looks, her lover is
> the very god of love for the courtesan.

'Now to become a god is to be elevated above the human
state, but it is also to become dehumanized, to lose one's
personhood. Eroticism strips lovers of their humanity.'

'Why do we need variety?' I asked, puzzled. Reminded
of my own, continuing encounters with the courtesan in
Varanasi I had first visited with Chatursen, I knew that
any additional sexual variety to what I had already
sampled would leave me frozen with fear rather than
tingling with excitement.

'The manifest aim of the science of erotics—I will talk
of its hidden goal later—is to help men and women
increase sexual pleasure, a pleasure made possible by
excitement. Now sexual excitement is a fragile state, a bud
constantly endangered by the frost of boredom. Much of
the *Kamasutra* is therefore devoted to saving the sexual
encounter from becoming mechanical and predictable. In
essence, sexual boredom is the loss of a sense of risk. The
variety of positions, scratches, bites and blows introduces
just that little bit of uncertainty to the sexual encounter, a
small possibility of failure in a larger anticipation of
triumph. The risk is not only at the gross level of the body
but also at the subtler level of mind. With every new
partner, for instance, there is the possibility of a damning
verdict, of one's undesirability being revealed in the eyes
or felt in the limbs of the lover, the chance of a revival of
the hare man's shame or the elephant woman's
mortification.

'Even the most accomplished courtesans I have known are not immune from sexual boredom. "In the first few years of my professional life," Chandrika told me in one of our last meetings, "there was a good deal of sexual excitement in seeing and touching men's genitals. Innumerable men. wanted me, and I found that exciting. Orgasms were easy. Gradually the mystery wears off. Men's bodies become familiar. To climax becomes a struggle, although you can sometimes achieve one during intercourse by becoming selfish, withdrawing totally into your imagination while pretending involvement in the flesh. In later years, I was sometimes aroused only when the man and I had our clothes on and we were embracing and caressing each other through the cottons and silks separating our naked bodies. My excitement would suddenly disappear once we undressed and got into bed."'

I confess I was deeply disturbed by Vatsyayana's discourse. Was he questioning the enduring truths bequeathed to us by ancient sages and passed down from generation to generation? Was he in secret sympathy with some of the new sects which acknowledge the existence of no other life except this one, accept the reality of no other realm other than the material, believe in no other body besides the gross physical sheath? Had I made a mistake in confusing his vast knowledge with wisdom? All those years of theological study are responsible for an ingrained scepticism that continues to shackle me, even while I express an impatience with the subject and refuse to follow it as a career. I can rebel but not overthrow what has shaped me.

'Acharya, is eroticism then a separate realm of existence altogether, serving no other god but its own?' I asked.

'No,' Vatsyayana said. 'Kama may be incompatible with dharma but like the latter it too is subordinate to the highest goal of man's life—the unity with the supreme soul in moksha. Just as the dedicated musician endeavours to reach moksha through the subtlest experience of sound, the erotic man, the kami, strives for the same goal through the highest refinements of touch. The Nad-Brahman of the musician has its counterpart in the Sparsh-Brahman of the kami. Because of the power of sexual excitement which creates a tumult in the smallest atoms of a man's or woman's being, shakes up the whole body-mind-soul system, frees the lover for a moment from the karma of all past lives, the kami with his sensuality is better situated than the yogi with his asceticism to cross the gulf from the human to the divine, to become enlightened, as the Buddhists would say.'

He closed his eyes.

'Let us now contemplate for a while this most profound of human experiences which touches us with the breath of the sacred, blesses us with the revelation of the true nature of things.'

Obediently, I shut my eyes to meditate together on the essence of Lord Kama and the gravity of the vision he bestows upon us. What I received from the god were images of Malavika that I had never let myself see before: Malavika lying naked on the grass under a tree in the forest clearing, uneven strips of sunlight let in through the leaves playfully gliding over her body; Malavika standing waist-deep in the pond, droplets of water glistening on her taut breasts as she raised her arms to take a shell comb from the hair gathered high at back of her head; and then all I saw was her face, flushed with pleasure and with her eyes shut tight, her uneven, quickened breathing infused with the god's own breath.

Chapter Ten

In love, all kinds of acts cannot be performed at all times with all women. In erotic practice, a man's behaviour should take the place, the country and the times into account.

Kamasutra 2.7.35

*I*n the beginning of the spring of the year in which Vatsyayana turned eleven, his father kept his promise and took him along on a caravan journey to Kashgar. Since there was no further word from the yogi and the time of the dangerous planetary constellation was over, it was assumed by everyone in the household that it was safe for the boy to travel, although his mother still insisted on taking the precaution of offering a seven-day sacrifice at the temple of Ganesha.

'As far as I was concerned,' Vatsyayana said, 'my mother asked me to immediately report any bad omens in the week before the start of the journey, omens like a trembling of the left arm, twitching of the left eyelid, coming upon an anthill in the garden, a snake crossing my path, or seeing a dove perch on the roof. There were none, and I would not have told my mother if there were any.'

Kashgar, which lies beyond the High Pamirs and at the

edge of the Taklamakan desert, is a meeting point of both the northern and southern trade routes from China to countries in the west and south-west. The journey took a little more than nine months and winter would have just begun to set in by the time they returned to Kausambi. Caravans from the middle countries of India to Kashgar, Yarkand, Khotan and other oasis cities at the periphery of the Chinese empire, usually started in the spring when the Himalayan snows had not yet begun to melt and the rivers were still fordable. During this time mountain ranges to the north, especially the formidable Pamirs, could be crossed and re-crossed on the way back by the end of autumn, before the bitter cold made such crossings extremely uncomfortable for the pack animals and men used to the hot summers and mild winters of the Ganga plain.

Vatsyayana's excitement began many days before the actual commencement of the journey. At his father's insistence, he accompanied him to some of the meetings with the merchants organizing the caravan. Vatsyayana would squirm with embarrassment, while at the same time he inwardly preened whenever his father smilingly introduced him as 'my young assistant'. He wished he was older and a real assistant, able to help his father with the preparations required for the journey. There were carts and wagons to be assembled, draught animals and horses to be procured. Jars for drinking water were bought, rice and oil for the men and forage for the animals arranged. Drivers, guards and cooks were hired. Arguments between the merchants on the place assigned to each one's wagon in the column had to be settled before the merchandise could be loaded.

Vatsyayana noticed that most of the arguments on who was entitled to the best places in the column (the ones in the middle, since irrespective of the direction of the wind these were the least exposed to the swirling dust once the caravan began to move) were between merchants representing the textile guild on one side and representatives of all the other guilds on the other. In the last few years, his father told him, because of the settled political conditions along the trade route to the north, the demand for fine cottons, muslins and silks had soared, and the cloth merchants had begun to question the traditional hierarchy where those dealing with precious stones and with incense and aromatic oils had claimed precedence over other traders. The head of the guild of textile merchants, an irascible man who was quick to take umbrage at what he perceived as affronts to his dignity, had become one of the more important and influential citizens of Kausambi. His guild spent the most money on charity and organization of public works in the city, and had become the biggest donor for the construction of the temples to Vishnu that were springing up all over the country. The guilds of the perfume and of precious stone merchants, on the other hand, continued to patronize Buddhist temples and monasteries, though on a reduced scale, diverting some of their donations for the construction and upkeep of Shiva temples. As his father explained all this, the boy felt that for the first time in his life he was learning something really useful about the ways of the world.

'Even in my excited state, I saw that my mother was upset at my leaving. My father had decided that after we returned to Kausambi in autumn, I could stay at home for a few weeks before going away to a gurukula for the last ten years of my studies. It was the first time I saw my mother sad at the prospect of losing something else besides her youth or looks. I know she wanted to talk to me, establish some kind of bond between us, but did not know how. All she could do was to translate her inarticulate feelings into a fussy hovering and a continuous barrage of instructions and reminders on what I was to do and, especially, not do, while I travelled with my father. Our few moments of connection were to come much later and those, too, were mostly silent while she lay dying.'

Vatsyayana's mood became sombre as he was transposed into another time in his life, of which I had no knowledge as yet. I sat quietly till he completed this particular journey and returned to the boy setting out on one.

'It was shortly before daybreak when the column of wagons began forming up. The night patrols were in the final hour of their duty and the men's warning cries echoing in the streets had lost much of their earlier vigour. Ganadasa had come to see me off and I clung to him for a while, inhaling the deeply comforting smells of our kitchen and the familiar feeling of his paunch against my cheek while he stroked my hair and tried to lighten the mood of our separation.

'"This is the last time I will wake up so early in the morning. No more of those early theatre performances in the temples for me," he said.

'By the time my father and his officers arrived after offering prayers at the temple of Yaksha Manibhadra, the presiding deity of caravan leaders, we had both wiped off our tears with the backs of our hands.

'Chandrika's farewell gift was to allow me to sleep in her bed the night before my departure. "You are a big boy now and will soon be a man," she said. She did not need to add that this was to be the last time. That night signalled the end of my intimacy with a body I had known so long and so well and which would always remain uniquely etched in my memory and enchanted in my imagination. I remember that I slept fitfully. Lying on my side, with my body moulded into the curve of her back and wrapped in the warmth of her bed, I often woke up during the night, conscious of a strange desire, exhilarating and shameful at once. Intuitively wise in such matters, Chandrika pretended not to notice—although her steady breathing became swift and ragged when, unable to bear the ache in my loins any longer, I pressed convulsively against her hips.

'She, too, was crying when I left the house just before dawn.'

The trading caravan finally moved off with a grinding of wooden wheels and the blowing of conch shells, sounds that were to herald the rising of the sun each day for the next many months. Their wagon, which also seated two of his father's officers, was at the head of a long, thin line of thirty-five other wagons. The sarathvaha always travelled at the head of the column as long as the day was calm, without a breeze, or if the wind was blowing into their faces. This was to avoid the dust churned up by the caravan and thus remain fresh and alert. When the wind was blowing in the same direction as they were travelling, the sarathvaha's wagon would let the rest of the convoy pass to bring up the rear.

With a midday stop for food on the way, the caravan travelled about twenty miles a day on the old Mauryan highway before it halted at nightfall outside a village. If there was no available space to spend the night at a rest house or in the village temple, the camp was generally set up on open ground next to a stream or a well. Care had to be taken that the site of the camp not lie on the way to a waterhole used by wild animals. The story of how a herd of wild elephants on its way to drink water at midnight had trampled many sleeping members of a caravan was familiar to all the caravan leaders. The wagons were drawn up in four circles and the oxen penned in their centres. Fires were lit to cook the evening meal while the travellers washed the dust and the sour reek of sweat from their bodies. The guards, who relieved each other every four hours, kept the fires in the corners burning throughout the night to keep wiled animals away. The meal was a simple one of boiled rice and lentils. The men ate in small groups separated less by caste—the merchants were all vaishyas—than by trade. After the meal they sat around the fires, talking, while Vatsyayana's father conferred with his officers before he went around inquiring about the day's journey and giving both information and instructions on the next day's leg. Initially Vatsyayana accompanied his father, but as he came to know the individual drivers and the merchants better, he often went off on his own to join one of the groups.

'To this day, those nights shine brightly in my mind,' Vatsyayana recollected. 'The darkness around the camp would become magically alive with the dancing pinpoints of fireflies, the balmy air pleasantly scented with the smoke from burning wood and cowdung. I would be lying with my head in the lap of one of the merchants I had become friends with, looking up at the canopy of a brilliant sky densely packed with glittering stars, listening to the occasional barking of a village dog in the distance and trying to understand the exchanges taking place between the men around me. Invariably I drifted off to sleep and the merchant would carry me back to our wagon.'

As the caravan wended its way towards the north-west, Vatsyayana was learning a good deal about the world from the talk around the camp fires. The general perspective was naturally of the merchant, although sometimes it might be tilted towards that of the warrior when Vatsyayana asked his father questions on a conversation he had not quite understood. For instance, although both his father and the merchants agreed that Samudragupta had proven to be an even better emperor than his father, their reasons for the common verdict differed substantially. In spite of the strong rumour that Samudragupta was contemptuous of the merchant caste and barely civil to the guilds who financed the wars he loved so dearly, the merchants admired him since he amply fulfilled the most important expectation they had of a ruler—peace and order within the borders of an empire and thus the facilitation of undisturbed trade in a large market. His father's admiration for the emperor had different grounds—Samudragupta's conquests and his valour in battle.

Brought up in a sheltered household with Kama as its presiding deity, Vatsyayana quickly discovered that he was ignorant of the issues and people that featured in the political conversations he overheard. He was unfamiliar with the names of the rising and falling stars in the emperor's court. He did recognize a few names when the merchants discussed the politics of Kausambi's court although here, too, he discovered that a name was only loosely associated with the image of a person. The senapati, who he had visualized in the context of his infatuation with the hairy legs and strong odour of a female Greek slave, also turned out to be a valiant commander of soldiers, a man who enjoyed even greater favour with the emperor than his nominal overlord, the king Rudradeva. Vatsyayana had not known that for all practical purposes of governance, Kausambi had been absorbed into Samudragupta's empire, although both Rudradeva and the emperor maintained a facade of the king being a feudatory who paid tribute rather than a vassal. From the merchants' conversations around the camp fires, Vatsyayana learnt that when after a few weeks they passed the ancient and now ruined city of Hastinapura, they would also be crossing the borders of Samudragupta's empire and entering the lands of his feudatories in the Punjab. Beyond the Hindu Kush to the north, they would travel through Bactria and other dominions of the Yavanas which extended as far as Kashgar to the east. The merchants were unanimous in their opinion that the Yavanas, although politically and militarily opposed to the Gupta empire, protected and encouraged all trade passing through their territories. In spite of their reputation as fierce warriors, the Yavanas were a civilized people and, like most followers of the Buddha, closer to the mercantile ethos. In contrast to their own countrymen's absurd admiration for priestly and warrior ways and an equally absurd nostalgia for the life of the forest and of the village—did the dharma texts not maintain that it was 'impossible for one to obtain salvation, who lives in a town covered with dust'? —most merchants felt themselves closer to the Yavanas' preference for the city and the urban lifestyle.

Their first long halt was in the city of Mathura, the birthplace of Krishna, where the pack animals had to be changed and the caravan freshly provisioned. Straddling the trade routes from the north-west and Kashmir into the Ganga plain as also the route to the western sea ports through Ujjayini, Mathura had once again become a pre-eminent trading centre after Samudragupta's defeat of its king Nagasena and its subsequent incorporation into the Gupta empire. Five other merchants were to join the caravan here.

'By this time, I was quite knowledgeable about the merchandise carried by our caravan and its various destinations,' Vatsyayana said. 'Most of the merchants were only travelling as far as Bactria, from where traders from Rome and other western lands would carry away their indigo, ivory, cloth, balsam, aloe, tiger and leopard skins and the cargo of long pepper we were picking up at Mathura. Merchants continuing eastwards to Kashgar were mainly taking perfumes and fragrances—myrrh and musk in bladders placed inside tightly sealed vases, alabaster jars containing aromatic essences from the dry western region and costus from Kashmir—as well as precious stones, glass beads and vessels, rhinoceros horns and teeth, and a small quantity of silk into the Chinese kingdoms. On the way back, we were to pick up Chinese silk, ceramics and lacquer, jade and cinnamon bark at Kashgar, animal hides and wine from Bactria and lapis lazuli from Kabul. This brilliant blue stone, which represents the acme of purity and bliss to the Buddhists, would be cut and polished into beads in Kausambi and Varanasi.'

As Vatsyayana talked, his shining eyes reflected more than the luminosity of his boyhood memories—the adult's pride in his knowledge of commerce was also unmistakable. I remembered how during the discussions of the *Kamasutra* at my guru's hermitage, my guru's irascible friend Palaka had levied the accusation of 'commercially-minded' at its author.

'The book is as amoral as Kautilya's text on artha. Kautilya is at least frank enough to say that prosperity and accumulation of wealth are the highest goals of life. This Vatsyayana fellow is a hypocrite who pays lip service to the supremacy of dharma. The man admires Kautilya's book so much that he has slavishly followed its spirit and structure in his own work on love,' Palaka said, spitting out the last word.

'Vatsyayana even copies the stylistic peculiarities of the text on prosperity. Like Kautilya, he too introduces quotations with an *iti acharyah* (so say the teachers),' a young scholar had sought to flatter Palaka by agreeing with his judgment.

Vatsyayana's fascination with the world of commerce, evident in the long sections he devotes to the matter of courtesan's fees and ways of extorting wealth from clients, had damned him further in the eyes of Palaka and other theologians. My own friendship with Chatursen and his friends has given me a greater tolerance for trade and commerce although, I confess, generations of brahminical disdain still stand in the way of my summoning up genuine enthusiasm for the mercantile arts. Vatsyayana's involvement in the details of commerce was touching, and I wanted to prolong the feeling of tenderness I felt for a man for whom my admiration had been growing.

'Why take silk into China and then bring silk back from China into our country?' I asked.

'Chinese silk is different from ours,' Vatsyayana replied. 'It is short-fibred since their artisans do not unreel the silk fibre before the moths have gnawed through their cocoons. But the major reason why Chinese silk is preferred in our royal courts is its high price and the fact that it comes from afar. I have no doubt it is the same with the Chinese preference for our silk.'

For the last few decades, the market for perfumes had been shifting from the Roman to the Chinese empire. Because of the spread of a new, puritanical religion—something to do with the crucifixion of the son of Brahma (although, it is well known, the Creator only had a daughter!) in a country near Syria, the demand for fragrances in the Roman empire had steadily decreased. In China, on the other hand, because of the spread of the religion of the Buddha, the use of fragrances was no longer confined to the circle around the royal court. Since the burning of incense is essential to Buddhist rituals, fragrances in the form of incense are used at all social levels. Merchants dealing with aromatics are not only acting out of pious motives when they donate so generously to Buddhist monasteries and orders to help spread the Buddha's word. It is the same with those dealing in precious stones who, too, are among the biggest supporters of Buddhism since for lay devotees of the Buddha, the way to the different heavens is through worship and donation. The donation of the 'seven treasures'—gold, silver, lapis lazuli or turquoise, crystal or quartz, pearl, red coral or garnet, and agate—is considered especially meritorious.

'We entered Mathura from the eastern gate,' Vatsyayana continued. 'Even in my tired state I was struck by the majesty of the city. The bridge across the surrounding moat was the widest I have ever seen, with space for two elephants to walk abreast. The gate-house was three storeys high. The city wall, topped with battlements, was wide enough to accommodate a galloping horse.

'Our caravan entered the city gate a little after sunset. The dark gray sky was fringed with vermilion. A haze of dust hung above the noisy caravan camping site. The bullocks, horses and camels were being settled for the night by their keepers while the merchants and other members of the caravans were preparing to go out to sample Mathura's evening pleasures.'

From the merchants' conversations, Vatsyayana had gathered that Mathura's reputation was that of a city with loose morals. Its women were said to be adept in perversions which were otherwise only found among women of the north-western countries beyond the Gupta empire. Mathura's morality, many centuries earlier, had led the venerable lawgiver Manu to characterize its inhabitants as an ideal people from whom all other peoples on earth were to learn rules of good conduct. The decline in standards was attributed to its occupation by foreigners over hundreds of years. Successively ruled by the Greeks, Scythians and then by the Kushana kings, Mathura's citizens, especially women, had assimilated the vices of each of these nationalities. It was a wonderful city for a short halt, the merchants agreed, but would inevitably corrupt and enervate if one lived in it for any length of time.

In the morning, Vatsyayana's father sent a servant around to the house of his occasional mistress Padmavati, a well-known courtesan. The messenger's announcement gave Padmavati time to cancel her evening appointments.

'At the time, I took it for granted that any woman would leave everything else to be with my father if he wanted her. It did not occur to me to speculate about the secret of his attraction. He was not exceptionally wealthy, although he was generous enough with presents and gifts. Nor was he particularly handsome, even if my eyes convinced me that his was an ideal beauty, equal to that of Lord Kama himself. As I said the other day, the secret of his attraction lay in the manner he opened his heart to women and invited them to do the same with him. The teachers rightly say that to hold an elephant you need a post, to hold a horse you need a bridle, to hold a woman you need a heart. "Visits to a mistress are occasions to be celebrated," my father said as we walked toward Padmavati's house that evening, a servant carrying our chest of clothes. "They must never be so frequent as to become a boring routine. Fortunately my profession ensures that I cannot visit any one of my mistresses more that twice a year, and most of the time, not even that frequently."

'On the main street of the courtesan's quarter, its dust settled by the evening sprinkling of water, the breeze rising from the river was cool against my face. The music and dance halls of Mathura brothels are on the first floor. The tinkling of anklet bells, the sounds of the flute and the vina, snatches of conversations and fragments of laughter drifted from the music halls onto the balconies before merging with the street sounds below. Perfume wafted around us as courtesans on their way to assignations for the night rattled by in curtained carriages or were borne along in covered litters on the shoulders of trotting palanquin bearers. I clung to my father's left hand. His other hand held his present for Padmavati, a silver box with five compartments containing red lac, red arsenic, yellow orpiment, vermilion and a blue-black vegetable dye. He had bought five such boxes in Kausambi, each a gift for a mistress he planned to visit in five cities along the route to Kashgar where the caravan would halt for a few days.

'Padmavati's house was not a bit like ours. It was far grander, with five other courtesans, many more rooms and over a dozen servants. Padmavati, though, reminded me of Chandrika. The resemblance was not physical. It lay more in the quality of their animating spirit. Both exuded a vitality and an exhilarating sense of life in which everyone near them longed to be a participant. When my father introduced me to her, I had a strong impulse to run the tip of my fingers over her flawless, honey-coloured skin. I wished it was not my father but I who could be the sole focus of her charcoal-gray eyes. The evening entertainment had not yet begun and the other girls, dressed in their colourful finery, came running when they heard of my father's arrival. They cooed over him like excited tropical birds before swooping over me, clucking their praise, warbling their admiration.

'"Ooh, what a handsome boy!"

'"Look at those eyelashes! I wish I had them."

'"And that hair!" said another as she ruffled it with her perfumed hand.

'"I still prefer the father," Padmavati said, laughing.

'It was all good humour and I was grateful to be included in their adult world, to which I now felt tantalizingly close.

'Sometime in the early hours of the morning I had my nightmare again, although this time I was falling into a deep well rather than a lake. I must have screamed in my sleep. My father, who was spending the night with Padmavati in the adjoining room, came rushing back to my bed. Enclosed in the granite solidity of his strong arms, feeling his stubbled cheek against mine, my body ceased to tremble as the nightmare rapidly receded.'

The countries immediately beyond the borders of the empire were poorer than the Middle Kingdom and bore visible scars of the wars which had ravaged them a few years earlier. For two days the highway here crossed a wide plain, skirted by hills to the north that provided hideouts for bands of robbers which often swooped down on lightly-protected caravans at night. Because of the danger from bandits the sarathvaha increased the frequency of night patrolling by the caravan's guards. The merchants too seemed tense, with much less joking and talk of women around the campfires. The highway, though, was safe enough. The caravan encountered more than a dozen posses of the emperor's soldiers stationed in these countries with the permission of his feudatories, for the protection of trading caravans which were often pillaged. The general consensus among the merchants, echoing a judgement by ancient sages, was that this land of five rivers was unfit for the habitation of the Aryas. Moreover, its inhabitants were fond of the filthy practice of aupratishka.

'Actually, in all the months of travelling there was no real attempt to rob the caravan. A few merchants and guards were robbed in different towns where we had halted, but this was when they were drunk and the robbers generally low whores with no inkling of the prostitute dharma. My father and I were the victims of one attempted theft during our long halt at Bahlika. Thieves broke into the room of our inn one night by first wetting the mud wall and then cutting through the soft portion with a sword. Luckily, my father woke up at their noise and the thieves fled into the darkness with just one saddle my father had bought in Bahlika.'

Their next long halt was at Takshashila, the last stop on the old Mauryan highway. Vatsyayana's father explained that the name of the city meant 'the rock of Taksha' in Sanskrit but 'cutting off the head' in Chinese. The Chinese name derived from a story of the Buddha when he was still a bodhisattva. During this stage he sacrificed his head for a fellow creature. A great stupa covered with a thin foil of gold and adorned with precious stones was built to celebrate the event.

Away from the quarter where caravans halted, which looks the same from one city to another, what struck Vatsyayana about Takshashila was its distinct Buddhist character. It contained hundreds of stupas and scores of monasteries, many of which now lay in ruins after Takshashila was sacked by a Persian tribe some twenty years ago. Shaven-headed monks in crimson robes were a common sight in the bazaars, pouring out from the monasteries into the streets at specific times in the morning and at sunset when they strode purposefully through the city with begging bowls, collecting food.

'Takshashila is a most ancient city,' Vatsyayana remarked. 'In the *Mahabharata*, which has existed since the beginning of our race, it is mentioned as one of the cities conquered by Janamejaya, the king who threw thousands of snakes into a blazing fire to avenge the death of his father caused by the snake-king. Its famed Sun temple, to which my father took me, is almost as old as the

Mahabharata itself. Fortified like a Greek city by the successors of the barbarian conqueror Alexander who passed through it, Takshashila has been the capital of generations of Kushana kings.

'In reduced intellectual circumstances now, Takshashila was a famous centre of learning when I was a boy. Students from all parts of the empire and from countries beyond its borders flocked to the monasteries and hermitages of its renowned teachers. Its sculptors were considered peerless. One of the better known of Takshashila's scholars was Kunala, whose fame as a master of erotic arts had spread far beyond the confines of his discipline. Reputed to be especially well versed in the secret arts, Kunala was much sought after by travelling merchants and other visitors to the city. Some wanted help with problems of potency while others came for salves and devices Kunala had invented to increase the duration and enjoyment of union. The recipe for a permanent increase in the size of the penis by rubbing it for ten nights with a mixture of the hair of the shuka insects in oil, which I give in the seventh part of the *Kamasutra*, was actually discovered by Kunala.

'My father, who scoffed at the idea of using special creams or occult methods to increase erotic pleasure, nevertheless held Kunala in high esteem. Kunala was a pioneer of a whole new branch in the study of women's sexuality. I remember pestering my father with questions. What are the erotic arts? How does one become a scholar of these arts? What is sexual enjoyment? My bemused father patiently tried to tailor his answers to the understanding of an eleven-year-old boy. He had had a particularly good visit with his Takshashila mistress, a woman whose boldness of manner and the confident way her body moved once again reminded me of Chandrika.'

'You do not mention Kunala anywhere in the

Kamasutra,' I said, intrigued by Vatsyayana's omission.

'Kunala's ideas are still relatively new, their validity yet to be fully established. They lack the imprimatur of authority. The *Kamasutra* is a textbook and texts must not only be comprehensive but also conservative. Perhaps future generations of scholars will honour Kunala's contributions more than I could. Your own commentary may be the first to do so.

'Briefly, Kunala is of the opinion that because of the soft and liquid nature of a woman's sexuality as compared to a man's which is hard and dry, the waning and waxing of the moon have a strong influence on women's sexual satisfaction. During different phases of the moon, different parts of the female body become erotically sensitive. He has worked out a whole chart linking the phases of the moon to a woman's body parts and the man's caresses. On the fifteenth day of both the light and dark fortnights, a woman's head and hair have great sexual energy. Running fingers through her hair and' gently massaging the scalp spreads the energy to the rest of the body. On the fourteenth day, the eyes should be repeatedly kissed, the right eye on the light and the left eye on the dark fortnight of the moon. On the thirteenth day, the lips should be kissed, bitten and softly chewed. On the twelfth day, the same caresses should be applied to the cheeks. On the eleventh day, the throat becomes particularly sensitive and the caress it craves is a gentle scratching with the nails. On the tenth day, the woman's side should be scraped with the nails. On the ninth day, the breasts are to be cupped and kneaded. On the eighth, the whole bosom is responsive and should be tapped with the base of the fists. On the seventh day, the navel should be tapped with an open palm. On the sixth day, the buttocks are squeezed and tapped with the fist. On the fifth day, all of a woman's responsiveness is drawn into her vulva and she needs nothing more than the friction of the penis. That is why the fifth day of moon's light and dark fortnights are known as the lazy man's days for sexual union. On the fourth day, the woman's knees must be pressed by a man's own, and on the third the calf of her leg is to be massaged with alternating gentle and hard movements of the hand. On the second day, the woman's foot should be pressed with the man's toes, and on the first day, her big toe should be similarly manipulated.

'These are the general touches which apply to all women. Kunala has gone further in working out specific caresses for each type of woman. For instance, the elephant woman is especially responsive on the ninth, fourteenth, full and new moon nights. Each of these nights demands a different caress. When making love to the elephant woman on a new moon, scratch and tickle her armpit, kiss her eyes, pass the palm lightly over her nipples and rub them between thumb and forefinger. Scratch her chest with the nails till they leave marks, kiss and suck her lips and open and close the lips of her vulva repeatedly till the moment of entry when the vulva lies open under the tip of the penis like a crimson palm.'

Given my own scholarly background, I could appreciate Kunala's staggering achievement in working out the most responsive nights for different types of women, and the combination of caresses suitable for each type on each of these nights.

'Kunala, however, was not only a dedicated scholar but also a famous rainmaker who was popularly known as the Moist Sage,' Vatsyayana continued. 'The story goes that once upon a time Takshashila had abundant rains for three years in a row while the neighbouring kingdom of Madarakas, barely two days march to the south, suffered from a terrible drought. The king of Madarakas was baffled by the wrath of the weather gods, especially since he was a pious man who patronized Buddhist monasteries, welcomed brahminical ascetics into his kingdom and discouraged brothels by taxing them heavily. Charged with finding the reason for the drought, the royal astrologer and chaplain came to the conclusion that the misfortune of Madarakas was due to the influx of a large number of young ascetics, all fiercely celibate, into the kingdom's forests. Ascetic practices are the chief enemy of fertility, they said, and it is the spiritual heat generated by these yogis which is scorching the land with drought. The king was properly repentant. In the spring of that year the festival of Kama was celebrated all over the kingdom with enthusiastic royal support. Courtesans from the central countries were encouraged to migrate to Madarakas, and to counterbalance the excess of ascetic heat, Kunala was invited to visit the kingdom. It is said that the day Kunala reached the capital, the air became moist and clouds began to appear in the sky. Within a week of Kunala's arrival, there were heavy rains. Alas, the life and work of this great master of erotics were both cut cruelly short when the Persians sacked Takshashila.'

Vatsyayana did not have distinct memories of some of the towns—Pushkarvati, Nagarhara, Kapisha—along the caravan's route where it halted for re-provisioning as it travelled further towards the north-west. One of the merchants told him about a rock inside a cave, five miles south of Nagarhara, on which the Buddha had left his shadow. From a distance of ten paces the shadow is startlingly like the image of Buddha's actual body. His golden complexion, thirty-two greater and eighty lesser characteristic marks, are all brightly visible. The nearer one approaches, though, the more indistinct if becomes. Kings of many countries have sent their most skilful artists to sketch the shadow, but none has succeeded. Vatsyayana remembered the story but not the town.

After Kapisha, on the middle reach of the Panjshir river, the route became sandy and rocky as it climbed up the Koh-i-Baba range. It became uncomfortably hot during the day after the granite rocks were heated by the sun. It also became dangerous. Hugging the side of the mountain, the road sometimes became so narrow that a stumbling bullock could send the cart hurtling down a steep cliff. There was constant threat of landslides. The dark boulders perched on the bare slopes were like motionless vultures which could at any instant come swooping down on the caravan. Many statues of the Buddha had been carved into the rocky hillside by merchants anxious to ensure divine help in case of emergencies and calamities.

Descending from the Koh-i-Baba, they passed through a valley dotted with many vineyards. Along the road there were small Buddhist settlements and monasteries. Their bells filled the valley with music through the night. Vatsyayana found the bells comforting. They were unseen but friendly presences guarding his sleep.

The caravan rested for a day in Brahmayana before crossing the mountain range into the plains of Bactria. Here, for the first time since they left Kausambi, Vatsyayana felt he was in a foreign country. One reason was his father's instructions to members of the caravan not to taste anything unfamiliar, to eat no unknown root, flower or fruit without first showing it to him or his chief officer. And if anyone unwittingly did so, he was to immediately ask the sarathvaha for an emetic.

Bahlika, the capital city of Bactria, was the node of international trade between Rome and Syria in the west, China in the east and India in the south. Although a major trading centre, Bahlika was an odd city in the sense that its floating population was larger than the number of its permanent residents. The number of foreigners living in the city was larger than that of the native Bactrians, who preferred a nomadic life.

There were colonies of Chinese, Scythians, Romans, Persians and Indians to provide the services required by the caravans from their countries. All these groups led segregated social lives. Even the brothels were separate. My father received many invitations for a meal to the houses of our countrymen, and I accompanied him on his visits. Homesick for the sights, smells, sounds and tastes of Ujjayini, Saurashtra, Avanti, Pataliputra, Vanga, Kalinga or wherever else they originally came from, the residents plied us with food and the splendid Bactrian wine my father loved. All we were expected to do in turn was to listen to their nostalgic outpourings and offer them bits of news from the home countries.

Most of the Indians had lived a major part of their lives in Bahlika, yet each regarded himself as a temporary visitor to the city and one who would soon return home. They talked of the mango season which was just beginning in the Ganga plain at the onset of summer. They spoke of the joy of sleeping on the terrace on summer nights, of parrots and peacocks and of long-forgotten plays seen years ago. They recited old verses and asked my father if their favourite poets had composed new ones. They were strongly religious—many were still Buddhist—and carried out the rituals in older, more conservative fashion. They would have strongly disapproved of the lax morals in the towns of the home country. Our countrymen were also disparaging of the country they lived in. They believed that their Yavana rulers were barbarous and sinful kings about whom it had been prophesied that they would rule the earth at the advent of Kaliyuga. The mixing of the people of Bahlika with Persian tribes, Greek invaders and other foreigners from east and west had considerably modified Bactrian customs and standards from those prevailing at home, and the Indians in Bactria considered the people they lived with as the very dregs.

To a boy, people who are classified as dregs are unfailingly interesting, and Vatsyayana tried to discern the supposed evil lurking behind the smiling countenances of these handsome and happy people. He observed that the Bactrian women drove wagons more often than men did and that women were in the forefront of family groups strolling through the bazaars. Like the people of Strirajya to the north-west of Bactria, they followed a form of polyandry where a woman had three to four husbands. Whereas the women of Strirajya exercised power in state affairs, the dominance of Bactrian women was limited to the family sphere. The Indians grudgingly admitted that women of Bahlika, unlike the depraved females of Strirajya, were decent and averse to kissing and similar unclean practices.

Although Vatsyayana is too modest to say so in his treatise, the *Kamasutra*, as compared to earlier works, is distinguished by the attention it devotes to variations in sexual mores according to the country. It emphasizes the relative nature of sexuality within the universality of sex or, as Vatsyayana once remarked in a discussion of another chapter, 'Erotically, we all react the same way but very differently.' When the present controversy surrounding the *Kamasutra* comes to a close with the death of its critics, the way in which scholarly differences are most often resolved, I am convinced that future generations will recognize Vatsyayana's methodology as a path-breaking contribution to the erotic sciences.

I had often wondered about the origins of his interest in comparing the sexual mores of different countries, and asked him whether the journey with his father was instrumental in the awakening of this singular pre-occupation. Vatsyayana laughed. 'If you are looking for origins then you must go back earlier to Ganadasa's discourses on the food regimens of different peoples. Later, when working on the *Kamasutra*, I wondered whether nations also had different sex regimens. My interest in comparative research was certainly reinforced by the travels with my father, but you must remember that as a small boy I was only exposed to veiled hints regarding the sexual mores of different countries we passed through. The information I was able to gather when writing the *Kamasutra* was much less than I would have liked. Moreover, this information was mostly limited to the preferences of women. This is understandable since my informants were men and among men, merchants. Men travel more and have a greater chance of coming into sexual contact with women of different countries than do women.'

There are scattered references to the sexual habits of different peoples, especially in the fifth but also in other chapters of the second part of the *Kamasutra*. The women of our own central country are rather puritanical, Vatsyayana tells us. They dislike being kissed, bitten or scratched for fear of becoming polluted. The women of Dravida country in the south, although they like to be rubbed and pressed at the time of sexual enjoyment, are very slow in the act of coition, taking a long time to become fully wet. The women of Andhra, normally gentle by nature, are shameless in bed and their sexual tastes are not very decent. In intercourse, many of them prefer the position called the 'mare' in which a woman rubs her sex against the man and, like a mare with a stallion, seizes it with her vagina in a sucking motion, without a preliminary embrace or a kiss. This requires a certain skill and is used by the cheaper whores in our own country since it reduces the time of intercourse and adds to the number of customers they can entertain in one night. Whores in our country also increase the number of their customers by insisting that they first wash the customer's penis in the interest of cleanliness. The slow movement of her soapy hand not only excites the man but often brings about an ejaculation, obviating the need for intercourse and thus provides the whore both extra income and respite from her labours.

Anal intercourse is more prevalent in the south. The women of Malwa and Abhira like embracing and kissing, scratching and biting, but not wounding. They are very fond of sucking the penis. The women of Maharashtra utter coarse and obscene words during intercourse and like to be spoken to in the same way. The women of Gujarat, according to the whores of that country, enjoy licking the labia, the crotch, the armpits and the pubis. The women of Koshala and those belonging to regions where women are politically powerful and socially ascendant, are fond of violent practices and brutal sexual behaviour. They are also great users of dildos.

'The other countries I was thinking of when I wrote about the dildo were Bahlika and Strirajya,' Vatsyayana said. 'I also wondered why the dildo, used to supplement the weakening sexual power of men, is so frequently used in countries where women are the dominant sex. Is it the women's dominance itself which causes impotence and weak erection in their men? Could it be that strong women like their sex to be violent? In any event, my recommendation of a wooden dildo comes from its prevalence in Bahlika and Strirajya, although in Strirajya the women also use one made of copper and filled with hot water.'

He smiled and waited for the quotes. By now, it was a game we played with a degree of ease.

According to the Babhravyas, penetration with instruments made of tin or lead is soft. They are pleasantly rough and have the effect of fresh semen. However, according to Vatsyayana, dildos made of wood are more desirable.

'You should not exaggerate my interest in comparative sexual habits,' Vatsyayana continued after I had finished quoting from the *Kamasutra*. 'Although local customs must be given consideration with regard to dress, behaviour and the times of making love, the sexual preferences of different countries should not be given undue importance. Here it is important to remember Suvarnanabha's opinion that what is agreeable to the nature of a particular person is of more consequence than that which is agreeable to a whole nation, and therefore the peculiarities of the country should not be observed in such cases. This is eminently sensible: one has sex with an individual woman, not with a nation.'

Chapter Eleven

Those whose sexuality follows their imagination
and local customs, inspire affection, desire and love
in women.

Kamasutra 2.6.52

The first sentences of my commentary on Vatsyayana's biography were yet to be written, but the obvious dedication with which I was going about these tasks seems to have impressed my father favourably. Not that he now approved of my enterprise, but my industry had won his grudging respect.

'I wish you could work equally hard at something more worthy of your talents and the traditions of our family,' he would sometimes say with a sigh, but his curiosity about my meetings with Vatsyayana and his wish to share my discoveries were unmistakable.

Whereas my work with the sage drew my father closer, it pushed Chatursen away. He could not understand that scholarly work could be so absorbing as to turn me into a near-recluse. He was baffled by my reluctance to join him and his friends in their nightly carousing just because I wanted to wake up fresh in the morning for my trip to the Seven Leaf hermitage. He refused to believe that the mind has pleasures which are unknown to the senses. Instead, he took my enjoyment and commitment to my work as a rejection of his friendship. The gulf between us was growing, with politeness replacing our earlier familiarity, although I tried hard to bridge it by regaling him with incidents from Vatsyayana's life which I thought would resonate with his adventurous soul, such as the sage's journey to Kashgar as a boy.

In Bahlika, Brahmagupta, a young Buddhist monk in his twenties, joined the caravan for the next leg of the journey to Kashgar. He was to be Vatsyayana's first friend, a man who influenced the choice of scholarship as his future career. Brahmagupta was returning to his monastery after visiting some major Buddhist centres of learning in the southern kingdoms. He had been away for more than a year, copying valuable manuscripts of his faith which he was now taking back, a camel-load of documents testifying to his pious industry.

'Brahmagupta's monastery lay two hundred miles east of Kashgar, a three-hour camel ride from the oasis-town of Kurfan on the southern rim of the Taklamakan desert at the outskirts of the Chinese empire. Clinging like a swallow's nest to an almost perpendicular slope, the monastery had been established a hundred years ago by Buddhist monks from Kerala at the southern tip of our land. Over the years, cave temples and shrines were hewn out of the cliff. Since the trade route after Kurfan passes through a particularly desolate stretch, merchants leaving China prayed at the shrines for protection from the physical and spiritual dangers such as the terrifying demons of the desert, while those who had crossed this stretch on their way to China offered thanks for deliverance from the desert's perils. They have been generous with their offerings—the temple are richly decorated with frescoes and silk paintings as well as gem-studded statues of silver and gold. The monastery is also famous for its collection of brilliantly illuminated manuscripts on silk, parchment, leather and something which the Chinese have invented and call "paper"—a thin, smooth parchment on which the ink does not run and calligraphy is clear and distinct.

'Brahmagupta was an assistant librarian at the monastery, responsible for the storage, upkeep and cataloguing of manuscripts. Since the monk in charge of the library was old and suffered from gout, Brahmagupta also travelled to our country to procure manuscripts as well as paints unavailable in China, such as precious ultramarine from Takshashila, the brilliant blue pigment used extravagantly in the wall paintings of Buddhist temples and chapels.

'Most of Brahmagupta's brother monks were now Chinese and Sogdians, although, like Brahmagupta, there were still a few who had come to Kurfan from the mother monastery in Kerala for specialized tasks such as running the library or teaching advanced spiritual techniques. The monastery had survived many dangers in its short history. Whenever the central authority in China waned, Kurfan on the outskirts of the empire was vulnerable to pillage by rogue warlords and brigands. Shortly after its establishment, there was a time of political chaos when Kurfan was ruled by the Huns for some years. The monastery suffered a harsh period of political oppression. Brahmagupta told me the story of its founder, the virtuous monk Gunabhadra, depicted innumerable times in the monastery's frescoes with a short beard, dark skin and bulging red eyes, whose compassion for all sentient beings was legendary. Gunabhadra had been brutally tortured for much of his three years in prison. After his release, when asked by a young disciple if he had ever felt himself to be in deadly danger, Gunabhadra replied, "Yes, twice."

'"The reverend father was close to death?" the disciple asked.

'"No," the old monk said. "On two occasions I almost hated the Huns."

'In spite of a life devoted to meditation, prayer and books, Brahmagupta was like many other monks I have come to know and admire who are perpetually cheerful, who laugh easily and loudly, the laughter not springing from a sense of humour but from an evolved spirit of mischief and playfulness. Sometimes, watching the frequent and obvious merriment of these monks, I have wondered whether the Buddha's message is indeed about the world being full of pain and sorrow; or perhaps, the Enlightened One has left a secret message for his monks, a cosmic joke which never palls with any number of re-tellings, which makes them laugh so much.

'I was enchanted by Brahmagupta's high spirits and spent four wonderful days in his company when my father went off to stay with his fifth (and last) mistress of the journey. During the day we wandered through the town, taking in the fascinating life of the bazaar. (Our favourite source of entertainment was the fights between the merchants and their customers which we watched with undisguised glee and with the hope that the altercations would soon result in fisticuffs. We stuffed ourselves with melons, peaches, grapes and shelled almonds, much of the fruit given as alms by the pious people of Bahlika and accepted by Brahmagupta with a benign smile and a perfunctory blessing. In the evening, we sat in the inn's garden, escaping the stuffy heat of our room but burdened with the unwelcome company of the largest mosquitoes that have ever bitten me. Brahmagupta talked about monastic life and the world of scholarship and I listened with fascination, asking many questions which he patiently answered. His secret passion was the translation of Chinese manuscripts into our language. The manuscripts that interested him the most—and these were also the rarest (he had only obtained three so far)—were on the science of erotics. Our later friendship, enriched and reaffirmed by our occasional meetings whenever he came to Kausambi, was based not only on mutual affection and shared memories of Bahlika and the journey to Kashgar, but also on a solid base of common intellectual interest.

'In one of his trips to the Gupta empire, when Chandragupta Vikramaditya was the ruler and I was in the middle of composing the *Kamasutra*, Brahmagupta presented me a roll of paper about a foot wide and seven feet long on which he had copied his translation of the Chinese erotic treatises. We spent two wonderful days together reading the texts. Brahmagupta was cheerfully patient in explaining the context and the Chinese sexual vocabulary which mystified me during that first, quick reading. The yoni, for instance, is variously the Purple Mushroom Peak, White Tiger's Cave, Dark Gate, Red Ball or Jade Gate, while the lingam is called the Jade Peak, Jade Stalk or other such poetic names.'

'Acharya, you do not mention any of the Chinese views in the *Kamasutra*?' I asked, surprised.

Vatsyayana lowered his eyes, as if seeking the answer in the clay floor of the clearing outside the hut.

'I was young then,' he began hesitantly, 'and still unsure of my acceptance by scholars, also because I was not brahmin-born and therefore disdained by many as an interloper in the field of letters. In my own area of erotics, Shvetaketu, Babhru, Ghotakamukha, Gonardiya, Suvarnanabha, Gonikaputra, Dattaka and Kuchumara were the only recognized authorities. A new work on any aspect of sexuality had to necessarily begin with their views. One could then advance one's own arguments and opinions but it would have been a scandal to bypass the traditional format entirely and quote Chinese teachers who no one knew even existed. You must remember I possessed the only copy of their work in our language. Scholarship, you will find out soon, is a highly sectarian activity with a very fine line between acceptable innovation and heretic dissidence. Scholars are generally dull people with intelligent but conventional minds that follow the prevailing fashion in the way they approach a problem and the language they use in its formulation. Straying from an already mapped out path will at best invite ridicule and, at worst, rejection through a deafening silence. Yes, I had already established a reputation and could have taken more risks. But remember, what I had then was the dubious reputation of an iconoclast, though one who was still within the faith, and playing with Chinese notions could have spelt an end to my career. But, yes, I was more cautious than courageous.'

Here Vatsyayana paused and looked at me with something like a plea for understanding in his eyes.

'Today I might have acted differently. Perhaps you will make amends for my failure in your commentary.'

'Are the Chinese texts so different from ours?' I asked.

'That is a difficult question to answer. At a fundamental level there is no difference. Like us, the Chinese, the Persians, the Greeks, the Romans, and every other nation must base its sexual knowledge on what the Divine Force has created: the architecture of the human body and the imperatives of human desire. The basic positions in sexual intercourse, for example, are only four: male superior, female superior, male and female facing each other side by side—whether lying down, sitting or standing, and male entering the female from behind. The variations can be many. The Chinese sage Li Hsuan lists twenty-six positions, our revered Babhru sixty-four. Most positions are identical in the two lists. Li's "Leaping Wild Horses" in which the woman raises both her legs and places them on the shoulders of the man so that he penetrates her deeply is the "Gaping" position of the *Kamasutra*; their "Phoenix Holding Her Chicken" in which a woman with a large yoni—an elephant or even a mare woman—crosses her raised legs to restrict the vulva and thus make it pleasurable for even the hare man, is our "Tight" position. Some of the variations invented by each nation perhaps tell us something about the collective sexual imagination of that nation but nothing more than that. All erotic texts must believe that sexual activity functions independently of any reproductive concerns; the Chinese scholars of erotics would thus agree with us that gods of fertility and love have nothing in common except the human body as the physical instrument of realizing their different divine purposes.

'What is more interesting in a comparison of erotic texts is the difference in general attitudes toward kama and the varying significance other civilized nations attach to some of its manifestations. Since our sages, beginning with Shvetaketu Auddalaki, have always maintained that a man in love feels its fervour more violently than physical desire, our texts tend to be broader in their conception of sexuality, discoursing on desire when it is but a seed and following it through to its flowers, fruits and seasons. The Chinese texts, on the other hand, focus more narrowly on intercourse and especially on the sexual arousal and satisfaction of women during the act. In their chosen emphasis, though, they are more comprehensive.

'The Chinese also play down the pleasures of orgasm, insisting that a man can learn to thrust one thousand times without reaching culmination. In this miserly insistence on withholding ejaculation, the Chinese are similar to some of our own ridiculous sects who too seek to propagate the absurd notion that longevity, creativity, physical and mental vitality are enhanced through the conservation of semen.

'I do not deny the many virtues of Chinese erotics which we could profitably incorporate into our own. Their advice to beginners entering the domain of Kama is exemplary, even though I doubt if a man is capable of counting when the tide of passion comes upon him. They tell the beginner to start with a woman who is not too attractive and whose vulva is not too tight. With such a woman it is easier to learn self-control. If she is not inordinately beautiful he will not lose his head and if her vulva is not very tight, he will not get too excited. They recommend the novice to first try the method of three shallow and one deep thrust and to carry out the thrusts eighty-one times as one set.

'On the other hand, noble-born Aryans will find some of the Chinese recommendations on love fluids abominable. Since they believe that the production and partaking of "jade fluid"—their generic term for saliva and for secretions produced during sexual excitement—is vital for the harmony of the female and male essences (what they call the Yin and the Yang), the texts celebrate these fluids without regard for questions of purity and pollution.

'You can understand the attacks the *Kamasutra* would have been exposed to if I had mentioned these Chinese practices, even if I did not openly endorse them. Even well-inclined critics would have been quick to point out that like everything else in the world kama has its own maryada, limits within which it is divine, and demonic if it transgresses these bounds. I took the safe road by making the general observation that everything is permitted at the height of passion, leaving it to future commentators to map the territory of this "everything".'

The caravan was reduced to half its original size by the time it moved out of Bahlika. Many merchants whose merchandise was intended for the Roman empire were staying on in the city. Some were waiting to sell their goods, others to buy. They would rejoin the caravan six weeks later on its return.

The road to China through the Bactrian plains followed the course of the Amu Dariya, or the Oxus as the Bactrians call it. Ahead of the travellers lay the Pamirs, said to be the highest range in the world after the Himalayas. The caravan would move for fourteen days through the mountains of the Pamirs, traverse Taghdumbagh, the highest pass on earth, before arriving at its final destination, the town of Kashgar. The wagons and oxen were left behind in Bahlika and replaced by twin-humped camels with long hair, almost fur. These animals are better able to withstand the rigours of travel through the Pamirs.

'Even though it was summer,' Vatsyayana recalled, 'the nights high up on the plateau were extremely chilly. No birds flew here due to the height and the cold. In the evenings when we built campfires, these were neither as bright nor of the same colour as the fire in the plains. The food, too, did not cook well.

'For six days, there was no shelter or habitation. The only large settlement in this mountain fastness was the Buddhist kingdom of Tash Kurgan some eighty miles to the south, which was reputed to have over a hundred monasteries and thousands of monks and nuns meditating on the Buddha's perfection and pursuing their own enlightenment.

'As we began our descent toward Kashgar, the barren ruggedness of the plateau softened to a degree. High shivering waterfalls cascaded down the slopes. We passed lush green pastures nestling in shadows of snowcapped mountains where herdsmen had pitched tents. Their villages lay in the valleys below. In spring they plant green beans and barley in their terraced fields, harvest the crop in summer and then move up to the higher reaches with their herds of sheep and cattle. Here they live in tents and graze the animals till the end of autumn before returning to the villages at the onset of winter. We encountered some of their families on the road. The men, their long black hair tied in a loose knot at the crown, their feet cased in high black boots with felt soles, rode donkeys not much smaller than horses. The women and children were perched on light gray camels.

'The view was often spectacular. I clearly remember a day when for three hours we traversed a road cut into the mountain that had a sheer drop down to a lake with clear blue water reflecting the white peaks. The lake was spread out like a vast canvas.

'By the time the caravan reached Kashgar, the mountains and valleys of the Pamirs had been left far behind. The largest of the many oasis cities at the edges of the Taklamakan desert, Kashgar— "the land with a bad character" in Sanskrit—is at the meeting point of the northern and southern routes from China which skirt the great desert. Surrounded by sand and stone, the oasis at Kashgar produces fruits, vegetables, varieties of grain, and grapes with an extraordinary rose fragrance that persists as a bouquet in wine. Rows of trees around the oasis-city form a formidable barrier against the sand. Besides avenues of poplars, there are orchards of apples, peaches, plums and apricots. Kashgar's bazaars are well stocked with wares from all over the world but also have shops selling local specialities: fleecy carpets and Kashgar silk, fine material in elaborate patterns of many colours.

'We stayed at an inn for caravans. It was comfortable enough, although I hated its prolific insect life. Mosquitoes, fleas, sand flies, lice and cockroaches were bad enough. I could even tolerate scorpions. But the poisonous jumping spider, its body the size of a pigeon's egg and jaws that make crunching sounds, absolutely terrified me.

'Kashgar's inhabitants were Sogdians, a tribe related to the Persians. They had a natural affinity to business and trade. Their children were taught arithmetic before they could read. Making money was a highly respectable occupation, in contrast to the status of commerce in the minds of our own conservative elite. Newborn babies wore coins as ornaments so that they had money next to their skin from the very beginning of life.

'"They consider stealing as one of the most heinous crimes," my father told me. "It is almost at par with murder. Even cheating draws the same punishment as rape."

'I could not imagine how a people so spiritually impoverished as to believe artha was the highest goal of life could yet be as seemingly content as the Sogdians of Kashgar. I remember that once, while accompanying my father to the provisioning merchants, I witnessed the execution of a thief. The memory has become indelible. The execution took place in the square next to the central market and at first glance seemed to evoke little interest among the merchants and their customers who remained busy with their transactions. Looking closely, though, one could see that everyone was determinedly incurious, careful not to glance at the condemned man standing in a specially built wooden cage, hanging from a pole by a chain. Protruding from the slats, the thief's head was firmly secured to the pole with a leather thong. His feet were roped to a wooden board at the bottom of the cage. This board was lowered a little every hour till the man's neck finally broke.

'"The Hun rulers of this country are an odd mixture of the civilized and the barbaric," my father remarked on our way back to the inn. "Putting a criminal to death this way is particularly barbaric. I have heard that in the olden days one of the Varanasi kings executed the victim by burying him in earth up to his neck and with his arms tied behind his back. All the poor man could do to scare off vultures and jackals was to yell and shout till he could no longer do so. We should be grateful that we live in civilized times where the executions are more humane, the condemned man quickly trampled to death by an elephant."

'What I most remember about Kashgar is my father taking me into the desert one evening just before sunset, the barren sands starting from barely two miles outside the town. He had once led a caravan through this part of the desert to Sha-che, another oasis town about a week's journey away.

'"This was before you were born," he said. "I had just begun to visit your mother and was infatuated by her. She was very different then, lively, playful, although looking back now I see that perhaps there was already a trace of that sadness which today grips her so tightly in its ghostly embrace. The change came later, after your birth, when her possessiveness and complaints at my long absences were no longer the playacting of a courtesan but aggravatingly genuine. Her copious screams and tears during our frequent fights became a blight on my desire and a cloud over her own nature. But she was not emotionally burdened when I first met her. She was only eighteen, but people already talked about her as the next 'Lady of the Court'. She liked me too, and I was thinking about asking her to be as wife to me after I returned."

'As we sat together on the flat surface of a large high rock, looking out at the immensity of the desert and its awesome stationary waves of sand, he told me the story of the last leg of their journey from Kashgar to Sha-che.

'"Desert travel is always dangerous, and nowhere more so than in the Taklamakan. Our caravan got under way at sunset. Travelling was done entirely at night since the days were unbearably hot. The journey was slow, never more than fourteen miles a day, and it was excruciating for both men and camels. Around the fourth day, some of the camels began to develop sore feet. We stitched pieces of leather to their feet to relieve the animals' distress. After a while the men who had to dismount and walk began to suffer the same way. Though nominally the sarathvaha, I had little control over the caravan's fate since the route through the desert was decided solely by the land pilot we hired at Kashgar, who found his bearings by the stars at night. My heart beat faster each time our pilot showed the slightest hesitation in deciding the direction. I could do nothing except try to hide my fear that he could lose his way, condemning us all to certain death in this ruthless place.

'"Yes, there are moments of beauty in a desert journey: sand shimmering golden at dawn; the clear night sky so densely packed with stars that some look ready to fall to the ground. Even on quiet evenings there is an awareness of the desert's terrible malevolence when one hears a sandstorm raging a few miles away, sounding like the clash of armies in battle. For a caravan, there is nothing more terrifying than the black whirlwinds of the Taklamakan. Close to Sha-che, no more than half a day's travel, we were struck by one such storm. Quite suddenly, without warning, the sky changed colour. The spiralling sand began to choke the sky, dyeing it a blinding yellow.

Glimpsed through a fast-thickening veil of dust, the sun became a dark crimson ball of fire. And then, after a few minutes, the sandstorm burst upon the caravan with appalling violence. Enormous masses of sand, mixed with pebbles and rocks, were lifted up by a whipping gale and hurled down on man and beast. The darkness increased. Strange shattering noises caused by the violent contact of great stones being whirled through the air mingled with the roar and howl of the storm. In spite of the great heat, men had to wrap themselves in thick felt so as not to be injured by the stones flying around with insane force.

'"Cowering under the flimsy protection of a tent which threatened to fly off at any second, I confess I was afraid I would not survive such elemental fury. At that moment I had a vision—I saw your mother, glowing after her bath in red and gold silks, enter the dance hall followed by a small boy. The fearsome sounds of the storm vanished, to be replaced by the swish of her silks, the jingling of her anklet-bells and a light glide on the vina. You were the boy, Malli, born in my mind in the Taklamakan at a time I thought I was near death, before you emerged from your mother's body in Kausambi two years later. This is why I decided your first journey with me must be to Kashgar, from where I could show you your other birthplace.

'"When the storm died down the desert looked quite different. The gale had shifted most of the sand dunes and created new ones, some more than a hundred and fifty feet high. We had to wait till after midnight when the dust settled and the stars became visible, allowing the pilot to chart our course."

'I was proud of my father, of the ordeals he had undergone and the dangers he had faced. Sitting at the edge of the desert, the oil lamps of Kashgar blinking behind us through the poplar trees, I had never felt as close to him as I did then. There had been other moments of closeness earlier: sitting together in the wagon, our shoulders touching as it lurched forward; walking side by side through strange towns with his comforting arm around my shoulders; the visits to his mistresses where he proudly introduced me as his son. But this closeness was of an altogether different kind, a source of much more powerful nutrients for my soul. He was letting me share in his profound engagement with his work. Because of his competence and pride in the exercise of his craft, I was being given access to what lay at the very core of his being. This is one memory of my father I hold very dear: my face looking up at his as he sat on the rock that evening, talking of journeys he had undertaken and the journeys we would go on together when I grew up, while before us stretched the vast unknown space of the Taklamakan desert and above us the mysterious infinity of the sky.

'Exactly a week from that evening, he was to die in an accident on our return journey through the Pamirs. He had ridden to the back of the caravan when his horse reared violently—stung by a scorpion, said the accompanying guard—and my father was thrown off the mountainside, falling hundreds of feet to his death into the beautiful blue waters of the lake we had passed on our way to Kashgar, the lake as still as a painted one.'

On the return journey and for many months afterwards, Vatsyayana's grief was not for the father he had come to know and love. It was for a father he would not know. He dreamt of journeys with a father who was much older in the dreams than the man who had fallen to his death off that mountain cliff in the Pamirs. It was a father who dozed at the back of the cart like an old man, his cheeks and chin darkened by gray stubble, while the dashing young rider on a horse trotting next to the cart was Vatsyayana himself. They took many journeys together in the boy's dreams: through unknown landscapes of forests, deserts and mountains, in which the son gradually came to resemble the father—fearless, self-confident and audacious.

Whenever he woke from such a dream, Vatsyayana was gripped by devastating cycles of emptiness, regret and sorrow. The intensity of the grief gradually abated, although for many years afterwards his sense of loss would flare up at unexpected moments, requiring a good deal of effort to keep his face from crumpling and his eyes from overflowing with tears. He mourned not so much for what had disappeared with his father's death but for what had not been allowed to develop and now would never exist.

Chapter Twelve

The fantasies invented by man in grip of sexual excitement are unimaginable even in dreams.

Kamasutra 2.7.32

In the following week I swiftly suppressed a surge of excitement when Vatsyayana told me one morning that Malavika wished to attend the Shivaratri ritual in the royal temple in Varanasi. 'She has never been to Varanasi,' he said, 'and there is no better time to visit the city of Lord Shiva than the occasion of His night. Will your father accept her as his guest?'

Of course, he would, I reassured him, keeping the signs of pleasure I felt away from my voice, eyes and, I hoped, his astute perceptions.

'Sometimes I feel that she will make a reluctant renouncer,' he said. 'Perhaps it would have been better for her to experience all the amusements and pleasures of youth before marriage—the young girl's delight in ornaments and delicate silks woven from threads as thin as air on your Varanasi looms, picnics in parks, moonlight excursions on the river with young admirers. But she was always a serious young woman and now here she is, trapped in a hermitage while I make up my mind about living the rest of my life in one.'

I was embarrassed.

'I am sure she is happy here, Acharya,' I said. 'She is different from most other women.'

Vatsyayana nodded. 'I am so glad you spend time with her,' he said, looking straight into my eyes though without any hint of intrusion or intimidation. 'She tells me how much she enjoys your company and the walks in the forest. I am grateful to you for alleviating her loneliness. You are almost like a son to us.'

Somehow I was less pleased by his rare and open expression of affection than I would have expected.

It is well known that the blue-gray basalt lingam in the sanctum of the royal temple is located at the very centre of the universe. On this great night of Shiva, there is not another lingam in the one hundred Shiva temples in Varanasi, or indeed in thousands of temples all over the country, which is as revered, as pervaded by the god's presence and as full of his energy as the four-foot high dark column, heaped with flowers at its base, that stood brooding above the mass of squatting worshippers.

My father had kept his promise and arranged for invitations from the head priest that allowed Malavika and me to attend the worship on this auspicious moment of Shiva's manifestation as the great lingam. An invitation to participate in the ritual at the royal temple is highly prized. It attests to the invitee's exalted social status and confirms his membership in the elite of Varanasi. Within this elite, there is a further differentiation according to the invitee's seating position in relation to the king who sits in the front row, just outside the opening to the sanctum. The royal family—the queens and their children—sits to the king's right while the seat of honour to his left is occupied by the chief invitee, usually the king of a country that needs to be cultivated by the kingdom of Varanasi for reasons of state.

In contrast to the dim light given off by the lamps flickering in alcoves around a hall crammed with the dark mass of over two hundred men and women, the sanctum was brightly lit by flares in its four corners and a large gold lamp hanging by chains a few feet above the lingam. Light bounced off the shaved pates of the priests, slid across their sleek, bare chests and slithered over the oiled surface of the god's organ as the lamp swung above it in a lazy arc.

Then at the stroke of midnight, the moment of Shiva's appearance, the temple bells tolled and the congregation became still. The six senior. priests, sitting cross-legged around the lingam, began the worship with the recitation of Shiva's thousand names. For three hours the ancient chant would swell up, subside and swell, again and again, in profound harmony but with a subtle heightening in its tempo. At exactly the same time all over the country, as if divinely synchronized, the same chant was rising up to the heavens, inexorably pulling down the god by a rope of love and devotion from his abode on Mount Kailash towering above the other snow-covered peaks of the Himalayas. And then Shiva was among us; his presence was felt in our bodies and heralded by an easing of all thought and imagination. My first awareness (but can one say 'first' when all awareness is simultaneous?) was of a sharp increase in the feeling of warmth coming from other bodies. The heat was not an anonymous mass of energy but flowed in individual currents which bore the specific, though illegible signatures of anonymous devotees. Such exchanges were taking place everywhere—the muscle tension of other men and women reverberating against the tension in my own arms, shoulders and thighs; the skin of bodies pressing against mine a conduit for the collective touch of the whole congregation. My limbs and organs, flesh and bones, nerves and arteries, muscles and ligaments, blood and marrow, all lay wide open to those of other worshippers as Shiva roamed freely among us, connecting not minds and hearts but the very atoms of our bodies.

Om Namah Shivaya, the priests chanted. The frequency with which they poured cups of cold milk over the lingam increased as they strove to keep the god's energy confined to his organ and preventing it from exploding into a ball of fire that could destroy all creation. I could see the black stone lingam glow from within like red-hot coal as rivulets of milk dribbled down its sides.

Om Namah Shivaya, the chant began its final descent. As the priests' voices faded the lingam's glow started to dim, and we felt the god's presence ebbing. 'Ah-h h h h h!' There was a long-drawn-out sigh from the worshippers as we felt the god withdraw from our collective body. The temple bells began to ring, as much in joy as in desolation. Full-throated shouts hailing the god rose from the congregation around the sanctum and the crowd gathered in the temple grounds. Our eyes beginning to focus again, Malavika and I turned toward each other, retreating into our separate bodies and minds even as we did so. What we had just shared had added that elusive depth to our closeness which transformed it into intimacy. We both sensed that Shiva's night had removed any remaining barrier between us. I believe Malavika too felt some of the enormous tenderness I enveloped her in as we walked back to my house through the rapidly-emptying alleys of Varanasi, careful to talk of everything else except the love which had flowered between us and which now infiltrated even the most banal of our conversational exchanges.

I have never been as happy as I was in the two days immediately after Shivaratri. Our intimacy of the previous night lay quietly between us, devoid of tension or demand for action—a state that would express itself in its own way when the time was ripe. An unseasonable cold spell, extending into spring, was prolonging winter's end that year. The lotuses were still withered, the water in the ponds cold. At night the stars were wan and the moonbeams glittered icily. We woke late, well after the gentle warmth of the morning sun had begun to seep into the earth. My father, who was an early riser, looked disapproving when he caught my eye as we left the house but remained unfailingly courteous to Malavika, who as the sister-in-law of the king of Kausambi and the wife of a well-known if controversial scholar, was an honoured guest.

We wandered through Varanasi's famed alleys, rich with shrines, temples and monasteries. We observed the river from the top of the stately flights of steps descending to the bathing ghats—pilgrims taking a dip in the Ganga, ash-smeared sadhus sitting on the steps in solitary meditation or in animated groups, barbers shaving the heads of men who had come to cremate loved ones, mourners gathered around burning pyres. Cremation at this holiest of spots ensured the dead almost certain freedom from rebirth and promised a stop to the cycle of birth and rebirth. We roamed through bazaars crammed with merchandise of every kind and crowded with visitors to the city from as far south as the Tamil kingdoms, people who had come to Varanasi for the Shiva festival and would stay on for a few days of sightseeing and accumulation of good karma.

Thanks to my father's connections at the court, I showed Malavika the workshop of the royal weaver, an acknowledged master craftsman in a city boasting the finest weavers in the world. In appearance he was quite ordinary, a middle-aged man squinting over his loom in complete concentration while his three apprentices kept everything he needed for his work in readiness. It took the weaver six months to weave three yards of cloth—the apprentices told us, the master having bent down to his work after a greeting kept so brief as to almost slip into discourtesy—so intricate were his patterns and so fine his workmanship. The brocade design he created on the loom by skipping the passage of the regular weft over a certain number of warp threads and instead interlacing gold, silver, silk or cotton threads into the warp with fine bamboo sticks, lay painted to the very last detail on an invisible screen in his mind. Unlike most other weavers, he did not need to keep the design, to be used as a guide in placing the cut threads, underneath the warp. Although lavishly paid and rewarded with gold coins and pearl necklaces whenever the king was especially pleased with his work, the royal weaver was known to be a sombre, even gloomy man. For one, the appreciation of his creations was confined to the court of Varanasi since he could exercise his skill only in service of the king and the royal family and, unlike his less gifted colleagues, was forbidden to export his creations to other royal courts. For another, he lived in constant fear of the day when in the king's judgment he had finally woven his masterpiece, a piece of cloth so beautiful that the king would order his right thumb lopped off to forestall any danger of duplication. The conflict between an inner drive toward perfection and the dread of achieving it was etched in deep furrows across his forehead. Our present ruler had never bestowed this ultimate mark of royal favour on a weaver, but his father was known to have done so twice during his long reign. I pointed out to Malavika the two large, rather grand houses in the weavers' quarter where the 'thumb-cut masters', as they were called, objects of people's awe, admiration and commiseration—continued to live with their families on generous pensions from the royal treasury.

Later in the afternoon of the second day, we hired a boat for a pleasure trip down the Ganga. We sat close together, leaning back against the cushioned backrests of our seats, our shoulders almost touching, the boatman's short, choppy strokes the only other sounds besides our voices. Not that we talked much or even felt the need to. Unspoken promises had been exchanged the previous night in the temple, unwritten agreements signed and sealed. Besides, like the forest, the river, too, nurtures silence. The last warm rays of the sun caressed our faces, the breeze rising from the surface of the river pleasantly cool. By the time the boatman rowed us back, the seven horses of the sun were about to vanish below the horizon, turning the golden spires of the temples lining the river into flaming spears at the moment of their disappearance. In the fast descending darkness that followed, another barrier to our intimacy collapsed, as I found Malavika's fingers clasping mine. We held hands swiftly, instinctively, unselfconsciously, both exquisitely aware that our touch was also a moment of stillness in the eyes of the storm that was set to break within and around us.

Vatsyayana's inner turmoil at the loss of his father, a father still in the process of being discovered before he had to be mourned, was reflected in the turbulence the Gupta empire was thrown into with the sudden demise of the emperor Samudragupta. Both deaths occurred within a few days of each other. The outer tumult is easier to describe than the inner one of a child's heart. Even while the coronation ceremonies were going on, Ramagupta, Samudragupta's eldest son and successor, began receiving news of revolts

brewing in the border regions of an empire still in the
process of consolidation. Ramagupta had little appetite for
the inevitable wars he would have to become embroiled in,
especially since the young man was being driven insane
with jealousy by the affair between his beautiful wife
Dhruvadevi, and his younger brother, Chandragupta.

Ramagupta detested his brother. With his slender frame
and finely formed, almost feminine features and ready wit,
all too frequently exercised at his elder brother's expense
although in such a subtle manner that it would have
seemed churlish for Ramagupta to take offense,
Chandragupta was a favourite of both the court and the
harem. Even his affair with his sister-in-law, although not
exactly approved of, was viewed more indulgently than
would have been the case with any other member of the
royal family. Smarting under a sense of injustice,
Ramagupta longed for the chance to perform glorious
deeds which would earn him respect, especially from his
wife, although he hoped he would not have to prove
himself on the battlefield. Since one's fears turn out to be
true more often than one's wishes are fulfilled—at least in
Ramagupta's experience—the opportunity for earning
glory presented itself through a military challenge on the
north-western borders of the empire. Piro, the son of the
Kushana king Kidara, Samudragupta's satrap in
Gandhara, entered the land of the five rivers at the head
of a formidable force. Goaded into action by his ministers,
Ramagupta ordered the mobilization of the Gupta army
and marched towards Jalandhara where the Kushana army
had set up camp.

'And then we heard a strange story,' Vatsyayana said.
'Even in the hermitage where I had begun my studies after
returning from Kashgar, the boys discussed it as avidly as
our teachers. We heard that Ramagupta had been
murdered by his younger brother who had married the

queen and assumed sovereignty. The story, which spread rapidly through out the empire, was that Piro's offensive had succeeded in cutting the Gupta army in two. Instead of pressing the attack further, Piro sent a message to the besieged emperor that if he ceded his beautiful wife Dhruvadevi, Ramagupta's forces would be allowed an orderly retreat. Confronted with the dilemma of either losing his life and empire or swallowing the greatest possible insult to a man's honour, Ramagupta procrastinated. At this juncture, Chandragupta conceived and carried out a plan which saved both the emperor's life and honour. Dressed in Dhruvadevi's clothes and ornaments and with a band of equally fine-featured young soldiers who could pass for women, he entered Piro's camp, slew the king and returned safely to the Gupta lines. It was said that this act of cunning and bravery enhanced his reputation within the army and endeared him even more to the queen. It also further heightened Ramagupta's jealousy, which now bordered on the insane. Perceiving an immediate threat to his life, Chandragupta killed his elder brother and in accordance with the ancient custom of a younger brother marrying the wife of the elder one at his death, took Dhruvadevi as his queen.

'Even at the time, there was no dearth of sceptics who disbelieved the story; Chandragupta's affair with Dhruvadevi was too well known. As in other such cases the people's scorn, afraid to express itself against the mighty and the powerful, focused on the hapless queen as its object. She began to be sarcastically called Dhruvaswamini—"one who is fixed in devotion to her husband"—a name she bears till today.

'The real story emerged much later, first in the form of a strong rumour, although I have known the facts for some years. Udayana told me. His father, worried that his son was not showing enough evidence of manliness, had taken him along on that particular campaign. As it sometimes happens in confrontations between armies, the battle never took place. With each army deployed defensively, none of the commanders wanted to risk an attack. Both the young kings had succeeded illustrious fathers, and a disgrace in their very first campaign could do their reputations irretrievable harm. There were minor skirmishes between scouting parties and a couple of probes of opposing defenses, but otherwise the battlefront was quiet. And then Piro suddenly died of food poisoning. Whether his death was due to eating contaminated fish as some said, or whether he was poisoned by one of his rivals to the throne, will never be known. The Kushana army withdrew without giving battle. Flushed with this "victory", Ramagupta decided to make his leisurely way back to the capital, with frequent stops for hunting excursions into the forests along the highway. On one of these hunts, Chandragupta murdered Ramagupta and became our emperor.

'As cunning as he is amoral—or at least he was like that in his youth, although I must admit he has changed for the better as he has matured—Chandragupta sent his trusted men to fan out in different parts of the empire. They spread the story about Piro demanding Dhruvadevi from her husband, Chandragupta redeeming a desperate situation and his being forced to act to forestall a certain death at the hands of a jealous brother. I believe the change in the emperor over the years, his acquisition of a calmer, gentler sensibility for which his musician-warrior father was well-known, has something to do with the guilt of fratricide. If great sins make some into unredeemable sinners, they can also transform a few into saints. Our emperor is not a saint—no one who rules an empire can afford to be one—but over the years I have seen him become more compassionate. First, there was his declaration that he intends to govern without decapitation or corporal punishment for criminals. And now comes his recent pronouncement that even in cases of repeated attempts at rebellion, which every ruler in the world punishes with death, the rebel would only have his right hand chopped off.'

The hermitage Vatsyayana's father had selected for the son's studies before their departure for Kashagar lay in a clearing at the edge of the royal forest, some twenty miles from Kausambi. It consisted of fifteen one-room bamboo huts arranged in a wide semi-circle. Thatched with fronds, the overhanging eaves sheltering a narrow veranda, each with a single door on a raised hearth and a small arched window to let in the light, the huts were very similar to the one Vatsyayana and Malavika now lived in at the Seven Leaf hermitage. At the centre of the space between the huts the hermitage's ritual fire burnt under a large banyan tree where the ground was strewn with a layer of sand and sheltered from the elements by a pavilion raised on columns of bricks.

The hermitage was presided over by two brothers—Mihirpal and Amarpal—both in their early forties. Mihirpal, the elder brother, taught the Dharmashastras but was also considered an authority on the hymns of the Rigveda. He was a widower. His hut, where he lived with his sixteen-year-old son, was at one end of the semicircle and at some distance from the one occupied by his younger brother Amarpal, who had never married and lived alone. Amarpal specialized in literary studies but also gave students introductory classes in a range of other subjects, from astrology and astronomy to medicine, without which the education of a civilized man remains incomplete. The brothers were fussy little men constantly deferring and bowing to each other in public, like two paddy stalks in the breeze.

Less than fifteen years old, the Mihirpal hermitage (all academic institutions except large universities and Buddhist monasteries are known by the names of their founders) had twenty-five students, including Mihirpal's son. Each hut was shared by two to three students while the remainder were left vacant for the use of visiting scholars—Mihirpal believed they enlivened the intellectual life of the hermitage—and former students who returned for a couple of months at a stretch, pursuing their own studies but also assisting with the instruction of the younger ones.

The Mihirpal hermitage was regarded as a progressive school of general education rather than an institution for the training of Veda specialists, merchants or barons. Not regarded as a centre of learning in any of the Vedas or in a particular science, the chief attraction of the school lay in its relaxed admission requirements as far a student's lineage was concerned. Both brothers declared themselves to be followers of Baudhyana who, in contrast to other legal scholars, held the opinion that the Upanayana ceremony which heralds the stage of study, did not have to exclude the shudras and could be held for all the four castes. Not that the students of Mihirpal school were shudras. Most were children of mixed castes. Like Vatsyayana, they were offspring of wealthy and powerful upper caste fathers and beautiful and accomplished mothers of lower castes, unions which automatically assigned the caste of the mother to the son.

In the Mihirpal hermitage, the mantra of Savitri, daughter of the Sun and wife of Brahma, who presides over the Upanayana ritual initiating the student, was not the Gayatri verse of the brahmin but the Trishtup of the warrior or the Jagati of the merchant caste. Except for Mihirpal's son, who wore the sacred thread and carried the bamboo staff given to brahmin students at the time of Upanayana, all other students wore the threads and carried the staffs (up to the height of the forehead for the warrior and up to the nose for the merchant) of the other twice-born castes. The time of the Upanayana, the ceremony heralding second birth—not of the body but of the mind and spirit—was when Vatsyayana discovered that the world regarded him as a member of the merchant caste, the question of his caste having never risen before or perhaps deliberately avoided in his mother's household.

'To forget one's second birth is as difficult as to remember one's first. Sitting alone throughout the night in a bare, unlit room, the naked body covered with yellow haridra paste—an embryo which is to be born in the world of knowledge the next morning with Savitri as the mother and the teacher as the father—is an experience a child can never forget. Although the whole ritual is supposed to dramatize childhood's end, I felt my own childhood had ended many months ago on the day I began the journey with my father. There was little sense of anticipation, only sadness, when Ganadasa and my mother, followed by Chandrika and the servants, entered the room the next morning with what was supposed to be my last meal with my mother: sweetened milk flavoured with cardamom and camphor and cooked with ripe bananas, rice flavoured with pomegranate seeds and tamarind, served with curds containing honey, ground cinnamon and mace. After the meal, which was quickly over since neither of us was hungry, we all sat around quietly, waiting for Mihirpal's arrival.

'"How ridiculous you look, Malli. Just like a yellow frog!" Chandrika said, trying to break the gloomy silence that seemed to have gripped everyone in the room.

Squatting on the floor with my back leaning against the wall and my arms tightly embracing my knees to hide my nakedness, I did indeed feel like a frog poised to jump.'

Vatsyayana's Upanayana ritual was short; it barely lasted a couple of hours. In spite of his reputation for tolerance and unconventionality, Mihirpal did not want to stay in a courtesan's house longer than was strictly necessary. He scarcely gave Vatsyayana time to dry off as he came out of the bath before he began to tie the lower garment of rough cloth he had brought with him around the boy's waist, securing it with a girdle made of three cords, indicating the protection of the three Vedas. As Mihirpal put the sacred thread around Vatsyayana's bare shoulder and touched his heart with the right hand, he chanted the initiation mantra in a tempo faster than its normal measured cadences.

'Even as I went through the ceremony, my head bowed, repeating the mantras I was asked to, there was a heavy mass in my heart which refused to budge, no matter how hard he tugged. He was trying to usurp my father's place and I could not let that happen.'

Vatsyayana was homesick during the first six months of his stay at the hermitage. To weaken the bonds with their families, entering students were not allowed to go home on school holidays at the time of festivals, new and full moon days, and the three-day vacation on each of the three ashtakas.

'At first, my homesickness was less for people than for food. It expressed itself in a profusion of remembered images of Ganadasa's delicacies: roasted quails wrapped in bitter leaves, slices of gazelle meat basted with melted butter and served in a spicy sauce made of sour fruits.

'I was perpetually hungry; the bland hermitage diet without meat or honey, and even without salt and spices on fast days, was an imposition against which my palate protested strongly. Now I realize that homesickness is a mourning for the end of childhood. At the hermitage I was called by my full name; I was no longer "Malli". Childhood begins to end when fewer and fewer people call you by the name you had as a child. When Chandrika and Ganadasa die, there will be no one left to call me Malli. I too will then disappear, and become a part of the story of my parents and their generation than of mine.

'The first time I saw my family again was after I had been at school for almost five months. I remember it was a day at the end of winter when we were taken to Kausambi, a day set apart for compulsory begging to teach us humility. Unlike the situation in other hermitages, our students came from rich families who had paid Mihirpal considerable sums of money in advance as fees. For them, begging was an annual ritual rather than a daily chore. I persuaded Mihirpal's son, who was assigned to me as my begging partner, to begin our day at my house. All I remember about the day is that while I stood formally in front of our gate, forbidden to enter my home by custom, my begging bowl held in front of me, my mother, Chandrika, Ganadasa and the servants standing in the courtyard on the other side of the gate, we were all crying, even my mother. Quietly controlled and unobtrusively she wept by herself a few feet away from the group while Chandrika's loud wails and copious tears which smudged kohl all around her eyes demanded our full attention.

Tears began to well up in my own eyes. I remembered running after my father's carriage, weeping loudly, as it took him away from Brahmdatta's hermitage where he had come to leave me on my seventh birthday. I could see the distress on his face while my guru's assistants held me back, oblivious to my breaking heart.

'And your life at the Mihirpal hermitage?' I asked, compelled to distract both of us from a long-forgotten, shared despair.

Vatsyayana looked curiously at me, registering the quaver in my voice, before deciding to go along with my purpose.

'In many ways it was no different from that of every other hermitage, its flow channelled by the same ancient rules that apply to the student stage of life. Like my father in his time and you in yours, I too learnt to correctly perform the sandhya rites, beginning the morning one when the stars are still visible and ending it at sunrise, the evening one performed between the times when the sun still stands above the horizon and the appearance of the first star in the sky. For these prayers, I learnt to recite the Savitri mantra given to me at my initiation, sprinkle holy water around the altar, and pour libations into the hermitage's sacred fire in the prescribed manner. Like you, and all other students through the ages, I too suffered the student's principal task outside the many hours he devotes to study—cutting wood and replenishing the logs needed to keep the fire burning, chopping the logs into equally proportioned faggots, cleaning the emplacement with my hands, watering it, and gathering cinders and ash from the hearth for the execution of sacred marks on the body. Of course, there were also differences from life in other hermitages. For instance, how did you wear your hair as a student?'

'We had our heads shaved every fourth day,' I replied.

'We wore our hair long and coiled at the back. Many of the younger boys looked like girls when they washed their hair or lay down on their sleeping mats for the night with their hair open. Later, I learnt that our hermitage was not as strict as the Veda schools which enjoin that no powders, pastes or the like be used in cleansing the body during a bath. We were allowed to soap our bodies during the third, evening bath. But we envied you Veda scholars for all the time you could take off from your studies. Among the younger boys there were rumours that in your hermitages the Veda study had to be interrupted for a day and night when any of the inauspicious sounds such as the howl of a jackal, the barking of a dog, the braying of a donkey, the grunt of a camel, the cry of a wolf, the screeching of an owl or the wailing of a person were heard. We joked about Veda students becoming specialists in mimicking the screech of an owl or the grunt of a camel for the immediate reward of a break from study, rather than devoting themselves to the recitation of hymns which promise a doubtful salvation in some future life.

'Although the rhythm of our daily life was the same as in the Veda schools—studying till eleven in the morning after the prayer and the bath, eating the midday meal with teachers and other students, classes starting again at two in the afternoon, exercises in the evening, dinner and then retiring to bed after the evening prayer and bath—only the content of our studies varied from theirs. For instance, in the months from July to January, exclusively reserved for Veda studies which prepare the ground for the study of other subjects—the sacred knowledge whose assimilation transforms the student's nature—we did not have to memorize the Vedas but only learnt a few short hymns. Our studies concentrated on religious law rather than sacred ritual and contained a much higher proportion of instruction in literature, aesthetics and political economy.

'Much of the learning of school years takes place outside classes. For instance, it was in Mihirpal's hermitage that I had my first experience of someone of the third sex, a person who is neither man nor woman, a person who lacks either the capacity or the will to procreate; Manu calls him—her "non-man". This was Sukumar, a fourteen-year-old whom the other boys called Sukumari—"Pretty Girl". With his soft body, plump arms and thighs and wide hips, Sukumar's appearance was certainly effeminate. There was also a lot of "Pretty Girl" in his behaviour. His talent for self-dramatization and his preening vanity reminded me of Chandrika in her more capricious moods. Sukumar was the senapati's son, fathered, it was rumoured, on the commander's favourite foreign slave. The rumour about Sukumar's mother may well have been true. Besides a pronounced brownish tint to his soft, straight hair, Sukumar's fair complexion had more ruddiness than the pallor that marks the fair-skinned of our land.

'Now Sukumar, I soon discovered, was a regular sexual partner to some of the older students in the final years of their studies who were no longer boys but young men.

'"Pretty Girl is better than any woman," they joked among themselves. "His breasts do not get in the way of a really close embrace. There are no menstrual periods to impede passion and no danger of pregnancy that would create problems for the man and ruin Pretty Girl's own youthful beauty."'

'Acharya,' I said, 'You do not elaborate on persons of the third sex in the *Kamasutra*. Are they only of two kinds according to whether their appearance is masculine or feminine? What is the cause of this third nature? Are they distinguished from normal men and women only by their compulsion to orally perform the act that in most cases is performed between the thighs?'

'In the *Kamasutra*, I dealt with non-man only as a sexual partner for the normal man. The third sex is otherwise a matter of some complexity—and fascination. In his textbook on Ayurveda, the sage Susruta lists six types of non-man. There is the fellator who derives pleasure by taking the penis of another man in his mouth. He has a manly appearance and often earns his living as a hairdresser or masseur, occupations which bring him in intimate bodily contact with men. He first excites and then satisfies the man by using his mouth, often feigning initial reluctance. Then there is the non-man who takes the penis of another man in his anus, an act forbidden by all law givers. Men who penetrate the anus of a non-man are unchaste and lascivious. Those who use the anus of a woman in this way are generally of weak sexual desire who need to engage in anal congress as a preliminary to intercourse in the yoni. Both the fellator and the anal-receptive are capable of being potent. They are still called non-man because their potency derives from their pleasure in such practices.

'The third category of non-man is a person aroused exclusively by the odour of the yoni. The fourth derives pleasure from looking at the genitals and congress of others. The fifth is the man of effeminate appearance and behaviour, the Pretty Girl of Mihirpal's hermitage. He drives pleasure from taking the penis of another man in his mouth or by assuming the passive, bottom position with another man and having him ejaculate in his pubic hair. Finally, there is the narisandha, the masculine-looking, female "non-man", with body hair. She is breastless and manhating, and prefers another woman as a sexual partner, both women licking each other's yoni in the inverted position of "The Crow". Susruta say that when two women perform this act and somehow achieve orgasm, emitting and mixing their love fluids, the feminine lesbian can give birth to a boneless being without features or life.

'The sage Charaka mentions yet another category: the possessor of the "bent penis". This is a non-man who obtains pleasure by introducing his flaccid penis—which is long enough or has been lengthened by artifice—into his own anus, permanently bending the penis with such usage.'

'Why does a person have the third nature which is not clearly male or female?'

'There are different causes for different kinds of non-man. The anal-receptive and the effeminate non-men who take the bottom position in intercourse will either have had fathers whose seed was defective or who played the female role in the coitus that conceived the non-man. He also takes birth when the putri and the duhitrini nerves at the bottom of his mother's vagina are equally stimulated at the time of his conception. The fellator who takes pleasure from another man ejaculating into his mouth will have a father with a paucity of semen. The female non-man suffers from a disease of the yoni which is either caused by reverse intercourse of the parents during conception or by embryonic damage during the mother's pregnancy.

'Non-men are defective, not evil. That is why when Manu lays down the law that no share of property be given to a non-man, an idiot or madman, or to one who is blind or deaf from birth, he also says that these persons should be given food and clothing without limit and that a king shall never slay a non-man.'

From my own studies, I knew that the dharma texts are unambiguous in their disapproval of mouth congress. Manu declares that if a man has shed his semen in a non-human female, in a man, in a menstruating woman, or something other than in a vagina—mouth, anus, the hand of one's own wife—or has intercourse in water, then he should carry out the 'Painful Heating' vow where he eats only in the morning for three days, in the evening only for the next three and not eat at all on the following three day. The *Kamasutra*, although it does not exactly approve, shows greater tolerance for mouth congress, another instance where the paths of virtue and pleasure diverge.

'You are not quite correct to observe that I neither approve or disapprove of the practice,' Vatsyayana said.

'At various places in the text I do outline my misgivings and suggest restrictions. The nipples of the partner who performs mouth congress may be pinched but it is not becoming to clasp him in one's arms. All those who set an example to society—brahmins, men of letters, ministers and other officials, the famous—should avoid this practice. I do not recommend mouth coitus with a partner outside one's own caste, and endorse the view that ritual purification is required when the act is done with a man of low castes. Also, whoever puts his penis in the mouth of his legitimate wife destroys fifteen years of his ancestors' life in the other world.

'It is true that I do not share the blanket condemnation of this practice by most Acharyas of dharma who find it contrary to sound morality and assert that a person is defiled by the contact of genitals with the face. Their disapproval seems to apply only to the act of putting one's penis in a strange mouth. Licking the vulva is not forbidden by the Acharyas or the texts—if it is a custom of the country. I have also presented the minority view which holds that the practice is not impure if done with a woman.

> Some say the calf is pure when it drinks milk, the god's mouth is pure when it seizes game, as also the beak of the bird when it makes fruit fall, and the mouth of a woman during the act of love.

There are many countries where mouth congress is enjoyed. Women from eastern countries and the land of Panchala north of Ganga like to suck a man's penis. People of Ayodhya practice it without embarrassment, as do those of Pataliputra. Our own neighbours to the south, the Saurasenas, indulge in mouth coitus without hesitation; but their general notions of purity are notoriously lax.

'I give my considered opinion at the end of the chapter

only after reflecting on all the factors:

> It is after one has taken the country, the period, custom, the injunctions of sacred texts, as well as one's own tastes into account, one can decide whether or not to practice these kinds of sensual relations.

'Anal intercourse is a very different matter altogether. It is an abomination. Even the law givers who prescribe mild punishments such as a ritual bath or small fine for those using the mouths of non-men, come down heavily on a man who uses the anus of another man or woman as he would use the vagina; he is to be punished with the loss of his caste. What a dreadful fate! But then, to enter the orifice of defecation is the worst possible pollution for a man, which no amount of ritual purification can undo.

'Yes, I have heard that in countries like Greece and Rome there are men who have intercourse with each other in the anus; the practice is called "taking turns". There are houses of prostitution in Persia where young men and boys offer their rectums to customers. In Bahlika, I saw a Persian trading caravan accompanied by a number of boys and lads, eyes dark with kohl, rouged cheeks, long tresses, hennaed fingers and toes, riding in camel-panneries. They were the travelling wives of the merchants who were devoted to them, and with whom they had intercourse in the anus. The Chinese, too, enjoy this practice, my friend Brahmagupta told me. But, then, the Chinese are notoriously indiscriminate in both their eating and sexual habits; their usage of ducks, goats and other animals for sex is equalled by the pleasure they take in anal intercourse.'

❀

'We all know that celibacy is the central virtue of the student stage of life. A twelve-year-old gives little thought to celibacy; for a sixteen-year-old it is a major source of anxiety. The first boy I shared a hut with at the Mihirpal hermitage was seventeen at the time. In the three years we lived together, I was witness to his frequent agonizing over what the dharma texts have decreed as the chief goal of life before a person marries and moves into the householder stage. Heir to a small barony at the border of the kingdoms of Kausambi and that of the Saurasenas, Virasena was less sophisticated than most other boys who were from the capital city. He thus lacked that streak of scepticism which urban boys absorb from their environment form the earliest years. For Virasena, celibacy was not only a more serious affair than it was for the rest of us, but absolutely critical for his progress up the ladder to salvation. Each deviation from the ideal was a momentous lapse, followed by a bout of self-recrimination and purificatory rituals far in excess of those specified by the texts. An otherwise kind and friendly boy who helped me to settle down to hermitage life and was always ready to answer questions I did not dare to put to our two teachers, Virasena was a different person altogether when he was punishing himself for a lapse from celibacy; the lapse in his case consisted of nothing more then the shedding of semen during sleep. At such times, Virasena broodingly retreated into his own mind, snapped at me when I tried to draw him out, and washed himself often in an effort to become as stainless as the crescent moon.

'One scene still stands out in my memory. It is late at night and it has been raining. I am woken up by a beating drum of thunder and the flash of lightning through the window. I lie awake on my mat, drowsily listening to the medley played by the raindrops: sharp on the roof's palm fronds, gentle on the trees, clean on the stones and splashing in the puddles. Then I see Virasena sit up with a start next to me. He throws away his loincloth with a convulsive movement, as if a lizard or a snake had crawled between his thighs. He stands up and rushes out of the hut. I can see him through the door, standing naked under the heaven's gloomy bulk, the shooting shafts of rain washing away the unseen pollution from his body but not the unknown sins of his heart.

'Today I can look back with a greater understanding at Virasena's predicament which is shared to different degrees by every youth,' Vatsyayana continued. 'He must be celibate during the years in which nature is implacable in its resolve to the contrary. In spite of exercising utmost vigilance during the day, even the most determined celibate has been laid low by Lord Kama in sleep. We were lucky that in our hermitage dream-fault was neither viewed as a terrible disease nor frowned upon as a breach of morality. It was simply ignored. In your schools, where the Vedas cannot be studied if there is even a hint of impurity in the student, any boy who has a nocturnal emission of semen is not only medically treated for dream-fault by having to drink the juice of bitter gourds for five days, but must also publicly atone by a ritual partaking of the cow's five products.

'Sometimes, I have wondered whether the use of kusha grass for weaving the sleeping mats used in hermitages is not deliberate. This grass reacts oddly to semen, leaving a stain that gets darker after it is washed. The mats of many older boys in our hermitage were mottled with patches of varying shapes, sizes and shades of darkness. Even the boys who used their hand as a female vagina—every hermitage has more of these than the Acharyas like to believe—were careful to let the sleeping mat absorb the ejaculation, thus giving the transgression an innocuous interpretation and a more acceptable label.'

Sitting outside another hermitage awash in wintry sunshine, the pale sun sheltering in unseasonable dark clouds, the sounds of the hermitage's life barely filtering through thick foliage, I found myself unable to ask the inevitable question. And you, Acharya? What were your youthful struggles with Lord Kama like? How did they end? Did you accept your defeats calmly or did they throw you into despair?

Vatsyayana sensed but ignored my straining questions.

'Between the extremes of Virasena's suffering on account of his involuntary transgressions and the blithe unconcern of a few older students who used Sukumari as a woman, sexual life at our hermitage was no different from what goes in other hermitages around the land. There were boys who gave pleasure to each other with their hands, others who broke their vows of celibacy by coupling with a servant girl or a prostitute on visits to Kausambi during the holidays. Perhaps there were even one or two boys, although I never came to know of such instances, who sought sexual pleasure from female farm animals. The older students warned new entrants against this filthy practice. They told us of the scandalous incident a few years ago when one of the young boys attempted to have intercourse with a bitch who had become very attached to him and happened to be in heat. The bitch, as is its wont, clamped its vagina around the swollen head of the boy's penis, making it impossible to pull it out after ejaculation. In a dog the semen is emitted very slowly and the bitch's vagina does not unclamp till the semen has been shed. Here, confused by the unnatural coupling, the bitch's vagina did not receive the signal that intercourse was over, and held the boy's penis locked in. Mihirpal, otherwise a tolerant man, shamed the boy by having buckets of cold water poured over the wedged couple in front of the full assembly of hermitage residents. He also could not resist warning us of the degradation sexuality can bring in its wake by drawing the moral that the coupling of a dog and bitch is not unlike that of a man and a woman, who, too, cannot free themselves of desire even long after it has turned into disgust.'

'Acharya!' I could not contain myself, 'The same incident is also supposed to have happened at our hermitage and every new entrant was told about it by an older student.'

Vatsyayana chuckled, a low sound of pure enjoyment.

'Perhaps this story is told in all hermitages and is part of every student's informal education,' he said.

This was our second meeting after Malavika's return from Varanasi, and I noticed that a subtle shift in Vatsyayana's attitude toward me had taken place. Without quite losing his grave formality, his manner had become familiar-like that of a father or perhaps more like that of a mother's brother. There were occasional hints of complicity in his voice, of secrets in common and of a web of unarticulated memories and expectations binding us together. He now regarded me with a fondness quite different from the benevolence of a guru—the former arising out of shared moments is always more personal than the latter, which is not a product of time.

Chapter Thirteen

A *woman who does not receive signs of love is wounded and becomes hostile, a foe of men. She will either reject all of them or go with another.*

Kamasutra 3.2.35

In our following meetings. Vatsyayana became increasingly candid in revealing himself as he recalled other memories from his seven-year stay at the Mihirpal hermitage. He was of the opinion that in his case the movement from being a boy to becoming a man was decisively shaped by his close physical proximity with other boys and young men, fostered by the everyday life of the hermitage. This was radically different from his childhood experience of intimate contact with women and their bodies. In the first two years of his stay, between the ages of twelve and fourteen, Vatsyayana was fascinated with male bodies, especially those of older students entering the full glory of manhood. Catching glimpses of their nakedness while bathing in the stream, or looking at Virasena's exposed genitals as he lay sprawled on the sleeping mat, his loincloth having slithered up well above his thigh, Vatsyayana was spellbound by the sight of the lingam, especially when erect. Later, when he was older and lived in a hut with a young boy who had just entered the hermitage, he discovered that all young boys of that age share an intense preoccupation with the difference between the adult lingam and their own inconspicuous genitals.

'Our small penises were mostly alike and of the same colour as the body,' he recalled. 'They were not the big organs of grown men which vary in shape and are darker in colour than the rest of their bodies. Whenever I watched Virasena's majestic organ grow hard in his sleep, I found it endlessly interesting in its detail, with all those fine veins and ridges etched in its dark silky skin. I would have a strong urge to hold it in both my hands. I would begin to feel a warmth in my loins the longer I looked at it, and my own small penis would start to swell.

'Later, when I saw the same desire in the eyes of younger boys assigned to live with me in my hut, I would let them hold my lingam. I told them not to be embarrassed by this urge since it did not come from Kama but from Lord Shiva himself. For a young boy, the lingam represents the grown man's greatness, strength, independence, courage, wisdom, knowledge, potency, mastery of other men and possession of desirable women—all the qualities and achievements that a devotee seeks in Lord Shiva and that a boy looks up to in men and desires for himself. Yet I never let a boy take my penis in his mouth or squeeze it in his hand, even when I saw the urge flare up in his eyes and felt the intoxication of Kama begin to course through my own limbs. It was vital, for both of us, to keep the moment of Shiva's glory intact, to protect it from Kama's onslaught and not to confuse it with sexual love between men.

'In some ways my curiosity about genitals was the continuation of an early interest. Ever since I can remember, I have been absorbed by the wonder of bodies—Chandrika's, my mother's, my own, by the sensations they produce and the pleasures they provide. As a grown man, I have spent my years in the dedicated service of Lord Kama, studying and reflecting on the myriad ways he manifests himself in men and women. Yet all through this preoccupation with pleasure I have remained celibate. I have been curious about sexual pleasure, indeed it has always fascinated me, but I have not especially wanted to experience it myself.

'It is not as if I have never been with a woman, but that was only at the level of the gross body. On the two occasions I had intercourse, my mind did not register any sexual pleasure. It remained indifferent to my physical sensations till the moment of ejaculation, when something very strange happened. We'll talk of these secret matters another time.'

The major event in the last year of Vatsyayana's stay at the hermitage was set in motion with Mihirpal's marriage. It came as a surprise to the students, since no one had thought of the teacher as the marrying kind. As someone who specialized in religious law, Mihirpal impressed the students as an ageless, sexless being whose thoughts hovered solely around the Divine and who saw the flow of life only in terms of what was dharma and what was not.

'In retrospect, I understand better his decision to remarry. Our Acharya was now a man in his late forties who came to realize that in some essential way he had not lived, that he was not ready for the conclusion of life. Married at the age of twenty to a fifteen-year-old girl who died in childbirth the following year, Mihirpal had spent his adult years exclusively in company of men, either scholars or young students. He had neglected the sensual balance of life. Sexual intimacy, the unlived part of his life, was a commitment he now made at a late age and, many of us thought, somewhat foolishly. Like most older men who have achieved some eminence in life and marry much younger women, Mihirpal was aware of the foolishness of the step he was taking but he had become too self-indulgent not to go ahead with it.

'The girl he chose for his bride was barely twenty, two years younger than his son who had recently finished his studies at the hermitage and now lived in Kausambi. She came from a destitute brahmin family belonging to his native village of Lavanka in Vatsa country. The combination of poverty and high caste, which made it impossible for her family to find a suitable match for the girl, was the reason why she had remained unmarried. Now, the right age of marriage for a woman is half the prospective husband's age plus seven years. This traditional formula has proved itself in practice over the centuries. It reduces the age difference if both the man and the woman are young so that they can mature together, while it permits a greater disparity if an older man wants to marry again. Ideally, Mihirpal's wife should have been twenty-nine years old; the presence of a twenty-year-old woman was likely to create problems. These were not long in coming.

'Gauri, our Acharya's wife, possessed an attractiveness which did not lie in any distinction of feature or form but sprang from an abundance of youth coursing riotously through her, an inner heat ripening her femininity. Her wheat-coloured skin was warmed from within by this youthful flush, giving it a tawny glow and a musky smell very unlike the male odours we were accustomed to in the hermitage. Being perhaps inordinately sensitive to smell, I registered Gauri's compelling fragrance more keenly than others. Although Gauri took care not to flaunt her presence—indeed she tried to underplay it—she could not help the turmoil she caused in the older boys. This was in spite of the fact that every boy reflexively tended to lower his eyes to the ground when she passed by close to him. The injunction that the guru's wife may be looked at without offence only at a sacrifice, wedding or in times of calamity like fire or flood, had struck deep roots in minds of the young celibates. For most boys, Gauri's shapely, red-tinted feet, with lines painted on the instep, were more familiar than the shape of her breasts or her face. The boys marked her fugitive presence on the hermitage grounds not through an exchange of greetings or smiles but by the rustle of her garment and the faint whiff of her seductive odour, mixed with the scent of her garland, that drifted in Gauri's wake. That is, all boys except the ones who had worked in Mihirpal's hut and could permit themselves a greater familiarity with its mistress. Suddenly, the obligatory service—every boy had to sweep, clean and help in cooking at Mihirpal's hut for ten days in a year, an act of service symbolic of the student's veneration for the guru—became deeply desirable. It was no longer a chore to be got through, like the conjugation of Sanskrit verbs, but an event eagerly anticipated by the older students. The boy selected for service by Mihirpal at the fortnightly assembly was much envied and sought after for a couple of days after his period of service was over, when others beseeched him for details about Gauri and her conjugal life. She was a friendly woman, we came to know, but spirited—standing up to Mihirpal whenever she felt his demands were unreasonable. She took good care of her hair and skin, had a mole on the right side of her neck, loved to eat sweets and was full-breasted and wide-hipped. Her sexual life with Mihirpal was sporadic or perhaps only very quiet. The sounds of love coming from inside the hut were so infrequent as to be non-existent; some boys were uncertain about whether they had dreamt of the Acharya's quick grunts.

'My period of service in Mihirpal's hut coincided with his ten-day absence from the hermitage. In fact, his impending departure for Varanasi to attend a symposium was probably the reason why he called out my name in the assembly. I had the reputation of being a serious and responsible boy who kept to himself and was not a part of the boisterous group of other nineteen- and twenty-year-olds.

'It is not easy for me to talk about all that transpired during the fortnight I was alone with the guru's wife. Amarpal occasionally dropped in to inquire about his sister-in-law's welfare, but he was kept busy with the administration of the hermitage and in negotiating his brother's teaching load in addition to his own. Gauri and I were constantly together. I helped her with housework and listened to her talk about her village and her life with her parents. She was homesick. I shall keep silent about our rapidly growing intimacy and the turmoil it caused. It is such a long time ago. I still carry within me the knowledge and consequences of my sinfulness. I will only tell you the secret I talked of the other day. It is the secret of Kama, revealed to very few and fated to be forgotten even in the moment of its revelation by most of the chosen ones. It was revealed to me the first time I made love to a woman—my guru's young wife.'

For a devastating moment, my ear turned deaf. Then, as the import of his words forced a passage into my consciousness, I was struck dumb as well, looking at Vatsyayana in wide-eyed shock. His own eyes were closed, his breathing rapid. A chaotic blur of expressions, of which I could only decipher anguish, was flitting across his face. After few seconds of a silence that stretched like the eternity between the end of one yuga and the birth of another, he opened his still-unfocused eyes and quickly tossed his gray mane of hair. I saw the effort he was making to regain composure but could feel no sympathy, only a deep revulsion. An invisible screen was dropping behind his eyelids as he surrendered to waves of memory and began to talk again, unwilling or unable to stop.

'The ecstasy of my orgasm, in which all past and future pleasure came flooding in, was not of the heart-pounding, blood-pulsing kind but a calm sensation of utter bliss in which the universe is created. Semen was spurting from my penis in vivid streamers of green, blue and violet light that climbed from the horizon. I dissolved into the radiance of that ecstatic release as it surged across the night sky. But as my orgasm ebbed away the terror came, rushing to occupy the space being vacated by ecstasy. What if I had disappeared, and had never returned to my body? Both the terror and the longing for the experience from which I had just emerged were so intense that I fainted. The loss of consciousness must have been for the briefest of moments. When I came to, the woman under me was just surfacing from the private throes of her receding pleasure; the hut entombing our still-entwined bodies was gray and lifeless, the heavens above it indifferent. Cleaved to Gauri's warm flesh, I was still cold and gripped by a feeling of utter loneliness, an unbearable desolation, which made me want to rush outside and scream out to the stars, force the gods to respond with reassurance.

'The second experience followed a few hours later on the same night. After getting up from Gauri's bed and going to my own, I had slept the sleep the sleep of a yogi, dreamless and empty. Later in the night I suddenly woke up with a start. My first dreaded thought was that I was late for the morning sandhya. Looking up at the sky, I was reassured by the brightness of the stars, undimmed as yet by an approaching dawn. To my infinite shame, my body moved by a force beyond my volition, I went back to Gauri's bed. She was waiting for me.

'Glinting like mercury, semen rushed from the urethral opening and hurtled five, six hundred feet into a lake of sperm as bright as liquid silver. The infinite shining column flickered like the high, distant waterfalls I had seen in the Pamir gorges. The sequence of ecstasy that accompanied my fall as I became a part of my own semen, followed by the terror that gripped me as I felt the molecules of my body fly apart in liquid drops, was identical with the earlier orgasm. The second orgasm only reiterated the secret revealed by the first: what Kama desires is not pleasure but disappearance of the "I", of ahamkara, the former only a bait for the latter. Ecstasy and terror are inseparable companions of the person who would make the god's quest his own. After glimpsing the hidden face of Kama in my orgasmic visions, I knew he was the only god I would ever serve—but as a celibate. I must study and become familiar with the vast territory of the god but never again venture into his depths. We human beings live on the surface—the depths are for gods—and the precise understanding of the surface is vital for our lives. Do you understand?'

No, I did not, not immediately. I was still horrified. My thoughts whirled around the revelation of Vatsyayana's acts of incest with his guru's wife. His fevered imaginings were a consequence of his transgressing a sacrosanct law: the violation of the guru's bed, I told myself. My compassion for him was to come later as I walked into the forest that afternoon, almost a fortnight after Malavika's return from Varanasi, during which I had avoided even chance meetings. As my steps took me towards her favourite spot, I found that the pity I now felt for Acharya subverted my conditioned reverence for the guru. Seeping into the foundations, it was seriously weakening the edifice of devotion in which I had housed Vatsyayana these many months. The protective aura around Malavika, however, was not only intact but had become increasingly luminous by the day. I found my stride lengthening in anticipation of our meeting, unchecked by the moral qualms which had often made it hesitant in the past.

Chapter Fourteen

A vision evokes desire which, taking hold of the mind, becomes an obsession. He can no longer sleep, his body weakens, he loses interest in everything, loses all sense of propriety, loses reason, loses consciousness, and ends with dying. These are the ten stages of erotic passion.

Kamasutra 5.1.5

In the fortnight since Malavika's return I had avoided meeting her alone. I no longer went into the forest in the afternoon, pleading my father's illness as an excuse for an early return to Varanasi. On the first morning I made a trip to the Seven Leaf hermitage after her return, I could barely contain my excitement as my carriage rattled along the road. It was at the end of spring, a time of the year when the earth begins to heat up. By midday the countryside lies largely empty in a sun-drugged silence. The few signs of life are provided by the kites swooping across the sky in lazy arcs, occasional families of peacocks pecking their way through ploughed fields, buffaloes immersed well above their knees in ponds carpeted with green slime, swishing their tails to keep the flies away.

The nearer I came to the hermitage, the greater the dread that began to blunt the edge of my excitement. Malavika was standing in front of the hearth with her husband as I went up to the hut. The afterglow of the three days we had spent together in Varanasi was still strong enough to make us greet each other with delighted smiles.

'Was your journey comfortable?' I asked, masking my exhilaration with ritual dialogue.

'Malavika has been just telling me how well you looked after her in Varanasi,' Vatsyayana answered on her behalf, looking fondly at his wife. 'Why shouldn't he, I said to her, he is the son we did not have.'

I began to feel very uncomfortable.

'Will you come to the forest later?' Malavika asked.

'Not today. My father is ill. I have to go back early,' I answered, the lobes of my ears burning at the lie.

Malavika's eyes went wide with shock. She looked at me in utter disbelief. Under Vatsyayana's politely inquiring gaze, she quickly composed herself, her face resuming its morning mask. 'Please treat this house as your own while I'm out,' she said with a distant formality.

I have often asked myself why we did not become lovers in Varanasi. The hesitation was solely mine. It was my father's house and she was his guest, I said to myself. The phrase 'she is your guru's wife' kept on echoing in my head, at the same time as did Vatsyayana's oft-repeated verse that when the tide of passion is high, everything is allowed and prohibitions disappear. But I know I hesitated because I was not yet ready. I was only setting deliberate impediments in the way of a desire mercilessly heating up our blood.

We became lovers at the end of spring, on the afternoon of Vatsyayana's revelation, in a secluded spot at the edge of the clearing in the forest, on a grassy carpet hidden from any casual spectator by a depression in the ground and surrounded by the love-mad murmur of wild geese.

Malavika laughed when I showed her this awkward sentence yesterday. 'Even now, after so many years, you still become anxious when you remember the afternoon we first made love. I waited for you in the forest every day during that fortnight.'

'But you were so angry with me! I saw it on your face the first morning we met after Varanasi. Of course, you had every right to be angry. I was scared. I felt like sinking into the ground with shame each time Acharya looked at me. I felt he knew.'

'What does anger have to do with desire? Do you believe one can only have either the one or the other? *He* has always maintained that in lovers anger and desire are often bound together in a terrifying unity; lift the lid for one and the other might pour forth without rhyme or reason.'

'The morning you left Varanasi for the Seven Leaf hermitage and your presence began to fade, all my fears came rushing back,' I said, trying to explain my abject withdrawal. 'Why would Acharya's beautiful young wife ever want someone like me—I asked myself, hopelessly. I even turned to the *Kamasutra* to look for answers.'

'To the *Kamasutra*?' Malavika was surprised.

'Yes. There was no one else. I could not confide in Chatursen. You were sacred for me—an infinitely superior being, a goddess. Chatursen would have made some coarse remarks intended to rip the sheath of my devotion and I could not bear that.'

'And did you solve the mystery of my desire for you?' Malavika asked with a mischievous smile.

'No, but the chapter on how to seduce a married woman gave me a range of possibilities to think about. Acharya's remarks on the kinds of women who are easily seduced can also be read as a discourse on why women become unhappy with their husbands and thus susceptible to seduction. Knowing what I did about you, him and your life together, there were some possibilities that I immediately rejected. Your husband was not irascible, dirty, lazy, fearful, hunchbacked, dwarfish, deformed, dissolute, loutish, evil—smelling or sick. He did not have a first wife nor did he have many brothers. He was not away on a long journey. He neither humiliated you in front of your equals nor denigrated talents on which you prided yourself. You yourself were not of a quarrelsome nature nor had become dissolute. And I knew you were not one of those women who are married off by force in their youth and not allowed to marry the man they wanted.'

'What are the remaining reasons which could apply to me?'

'A woman becomes unhappy with a husband who is old or impotent. A woman who is vain but scorned by her husband is vulnerable to seduction as is the woman who is a man's equal in mind, intelligence, character and aptitude.'

'And? Which one am I?' Malavika persisted.

'I am not sure,' I said unhappily, wanting to end the conversation. 'Perhaps all of them.'

Malavika laughed out loud, a sound of pure but fond merriment.

'Oh, you men! You know so little about women. You were so sweet when I took you in my arms and pulled you down to me on the ground. Trembling like a frightened flamingo at first, suddenly you were a rutting elephant who would not be stopped.'

I had not been unprepared for the moment. In the last few months, before Malavika's trip to Varanasi, I had visited Kalavati regularly at the brothel. Yes, that was the name of the woman with whom I had shared my less than glorious first foray into Kama's realm. I could not be her steady lover—I was too poor for that—but thanks to Chatursen's generosity I was able to spend one night a week with her. We had quickly become friends, companionably making our way to bed after the beginning rituals where I hesitantly put into practice some of the lessons I was learning from my conversations with Vatsyayana.

Running her hand through my hair, absently stroking a cheek, Kalavati was not overly enthusiastic but tolerant enough of my sexual wishes and generous enough to lend her body. In the beginning these amorous sessions were incredibly exciting—and excruciatingly painful. Wrapped in the blissful promiscuity of touch, my penis would harden to a point I felt it would break in two without the vaginal salve of the love god. Yet any move in that direction brought on a panic which quickly swamped the excitement. I had not dared to enter her again, convinced that my penis would repeat its refusal. Perhaps a man's penis is more reflective than its general reputation gives it credit for, aware at some primal level of the danger a particular woman might pose to its owner, although given Kalavati's easygoing nature, I could not imagine what this threat might be.

As I became more comfortable with my dips into the stream of sensuality, I became bolder in my experiments. The day after Vatsyayana's discourse on odours, for instance, I had expressed my inclination to explore this particular path. Kalavati had no objection although I thought I saw her eyes glint in amusement. Once we had taken off our clothes, I went on a nuzzling spree. I burrowed into her soft cleavage but the faint scent of saffron mixed with that of light perspiration was too tame for my highly aroused nasal needs. My next stop was the hollow of her armpit, its stubble tickling my nose, the strong odour of her perspiration aggravating my desire. I shall not even try to describe the wonderful redolence of my final destination. I lay enthralled and aroused as I deeply inhaled Kalavati's intoxicating labial musk.

After that night, I felt I was ready for intercourse. When I was in bed with Kalavati my terror was ephemeral, only occasionally brushing my swollen genitals with its black wing. Although I ejaculated too soon the first couple of times, my subsequent attempts at intercourse were not unqualified failures. But somewhere I knew I needed to wait, that I should make my obeisance at Kalavati's sanctum a little longer before I presumed to worship at the temple of my goddess, the incomparable Malavika. I knew that to sleep with my guru's wife would be a far more serious affair. But I did not know how wonderful, how wildly intoxicating for the senses and how utterly absorbing for the mind our mutual immersion was destined to be.

'I know you want to ask me about the aftermath of my great sin,' Vatsyayana began the next morning. 'But except for a brief, mysterious illness, there was none.'

We had been sitting in silence, reluctant to begin the day's work, hesitant to engage with each other after yesterday's deeply unsettling events. Each was absorbed in his own thoughts, though Vatsyayana's words suggested that he believed his own preoccupation was also mine.

The next morning at Mihirpal's hermitage, Vatsyayana had woken up with a high fever. With fluctuations, the fever was to last for more than two weeks and baffled the doctor called in from Kausambi. The doctor had no difficulty in immediately lowering the temperature by pacifying the disturbed humours with a general anti-fever medicine and the application of a cooling paste made from mint and basil leaves. But after every few hours the temperature shot up again, taking Vatsyayana into a state less than delirium but more than a mere dimming of consciousness. Since he was unsure of the cause, the doctor could not prescribe a more specific treatment. The boy had many symptoms of the sannipata fever in which wind, bile and phlegm are all agitated—alternating sensations of heat and cold in the body, headache and pain in the joints, watering eyes, a dull ache and a ringing sound in the ears. Yet the doctor hesitated to assign the cause of illness solely to the bodily order. For whenever he brought the temperature down, Vatsyayana also exhibited the distinct symptoms of mind-fever: apathy, depression and, more specifically, the breathlessness associated with erotic-fever. Since there was no occasion for the excitement of kama in the celibate life of the hermitage, the doctor was naturally confused. As the intermittent fever continued, the brothers decided to send Vatsyayana back to his home in Kausambi. Except for the vital 'returning home' ceremony, Vatsyayana's education was in any case complete. Mihirpal felt that the final ritual which marked the end of the student stage of life could be held in an abbreviated form at a time when the fever had temporarily abated.

Thus on the afternoon of an auspicious day selected by Mihirpal after a careful consideration of Vatsyayana's horoscope, the youth's hair and straggly beard were shaved off even as he lay on his mat. Instead of a full bath with a liberal use of powders and perfumes—forbidden to the student—which would change his status to that of 'one who had bathed', the snataka, Vatsyayana's forehead was symbolically moistened with water and sandalwood paste. In presence of the full assembly of students, with Gauri watching from the window of her hut, he was undressed; his upper and lower garments, girdle and staff were gathered in a heap and thrown into the hermitage fire. Vatsyayana was then wrapped in fine silks, not without difficulty since he could barely lift his arms, and his ears were studded with new gold earrings. The sacrifice ceremony was shortened and the long concluding valedictory verses to be spoken by Mihirpal were reduced to a single sentence: 'Apply thyself henceforth to other duties'. Vatsyayana was again feverish by the time he was lifted into the oxcart which was to take him home. Two days after his return the fever disappeared as mysteriously as it had flared up, although the doctor claimed and was given the credit for its cure by the young man's grateful family.

'The fever permanently deprived me of all sexual desire. It made me an ascetic even as I was entering the householder stage. Images of that night with Gauri sometimes came unbidden as I worked on the *Kamasutra* but they lacked the power to move me. They remained just that—images. I could observe them and release them dispassionately, without feeling shame or remorse.

'A few years ago, I recounted the symptoms of my illness to the court physician. He was of the opinion that it may have been a case of temporary madness initiated by a demon through the sense of smell. The demon-madness also disturbs all the three humours and leads to a sickness which takes the same course as mine did.

'"Did you notice any of its incipient signs such as the urge to blaspheme, rage against brahmins and ascetics or the wish to kill your gurus?"' the doctor asked.

'I could not truthfully say that I remembered any such signs. The wish to kill Mihirpal? Even the thought was abhorrent.

'"And dreams? Do you remember being scolded in your dreams by a god?"

'"No," I again answered truthfully. I could see that the

doctor was puzzled. The illness remained a mystery.'

I did not comment, keeping my eyes fixed firmly on the ground in front of me. My thoughts were with Malavika. I longed to be with her. I imagined her waiting for me at the edge of the pond in the forest clearing, the toe of her arched left foot hesitantly touching the placid surface of the water that lay at her feet like a tame deer.

Udayana had been king for two years when Vatsyayana returned home from Mihirpal's hermitage. With the end of Rudradeva's bluff, soldierly reign, signs of a more aesthetic dispensation had begun to appear all over Kausambi. Nowhere were they more visible than at the royal palace, which was the first to reflect the tastes of the new sovereign. Overlooking the central square where the two royal highways connecting the four directions intersected, the palace was surrounded by an outer wall. The hall of the main gate, like that of the four city gates, was a place of congregation till its closure late into the evening. Whenever he returned to the capital from one of his dearly loved military campaigns, Udayana's father passed most of his free time in the outer courtyards of the palace which housed the stables, cow sheds, elephant stalls and coach houses or in the workshops of the royal arsenal. He spent hours watching the grooming of the horses and elephants and contentedly wandered around the workshops of the arsenal where skilled men laboured through the day to make bows and swords, quivers and arrows, lances, pikes, shields, daggers, elephant goads and protective armor for the soldiers and war animals. The sight and smells of horses and elephants, and the sounds of the arsenal workshops, was all the relaxation the old king needed to recover from dealing with irksome affairs of state.

One of Udayana's very first acts on ascending the throne was to begin with a renovation of private sections of the palace, a three-storey building in the innermost courtyard with living apartments on the upper floors, that had long suffered from the soldier-king's neglect. More concerned with the stock of sandalwood and aloe in the warehouses than with the decreasing pile of gold in the treasury, the king spent lavishly to realize his vision for the royal palace. Halls for dance, music concerts and theatrical performances that had lain unused for years were repaired, their pillars coated with blue and red lacquer and decorated with a circular gold-wrought motif incorporating gems and precious stones. The palace windows were resurfaced with sparkling crystal. New marble chessboards were inlaid in the floors of the games rooms, reception and assembly rooms decorated with painted and sculpted panels. The walls of the king's apartment, a self-contained and separately roofed pavilion on the top floor, set back from the parapet to provide an exterior terrace, were lined with ivory sheets and the terrace floor inlaid with turquoise blue ceramic tiles.

Architects were invited from as far away as Takshashila to build new pavilions on the palace grounds. Avanti's best known landscape artist was asked to lay out gardens complete with fountains, canals, artificial lakes and the fish ponds which had become fashionable in the last few years ever since the emperor Chandragupta had one made for himself in the palace gardens of the imperial capital. There was a steady influx of architects, stoneworkers, carpenters, sculptors, painters and other craftsmen as Kausambi's nobility and rich merchants followed the king's lead in transforming the capital's garrison ambience into an elegance for which it is justly famous today.

Udayana's appreciation of the arts and inclination

towards the sensual side of life gradually suffused Kausambi with an ineffable shringara rasa—the essence of all that is bright, charming and beautiful. The city also began to attract people other than those connected with the building trades, notably poets and courtesans. The advent of the latter was to prove especially damaging for the fortunes of Vatsyayana's household.

'The decline had set in earlier,' Vatsyayana said. 'My mother had virtually retired and spent most of her time at the Goshitrama monastery, listening to discourses of Buddhist teachers and their message of suffering and impermanence. The burden of generating enough income to run the household was now solely Chandrika's responsibility. Chandrika, though, was no longer the same person she was before her violent encounter with Kirtisen. Except for a coin-like crimson scar on her right breast from where the merchant had bitten off a piece of her flesh, the other marks left on her body by his nails and teeth were now faint jagged lines and spots many shades lighter than her golden-brown skin. For Chandrika, though, they were disfiguring welts that damned her to perpetual ugliness. A woman's looks are as much a matter of her belief as they are a physical quality, and Chandrika had lost confidence in her beauty. She was also getting older, even though the lines and creases of aging had yet to manifest themselves on her still flawless skin.'

In the years Vatsyayana was away studying at Mihirpal's hermitage, the number of clients coming to Avantika's—as their house was called—had steadily decreased. At the time Vatsyayana returned, this drop had become precipitous. The competition from newly-arrived courtesans had dried the stream of Chandrika's suitors to a trickle. On most evenings the entertainment room was empty except for the two musicians sitting in a corner, listlessly tuning their instruments or engaged in desultory conversations. Chandrika remained cloistered in her room upstairs, waiting till late into the night for the customers who did not arrive. The aging chief of prisons still sent her a monthly allowance. A generous man, he had increased the sum by an extra hundred panas to compensate for the shortfall in the household's finances caused by the death of Vatsyayana's father. But without a constant flow of presents of ornaments and money by new lovers and hopeful suitors, the financial situation of the household rapidly deteriorated. Once every few weeks merchants from the bazaar came to the house to appraise and buy pieces of the sisters' jewellery, precious rugs and other expensive household furnishings that were for sale. The bullocks were sold and the number of servants sharply cut down as the house began its inexorable slide into a decrepit melancholia.

Absorbed in her spiritual pursuits, Vatsyayana's mother remained indifferent to their descent into poverty. Chandrika's efforts to involve her sister in a search for solutions to their money problems were of no avail. As long as her collection of mirrors was left untouched, Avantika did not care if everything else in the house was sold off. Recently, Chandrika had taken on a few young prostitutes, newly arrived in Kausambi, who aspired to the courtesan status, as advanced students of the erotic arts. Although Chandrika was a recognized adept herself in many of the sixty-four arts required for a courtesan's education, her elder sister's reputation for proficiency in these arts was legendary. Her joining Chandrika in this educational project would not only have attracted more students but also enabled the sisters to charge substantially higher fees. Vatsyayana's mother, however, remained stubborn in her refusal to resume any part of her former life. She bore Chandrika's complaints and remonstrance with a patience that was maddening to the younger sister.

Vatsyayana thus returned to a household stricken by Chandrika's resentment and discord between the sisters, and gripped by the fear of impending destitution to which even Ganadasa did not remain immune.

To save money on kitchen expenses, he had to let all the helpers go. He did not object to extra work or the lowly tasks of cutting the vegetables and cleaning the kitchen. He even accepted with equanimity the drastic reduction in the number and variety of dishes he was allowed to prepare. What rankled most with Ganadasa was his loss of status as a teacher of the cooking arts. Without students he was only a cook, a mere practitioner. He shuffled around the kitchen like a defeated general revisiting the battlefield and the site of his humiliation. His paunch was no longer sleek and gleaming but dulled by apathy. His welcoming smile as I ran to embrace him soon vanished from his eyes.

It was clear to Vatsyayana that Ganadasa looked up to him as a potential saviour who could reverse the turn in the family's fortunes. Except for his sublimely indifferent mother, this expectation seemed to be shared by every one else in the household. It was evident to the twenty-one-year-old youth that he had to begin earning money, and soon. He had to rapidly generate income in quantities large enough to arrest Avantika's depleted finances.

'Kausambi at the time was a bustling city full of opportunities, though not for a young man lacking every useful skill whose only accomplishment was a familiarity with literature. I suppose I could have helped Chandrika by teaching her students three of the arts which occupy places fifty-four to fifty-six in my own list of the sixty-four arts in the *Kamasutra*: knowledge of dictionary, poetic meter, versification and literary forms. Chandrika did not encourage me. She doubted whether the women would welcome lessons from a student fresh from his guru's hermitage, when there was no dearth of older and renowned kavis who were eager to augment the women's physical beauty with nuggets of literary sensibility.

'And then I had an idea. If I had not been so young I would have never pursued the idea to its conclusion. I would have convinced myself that the task I was about to set myself was far beyond my capabilities, that I was trying to cross the ocean in a paper boat. But the confidence of youth compensates for its failings. For one week I worked fifteen to sixteen hours a day, writing feverishly.'

Vatsyayana's idea was to write a romantic play that would catch the fancy of the king. Udayana was eager to be known as a patron of arts and learning, and although kavis from Avanti, Magadha and other kingdoms were being drawn to Kausambi, there were rumours that the king was disappointed at the dearth of local talent. Vatsyayana's idea was to write a play that would have Kausambi as its locale and which would appeal to Udayana's vanity at the same time as it captured his interest.

'I decided to write a play about Udayana. No, not the present king—I was not going to be that obvious—but about his legendary predecessor who ruled Kausambi at the time of the Buddha. I felt Udayana would be flattered if Kausambi's citizens were again reminded of his illustrious namesake. The plot was taken from one of the many stories about that ancient ruler which were still sung by itinerant bards.

'The story I chose was about Udayana's inordinate love for his wife Vasavadatta, and his consequent neglect of the affairs of state. Alarmed by the king's infatuation, his ministers decide to make the king believe that Vasavadatta is dead, and to persuade him to marry Padmavati, the daughter of the king of Magadha. Given a magical potion by the ministers which enables her to change her appearance, Vasavadatta disguises herself as a brahmin woman and goes off to serve her rival Padmavati at the court of Magadha. When Udayana returns to his capital after marrying Padmavati, Vasavadatta accompanies the new queen as part of her retinue. She makes garlands for Padmavati, using a special technique that she had been taught by the king. Udayana recognizes the garland and asks Padmavati where she got them. The queen replies that her maid has woven them. The king realizes that this maid must be Vasavadatta. The ministers confess everything to the king who lives happily ever after with his two wives.'

'But Acharya!' I exclaimed. 'Your plot is very much like that of Bhasa's great play, *The Dream of Vasavadatta.*'

'Not exactly,' Vatsyayana laughed. 'My friend Bhasa also uses the same story for his plot but adds elements from other stories. He replaces Vasavadatta's disguise and the king's recognition of her through the garland by the justly famous dream sequence in which Udayana dreams of Vasavadatta while sleeping in Padmavati's bed, while Vasavadatta is sitting on one corner of the bed carrying out a real conversation with the sleeping king who is talking to her in his dream.

'You must remember that I was not even aspiring to be a playwright, while Bhasa was an acknowledged master of the genre when he wrote his play about Udayana and Vasavadatta. My aim was not to produce a literary masterpiece but to earn money by attracting the king's attention and patronage. All I knew about theatre came from being an avid spectator as a child, and from the theory and philosophy of drama taught to us by Amarpal during my studies. Although both plays describe the supposed death of a beloved queen and her final recovery by the husband who was convinced that he had lost her, my own effort was trifling compared to Bhasa's masterpiece.

'It is not difficult to understand why, if one analyzes both plays. I, too, tried to construct my work according to the rules of drama: for instance, the principle that the narrative should always hinge on separation and reunion. I dutifully followed the axiom (as does Bhasa) that dramatic action should pass from happiness to misfortune and back to happiness again, that the end of the play should in some way recapitulate its beginning. Yet my play remained a skeleton of theories, whereas Bhasa could put flesh on the bones, breathe soul into the frame and thus produce a drama vibrant with life.

'Today I can understand the reason for my failure: a false grasp and application of what constitutes harmony, the highest principle of aesthetics. The poise between opposites, the delight of serenity, does not come from a mechanical avoidance of the harrowing depths of tragedy or the irresponsible hilarity of pure comedy. Bhasa does not achieve equilibrium by an academically recommended avoidance of extremes, but by an immersion into contrasts, conflicts and opposing forces in such a way that they are never in collision, never restless. Add to this his masterly conceit of the dream sequence, which makes his play incredibly rich in complexity and nuances as it proceeds to deal with the rival claims of actuality and memory, reality and illusion, the living eye and inner vision. I have learnt a lot from Bhasa and am proud of his friendship. He sharpened my awareness of balance and harmony, lessons I learnt too late as far as my literary effort was concerned but which stood me in good stead in the writing of the *Kamasutra*.

'The aesthetic failure of my play constituted its success as far as Udayana was concerned. To capture his interest I had imbued the initial happiness section part of the happinessmisfortune-happiness cycle with a goodly dose of eroticism. I had wanted to make Udayana's infatuation with Vasavadatta at the beginning and their final reunion physically realistic. I succeeded too well. The chief of prisons who had financed the play's production and was also instrumental in getting it staged at the palace theatre told me of the outrage it created. To a man, Udayana's poets and scholars were shocked by its lack of balance, by its undue emphasis on shringara rasa and the crudity with which I apparently treated the erotic sentiment. And they alleged that the sentiment of pathos was woefully under-represented. But I knew that if I had applied the principle of balance and harmony demanded by the canons of drama, my play would have been competent . . . and unremarkable. I certainly did not possess the genius of Bhasa.

'A week after the play's disastrous reception, I was in a despondent state of mind when I was summoned to the palace for an audience with the king. I was naturally apprehensive, expecting a vituperative critique at best and exile from Kausambi at worst. On my way to the palace I kept a lookout for any bad omen but except for a slight twitch in my right eyelid, which may or may not have been imaginary, there were no disquieting signs. To my surprise, Udayana received me alone in his private chambers, its walls resplendent with frescoes in ivory and gold, with only a scribe present to take down the king's instructions. Dispensing with all but the minimum of courtesies he came straight to the point.

'"My dear Vatsyayana," he began, again surprising me with the intimacy of his tone and the mode of his address, "The feelings against a 'violator of tradition' and 'defiler of culture', as some of the kavis called you, are still so strong as to preclude any kind of royal patronage. They detect the insidious influence of the western kingdoms, Bahlika and Strirajya, in your attitudes and writing. They especially dislike your irreverence and your questioning the authority of ancient sages who are like gods in their wisdom."

'My hopes began to revive since the warmth of his voice and a conspiratorial smile belied his words.

'"I do not disagree with the judgment of my most accomplished men of letters although some of them may have been too harsh," he added, watching my expression as I tried to control my soaring spirits. "Your preoccupation with the erotic, sensual side of life is indeed excessive, even disgraceful. It is better suited for writing treatises on kama than for composition of poems and plays."

'"Hmmm," he appeared suddenly thoughtful, as if surprised by a novel idea. "What I *could* do is send you eight hundred panas a month for three years if you are willing to compose a new treatise on kama that distills the essence of all extant texts. Our arrangement must remain a secret. If and when you produce a work of a quality that can be presented to the assembly, we can review our understanding."

'I quietly thanked him, too overwhelmed by what had just transpired to be able to say anything else. Later I realized that what appealed to Udayana in my play were precisely its excesses. Besides his proclivity for questioning all conventional judgments, perhaps an expression of the uncertainties of his own sexual nature, Udayana liked the erotic coarseness of the play. He interpreted this as the manifestation of a youthful awkwardness in sexual matters which he found as endearing in me as he did in himself.

'"I do not want you to become a hermit," Udayana added, more a friend now than a patron. "We have enough of them. I expect you to come to the palace regularly to keep me informed about the progress of your work and amuse me with the interesting bits of information you gather in the course of your researches—especially on the amorous escapades of other kings of the land."

'I remained silent, refraining from foolishly protesting that I was incompetent for this task. I assumed that Udayana was as aware as I was of my lack of preparation to assume the role of a scholar of erotics. He was trusting my potential and my passion, not my credentials and capability.'

Chapter Fifteen

Interest (monetary) and love are not opposed, but the search for the means of subsistence must predominate.

Kamasutra 6.1.19

*W*ith Udayana's unofficial patronage making up for the shortfall in the household finances, Vatsyayana could begin his career as a scholar of erotics without monetary worries. Of the seventeen works on the erotic sciences and their forty-two commentaries, all but a handful were listed in the catalogue of the Goshitrama monastery which, befitting its status as a renowned centre of learning, boasted a magnificent library. The available manuscripts included the classic texts: Dattaka's *On Prostitutes*, Suvarnanabha's *Erotic Approaches*, Ghotakamukha's *The Art of Seduction*, Gondardiya's *On Wives*, Kuchumara's *Occult Practices*, Charayana's *General Remarks on Sexuality* and the standard textbook by the Babhravyas, *Kamashastra*. The librarian, an old monk who did not pretend to hide his disapproval of Vatsyayana's research interests, told the young scholar that to consult the texts unavailable in the Goshitarama collection, he would have to travel to Varanasi. There were at least four other scholars in that holy yet academically sinful city, the monk sniffed, who shared Vatsyayana's prurient concerns and who could guide the young man to libraries housing these manuscripts. As a monk belonging to the ascetic Lower Vehicle sect of Buddhism, the librarian shared its sombre view of life, its identification of Kama with the god of death Mara, and its general disapproval of sexuality and sexual pleasure.

For almost a year, Vatsyayana spent a major part of his day at the monastery library, copying the manuscripts as a first step towards their rigorous study. Observing Vatsyayana's diligence and dedication to the task, the old librarian thawed towards the student, though not to the subject of his study. Although he had little knowledge of the erotic arts, the monk's vast learning in other fields and linguistic proficiency was of great help to Vatsyayana in grasping the intended meaning of many difficult passages in the texts. Even the librarian's implacable opposition to the aims and goals of Vatsyayana's research was to prove beneficial to the aspiring scholar's enterprise.

'He made me realize the difference between the student and the scholar. The optimal conditions for learning arise when the student fully opens his mind to knowledge and his heart to the teacher. A scholar needs to close both, just a little. Learning demands the greatest possible identification of the student with his subject and his teacher whereas scholarship demands some distance, a critical rather than a reverential attitude towards received knowledge. I was still a student, overawed by authorities and the written word, especially if both came down from ancient times. As a Buddhist monk, the librarian could openly scoff at the assumptions and values contained in what were essentially texts in the brahmin tradition. Even though I did not share his prejudices, his irreverence shaped a sceptical perspective which otherwise would have developed at a much later age. His ruthless interrogation of principles I had held sacred took the edge off my youthful enthusiasm without making me lose an essential respect for the works of ancient sages. I still feel a great affection for that irascible man who was truly one of my teachers, without either of us acknowledging it at the time. He died before the completion of my work and my triumph at Udayana's court.'

Vatsyayana's life was not all work, though. His periodical visits to the palace to report on the progress of his undertaking ensured a certain participation in court life and in the rhythm of the king's day. In the beginning, he was expected to present himself before the king once a fortnight. The meeting would take place at noon after Udayana was free of his obligations of presiding over the council of ministers, receiving the daily reports of his officials and secret agents, hearing the complaints of Kausambi's citizens and, for him, the tiresome task of inspecting his treasury, arsenal, war elephants, horses and chariots. Vatsyayana would be led straight to the king's bathroom in his private apartments, a small pavilion with a blue-tiled floor, painted pillars and brightly-coloured tapestries hanging from the walls. Here the young scholar would find the young king lying naked on a rosewood platform in a corner, its dark surface radiant with an oily sheen, being massaged by his two favourite masseurs while an attendant fanned his face with a moist lotus-leaf fan. In a voice loud enough to carry above the sounds of the vigorous rubbing of the royal limbs with oil and the king's grunts and sighs of pleasure, Vatsyayana reported on the progress of his work. Udayana's expectation, he soon discovered, was that Vatsyayana regale him with amusing anecdotes on the sexual mores of different countries and with stories of sexual misadventures of gods and ancient kings.

'For instance, reporting on a king's pleasures, I told him about the custom in the kingdoms of Vatsa and Gulma, where the harem women belonging to ministers and high officials are sent to the ruler for a night every month; that in Andhra, a newly-wed girl is sent to the harem on the tenth day to be enjoyed by the king for the night; that in Vidharba, pretty country girls are sent to the harem for fifteen days in order to learn the art of making love. Or, illustrating the dangers to which a king exposes himself if he enters another man's home for amorous purposes, I told him the story of the king of Abhiras who sneaked into the home of a merchant to make love to his wife and was assassinated by a laundryman at the behest of the merchant's brother. Similarly Jayasena, the king of Varanasi, was killed by his cavalry commander who found him in his bed with his wife.'

After the massage was over, Udayana proceeded to a crystal seat in the middle of the bathroom where female attendants poured perfumed water over him from great ceramic jars lining the walls. Later, as Udayana sought him out more and more, Vatsyayana's visits to the palace were not limited to any particular time of the day. He could be summoned to accompany the king on his inspection of the palace gardens in the late afternoon, asked to join him in the evening to listen to a musical concert or to bards reciting the adventures of Udayana's ancestors, or even late in the evening after dinner when the king might be in a mood to play a game of chess or dice.

'Why did Udayana seek me out? I have some answers, although I do not find any completely convincing. We were of the same age and perhaps he felt more comfortable in my company than with his nobles who were a part of what was largely an inherited court. As Rudradeva's men, most of the courtiers were far from being animated by Udayana's aesthetic sense of life. In a drunken moment, Udayana himself described the feeling of affinity he felt for me as "that of a non-man with the son of a whore". This was much later, almost five years after our initial meeting, when we had become friends, or rather as friendly as one can become with one's sovereign and benefactor. By this time the king allowed himself to get drunk in my presence. He let himself weep when he talked of his mother, to whom he was extremely close all through his childhood and up to the age of fifteen, when she died. He would rail against his father who had mortified him and mocked what his mother had most adored—her son's physical beauty. "What a pretty son I have!" Rudradeva would say to his companions whenever they encountered each other. "Admire his pretty hands and shapely arms which cannot even wield a child's sword!"

'Udayana had always been afraid of his warrior father who was rarely available to the son when at home. Yet, for many months of the year when Rudradeva was away from Kausambi on his military campaigns, the boy yearned for his father's presence. Once Rudradeva was back, Udayana again found him frightening, frustrating and overpowering.

'"It is the just revenge of the gods that his son prefers men to women, thus demonstrating to the world that the great warrior either had defective seed or took the female position in intercourse," said Udayana with a bitterness of which I had not suspected him to be capable.

'On many an evening in his bedroom, with just one servant to keep the wine cups filled, I listened to Udayana talk without interrupting his flow. He hated to be alone and on the nights when his favourite slave was unavailable or unwanted, he asked me to stay back, his drunken talk becoming frenetic as the night advanced. In one of the lucid intervals during one such evening, he once said to me, "What I value the most about you, my friend, is the solitude that surrounds you, not like an armour but like a cloak under which a passerby can warm himself before he goes his own way. It is the solitude of the sage even when he is not alone in the forest but among other men in the city. You can be so wonderfully solitary even while you sit here with me.""

Hearing Vatsyayana repeat Udayana's remarks, I experienced a flash of recognition. Yes, this was one of the keys to the man and his composition! I suddenly realized that people were quite right to believe the rumour that the *Kamasutra* was written by an ascetic. But they went wrong in equating asceticism only with celibacy; they forgot the other distinguishing mark of the ascetic—solitude.

Vatsyayana's work progressed well in the next few years, a period of cultural flowering and increased prosperity for Kausambi. The Gupta empire had secured its borders against all external enemies and was vigorous in enforcing peace between its constituent kingdoms. The only occasion war touched the lives of Kausambi's citizens, and that too in an oblique way, was in the year 83 when Chandragupta decided to push the empire's western border right up to the sea through the conquest of Gujarat. Rudrasimha, the Shaka king of that country, was a civilized monarch, well known for his patronage of monasteries, temples and the arts. To Chandragupta's credit, the emperor did not try to blacken Rudrasimha's character to justify the war he was contemplating. He did not even stress the foreignness of the Shaka ruler to whip up patriotic sentiment.

Conquest of other countries and the extension of the empire's borders has been mandatory if an emperor wishes to be recognized as chakravartin, and Chandragupta had always been unabashed in his pursuit of greatness. Considering the number of poets he patronized to compose verses in his praise, and the extravagant claims about his sagacity in civil affairs and prowess in battle which he had caused to be inscribed on stone and iron pillars at various sites throughout the empire, the task of establishing the emperor's greatness became a minor industry in itself.

Udayana ceremoniously placed Kausambi's army at Chandragupta's disposal when the emperor passed through the kingdom on his way to Gujarat. As for his personal participation, Udayana requested the emperor's permission to join the campaign a few months later at the beginning of spring. It was not only because of the indifferent health he was keeping lately, a lung condition which was apt to be worsened by the cold dry climate of Gujarat, he told the emperor, but also because he wanted to personally design the coins commemorating the Gupta empire's eminent victory over the Shaka kingdom. Chandragupta consented, though with ill-concealed grace, his ire somewhat mollified by the splendid reception Udayana arranged for the imperial army as it marched through Kausambi.

Floral arches, high enough for the passage of war elephants in the vanguard of the army, were constructed on the royal highway at a distance of every arrow-shot. The capital's citizens, garbed in their best finery, thronged both sides of the highway, cheering the parade of war chariots, cavalry and foot soldiers which followed the elephants. Udayana came out of the palace along with his ministers and other dignitaries of the state at around noon, when the army had passed and the sweepers were cleaning elephant and horse dung from the streets before the arrival of the emperor. There was an interval of about twenty minutes before Chandragupta's elephant, preceded by the mounted soldiers of his personal bodyguard, strode into view. Full-throated shouts of 'Victory to the Emperor' were raised by the crowds lining the opposite side of the street. Temple bells began to peal and conch shells were blown from the ramparts of the palace, while Kausambi's ruler and his court paid homage to their overlord with bowed heads and joined palms raised to forehead.

On the first leg of the journey to Gujarat, Kausambi's army contingent took the same route Vatsyayana had taken with his father many years ago when their caravan had set out for Kashgar. The road led through Mathura before veering south from the old Mauryan highway and then turned west after Ujjayini, ending at the port city of Barigaza in Rudrasimha's kingdom. On the road to Mathura, recollection of the landscapes Vatsyayana had travelled through earlier fused with the actual journey, confusing his sense of time. The memories—the fireflies outside the circle of wagons where the cavavan had camped on the first night, the barking of village dogs near the temple where they had stopped on their second evening—were more vivid than the faded impressions of the places he now rode by in Udayana's wake.

Udayana was fretful throughout the expedition to Gujarat. He hated being on horseback which made his buttocks sore, hated the discomfort of camping out in the open, missed the food of his palace cooks. He was not unduly worried about the prospect of the actual fighting—which he would have preferred to avoid—since he would be almost as protected as the emperor himself. In battle order when the conches, gongs and drums sound the charge, there is always a massive line of elephants drugged with wine plodding close together in the front, providing cover for the following infantry. Chariots, each carrying three archers, would be massed on each flank with the cavalry immediately behind. Udayana's elephant would be next to Chandragupta's in the centre of the rearguard, difficult to reach even for the most intrepid enemy formation. As it turned out, Udayana never got to take part in the fighting. The Kausambians arrived at the emperor's camp after the war was over. Actually, they reached the battlefield on the evening of the day Chandragupta won the decisive battle against Rudrasimha.

On the way to the emperor's tent, following Udayana and his generals, Vatsyayana passed groups of soldiers laughing and singing, many already sprawled on the ground in drunken stupor. Horses and elephants were being washed and groomed by their keepers. Cooks were roasting deer on spits for the victory meal. Stretcher-bearers were taking the wounded to the field hospital set up in a distant corner of the camp, the agonized groans and cries muffled by the sounds of revelry. After Udayana had disappeared into the emperor's tent, crowded with his commanders and feudatories celebrating the Gupta victory, Vatsyayana decided to go to the battlefield, an hour's walk from the western gate.

The smell of blood and decaying flesh became stronger as he approached the open ground where the battle had taken place. The stench forced him to stop a few arrow-shots away. The sun had set and it was gradually getting darker. In spite of the light from a series of funeral pyres—one for each caste among the slain soldiers—the men moving around the battlefield were little more than dark shapes. Vatsyayana was surprised to observe how busy the site of battle remained even after the fighting had been over for some hours. Slaves of the victorious army were gathering up used arrows for straightening or mending in the field workshop. Corpses were being collected and identified according to caste, irrespective of the army they had fought in. Veterinarians were caring for the wounded horses and elephants. Physicians and orderlies from both armies were bandaging and treating the lightly wounded while stretcher-bearers were carrying the more serious cases back to their respective camps. There was a peculiar camaraderie between all those who dealt with the refuse of battle, who cleared the litter of war; the brotherhood of pain was infinitely more inclusive than that of well-being.

And, yes, Chandragupta was not unduly upset over Udayana's late arrival. In part, this easy forgiveness was due to the victory coin Udayana had designed. The Gupta emblem, the Garuda—the swan-vehicle of Vishnu—was on one side and the image of the emperor slaying a lion on the other. Udayana was greatly pleased with this particular inspiration. The lion shown being killed was at the same time the real animal, so numerous in the forests of Gujarat, a tribute to the emperor's otherwise indifferent hunting prowess. It was also the 'Ferocious Lion', which was the name of the Shaka king. The image further flattered the emperor by comparing him to his great father who was shown slaying only a tiger in *his* coins.

A few months after their return from Gujarat, Udayana invited Vatsyayana to move into one of the smaller guest houses in the palace grounds. Vatsyayana's brief hesitation in accepting the offer, which was also a great honour, was merely a perfunctory bow towards the dictates of courtesy. He was glad to get out of an increasingly sepulchral house where the corpses of past gaiety lay unattended in dark corners. From being a famed temple of shringara, the house was fast becoming its neglected tomb. The improvement in its finances had stemmed the tide of panic but did nothing to dispel the gloom that had taken a firm hold of Avantika. The panic had at least tenuously bound the members of the household together. With its disappearance, each person—Vatsyayana's mother, Chandrika, Ganadasa—drifted away from the others, like rogue planets spinning in their own orbits.

'Time had brought about this change, and eroded the charms of the sisters, demanding back the loan of beauty it had made in their youth, and which they had believed was a gift to keep. My mother realized the nature of time better and was therefore more at peace with its inexorable march than Chandrika who was being dragged to time's court. Both women were intelligent and educated, adept not only in the sixty-four arts but also intimately familiar with the epics. I had often heard my mother reciting from the *Mahabharata*:

> Time makes the wind blow with the force of gale, time makes the clouds give rain.
> Time makes the lotus flower and time makes the tree grow strong.
> Night becomes dark or light through time and it is time which gives the moon its fullness.
> If the time has not come, trees do not bear flowers or fruits.
> The current of a river does not become fierce if its time has not come.
> If the time has not come, women do not conceive.
> If the time is not ripe, a child is neither born nor dies, nor does it pick up speech.
> Without its proper time, youth does not come and the sown seeds do not sprout.

Whereas my mother accepted the overlordship of time, the

collection of mirrors in her room her one defiant gesture staking claim to a past she would not let go, Chandrika, still handmaiden of Lord Kama, could not reconcile herself to time's passing, to the change of gods in her life.

'By the time I moved out of our house, my mother had become largely detached from all of us. Her greeting when we encountered each other on my visits home or in the Goshitrama monastery where I worked in the library, were kindly and serene but distant, like that of a nun, without a trace of that personal engagement that quickens the sense of life in its recipient. From listening to Buddhist discourses, praying and performing acts of charity and compassion, she began to travel the even more ascetic path of the Jainas. Most of her jewels were already sold. She donated the rest to the asylum for diseased and decrepit animals run by Jaina monks and nuns where she worked long hours every day. Soon she began to spend most of her nights at the asylum. Her visits home became rarer, the mirrors in her room acquired thicker and thicker layers of dust. Chandrika and Ganadasa told me about how devout she had become, and of her starting a small hospital for wounded birds. The birds she looked after were not the parrots and mynahs of palaces and mansions but the humbler sparrows, pigeons, doves and crows who had a chance of surviving their injuries. We heard of her increasing self-mortification and prodigious fasts that were the envy of the Jaina clergy and aroused the admiration of its laity. Those familiar with the religion were prophesying that she was destined to fulfill the vow of sallekhana, the starving of oneself to death, revered by the Jainas as the most fitting end to life. Indeed, my mother did keep that particular vow but not till many years later, when I was already married and our contact, so fragile at best, had become non-existent.

'For all the discourses she attended over the years, my

mother never really understood the Buddha's message. She believed that the Buddha asks us to forego attachment in order to avoid suffering, a prescription which at best only applies to the clergy. The Enlightened One says that the chief cause of human suffering is being away from people you love and being near those you do not. The more one meditates on this maha-vakya, the greater the truths it reveals. For instance, it tells us that we suffer not only by being with people we hate but also by putting up with the presence of those to whom we are merely indifferent. Then, again, to receive love passively can also be a cause of suffering if one does not actively love back. The solution to suffering can then never lie in cutting off and controlling attachment, in not letting yourself love, for then you are always fated to be with people you do not love and never in the presence of those you do. Perhaps my mother finally discovered that the only beings she could love were wounded birds. Perhaps she was happy in her hospital.

'Chandrika dealt with time the only way she knew—by falling desperately in love with a man, by becoming totally infatuated,' Vatsyayana said with a rueful smile that shyly revealed his own infatuation with his aunt.

'Ten years younger than she was, the object of her passion this time around was an architect from Ujjayini who was building one of Udayana's new pavilions. The young man had come to Avantika's with a group of his friends, less in pursuit of amorous dalliance than out of curiosity. Deserted by its regular devotees, our house had by now become a kind of disused shrine, a monument famed for its past glories, and well worth an evening's excursion for visitors to the city who appreciated the finer nuances of the courtesan tradition.

'I was later told by the musicians that Chandrika surpassed herself on that particular evening. They raved about the powerful images, clever and simple at the same time, which she wove with her face and body as she danced. They would never forget the way she depicted the tender turning away of the heroine and the importuning of her lover in one unbroken, undulating movement, or the lovers' kiss which she presented with an amazing and consuming tenderness yet without abandoning clarity of movement or expression.

'The young architect was flattered by the attentions of a legendary though aging beauty, and let himself be loved for a while. For those few days Chandrika was radiant with happiness. It was quite touching to see how she immersed herself in the arcana of architectural theory in an effort to be more pleasing to her less than ardent lover. Like the rest of us, she had not paid much attention previously to the intricacies of building a house. Her knowledge of architecture was like that of any other educated person, both scanty and vague. She knew, as we all did, that to ensure longevity the bedroom must always face east or south and that to eat while facing south increases a person's fame. Now, while waiting for her lover in the evenings, she would try to engage the musicians in a discussion about building materials.

'"Malli," I remember her telling me when I went home for lunch one day and we were sitting together in her room after one of Ganadasa's delicious meals, "I simply cannot remember all the different formulae for determining the layout, choice of site and the thickness of walls and columns according to the direction the building will face, the day and time when the construction should start and the position of the stars at that particular moment. I get confused about which god is the presiding deity of which square in a building plan. My lover won't think I am stupid, will he?"

'"No, masi," I replied. "You are beautiful, intelligent and will never be called upon to build a house."

'I was kept informed about the progress—or its lack—of the affair by Ganadasa who often visited me at the palace, ostensibly to cook my favourite foods but actually to gossip. Ganadasa thoroughly disapproved of the architect. Contrary to the prevailing fashion, Chandrika's lover wore a beard, an affectation that damned him in the cook's eyes as a person who admired the barbarian Greeks.

'"He is a smug youth who has tasted his first success," the cook sniffed. "He has an inordinately high opinion of himself unwarranted by either birth or achievement."

'I cannot comment on Chandrika's choice for I never met the man myself.

'Eventually, inevitably, the architect left Chandrika. He began his retreat by taking another lover, a young courtesan. Chandrika grew desperate. Every morning a servant was dispatched from the house with pleading messages and presents she could ill afford. She tried to tempt him with Ganadasa's delicacies and even offered to teach the finer points of the erotic arts to her rival as long as the lover was also present during the instruction. She even wanted me to intercede with Udayana and have the king *order* the architect's attendance at our house. She sulked when I pointed out the absurdity of her suggestion. She tried to cling to the callous lover as he slipped away. She cajoled, entreated, begged in panic, blazed in anger, had moments of ecstatic hope followed by long intervals of searing despair. She must have found her uncontrollable emotions very painful. She was a proud woman who was simultaneously struggling against the loss of her pride while she was busy undermining it. Much later, looking back at the episode as a respected nun, Chandrika would shake her head in wonderment at the force of the erotic gale that had blown away her self-possession. To be enslaved by what she had always used to enslave others—the press of sexual desire—was something she now regarded with a degree of bemusement.

'I now wonder if Chandrika's self-abasement was not a part of her karmic design. Perhaps she needed to shed her self-respect and sense of shame to go on to the next stage of her life. They were the last bits of clothing that covered her old self. Stripped naked, Chandrika could now don a new habit—that of the Buddhist nun—as she fled into the Goshitrama monastery in pain and humiliation. My mother, ensconced in her own little cell in the bird hospital, was indifferent when I brought her the news. "To gain tranquillity the mind must first cancel its debt with tears," was all she had to say about the upheaval in her sister's life.'

Depending upon the kavi one talked to, Vatsyayana's first presentation of his work, on the sexuality of women, was either a brilliant success or a great scandal. The two were identical as far as Udayana was concerned, and in the year 88 Vatsyayana was ceremoniously admitted to the assembly of Kausambi's litterateurs. Vatsyayana's arguments (which he naturally attributed to ancient authorities) for women's sexual autonomy, of her responses during intercourse not being solely determined by male sexual activity, his championing of love marriage as superior to the traditionally favoured forms and his open admiration for the courtesan and her crafts, ensured that he would draw upon himself the wrath of conservative scholars while finding passionate defenders among the more modern ones.

The conservatives in the assembly, a small group left over from Rudradeva's era, were led by Rajnikanta, a scholar of political science with the squashed face and bulging eyes of a frog, who had penned a commentary on the *Arthashastra* many years earlier and thereafter made a career and reputation out of repeating himself. Bemoaning the corruption of present day public life as compared to the purity of an earlier idyllic era, fulsome in his praise of the peasant and the self-sufficient village while scorning the evil city, the greedy merchant and the great empire, Rajnikanta was bloated with moral fervour and the smug arrogance of brahminical superiority. He openly reviled Vatsyayana as 'that low-caste son of a whore who lords over us high-born brahmins in the assembly'.

'I was aware of his intense dislike for me but did not feel the need to either investigate or mitigate it. As is always the case in such situations, the dislike was mutual. I had no use for his platitudes and his talent for repeating the obvious. If there was a blue cow on the road, Rajnikanta could be trusted to be the first one to point it out and say, "Look! There is a cow."'

Inflexible in their certainties and righteous in defence of a tradition which they sought to appropriate as their own, Rajnikanta and his group of theologians tried in vain to counter Vatsyayana's influence with the king and his growing reputation in the central countries as the most promising scholar of erotics of his generation. Udayana openly exulted in his friend's success. As one of the few native Kausambian stars illuminating the intellectual firmament of the Gupta empire, Vatsyayana was as much the kingdom's pride as was the workmanship of its goldsmiths or the expertise of its courtesans.

'Although he could not harm me in Kausambi, Rajnikanta belonged to a loose network of conservative scholars spread throughout the hermitages of the central countries, a clique that vigorously opposed what they called a general decline of morals in the Gupta empire. Among members of this group, he succeeded in painting me as a dangerous iconoclast, a threat to dharma and the ancestral way of life.'

Absorbed in the composition of the *Kamasutra*, his achievements recognized and liberally rewarded, Vatsyayana had every reason to be well satisfied with his life. He was happy alone, his days as long or as short as he wished them to be. Nevertheless, they had a certain rhythm determined by his work, his occasional evenings with the king and a weekly visit to his aunt in the Goshitrama monastery. Almost forty-five years old, Chandrika had aged in a manner that abolished most traces of the high-spirited girl and capricious beauty Vatsyayana had known all through his childhood.

'There was now a calmness about her, even gravity, which I would not have earlier believed possible. Whenever I met her, I involuntarily searched her face for reminders of the Chandrika I had known. In Goshitrama, she generally kept to herself, spending her day in a hidden nook of the monastery's large garden, far from busy monks and nuns and teachers discoursing on traditional wisdom.

'"Malli, I find I am happy enough to just sit under this tree, doing nothing and speaking to no one," she told me once. "These are the times when my mind is free of all thought and my equilibrium remains in harmony with all that I see around me: a bee alighting on a flower, a squirrel scampering up a trunk, a family of monkeys swinging from one branch of a tree to another.

'"You want me to talk of love and my lovers. They are now but flickers of memory. When I lie at night I gather no one in my arms now, not even in my dreams. And you know, Malli, I prefer this to the euphoria and despair of youth, to the swing I was on for all those years which, pushed hard by fate, rose and fell with a rhythm over which I had little control.

'"This doesn't mean that I am not happy to see you,"

she added hastily. "Tell me what is happening at the court. And why are you still unmarried?"

'"Only because I can't find a woman like you, Chandrika masi. Find me one and I will get married faster than the speed of Indra's thunderbolt," I said, deflecting her last question. My renunciation of sexual desire, a consequence of the fever after my return from Mihirpal's hermitage, was a secret I had only divulged to the court physician.

'For all her newly acquired seriousness, Chandrika was not immune to the attractions of court gossip. She particularly enjoyed hearing about the escapades of Bhasa, the poet who had recently joined the assembly and was assiduously cultivating me as a friend.

'Looking back, it is clearer than ever to me that Bhasa has been my only other friend besides Brahmagupta who I have met only thrice since our travel together from Bahlika to Kashgar. I know Udayana thought of me as a friend but I was never completely at ease with him. He was someone who remained unpredictable no matter how long I knew him, capriciously changing from being an affectionate friend to an imperious overlord and back again. Bhasa was excitable but never changeable.

'Bhasa had already earned a considerable reputation for his plays on themes from the Mahabharata when he was invited to join the assembly at Kausambi. An assiduous frequenter of brothels, Bhasa loved the company of courtesans and persistently tried to pay them with spontaneously composed verses rather than with money, of which he was almost always short. He tried to include me in his evening excursions, teased me as "the monk" when I refused, and then borrowed money from me for his sexual adventures. Before he went off to one of the reigning deities of his heart—he was a natural polytheist in matters of love—he would embrace me with considerable feeling.

'"That is why I love you! You are generous even if you are indifferent to female company. Normally, I hate ascetics!"'

'Bhasa also constantly sought my advice on the conduct of his various love affairs. In spite of the abiding turmoil in his love life, Bhasa was a serious and gifted poet who was responsible for many innovations in classical drama. He drastically shortened the traditional prelude which praises the work and its author, and would have ideally preferred to plunge straight into the play's action after the benedictory prayer to Vishnu. The plays he wrote while at Kausambi do not contain obligatory comic scenes and the speeches of the actors are as much verse as prose. His departures from tradition naturally attracted the ire of Rajnikanta and his group. Thus, besides the money I kept lending him and the sexual advice relating to courtesans that I refused to give, it was also the existence of a common enemy in Udayana's assembly of scholars which brought us close together.

'I did advise him on other matters, though, for instance on the choice of a theme for his inaugural play as a new member of the assembly. Given his chronic financial difficulties and recollecting my own effort to win Udayana's patronage after my return from Mihirpal's hermitage, I told Bhasa about the play I had written with the king's namesake as its hero. Bhasa was almost embarrassingly grateful for the idea. Of course, given his prodigious talent, *The Dream of Vasavadatta*, which he wrote and staged within two months of our discussion on the subject, has come to be regarded as a masterpiece of modern drama.

'Udayana, however, took perverse pleasure in rewarding Bhasa more with praise than with the large sums of money the poet continuously needed. Bhasa importuned me to intercede on his behalf, railed against Udayana's niggardliness in private, and recited flattering verses in public in praise of the king's imagined valour and sagacity. The flattery availed him as little as did the moral homilies he began to include in his plays, specifically directed at Udayana, which enjoined a king to be generous to highly deserving brahmins—such as Bhasa himself—who were worthy of the highest honours on earth. I still remember Bhasa looking meaningfully at Udayana from the side of the stage while an actor in one of his plays declaimed: "The king should hand over to brahmins the entire wealth of his kingdom and leave only a bow for his sons."

'Udayana only gave a broad smile. Leaning back and inclining his head towards me—I was sitting in the row behind him—he whispered, "I would rather leave the brahmins to my sons."

'The scandalous whisper was overheard, and further hardened the belief of the assembly's conservative faction that Kausambi was being ruled by a degenerate king who favoured kavis in the habit of mocking tradition and undermining dharma.

'Of course, Rajnikanta and his cohorts finally did succeed in taking their revenge when Bhasa's foolishness presented them with an opportunity. But this was much later, some years after Udayana's marriage to Madhavi and three years after my own to her sister. Fate indeed works like water buckets on an irrigation wheel; it empties these and fills up those, raises some and lowers others and others again it keeps in between, continuously teaching us bitter truths about our lives in this world.'

Chapter Sixteen

However virtuous a woman may seem to be, or however sensual she is in appearance, her true nature is revealed in intercourse.

Kamasutra 2.8.40

I was amazed at the ease with which our mutual passion overwhelmed my earlier feelings of shame. I carried out my interviews with Vatsyayana in the morning and walked into the forest in the afternoon without feeling a tremor of remorse. My shoulder muscles did not tense, as they sometimes did when I felt Vatsyayana watch my retreating back from the veranda of his hut. This is not to say that I was free of *thoughts* of my transgression. Abstract intimations of the shame I should have felt did arise, but desire unbound and love returned had severed these thoughts from their emotional moorings. I did not flinch when I looked Vatsyayana in the eye while we talked about his work; neither did I falter when I asked him questions about his life. Our work together continued as before, isolated from my intimacy with Malavika, although somewhere I sensed that the flimsy screen I had put up between the two was in danger of collapsing.

The many images of those late spring afternoons in the

forest are by now coalesced into one. We are lying together, Malavika's head on my shoulder, our bodies separating after union, each retreating into its own secrecy. Night jasmines fading in Malavika's hair, sun-warmed earth, fresh grass, the echoing silence of love—all fused into a happiness so intense we cannot speak. Insects murmuring frantically all around us, and the occasional flapping of wings as a heron takes flight from the pond. Above us the sky is awash in a deep turquoise. Fluffy young clouds not yet dark and swollen with rain, drifting across the radiant blue. Nestling against my side with her head propped up on an elbow, the weight of one breast on my shoulder, Malavika gently twining my chest hair around her index finger.

We were both caught up in the enchantment of passion. Meditating together on desire, we were intent on using our senses to seek what the senses cannot touch and thus never find. Initially, as our capacity to instinctively understand each other's moods increased with every meeting, words often seemed like intruders from a world we had left behind at the edge of the forest. Yet after a while, obeying the lovers' irresistible urge toward confession, we felt the need to speak. We exchanged information on our lives before love, on who we were before each became that special someone else recognized only by the other. I told Malavika about growing up in my Varanasi home where she had been a recent guest, about my father's hopes for my career and how I had disappointed him. I talked of my mother who died when I was five years old and whose face was dim in my memory, but whose presence was strong in my mind. Malavika talked of her conventional, happy childhood and her peculiar married life. Reticent about his marriage except for a brief narration of the circumstances under which they had met, Vatsyayana had clearly intimated to me that this was an area of his life he preferred to keep out of our conversation. The story of Vatsyayana's marriage is thus essentially told in Malavika's voice.

Malavika was the younger daughter of a minor king of the Vatsa country who recognized the overlordship of King Udayana. The sisters were close, and when Udayana chose the sixteen-year old Madhavi as one of his queens, the fourteen-year Malavika accompanied her to Kausambi. The parents were overjoyed at their good fortune in having the king for a son-in-law and did not object to the younger daughter's decision to make her home with the elder one. Doubtless, they also thought that living in the palace would vastly improve Malavika's chances of finding a good match from among Kausambi's nobles.

Consisting of eight pavilions in the innermost courtyard of the palace and grouped around a garden studded with ashoka trees, the royal harem of Kausambi was enclosed within its own ramparts. Its chief guardian was an elderly eunuch called Bhadraka, who in his white tunic and a cap disguising his baldness, limped around the harem with the help of a cane, grumbling about his many infirmities and the trouble that the women—the six queens and their maidservants—caused him. Except for Udayana, the royal priest and the physician, no other man was allowed inside the harem, its entrances guarded by female soldiers armed with lances and short daggers tucked into the waists of their uniforms.

Malavika was an interested observer but only an occasional participant in the lazy flow of harem life. The most exciting part of its daily routine was in the morning when the queens began to get ready for the day. Awakening to the strains of a morning melody appropriate to the season, played by the harem's female musicians, the pavilions soon filled with a purposeful bustle. Perfumed bathwater was prepared in huge bulging ceramic jars. Maids ground sandalwood bark with musk oil to a paste to be rubbed on the queens' bodies, diluted lac to paint the soles of their feet, prepared fresh collyrium for lining their eyelids. Others cleaned the birdcages while the queens personally selected the appropriate skirts, accessories and jewellery for the day. After the queens' toilet was complete and they was dressed in all their finery—a process which took about three hours—there was nothing much to do and a lull descended. The queens visited each other, exchanged gossip of the palace and the city, went out into the garden to sit on swings that hung from sturdy branches and were pushed to and fro by the maids. Once a week they went on a day-long excursion to the royal park outside the city. Of course, there were the many festival days, with accompanying rituals in which the queens were enthusiastic participants. In the evening another toilet was performed though it was less elaborate than the morning affair. Hair was perfumed with incense smoke, braided with fresh flowers and coiled high on the neck. Garments were changed and the queens assembled in the hall reserved for the king's arrival, even though Udayana rarely visited the harem. Here, they passed time listening to music, watching dancers or laughing at the antics of a female dwarf dressed in male costume who was an expert at mimicking the sounds and movements of an amorous man. On festive days, there was an evening performance of a play at the palace theatre, an event eagerly anticipated by the queens.

Both the sisters were renowned for their beauty—even if Malavika was still a little plump when she first came to Kausambi—but were of radically different temperaments. Madhavi was outgoing, pleasure-loving and surrounded by friends. Malavika was quieter, artistically inclined, and liked to spend her time painting in her room or making occasional excursions to the public park to sketch the motionless cranes and the ripples on the ponds. She preferred to remain aloof from the harem's bawdy talk. Malavika was a favourite of the tutors who came to instruct the girls in literary composition, painting and playing the vina. Madhavi on the other hand preferred the arts taught by their mother. She was too lazy to learn weaving and embroidery, but was happy to be in the garden among the trees and flowers. She took her lessons in the supervision of a garden seriously. What she really loved were the rituals of beauty treatment, the art of massage and the application of ointments and perfumes, although not their preparation, which was the province of serving women.

Malavika was also an avid reader, her taste tending towards dramas based on love stories from the epics, and here court life gave her ample opportunity to indulge her literary inclinations. The court of Kausambi was known all over the central countries for its brilliant assembly of scholars, writers, poets, philosophers, ritualists, theologians and grammarians. Some of Udayana's subjects, contrasting him with his warrior father, disparagingly observed that the young king aspired more to be a poet than a soldier, that he preferred the life of the mind to that of warfare. The royal palace supported a permanent theatre where festivals were observed through performing plays in a programme that judiciously combined the classics with new offerings by the court's own playwrights. The assembly of scholars and writers met twice a week for theoretical discussions on abstruse topics such as whether realism in art can be produced purely through the imagination. On Friday evenings there was an open meeting for interested courtiers, where poets submitted their recent work to criticism by reading it before the assembly. Udayana never failed to preside over the Friday meetings which ended with literary games, such as the completing of verses, in which the king was an enthusiastic participant. Except for the royal emblems of the two flywhisks and the white umbrella held above him, Udayana was indistinguishable from the rest of the kavis in his vocal expressions of pleasure and disapproval and in his often good-humoured and at other times acerbic literary repartee.

After she had settled down in the palace, Udayana readily acceded to Malavika's request, unusual for a woman of the harem, to attend the Friday meetings.

'I wish your sister had more of your tastes,' he said, somewhat wistfully.

'I was fifteen at the time,' Malavika said, 'and people told me I was beautiful, although I found my beauty a heavy burden. Men looked at me in that peculiarly hungry way, as if waiting for a chance to pounce on me and begin to devour me. The male gaze disgusted me. The poets were particularly bad. Old or young, they were equally lascivious. Whenever one of them used a conventional poetic fancy such as the chakora partridge drinking moonbeams or the ashoka tree flowering when kicked by a beautiful woman, he would look meaningfully at me in the lustful manner of poets, ruining my pleasure in the poem and provoking a wish to kick the man rather than the poor tree. The worst was Sudhakara, a poet in his late twenties but already balding. I suppose with his flashing eyes and impudent grin he was considered handsome, although I never paid attention to men's looks. He was well known as a great flirt and gossip, and the harem had it that he was a regular customer at the cheaper brothels in the eastern quarter. Whenever he spoke at the assembly he would first give me a conspiratorial look, as if we had already privately discussed what he was going to say. I hated that.

'My brother-in-law was one of the few men I tolerated because he did not see me as a commodity to be consumed. Oh yes, he made the obligatory innuendoes. "The wife's sister is half a wife," he would smile, especially if other people were about, but in reality, to my great relief (although to my sister's regret), he was not interested in women as women. Not that after a brief initial phase Madhavi had serious objections. She was certainly not one of those proverbial virtuous wives who have the power to make rain fall in times of drought. There were many handsome men at the court and Udayana was a tolerant husband. All he insisted upon, without ever putting it into words, was that his wives exercise a minimum of discretion.'

Udayana had six wives not out of personal choice but because of reasons of state. The status of being the monarch of a powerful kingdom like Kausambi demanded that the king's harem be as well stocked with women as his granaries were with grain, forests with game or court with learned men. Udayana rarely visited his wives. When he came to the harem it was only to sustain the pretence of royal virility in public view. Udayana was visibly ill at ease whenever he walked from his own quarters to the gate of the harem, a strapping young slave carrying an ivory phallus on a scarlet cushion behind him. The queens, too, dreaded their husband's show of conjugality. However, there was nothing to be done. With the traditional sanction for the use of the artificial phallus to 'satisfy' many women on the same night—Vatsyayana comments on this in the last chapter of the fifth part of his book—Udayana too had to go through the motions of copulation for which he had little desire. The women found it boring, often painful, and gave the appropriate love cries as soon as decency permitted, a signal that the king could stop the heaving of his body upon theirs. Udayana, too, was grateful for having this particular royal duty cut short. The rumour in the court was that both the ivory phallus and the slave served his own pleasures, though again, very discreetly.

'So in Udayana's harem the women did not need to employ the artifices listed in the *Kamasutra*?' I asked.

I remember we were sitting down on the grass in a forest clearing at the time, Malavika's eyes cast down on an idly moving foot. She looked up at me blankly. I reminded her:

Dressed as women, citizens are sometimes taken into the harem as maidservants.
Disguised as a guard, he enters at the right moment, unperceived.
It is also possible to enter and leave the harem if one is bringing food or drink; at the time of drinking parties or walks in the garden, when servants are running about; during changes of domicile or change of guard; during excursions to the country or departure for trips, and also if the king goes on a long journey leaving the queens behind in the palace.

As Malavika laughed, her teeth gleamed like raindrops in a flash of lightning.

'If he had dared, my brother-in-law would have commissioned his learned men to find even more ways for the queen's lovers to get inside the harem without exciting comment by his subjects,' she said.

The pressure on Malavika to choose a husband was mounting. Once a month, sometimes more, a messenger came from her parents with suggestions regarding possible grooms and reminders from her father that with every menstruation while she remained unwed he was incurring the sin of foeticide. Madhavi, otherwise feckless, suddenly discovered her responsibilities as an elder sister and became a nag on the subject of marriage. Even Udayana joined in. At the end of one of the Friday assemblies he pointed out two young nobles and asked Malavika whether she did not find them handsome. Malavika did not answer but looked straight into his eyes. The king blushed. Finally her parents moved to Kausambi for a longer stay. Determined to arrange her marriage that very year, they settled down in one of the smaller guest houses on the palace grounds.

As Malavika was a renowned beauty and sister-in-law of the king, there was no dearth of suitors for her hand. The problem was that she found the thought of sexual intercourse with men disgusting. All through her girlhood, while others her age relished the lessons on erotic science, whispering and giggling together after the teacher left, Malavika had sustained a look of polite interest on her face while she removed her mind from the classroom and the lecture. A sensitive girl who loved her family, Malavika was fully aware of her parents' unhappiness and their growing exasperation as she went on rejecting each prospective husband. There were heated scenes in which the father raged, the mother wept and Madhavi tried to soothe the parents while directing reproachful looks at the younger sister. Unable to bear this concerted emotional barrage and after declining the twentieth proposal, Malavika finally surrendered and agreed to marriage.

The family's choice fell on one of the senapati's two sons who was, therefore, almost certainly at the beginning of a brilliant career in the army. Madhavi tried hard to enthuse her sister about her future husband and his worldly prospects but Malavika remained disinterested. 'She acts if she is a polite guest who has just wandered in on a discussion of her life,' Madhavi grumbled to the parents.

The astrologers compared horoscopes and found no heavenly hindrance to the proposed match. The day after the astrologers' verdict, the senapati's family priest brought a tray containing eight small balls of earth, each prepared from a different ground. He was accompanied by the commander's supervisor of female slaves, Kanchan-mata's old friend, who was trusted by Malavika's future father-in-law to deliver an acute and unbiased evaluation of the girl. The ritual of the earth balls went off smoothly. Malavika did not choose the ball from the earth of the graveyard, which would have meant that she was destined to murder her husband. Nor did she select balls signifying barrenness or reckless temperament. She chose one of the auspicious balls, from the earth of a pool which never dried up, indicating that her married home would have an abundance of all things.

Malavika did not evince interest in the marriage negotiations, which now began in earnest. Expected to be present when the professional go-between from the groom's family came to her parents' house, she barely listened as he extolled the man's perfect education, irreproachable conduct, the respect and affection he had for the parents, and his immaculate physical condition without a trace of infirmity or deformity. The intermediary from Malavika's family was doing the same for her in the senapati's house. These were preliminary moves in a financial negotiation which ended after a week with her father agreeing to set aside a generous sum of money for her dowry. After the agreement was reached, the young man, accompanied by the family priest and two aunts, came to their house to officially ask Malavika's father for her hand. This was the first time she had seen him. She supposed he was handsome enough but she felt nothing;

she was going through the whole process with a numbed mind. From a distance she watched her future husband ritually introduce himself to her father by reciting his own name, followed by the names of all the ancestors of his clan. She watched them touch a ceramic vase filled with flowers, roasted seeds, fruit and pieces of gold and then her father bless his daughter by placing the vase on her head and wishing her wealth and prosperity. Astrologers from both sides were called in again. They calculated astral conjunctions, discussed the physical characteristics of the couple and examined other omens to fix an auspicious date for the marriage ceremony four months hence.

Three months before the wedding, the first strange incident in what was to become an inexplicable and frightening series took place in the Friday assembly. Bhasa, the talented poet from Ujjayini who was beginning to make a mark as a playwright and had recently join the Kausambi court, was giving a reading from his new play, *The Dream of Vasavadatta*. When the reading was over, the poet Sudhakara was the first one to rise to give his comments. As usual, after bowing towards the king, his gaze lingered for a moment on Malavika who sat just behind Udayana to his left. Malavika had turned her face away to avoid his intimate look. As Sudhakara spoke, Malavika kept her eyes firmly fixed on the back of the king's neck, staring at his shoulder-length curly hair. And then, without any warning, she felt the sharp tug of an unseen force lifting her head and directing her eyes to Sudhakara's groin. To her horror, she found she could not avert her eyes which were focusing on the bulge under the poet's pleated white tunic. Flushed with embarrassment and smarting with tears of shame, Malavika rose from her seat with effort, and fled the assembly.

She did not tell anyone what had transpired that evening. After a few nights of troubled sleep, she succeeded in putting the Friday incident out of her mind. Then the next one took place. This time she had gone with her maid to the royal park outside the city for a day's painting. As she alighted from the carriage, an old beggar approached her for alms. While she fumbled for a coin, she found herself unable to take her eyes off the barely perceptible bulge in his tattered undergarment. The old beggar, noticing the direction of her look, grinned and made an obscene gesture with his right hand, as if to release his genitals from their confines. This movement broke the spell and Malavika climbed back into the carriage, precipitately fleeing to the safety of the harem.

She now stopped going out of the women's quarters for fear of encountering men and repeating this frightening and bewildering compulsion. She was too ashamed to reveal it to anyone, and when Udayana inquired about her continued absence from the assembly, she warded off his curiosity by vaguely referring to an unspecified female malady. Udayana, who had a horror of mysterious female ailments, hurriedly walled off his solicitude and began to narrate all that had transpired in the literary meetings she had missed.

In the two weeks Malavika spent closeted in the harem after the second incident, there was a gradual return of self-possession. As with a bad dream, she was beginning to forget the intensity of her reactions while the incidents themselves remained etched in her mind. Then one morning while her maid was painting the soles of her feet, she found herself staring at the woman's breasts. Fortunately, unlike her experiences with men, it was not difficult to take her eyes off the woman the moment she became aware of what she was doing. The involuntary staring at women's breasts began to happen more frequently. These were disturbing breaches of equilibrium, but she doubted whether they lasted long enough to draw looks of puzzled attention from others. Nevertheless, they had the effect of making Malavika withdraw further from human contact and she spent more and more time in her room, painting.

Madhavi had noticed her sister's withdrawal and ascribed it to the girl's fears relating to her forthcoming marriage. She tried to reassure Malavika by talking, not very persuasively, about the bliss of conjugal life. She was more convincing on the topic of sexual pleasure that awaited her sister, although it was evident that the barely-disguised personal experiences she so enthusiastically recounted were occasioned by men other than her husband. To Madhavi's utter bewilderment, Malavika suddenly burst into tears. Clapping both her palms against her ears, she cried out, 'I don't want to hear it! I don't want to hear anymore!' Madhavi retreated. The outburst was just the manifestation of a young girl's tortured nerves, she said to herself. Marriage would soon take care of whatever was troubling the sister. It was the reliable remedy for a young girl's excessive emotionalism.

In the meanwhile, the marriage preparations were well under way. Malavika's parents returned to their family home which was thoroughly scoured. New clothes of fine silk and brocade were stitched for the whole household, the quantity and quality of the brocade decreasing as one descended down the household's hierarchy of servants. There was a constant coming and going of jewellers and tailors as Malavika's trousseau was prepared. Her father was personally supervising the erection of a wooden pavilion with elaborately carved lintels in the sprawling courtyard of their house; her mother was in charge of its floral and floor decorations. The young couple would stand under the awning of this pavilion for the marriage ritual.

The demonic force which possessed Malavika suddenly

changed its focus. It now seized her hand while she painted. Malavika could be painting a lotus when, suddenly, she would find herself emerging from a trance to discover to her horror that a lotus bulb had taken the shape of testicles or the stalk had taken the curve, thickness and veined texture of an erect penis. The girl was terribly frightened. She tried to continue painting by limiting herself to objects—birds, clouds, ponds—where there was no danger of such transformation. Once in a while, though, it would happen again; a bird's neck became obscenely elongated, a cloud hung in the sky in that distinctive shape she had come to dread, a pond sprouted a nipple in its calm centre.

Much worse was to follow in quick succession, as if the last act of the drama demanded a faster tempo. Sudhakara began to talk to her. She did not actually hear him. The poet talked in her mind, and here she could do nothing to keep out his insinuating voice. He was responsible for her condition, and had planned each incident, he told Malavika. He wanted her to be ready to surrender to him. He described in lascivious detail what he was soon going to do to her. She would especially like it from the back, he told her. She was that kind of a woman.

'Stop this talk! Stop it!' Malavika cried.

But Sudhakara was relentless. Malavika no longer followed a routine which could frame her daily life and control her turmoil. Instead of waking up with the rest of the harem, getting dressed and going to her easel to work at her paintings, Malavika lay in bed for hours. Her hair dishevelled, eyes staring at the ceiling, the rhythm of her life was now solely and helplessly dictated by his phantom voice.

Sudhakara first made love to her in a dream. He had entered the dream and the room without closing either door behind him. As he lay on top of her, she kept looking over his naked shoulder in fear that the maid might come in, willing her mind to ignore all other sensations coursing through her body. She wanted to push him away and then she did not. When the orgasm came she woke to find her body arched; as the orgasm continued, she fainted. Next morning there was a dull, throbbing pain between her thighs. In the afternoon he again came to her room. She was fully awake. This time she did not see him, only felt him enter her, again causing an orgasm.

'Please don't do this to me!' she pleaded.

He only laughed. In the next few days—or were they only hours?—he continued to enter her room and her body at will, inducing paroxysms of agonized pleasure which she loathed as soon as they began to ebb.

Malavika's maid noticed that her mistress had become increasingly withdrawn in the last four weeks. She was concerned about the uneaten meals, the terrified eyes and the long silences that persisted week after week. The maid discussed her misgivings with other servants, who reassured her that all these signs pointed to her mistress suffering from unrequited love. They wondered about the identity of the man. The maid was unable to satisfy their curiosity. On that particular morning, though, when she saw Malavika mumbling to an unseen presence, her incoherent talk punctuated with screams of refusal, prolonged moans followed by spasms and whimpers of tormented ecstasy, the maid ran to Madhavi's apartment for help.

Madhavi, who together with the other queens, had been away on a four-day hunting excursion with Udayana, was shocked at her sister's appearance. Malavika had become skeletal, her body drooping like a delicate creeper touched by a scorching wind. The gaunt face, now completely dominated by the large black eyes glittering with an inhuman light, had lost its youthful glow. The skin was dull and withered like a dry bed of lotus stalks, the lips chapped and swollen with bites.

Madhavi took her sister in her arms, stroked her hair and crooned the soothing sounds from their childhood, reminiscent of the times when the younger sister had hurt herself while playing. Malavika entered a brief period of lucidity when, between sobs, she told her sister the whole story before the demonic force possessed her once again. The court physician was urgently summoned. The doctor only had to observe the girl's behaviour for a few minutes before deciding that it was a clear-cut case for exorcism by a shramana of the Kshema Shira sect of yogis whose hermitage was a few leagues outside the city. A carriage with a personal request from the king was dispatched, and the most highly regarded shramana of the sect was in Kausambi by the evening.

The shramana, a small, shrivelled middle-aged and mild-mannered man dressed in an antelope hide and with a leather pouch stuffed full with roots and herbal remedies tied around his waist, was of the opinion that Malavika had been seized by a rakshasa who had first to be appeased before he could be exorcised. Malavika was forced to drink pig's blood, which ran down the corners of her mouth and spattered the front of the thin cotton stole covering her breasts. The calming effect of this brew on the rakshasa was immediately apparent. The girl's eyes lost their uncanny brilliance and began to focus dully on her surroundings. The shramana asked for a small brazier to be brought into the room. He added some herbs from his pouch to the burning pieces of wood and asked Malavika to inhale the pungent smoke while he chanted the exorcism mantras above her. This continued for some hours. Gradually, Malavika returned to normalcy. She even listened with interest but without reaction to the king's message to Madhavi that Sudhakara was being tortured in the palace dungeon to stop his black magic. News of the poet's punishment seemed to hasten the process of recovery. When she finally slept it was for thirty-six hours, during which time the shramana sat in one corner of the room reciting his incantations. When she awoke, he fed her the ritually pure products of the cow—a tall glass of uncooked milk, a spoonful of urine, a bit of cowdung—to cleanse her insides. He then pronounced her cured.

Although free of the possessing force, Malavika did not immediately return to her normal self. She soon slipped into a deep depression.

'It is impossible to describe what happened to me at that time and what I felt, for the simple reason that I have little memory of those feelings. I was cut off from the person I was before and would again become after the depression lifted.'

My look of incomprehension spurred her to try and give me some understanding of her condition.

'It was as if the world had suddenly become empty. Everything good in it was lost forever, a loss that irradiated everything around me—the sky, the earth, the people, the animals, the birds, the leaves on a tree. The loss and the deep sadness that accompanied it was not something I felt—it was who I was. It was a state of being with its own memory, its own story, its own way of perceiving the world, its own way of relating to other people.'

Afterwards, Malavika came to know that the physicians had diagnosed her depression as a rare form of erotic insanity which, instead of the more common kind that makes a person highly excitable, leaves the patient immeasurably sad. She was suffering from the aftermath of an illusory rape, especially horrific because she was a virgin. Erotic madness is an illness that originates in the body but manifests itself in the mind, driving body and mind further apart. It was treated with a prescribed medical and dietary regimen. Vatsyayana, on recommendation of the doctors, was especially commanded by the king to make Malavika familiar with the mysteries of sexuality and thus bring her mind in closer contact with the unwilling experiences her body had undergone.

Of course, since the news of Malavika's condition had become a matter of public gossip, the marriage had to be called off; the presents the families had made to each other were returned.

Chapter Seventeen

*Like a horse intoxicated by speed, flying at a gallop
and seeing neither craters nor ditches, two lovers
blinded by desire and making furious love do not
consider the risks involved in their behaviour.*

Kamasutra 2.7.32

'He was well into middle age at the time, almost
thirty-five, and already had the reputation of being the
finest scholar of erotics in the land,' Malavika said. 'I
noticed him at the assembly because he was the only man
who did not pay me the slightest attention. Do you know
that from all he said during our many meetings over the
next three months I have forgotten everything except two
sentences from the very first time we met? We were sitting
on low chairs facing each other. My eyes were fixed on a
dark stain on the carpet in front of me. After the initial
exchange of greetings, I was barely aware of his presence.
He must have waited for a while for me to say something
before he spoke in a strikingly gentle voice.

'"How does one deal with pleasure that is forced upon
one? A pleasure which comes unbidden?" he said, as if
musing to himself.

'The evident sympathy in his voice jolted me out of

whatever dark corner of my mind I was visiting at the moment, and pulled me back into the room awash with the bright sunshine of a summer afternoon. I looked up. His eyes were very kind.

'"I hated it. It was not a pleasure. I did not want it," I cried out.

'"What an impossible situation to find oneself in: to wish and not want," he said with a heartfelt understanding I could not share. I simply did not know what he was talking about. But he had succeeded in capturing my attention.

'Yes, later he did talk of women's and men's bodies, of vulvas and penises, of size, time and temperament but, noticing my disgust, soon stopped. Even then I had the impression that he not only understood but empathized with my aversion to sex. Not that I remember what he actually said. He did not need words to talk to me. From our very first meeting, what I listened to was the warmth in his voice. It flowed over and around me like the shallow waters of a slow-moving stream on a summer evening. I felt the compassion in his deep brown eyes. I began to look forward to our meetings so that I could enjoy the touch of his voice. And then, I became addicted to its caressing warmth, missing it dreadfully in the periods between meetings.

'It did not take long before Vatsyayana became aware of the intensity of my feelings for him. Indeed, he could hardly remain oblivious to the glazing over of my eyes whenever he addressed me. I saw he was acutely uncomfortable that I listened to his words as if to music, with rapture rather than understanding. He began to come to our weekly meetings with growing reluctance, eager to leave as soon as courtesy and his own sense of responsibility permitted. He tried to ignore the feelings which I no longer concealed, avoiding them as if they were the corpses of strangers. Whenever I met him on the palace grounds, meetings I pretended were chance encounters although I had set my maid the task of finding out his scheduled visits to the king, his greeting was no more than merely civil. He would then walk past me without a smile, remote, like some holy man close only to god.'

Malavika was aware of Vatsyayana's mounting irritation, sensed his withdrawal from her but felt helpless to change a situation equally discomfiting for her.

'Even as I longed for his touch I felt ashamed of my longing. Even as I wanted him to look at me with love I was terrified he might actually do so.'

The best course of action for her would have been to end the meetings, which had become painful for both. All Malavika needed to do was tell her brother-in-law that her instruction was complete and she no longer required the instructor. Unable to act, feeling disgusted with herself each time she felt a wave of pleasure run through her as Vatsyayana walked into the room, the decision was finally taken out of her hands. One day Vatsyayana announced that this was to be their last meeting. He was going away to Varanasi for six months to work on the final chapters of his manuscript.

For two days after his departure, Malavika felt nothing. She was neither happy nor sad; she neither felt greatly relieved nor excessively burdened by his absence. She tried not to dwell on her thoughts of him, although images from their earlier meetings sometimes flashed before her: Vatsyayana sitting gravely, his head inclined, listening, Vatsyayana speaking in his warm voice, Vatsyayana's brown eyes moist with compassion. On the third day, though, she succumbed. She woke up in the morning with no memory of her dreams but with a heavy heart and tears in her eyes. The feeling of desolation, of abandonment, steadily mounted throughout the day. She lost her appetite, picking at her food while the maids cajoled her to eat.

Malavika's unhappiness at her separation from Vatsyayana was not as overwhelming for her consciousness nor as unacceptable to her mind as were the horrific flashes of sexual union with the poet. Even if the pain of separation was unbearable at times, Malavika still felt she could control it. It did not consume her the way the excitement and revulsion of the sexual images did.

Nights were particularly harsh.

'While others in the palace were sunk in the sweetness of sleep, I lay awake, my eyes streaming with tears. The moonlight was a vicious enemy. I wanted to lie curled in total darkness and never see light again.'

Over time, Malavika's sorrow became a disease that ravaged all beauty. Like a water lily gnawed by a beetle, she began to droop, becoming thinner by the day. Her arms grew lean. Bangles slipped from her wasting hands. For the first time in her life, she who had always looked down upon love poetry began to appreciate verses upon the theme of separation and read them one after the other, soon exhausting the royal library's small stock. The lyrics consoled her and at the same time heightened the awareness of her suffering. Most verses were like flawed mirrors; they captured some of her emotions but did not reflect her exact sentiments. When Vatsyayana had been at her side, she had not felt 'as happy as a city in the rapture of a carnival' although it was true that with him gone 'she grieved like a deserted house where the squirrel plays in the front yard'.

'Curiously, the only poem that accurately portrayed my state was by that wretch Sudhakara, still rotting in the palace dungeon. Do you know it? I recited the verses so often to myself that I started to feel condemned to remember them for the rest of my life.

People say you will have to bear it . . .
Don't they know what passion is like?
Or is it that they are so strong? As for me,
if I do not see my lover
grief drowns my heart
and like a streak of foam in high waters
dashed on the rocks
little by little I ebb
and become nothing.

This time Madhavi did not wait long to act. After finding the reason for her sister's condition from a close interrogation of the maids and a long conversation with Malavika herself, she sought an immediate meeting with her husband.

'That girl feels and lives her emotions more than anyone else I know,' Udayana grumbled, half in exasperation and half in admiration, after the queen had finished describing her sister's state. 'Certainly more than my poets with all their virtuosity and so little heart-felt feeling. What do you suggest?'

'Get her married to Vatsyayana,' Madhavi immediately answered.

'Is he not too old for her? Then there is the matter of his caste,' Udayana replied hesitantly.

Madhavi sensed that the king was loath to share his friend with a wife, even if the wife was a sister-in-law he liked.

'Malavika is over sixteen, almost past the age of marriage. After what has happened—I am talking about the possession illness which everyone knows about—she hardly has a choice about a husband's age, family or caste. As for Vatsyayana, it is about time he was married. A wife will relieve him of all household chores. She will take care of the details of daily life which take up so much time and keep him away from his work and his friends.'

Udayana was not yet fully convinced.

'Perhaps he does not want to marry?'

'Are you or are you not the king?' Madhavi's loud voice had an edge of scorn. 'You only have to order him to do so. Already people wonder whether you are forceful enough to sit on Kausambi's throne. They compare you to your father whose each word was law, every look a command.'

'They say I am not forceful enough, do they? Inform your parents and begin the wedding preparations. The marriage will take place in a month from today,' Udayana said, as Madhavi, fully satisfied with the way the conversation had proceeded, respectfully took her leave.

'Not forceful enough!' Udayana muttered to himself. Tomorrow he would dispatch a rider to Varanasi commanding Vatsyayana's immediate return. If not immediate, at least within two months. That should give him enough time to finish consulting Varanasi's libraries. Udayana had begun to miss his friend and his fund of anecdotes on the vagaries of human sexuality. Of course, if needed, he would command Vatsyayana to marry Malavika but Udayana was certain that matters would never reach that unpleasant stage. Like most men, his friend was a reasonable man and would understand the imperatives of everyone's situation. As the king, Udayana was also in position of the father Vatsyayana no longer had. It was not only his obligation as a friend but also his paternal duty to arrange the marriage, even in the face of Vatsyayana's hesitations or protests.

Oddly enough, when the time came Vatsyayana did not object to the marriage. Nor did he evince any enthusiasm or excitement; but Udayana had not really expected him to show either.

'Yes, it is time for marriage and I am honoured that the

queen has chosen her own sister for me. She is exactly the wife I need,' was all he said.

After the wedding, a quiet ceremony to which only close relatives were invited—an exception was Ganadasa who came from his village to which he had returned after the dissolution of their household—the newly married couple moved into a bigger house on the palace grounds. Madhavi had insisted that her sister live next to the harem. Udayana not only welcomed the suggestion but actively helped her persuade Vatsyayana of the desirability of the move. Here, in the fifth year of Emperor Chandragupta's reign, Vatsyayana and Malavika set up household.

'Our days followed a pleasant routine,' Malavika remembered. 'The man and the maid servant—Vatsyayana insisted we only have two—were experienced and efficient and needed minimal supervision. The mornings were slow and lazy, mostly taken up by the minutiae of our toilettes and grooming. Vatsyayana has always been particular about keeping his body scrupulously clean.

'"The body is a temple," he often says. "It must be kept shining, sweet and fragrant for divine habitation."

'After waking up, he followed much of the same regimen he describes for the cultivated man in the *Kamasutra*. He bathed every day, had an oil massage every second day and lathered his body with soap every second instead of the recommended third day. He also shaved every third instead of the normal fourth day and had his hair trimmed by a barber every tenth day. After his bath, he perfumed his clothes with incense smoke, applied collyrium to his eyes and lac-dye to his lips. It was almost noon when, wearing a garland of fresh seasonal flowers and chewing perfumed betel leaves, he began his day's work. Under his influence, although he never insisted nor even directly suggested it, I began to take more interest in the intricacies of women's cosmetics and dress-matters I had scorned while living in the harem.

'Madhavi was delighted by my newfound interest and became an enthusiastic teacher. "By the grace of Shiva, marriage is turning you into a normal woman," she said, and sent me bottles, vials, jars, flasks of oils, lotions, powders, pomades and perfumes in a steady stream. I continued with my painting, though, working on pictures in my room in the afternoon while Vatsyayana read and wrote in his own room across mine.'

Malavika tried hard to follow the ideal of the good wife Vatsyayana describes in the *Kamasutra*. She personally ministered to his needs at the table. She shared in his fasts and vows although this did not pose any hardship since Vatsyayana, being unorthodox in such matters, kept only a few fasts in the year. She almost always asked his permission to attend festivities, social gatherings, temple sacrifices and religious processions. She never showed open displeasure. She looked after the worship of the domestic deities and personally offered them oblations three times a day. Every day, she supervised the house cleaning, the polishing of floors to a shining smoothness, the adorning of rooms with festoons of flowers. She looked after the buying and storing of provisions. But what she loved most was supervising the gardener planting beds of vegetables, herbs and plants while they discussed both the technical aspects of gardening and the various legends connected with flowers and plants.

Vatsyayana spent almost all his evenings in the palace with Udayana, who liked to hold small goshthis of a dozen poets and scholars. Each visiting man of letters was invited to present his work. The subsequent discussions, made livelier by wine from the royal cellar, lasted late into the night. The full Friday assembly, which Malavika had not attended since the Sudhakara affair, was a more formal occasion where the attendance of every court kavi was mandatory. It finished early in the evening, making it possible for the couple to dine together at home at least once a week. According to Madhavi, with whom she spent most of her evenings, Vatsyayana's contributions in both the goshthi and the samaj were always received with great respect. There was no doubt that he was the brightest gem of Kausambi's court, his brilliance reflected in Udayana's pride when the king introduced him to royal guests from other kingdoms.

Most nights, Malavika was already asleep by the time Vatsyayana returned home. Taking care not to disturb her, he would undress in the dark and silently slip into his bed a few feet from hers. The separate beds were a secret of which even the servants were unaware. At night, before going to sleep, Malavika was supposed to push his cot away. In the morning, when it was time for the servants to come in with the bathwater, the cot was pulled back.

'At first I thought he did not touch me because of the Sudhakara affair. He knew of my disgust with sex and dislike for most men. I thought he was being considerate. I did not mind his restraint and was actually relieved that he had not insisted on consummation of the marriage. To tell the truth, I was terribly frightened on the first few nights following the wedding. I became more self-possessed only after I realized that Vatsyayana had no intention of approaching me sexually. I was content with the way we lived. I was happy to be with him in the same house, feel his presence like a father's embrace, hear his deep breathing as he slept, inhale his scent whenever he brushed past me, and the mingled odours of our bodies when I woke up in the morning. He did not object to my walking into his room whenever I missed him. I would sit in a corner and watch him work on his manuscript, the reed quill held in the slender fingers of his right hand dipping gracefully into the ink pot, pausing above the birch bark and then authoritatively moving across its surface. I could touch him or ruffle his hair whenever the impulse overcame me. This was all I wanted—to be able to touch him whenever I felt so moved by tenderness, gratefulness and sometimes also by a baffling surge of unease.

'Some months after our marriage I became aware of an unmistakable shift in my feelings towards him. What had been light and shining between us became heavy and dark. The sporadic stabs of longing for his presence and touch gave way to a steady drumbeat of desire for frank sexual contact. I was embarrassed but no longer frightened by the imperiousness of my craving and the disquieting images it conjured up every night as I lay in my bed next to his. He was certainly aware of the change in me. It was impossible for the foremost scholar of erotics in the land to remain unaware of the ways through which a young girl shows her desire without speaking it. After all, in the *Kamasutra* he himself lists over twenty signs that reveal a girl's wish and readiness for intercourse. But he chose to overlook my sighs and the involuntary narrowing of my eyes as they tried to hide the enlarged pupils betraying my lust. He pretended that my fingers brushing his were not transmitting my intensifying sensations. Erect and unmoved, like the lingam of the great ascetic Shiva himself, he intimated wordlessly that our original understanding of a celibate marriage must remain intact. Now he even avoided my touch, his body becoming rigid if I came too close, as if I was afflicted with a loathsome disease visible only to his eyes. My need of him was still strong enough to stifle any protest. Meekly, I submitted to his resolve to place fresh limits on our intimacy and quietly spread ash on the embers of my desire.

'I know he found me beautiful. He often said so. In the mornings, he lay in bed waiting for me to get up. At first I was embarrassed to emerge naked after my bath. He himself was careful to wear at least a loincloth. With a shyness I found appealing, he told me how much he loved looking at my body after the bath when the slightly flushed skin was "so fresh, so clean". When I rubbed aloe cream on my legs and sandalwood paste into my breasts I saw adoration rather than desire in his shining eyes. He was like a priest in a temple adoring the perfection of the goddess, not a man lusting after a woman's body. He was a devotee asking for a boon when he implored me to shave my pubic hair every day rather than every sixth as is customary.

'"The dark stubble on the mound of the love god is the only blemish on your otherwise flawless skin," he said.

'As the days passed, his early morning adoration gradually receded and was replaced by a distant affection; the worshipful look gave way to an indulgent one. From the goddess of the morning I changed into an earthly woman.

'Later, even before he told me, I understood that in a woman, Vatsyayana was searching for a purity uncontaminated by bodily functions. It was as if he wanted to feed off this purity, drink it like milk from her breast to build a new body that was immune to Kama's arrows, was armored for life against erotic excitement. The signs were many, although it took me time to read them. He looked away from my mouth when we ate and would have closed his ears to the sound of my chewing if that had been at all possible. He found the sight of the remaining drops of the white liquid on my lips utterly distasteful whenever I drank milk or madhupalaka. A barely concealed expression of disgust would flit across his face when I hawked, blew my nose or used the spittoon. From the kind of impatient movements he made in bed, I knew he disliked the sound of the stream of urine hitting the bottom and sides of the pot I used at night. As for himself, he would go to the outhouse even on the coldest winter night rather than draw my attention to his urination.

'When we were more at ease with each other, he told me that I came as close to purity as any woman could.

'"Of course," he said, "you are not a goddess because you menstruate. But the smell is minimal. Even at the end of the day your odour is so faint as to be almost illusory. This has nothing to do with your youth, although it is true that the young smell less than the old. Smell nestles in bodily cavities and depressions, and with their wrinkles and creases old people naturally smell more. You do not have a smell in spite of being a woman; women smell more than men because of their one extra cavity. No, it's not your youth but your purity that brings you so close to an odourless goddess. Like a goddess you do not secrete love fluids in the vulva. Chandrika, too, was young and without a blemish on her firm, smooth skin; yet she had a woman's heavy odour which percolated through the pores even after she had freshly bathed, an odour that kept its essence through the perfumed oils I rubbed into her skin."

'I wanted to believe every word he said,' Malavika continued. 'I loved him. I revered him. After all, just as great seers know all the secrets of man's spiritual body, was he not an acknowledged master on the workings of the sexual body? To please him, I was determined to reach as close to his ideal of female purity as I could. I would be as pure as the white flowers of night jasmine gathered every morning, glistening with fresh dew and strung into the garland he liked me to wear plaited in my hair.

'"These are your flowers—flowers of sadness and impossible love," he said, referring to the legend of the princess who fell hopelessly in love with the Sun god.'

I knew the story well. Deserted by the handsome Sun god, the princess was heartbroken and killed herself. The body was cremated and from the ashes arose the 'tree of sorrow'—the night jasmine. Since the Sun god is the cause of the death of the princess, the tree is unable to bear its sight. It blooms at night and with the first rays of dawn, the white flowers with orange centres drop to the ground.

Perhaps I should have been more surprised than I was to learn from Malavika that the sage whose work aims to enhance the sexual excitement of men and women himself sought stillness. I was even less surprised to hear of Vatsyayana's disgust with the bodily functions of women. Both the revelations, if they can be called that, had been presaged in our conversations. I had come to harbour a suspicion that there was something contradictory, or at least discontinuous, in what he narrated of his life and what he professed in his work. Malavika made me realize the source of my discomfort more clearly. On one hand, many of Vatsyayana's childhood memories were wrapped up in and perhaps even evoked by odours: the sharp aroma of fresh elephant dung, the spicy smells of Ganadasa's kitchen and condiments, the light fragrance of the ashoka tree flowering in the garden, the sundry scents of the women in the household. His fastidiousness reminded me of the legendary brahmin who refused a plate of cooked rice because it smelt of burnt corpses and then found out that indeed the rice had been grown in a field next to a cremation ground. On another occasion, the same brahmin held his nose in disgust at a beautiful perfumed courtesan, claiming she smelt like a goat. It was then discovered that the woman had been fed goat milk as a baby.

Yet odour plays a minor role in the *Kamasutra*. Vatsyayana's discourse on different vulva smells which had so fascinated me is missing from his treatise, despite its claim to erotic comprehensiveness. Taste, too, is scarcely dwelt upon in the *Kamasutra*, although Vatsyayana's memories of various childhood foods is utterly precise. He does mention licking in his text, namely the licking of the labia, crotch and armpits practised in the land of Gujarat. Yet he does not exactly approve when in the very next verse he holds:

> Vatsyayana's opinion is that people lick these parts and places in the heat of passion, and according to local custom. This does not imply that everyone should do so.

I remembered his strong disapproval of Chinese practices relating to love fluids. Also, kissing as described in the *Kamasutra* is not a matter of tongue and taste but of lips and teeth. 'Tongue combat' is the only kiss involving the organ of taste and here, too, the competitive nature of the activity is emphasized rather than its potential for deep erotic communion.

Then Malavika met Sudhakara again. She knew that he had been released from prison. The same shramana who had exorcised her came to Udayana with the tale of a vision about the unfortunate poet. Sudhakara, it seems, had been an unwitting perpetrator of black magic, more a victim than master of the evil spirits he was supposed to have unleashed. To keep him longer in the dungeon would earn the king bad karma. The shramana's vision had contained a particularly horrific scene of the king's tongue being pierced by a thin red—hot iron rod—a punishment in hell for offences against speech, of which poetry is the highest manifestation. Many at the court, including Vatsyayana, doubted the authenticity of the vision. There were rumours that the shramana had been bribed by the poet's relatives and friends. Udayana, however, was a cautious man when it was a question of his well-being in this or a future life. Sudhakara was set free. Banished from the court, though not the kingdom, the poet now earned his living by instructing the children of rich citizens and aspiring courtesans in the art of composing verse, and by giving public recitations during festivals. At the festival marking the beginning of summer, six months after her marriage, Malavika met Sudhakara.

She had gone to the Sun temple that evening for what she thought would be a performance of *The Little Clay Cart* by a visiting troupe from Avanti. A drummer had advertised the event for a week in the bazaars of Kausambi, promising the citizens the finest theatrical experience of their lives. Malavika had misunderstood the date of the performance—the play was scheduled for the next day. When she entered the dance hall from the western door opposite the entrance to the main temple, she found herself in the middle of a poetry recital. It was too late to go back since she had dismissed her carriage, asking the coachman to return in another two hours. It was a long time since she had heard poetry, a time which now seemed to belong to a previous life. The poems recited from the dais set up at the centre of the dance hall were of love lost, betrayed, unrequited, but also cameos seeking to capture love's fleeting moments, arrest its flow.

> Women bathed in sandalwood scents
> flashing antelope eyes,
> arbours of fountains, flowers,
> and moonlight
> a terrace swept with breezes
> of flowering jasmine—
> in summer they stimulate
> love and the love-god himself.

As such recitals go, this one was lightly attended, with an audience of less than a hundred poetry lovers scattered in a space which could comfortably seat more than four hundred. Malavika sat down at the back of the hall near the entrance, partially hidden in one of the twenty-four niches, leaning back against the base of the statue of the goddess Chamunda, feeling some of the divine energy and power through the sculpted stone. Sudhakara was the last poet called up to the dais. When she saw him turn in all directions to respectfully greet the audience with folded hands raised to his forehead, Malavika involuntarily shrank back against the stone goddess, cringing so that she could hide behind the bulk of the man in front of her. Only after Sudhakara had begun reciting a poem did Malavika feel more composed. She slid out of the niche and looked up at the stage. Sudhakara looked different, no longer the fearful figure of her memory and imagination. He had lost weight in prison and with it the expression of sleek self-satisfaction that had so irritated her. His hair was all gone, or perhaps he had shaved his head as a challenge and a solution to advancing baldness. Thin and gaunt, the serious demeanour gave him the look of a Jaina monk who had perceived the illusory nature of the world and had only compassion left for the suffering of its creatures. As his deeply familiar voice chanted lines from poems she knew well, Malavika's heartbeat slowed. Relief at hearing poetry and not intimate obscenities flooded through her. She could have laughed out aloud, so great was her exhilaration.

> . . . and like a streak of foam in high waters
> dashed on the rocks
> little by little I ebb
> and become nothing.

Sudhakara had inflected the last lines of his recital with a tender despair of which Malavika would have never believed him capable. There were a few sighs of applause and a couple of murmurs of appreciation, but the poetry session was obviously little more than a modest success.

People got up to leave. Malavika too should have left but she did not move. She sat with her head bowed, not looking up even when she felt his shadow fall on her.

'There is still some time before my carriage is expected,' she said, and then immediately flushed. What was intended as an excuse had sounded like an invitation.

'Malavika!' was all he said, in a voice vibrant with desire yet also subdued by defeat.

Her pulse quickened at his voice. Looking up, she saw his face bend towards her, the full mouth, so insistent and carnivorous in her faded dreams, now soft and humble in entreaty. Impulsively, she held her hand out to him but he hesitated to extend his own. Her feeling of power and elation had changed into one of sublime warmth which spread through her body, down to the tips of her fingers and toes, tugging furiously at her memory. She smiled at him in encouragement but Sudhakara seemed paralyzed, torn between longing and fear. Malavika stood up and moved closer to him. It would have been the most natural thing in the world—a moment preordained by all their previous lives—that she move into his arms, vanish into him like water in the clay of a new jar.

The temple bells began to peal. The god was retiring to bed for the night, the bells announcing the final disappearance of the sun long after it had set. The bells startled her out of the imagined embrace. As she regained self-possession, every cell of her body screamed in protest against being yanked out of a deep feeling of oneness. She pushed back a strand of hair that had strayed onto her cheek and tore off the crushed bracelet of jasmines that now hung limply from her wrist. Worshippers were climbing up the steps of the temple for the evening service. Sudhakar and Malavika could not be seen together. Her carriage was due at any moment. She was feeling profoundly energized, her spirits buoyant. She would have to take the initiative in their affair if it was ever to become one; he was too fearful of who she was, the king's sister-in-law. Awakened by Kama's grace which garbed the world around her—the carved pillars of the temple hall, the flickering lamps in the alcoves, Sudhakara's voice—with a new-found beauty, Malavika knew she was ready to take any risk and pay a price to keep this sense of life intact.

'We will meet soon,' she whispered. 'Wait for my message.'

Without looking back, she hurried down the steps of the dance hall, through the temple courtyard, past the Sun tank, and into the street.

Trysts, all clandestine lovers discover to their surprise, are nerve-racking affairs. The most obvious practical difficulty is to find a place where they are not known. Potential watchers lurk everywhere—the servants of neighbours and friends, shopkeepers, gardeners in parks. But more than external factors, it is the lover's own inner state, combining excitement with terror, that infiltrates each tryst with a sense of disquiet. No lover ever strides confidently towards the meeting place. Fear and the thrill of the rendezvous go hand in hand, the arousal both sharpened and inhibited by the threat of discovery.

'I was too immersed in the intoxication provoked by the meeting with Sudhakara to make practical plans, and asked Madhavi to help arrange our trysts. She was surprised, even dismayed by what I wanted. Absorbed in my own feverish longings, beguiled by my fantasies, I ignored her disapproval—not of my undertaking but of my choice.

'"My darling, he is an evil man who will only give you pain," she said.

'"He has been changed by his suffering, Madhavi," I said, "I know it. I felt it."

'"How can such a man ever change? Does coal become white because it is washed in milk? Does a crow become a swan by bathing in the Ganga?"'

The exciting prospect of arranging illicit sexual encounters, however, soon permitted Madhavi to overcome her initial reservations. Her solution was to have Sudhakara come to the harem in the guise of an astrologer to give her lessons in this difficult science. Hidden from prying eyes, guarded against encroachments from the outer world and with an atmosphere where sexual liaisons of its inmates were indulgently tolerated, the harem was actually the safest place for amorous assignations. If Udayana, who had to give permission for the entry of any strange man into the queens' royal quarters, had doubts regarding Madhavi's sudden interest in horoscopes and planetary constellations, he kept them to himself.

'It was wonderful. He was strong, tender, passionate, though silent throughout the act. At the end, as he ejaculated, he let out a sound which began as a low moan and then changed into a long, shuddering sigh. It was a sound the like of which I have never heard before . . . or since. I do not know how to describe it. The sigh was infinitely more than an expression of pleasure or satisfaction. It was the sound of surrender but also of contained power, of dying and disappearing yet with whispers of immortality and enduring presence. It seemed to rise from unplumbed depths of his subtle body before falling into an abyss that had no location. I have never felt as pleased with a man's sexual homage as I did when I heard Sudhakara sigh. I had not experienced an orgasm while we made love, but his sigh brought me very close to one. At that moment I loved him more than I would ever do again.

'We could only meet in the late afternoon when Vatsyayana left for the palace, though I fervently wished we could meet at night. Only when I lay in his arms, my face pressed into his chest and my eyes tightly closed did I feel my excitement fully, released from its shackles—the fear of discovery, the guilt of betrayal, the cold stare of inner vigilance. It is less the safety and comfort of the lover's embrace or the delicious feel of his skin against one's own, but the darkness which is desire's protector, its silence which is excitement's friend.'

In the following months Malavika discovered that she was not only a passionate woman but that she craved the sexual act with a greed and intensity that surprised her and gradually came to frighten the poet. Perhaps her craving also had to do with the fact that although she felt intensely aroused, to the roots of her hair and the depth of her womb, she was unable to have an orgasm. Or, rather, she did not have those moments of culmination and explosive release which she had experienced with the phantom Sudhakara.

Madhavi, who had taken upon herself to guide her younger sister through the liaison, seemed to be more upset than Malavika herself.

'I remember we were sitting on my bed when she began to discuss—to my initial embarrassment but later curiosity—what could lie at the root of what she called "your difficulties".

'"It must be a mismatch in one of the three fundamentals of intercourse—size, time and temperament, which your husband too identifies as an obstacle in the way of a woman's orgasm," she said. "Orgasm comes most easily in an equal sexual union—of the hare man with the gazelle woman, the bull man with the mare woman and the horse man with the elephant woman. In the unequal, lower union, such as that of the hare man with the elephant woman, the penis does not rub hard enough against the walls of the vulva to produce enough love nectar to allay its itch. In an unequal higher union, such as that of the horse man with the gazelle woman, the pain in the tender vulva caused by the large penis prevents it from becoming fully wet. Think, Malavika. Is your union high or low?"

'I shook my head, not looking at her, keeping eyes resolutely fixed on my chipped right toenail.

'"Is it a question of time then? Women, like men, take a short, an average or a long time to reach orgasm. Here, too, the best union is when the times of the man and woman match. The matching is not simple. It must take the difference between male and female natures into account. In the first intercourse, the time of the male is short but becomes longer and longer during subsequent unions in the day. In the female, the reverse is true. In general, it takes a longer time to satisfy female desire. A woman desires a union in which the vulva itch is stilled for a long time, not one where it is too quickly allayed. Is he too quick?"

'I kept my head lowered. My toenails needed to be lacquered.

'"Could the cause lie in a mismatch of temperament then?" she continued. "Women, like men, can be of small, average or great sexual passion. Again, the matching of temperaments is important for woman's orgasm. The best union for a woman is when the penis closely fits the vagina and rubs it everywhere, and time and temperament of both are evenly matched."

'Even as I listened, I felt there was something vital missing from Madhavi's discourse. I knew from my own experience that a woman's pleasure is different at different times. Perhaps Acharya is right when he talks of the importance of size, time and temperament for female orgasm. Perhaps orgasm as the end of desire attains a simplicity which is otherwise absent in the complexity of all that constitutes a woman's pleasure as desire runs its course. Now I know that to speak of woman's pleasure is to take the risk of being simplistic, for this pleasure comes in many forms and colours. Sometimes just lying next to the lover, hearing him breathe, his whispered words and familiar scent can suddenly set off a spasm of desire and a throbbing disquiet in the abode of the love god. At other times, in the mutual caresses and touch of bodies, before lust takes hold, I am overcome by a deep tenderness that is difficult to describe. The tenderness does not seek the driven rhythm of intercourse but asks only for a light, cautious contact with the lover through a certain look, a particular gesture.

'As the excitement mounts, there is a pulsating warmth in my belly and vulva. I can feel the wetness and a slow opening of the vulva, indeed of the whole body, which requires careful attention from the lover. A good lover is intuitively attentive to this phase of woman's desire; Sudhakàra was a good lover. You, of course, are incomparable,' she added quickly.

'If, again unlike you, the man is not attuned to my slow opening and is already at the stage of intercourse in his thoughts and wishes, when there is a lurking feeling of dissatisfaction throughout the act and a lingering disappointment at its end. However, if the man has paid attention to my slow opening then there is release of an extremely pleasurable energy. The energy can spread throughout the body or be concentrated in a raging storm in the abode of the love god. I then feel deeply connected to the man. Feelings of love and tenderness come surging up from the depths to envelop the lover while at the same time I retreat into my own self, exquisitely aware of the pleasurable sensations of my body. At this moment I crave for the man's penis to enter me. I sometimes open my eyes as it slides in, seeking a contact which will pull me out of myself. All these feelings and sensations are so intense that often they feel choked and confined, with little possibility of release. At such times a certain aggressiveness creeps into my lovemaking, wherein my vulva would seize and devour the penis; I want to dominate, conquer the lover's body and incorporate it into my own.

'The actual intercourse, again, is experienced at different depths. Sometimes the friction of the penis moving against the walls of the vagina leads to extremely high levels of heat and wetness, to waves of pleasure lapping against a dam soon to be breached. At other times the friction and thrusts release a stream of pleasure, gently flowing through the pores of my body and into the roots of my hair. This stream ebbs away slowly, leaving rivulets of deep peace meandering inside my body which, I imagine, is like the aftermath of an orgasm I have never had. At yet other times, the rubbing of the umbrella of the love god can drive me wild with the desire to have the penis drive hard and deep inside me. But there are also situations when the man's concentration on the umbrella of the love god alone leads to a rupture of energy between my legs and the lower portion of the trunk. I fall out of what I am feeling as my mind becomes active. The sensual tingling in the tips of my fingers and the roots of my hair dries up. If the man has ejaculated, I take his hand and put it on my vulva, not to ask for further stimulation but to keep the fast-dissipating energy inside me for a little longer.'

When I finally come to pen Vatsyayana's biography and my commentary on the *Kamasutra*, I will have to be careful that both conform to the approved style for such works, and that my own fascination with the nature of woman's pleasure does not creep into my verses. Rules of scholarship and conventions of biography do not allow the expression of all of one's knowledge. What one writes is always less than what one knows. I always chafed under this restriction during my studies. It turned me away from scholarship as a career. I dreaded becoming like the kavis I saw around me who limit their knowledge only to what is allowed by the dictates of its expression. It is sad to realize that to be taken seriously I too must follow the same pattern in the work I am now contemplating, that in my own commentary I must strictly follow Vatsyayana's text and omit all I learnt from Malavika about the sexuality of women after we became lovers.

Malavika was concerned about the poet's flagging ardour but much more worried that whispers about her affair might reach Vatsyayana's ears. She noticed that a month after she started meeting Sudhakara, her husband's behaviour toward her had changed. In the morning when she stepped into their room after her bath, he looked at her with an agonized expression before turning his face away. He stopped paying her compliments on her beauty and her purity. The tranquil devotion in his eyes gave way to something that was uncannily like the devouring desire in Sudhakara's eyes when he used to boldly look at her during Udayana's Friday assembly. The look was much more fleeting in Vatsyayana's case, quickly replaced by one of distaste which, in turn, gave way to his habitual expression of benevolent neutrality. His nostrils twitched whenever she passed close to him. She knew that since he could sniff out the slightest odour of love fluids, obscure processes in his mind and body were debating whether what he could smell was pleasant or not, whether to approach or flee from the source of nasal excitation.

'Did Acharya ever find out about Sudhakara?' I asked.

'Yes, he did. It must have hurt him very badly. He did not stop talking to me—he was far too polite to take such extreme steps—but our conversations became minimal. They also became formal, devoid of all life and spontaneity. Sometimes he did make an effort to show interest, asking me about my day and affairs of the household, but mostly he shut himself in his room when at home, working on his manuscript; I believe he wrote the chapter on occult aids in those months. Our morning routines did not change, nor did the distant courtesy with which he treated me. He was implacably focused on severing his knowledge of my affair with Sudhakara from his awareness, perhaps not even allowing dreams to cross the border he had drawn.'

'But how did he find out about Sudhakara?' I persisted.

'In such a farcical way that it could well be part of one of those fashionable plays the kavis write these days. One evening, when Vatsyayana returned from the palace, he brought me an exquisitely carved ivory horse with a horn on its forehead, small enough to fit into a woman's fist, which Udayana had given him. I suppose it was less its actual price than the uniqueness of the piece—it came from China, which made it valuable enough to be gifted by a king. I gave the horse to Sudhakara. Lately he had shown signs of wanting to break off our affair. He came late for our appointments and often cancelled them on the flimsiest of pretenses. I forgot about this gift. There was no reason to worry that Vatsyayana would ever ask about the missing horse since he was sublimely indifferent to material objects and possessions.

'Then one day, the whole affair came out into the open in three scenes. The first scene, which took place on the terrace outside the king's apartment on the top floor of the palace, involved a determined Udayana, a scared prostitute, and an agitated Vatsyayana. The second, played out in Madhavi's room in the harem, involved a furious Udayana, a defiant Madhavi and an apparently penitent Malavika. The third scene took place in our house some hours later and had a cast of only two actors: a coldly glowering Vatsyayana spitting out questions and a calm Malavika hiding her underlying despair as she tried to answer them. Udayana was in such a rage that he ordered his guards to decapitate Sudhakara the moment they found him.

'Luckily for Sudhakara, one of Madhavi's maids who was a witness to the scene in the harem and fancied the poet—I am now certain that the fancy was mutual—rushed to his house with a warning. Sudhakara had fled the city by the time the royal guards arrived.'

I had not quite followed the sequence of events and asked Malavika if she could make it clearer.

'Well, what happened was that unbeknown to me Sudhakara gave the ivory horse to a courtesan he was interested in at the time. This courtesan had cause to complain against one of the king's ministers and went to the court as a supplicant before Udayana, bearing the ivory horse as a gift fit for a king. Udayana, of course, recognized the horse at once as the one he had given to Vatsyayana. The three scenes revealed the route taken by the horse in its canter back to the king.'

Chapter Eighteen

A desire arising spontaneously increases with experience. Ardour comes from mutual understanding which gradually becomes a permanent feeling.

Kamasutra 5.1.56

We live in a small but comfortable house at the edge of the Quarter of Entertainers on one of the few streets in Ujjayini where the castes are mixed. Our neighbours—merchants, scholars, craftsmen—are long-term visitors from all parts of the empire; they are more than travellers but less than migrants. We have lived in Ujjayini for four years now, longer than most of our neighbours, but we have no plans of settling down in this city. My income, like our house, is small but comfortable. I earn it by providing emergency priestly services to the temporary residents far away from their own family priests, and from drawing charts for one of Ujjayini's leading astrologers who is swamped by clients and in need of assistance. I am glad that my education in the Vedas, which I looked down upon in my youth, is finally proving to be of some practical use.

People know us as that friendly young couple from

Varanasi with a delightful little daughter. They know me as a competent ritual specialist but are unaware that I am also an aspiring scholar of erotics who is writing a commentary on one of the modern classics in the field. They do not know of my connection with the author of the *Kamasutra*, that Malavika is Vatsyayana's wife, or that we are not married. I am surprised how easy it is to construct a different past without deliberately lying but only through certain omissions, leaving false assumptions uncorrected and by not telling the truth loudly enough.

As I write this, I can hear my daughter in the next room argue with her mother in her lisping voice, trying to convince her that her hair does not need to be oiled and plaited. Malavika is gentle and patient with her but equally adamant. We have been happy in the years that have passed since we left the kingdom of Varanasi. After what happened, we could not have stayed on. We were not guilty of any crime, yet treated as outcasts. Even my father's normal reproachful look changed into one of pained distaste. Chatursen was the only person who did not turn away from me, although with him too I could sense a growing distance. Ujjayini, where our daughter was born, has been a good choice. Far from both Varanasi and Kausambi, its anonymity has not only helped to heal painful wounds but, in shutting out the outside world, brought Malavika and me closer to each other. This closeness, where concealments have fallen away with time, ripening our love, has not been at the cost of a decrease or inhibition of desire. Passion has not receded with familiarity. When we touch or brush past each other during the day, or lie in bed at night, my arm around her breasts, my body curled into her back, fitting together like two unstrung bows in a sheath, our touch continues to vibrate with amorous tension. Perhaps the hint of the illicit, the adulterous, that gives our lovemaking an edge of continuous excitement, composed of stolen snatches of time, has spared us from that certain blunting which comes from a long period of living together.

Our intimacy has also unveiled a very different face of Lord Kama, which Vatsyayana, following the ancient sages, has kept well hidden in his text. This face is invisible in a transient sexual encounter, no matter how vivid and how spontaneous. Only now, after these many years of living with Malavika, do I sometimes glimpse it in the aftermath of our nightly embrace. Like a rainbow after the passing of a cloudburst, I can see Kama's other face in those rare, blissful moments of ineffable intimacy when our bodies have separated and are lying together side by side, but are not yet two in their responses. It reveals to me that the goal of desire is its cessation; what a wish wants is to stop being one. What men and women long for is the abiding serenity that comes from desire stilled, not satiated, conquered or denied. When lord Shiva opened his third eye to annihilate the god of love, he did not realize that he was fulfilling Kama's most secret urge. I have seen this face of the love god but occasionally, yet the traces it has left behind have created a space in my heart which irradiates my body and mind with a deep feeling of tranquillity, a peace which is not complacency but voluptuous absorption and repose. It is a space untouched by passion even when I lie with Malavika—the eye of the sexual storm, Kama's rare gift.

Udayana did not really have much of a choice. He was fond of Malavika and Vatsyayana was his closest friend, yet he felt powerless to protect them. Normally, the subject of a wife's infidelity was not a matter of public interest; it could be safely left to the concerned couple to reach a private understanding. Given the example of the emperor's own adulterous relationship with his brother's wife when he was young, adultery evoked some curiosity but little moral condemnation in courts of the Gupta empire. In case of Malavika, though, adultery was a minor part of Udayana's difficulty. Her affair with Sudhakara involved the sanctity of the king's harem, traditionally as inviolate as the king's person. Udayana's father had executed people for lesser offences. Unable to seek counsel from either Madhavi or Vatsyayana, otherwise his closest advisers but personally involved in this vexing problem, the king did not know what to do.

Udayana's dilemma was compounded by Rajnikanta and his cohorts who were openly demanding the death penalty for the king's sister-in-law. As a self-appointed guardian of public morality and the healthy functioning of institutions of the state, Rajnikanta was trying to turn Malavika's case into a test of Udayana's willingness to conform to the king's dharma by administering impartial justice.

'I hear that in those weekly public meetings, the fellow goes around from one temple to other, raising the question as to whether I will indeed sentence Malavika to death as required by custom and tradition,' the king complained to Vatsyayana. 'I must say this for him; the fellow is clever. I hear he deports himself at these meetings as if he was an advocate of my own better self. "Let us pray to the gods to give our king the strength to fulfill his duty," he says at the end. "May he be guided by the example of Lord Rama who exiled his chaste wife Sita on the mere suspicion of infidelity voiced by a lowly washerman. May our sovereign remember the example of virtuous king Harishchandra who, reduced by fate to a base attendant at funeral pyres, carried out his dharma as a faithful servant by refusing to cremate his own infant son because his wife could not pay the required fee. Let dharma always prevail.'''

Udayana did not entertain the idea of Malavika's execution but had reluctantly reached the conclusion that his sister-in-law must be banished from Kausambi.

'It will only be for a couple of years till passions cool down,' he said to Vatsyayana.

'You know that I will go with her,' Vatsyayana said.

Udayana nodded.

'I understand. She has no one else,' he said.

'*I* have no one else,' Vatsyayana said.

'I promise you it will not be for more than two years, even if that frog-face whips up public sentiment against her return,' the king said.

'Although I will never see the face of my son's son, my hair has begun to turn gray,' Vatsyayana said. 'Perhaps it is time for me to retire to the forest, leave worldly attachments behind and devote the rest of my years in search of moksha, the highest goal of life.'

'No, no!' Udayana protested in alarm, stricken by the thought of his own aging. 'Renunciation is only talk of scholars whose mouths reek of stale wisdom. You will come back. We shall play chess and dice, feast on roasted quail and drink Persian wine. You shall write other books that add lustre to Kausambi's name and augment your own fame.'

Vatsyayana's answering nod was noncommittal.

'I hope you have forgiven Malavika,' Udayana said. 'Women are prone to such lapses.'

'There is nothing to forgive. Women make mistakes but goddesses do not; they are only testing their devotees.'

'Goddesses?' Udayana was puzzled.

Vatsyayana smiled, a strange smile of complicity and secrecy, as if he was privy to a revelation yet to come.

'Malavika is not a goddess—yet. She still has the bodily functions of a woman. But her female smell was becoming fainter and fainter till this happened.'

'Smell?' Udayana was now completely baffled.

'It is difficult to explain. All she needs now is time and further preparation to realize her true nature,' Vatsyayana said.

Udayana sensed his friend was both unwilling and unable to carry the conversation further. 'Malavika is a reliable woman,' he said. 'She is not as frivolous as many others of her sex.'

After initially being seized by cold rage, Vatsyayana was quick to regain his composure. In his own distant way he was once again unfailingly courteous to Malavika. Sudhakara's name was never mentioned again, nor did Vatsyayana allude to the affair when he informed her about the king's reluctant decision. Still in a state of shock, Malavika had numbly acquiesced to Vatsyayana's choice of the Seven Leaf hermitage outside Varanasi as their future home. Many years earlier he had spent a week there when working on his treatise, and had enjoyed its atmosphere of peace and unpretentiousness.

'Within a few days of our arrival,' Malavika said, 'I began to sense that behind his apparent distance he was acutely aware of my presence. In a strange, disembodied way, he seemed to hover all around me, his ear attuned to the slightest sound I made, his eyes quickly narrowing to hide the gleam in the pupils whenever I caught him surreptitiously looking at me. I felt he was expecting something from me, an expectation he tried to mask under the formality of his manner and an anxious concern about my well-being.'

'What did he expect?'

'He was waiting for me to turn into a goddess! "It is

very rarely that women become goddesses," he said. "The boundary between humans and gods is more easily crossed in the other direction. But we know from history that it is not impossible for women to become goddesses or for men to become gods." The forest outside the hermitage was going to play a role in my transformation, as were other unnamed trials I had to go through. When I returned to our hut in the afternoon, flushed with happiness since I loved to spend the day in the forest by myself, his eyes would light up in satisfaction, as if events were unfolding exactly according to a plan. I remember him once saying that the forest force to which I was daily exposed was preparing me for the test ahead of me, and that Sudhakara had come too early.

'When we sat outside our hut in the evenings after finishing dinner, he sometimes talked of purity. At these times I had the strong feeling he was talking to himself as much as to me, that he was trying to understand something that was still unclear in his own mind.

'"Purity," he would say, "is obtained by wrestling with the impure, not by avoiding it. The lotus, purity's foremost symbol, is rooted in mud. Do the secrets of the lotus lie locked in the mud? The chastest of goddesses was desired by her own father as soon as she was born. Did she not have to forge her purity in the fire of male lust that encircled her since birth?"'

I now know that just as I chose Vatsyayana as my teacher on my first visit to the hermitage, he was selecting me for the test his wife had to pass in her progress toward becoming a goddess. The test had to be real but not too difficult. It was essential that the chosen man be young but not especially attractive of face or figure, and not knowledgeable in the ways of women and love. I was naïve, inhibited, fearful of women and alarmed by my own lust—exactly the combination he was looking for in a man.

Both our choices were fated to belie our expectations.

I can still see the expression on Vatsyayana's face as he loomed above us in the forest clearing that summer afternoon while Malavika and I lay entwined on the ground, our clothes scattered all around our impatient bodies. We had not heard him. There was neither shock nor anger in the look he gave us, just utter anguish. He stood there for a few moments before he turned and walked away without saying a word. The sound of his feet, dragging slightly in the dry undergrowth, became fainter before the forest's silence, the hum of insect life, intermittent bird calls and the distant grunt of a deer, enveloped us again. We had closed our eyes, unable to immediately confront each other. The knowledge about what we had done was about to crash down upon us like a storm.

I never saw Vatsyayana again. By the time Malavika and I made our hesitant way back to the hermitage, terrified of his fury, he was long gone. He had commandeered Chatursen's carriage to take him to Varanasi, spent the night at an inn and then disappeared in the morning. No one has seen him since. There have been rumours of different sightings over the years. Someone saw him from a distance in a group of wandering sadhus high in the Himalayas near the foot of the glacier from which the Ganga springs. Others allege he is an ascetic in a cave in the mountains above Takshashila. Yet others have heard that he has become a Buddhist monk and lives in a monastery at the southern rim of the Taklamakan desert. A merchant from Kausambi whose caravan was attacked by robbers in the land of five rivers even claims to have recognized Vatsyayana in the leader of the bandits.

The rumour, in the process of becoming the historical truth about the last part of the sage's life, has been assiduously spread by the network of conservative scholars and orthodox priests, which remains influential in the Gupta empire and indeed is enjoying a resurgence. Since my work on Vatsyayana's life will perhaps never be written, Rajnikanta seems to have had his revenge after all by composing the last chapter of his story. In his version, Vatsyayana, sincerely repenting the folly of his youth in giving erotics such a radical interpretation, thus weakening dharma, first went on a year-long pilgrimage to the four major temples located in the four corners of the land, praying for forgiveness. He then retired to a remote forest in the foothills of the Himalayas to practice the severest austerities as penance. Avoidance of all contact with women and total silence are the two major vows he has taken as an ascetic.

My commentary on the *Kamasutra* is now almost complete. I have written it in the conventional form required for such literary undertakings, excising all biographical detail about the author or the commentator. The birch bark on which I have been composing my recollections of Vatsyayana and our work together is destined to lie unread in a corner of this room. Even after I finish these memoirs, put the last bark strip on top of the stack and tie them all together with a string, Vatsyayana's story will remain incomplete.

I did make an effort to find a conclusion when a few months ago, at the beginning of summer, I travelled to Kausambi to meet Vatsyayana's aunt. Malavika had been pressing me for a long time to undertake the journey; if there was anyone who knew Vatsyayana's whereabouts it would be Chandrika. My step became hesitant the nearer I came to the gates of Goshitrama monastery. I was fearful of the old nun's disapproval. I need not have worried. There was no condemnation in her eyes, only a warm understanding which I have come to associate with the followers of Lord Buddha who have travelled some way on the road to compassion. Yes, Vatsyayana had secretly visited her after he disappeared from the Seven Leaf hermitage.

'He sat at the same place under this peepul tree where you are sitting now,' Chandrika said. 'No, he did not talk about what had happened or why he had come. All he wanted at first was that I talk of the past, recall memories of the time I was young and he was a little boy hovering around me every afternoon while I got ready for the evening's entertainment. He seemed calm enough, though I could sense a certain disappointment under that composed exterior. His expression reminded me of the time he was six years old and our cook Ganadasa allowed him to prepare a sweet dish for our dinner all by himself. Although he tried hard to control his tears, he could not hide the look of stricken disappointment when he found the sweet was inedible because he had got the proportions of its ingredients all wrong.'

'And the rumours of his having become an ascetic?'

'I find it impossible to believe that he has retreated to a forest or to a mountain cave to practice austerities,' Chandrika said. 'Have you not realized that he is a very different kind of yogi? That he is someone who lived at the edge of the forest but never went inside? A man who has devoted his life to the service of Lord Kama but has never been his subject?'

Yes, I said to myself, he was a man who wanted a wife who should not be a woman; a man who reflected and wrote about sex all his adult life but shied away from its practice.

'Like a true yogi whose meditation is not separated

from his daily life but who seeks to transform each moment of life into a meditation,' Chandrika continued, 'Vatsyayana's contemplation of kama has to take place within the erotic field, not outside it. If you ask me, he is probably living in a noble brothel somewhere in a city outside the central countries. He could be a gardener perhaps, or even a cook in such an establishment, while he continues to meditate and reflect on the nature of desire.'

'Did he say anything to make you believe that?' I asked.

'Not directly,' the old nun said. 'But at the end when it was almost time for visitors to leave, I tried to divert his mind from a growing sadness at our parting, which I did not know then was a final one.

'"What happens to all of us older people, Malli, who are not worthy of Lord Kama's attention?" I asked him. "After all, the god is but a youth, who has neither understanding nor compassion for his effect on aging bodies. What do you think, Malli?"

'"Chandrika masi," he replied, obviously pleased to slip back into his role of an authority on erotics, "the ancient sages say very little about the kama of older people. The texts on erotics seek to provide instruction to those entering the householder stage rather than to ones who are nearing its end. Outside the texts, Abhirata of Purushpura has a few verses on sexual relations of older men and women in his poem 'Vilasaka and Manjari'. Do you remember the place where the old bawd Kamini-mata advises Vilasaka on how a courtesan whose charms are fading may still attract and hold onto young lovers?"

'I nodded, although my memory of this particular poem was vague.

'"But Abhirata's verses, although composed in the Arya meter of eroticism, are comical, even satirical," he continued. "The poet's intention is not to impart knowledge on the sexuality of old age but to caricature us scholars and our scholarly work, especially mine. Analogous to the gazelle, mare and elephant women of the *Kamasutra*, Abhirata mockingly sets up a three-fold classification of fish, turtle and crocodile for older women. These types, he tells us through the bawd's mouth, are not based on size but the texture of the aging yoni—from the moist and smooth to the dry and scaly. Similarly, he classifies older men according to the frequency and duration of their erections. Such verses may provide amusement to the vulgar but not insight to the discriminating."

'"What little we do know about sexuality in advancing years has been excellently summarized by Dattaka in his chapter on the aging courtesan. Dattaka quotes from medical texts to the effect that the sexual fluids of older women are less sweet and more astringent, sapping rather than increasing male vitality. He further tells us that erotic experience in later years is otherwise not much different from that in youth.

Yoni and lingam are the last parts of the body to age; the pubic hair last to gray.

Both male and female genitals remain supple and youthful, even as the skin on the rest of the body sags and wrinkles. The pleasure of intercourse, in so far as it is constituted of physical sensations radiating from the genitals, is unchanged well into the vanaprastha stage. The difference is that the bodily passion of older people does not surge as strongly, nor is it experienced as overwhelmingly as in youth. Their sexuality is more deliberate, like that of a mature painter who knows his possibilities and limitations well and is always conscious of the lines he draws and the colours he uses."

'No, Vatsyayana can never be an ascetic,' Chandrika

concluded. 'His engagement with kama, of the mind, not of the body, has always been too profound for him to be anyone else but a scholar of desire, a sage at the love—god's court.'

Goshitrama's gong sounded, a deep booming signal for the monks and nuns to go out into the streets to beg for their evening meal. Dusk was setting in. A flight of parrots descended on the branches of the peepul tree and raucously began to settle for the night. I held my hand out to help Chandrika rise. The back of her hand was veined and leathery but the palm surprisingly soft and smooth. There was a faint smile on her puckered lips, deepening the lines around her mouth.

'But you know both Malli and the venerable Dattaka were mistaken,' she said as she turned to leave. 'The very last part of the body to age is the heart.'

Acknowledgements

I wish to begin my litany of thanks with the Institute of Advanced Study in Berlin where I began writing this book in the summer of 1995, and where I completed it during another stay in the summer of 1997. I hope my friend Wolf Lepenies, the Rector of the Institute, is not too surprised with this particular result of his generous hospitality.

The fragment of the poem in Chapter Seventeen is from A.K. Ramanujan's translation of Kur 290 in *The Inner Landscape: Love Poems from a Classical Tamil Anthology*, published by Oxford University Press. The map of Vatsyayana's India is adapted from Joseph Schwartzberg's *A Historical Atlas of South Asia*, also published by OUP.

The quotes from the *Kamasutra* were selected and compiled by consulting the Hindi translation of the work by Devadutta Shastri and the recent English translation by Alain Danielou.

There are debts to other scholars, too numerous to mention, who have written on the history, art, literature and economic and cultural life of the Gupta period, and whose work I have gratefully appropriated.

My special thanks are due to my friends Wendy Doniger for her constant support and Catherine Clement for her encouragement to embark on this fictional venture. I am also grateful to Kunal Chakravarty, Professor of Ancient Indian History at the Jawaharlal Nehru University in New Delhi, who checked the manuscript for gross historical inaccuracies, to David Davidar of Penguin India for his invaluable editorial input, and to Smriti Vohra for her admirable copy editing skills.